PENDRAGON

THE RIVERS OF ZADAA

PENDRAGON

AN ADVENTURE THROUGH TIME AND SPACE

PENDRAGON

THE RIVERS OF ZADAA

D. J. MACHALE

SIMON AND SCHUSTER

SIMON AND SCHUSTER
First published in Great Britain in 2005 by Simon & Schuster UK Ltd.
1st Floor, 222 Gray's Inn Road, London WC1X 8HB
A CBS COMPANY

This edition published in 2009

Originally published in the USA in 2005 by Aladdin Paperbacks,
an imprint of Simon & Schuster Children's Division, New York.

A CIP catalogue record for this book
is available from the British Library

ISBN 978-1-84738-485-0

10 9 8 7 6 5 4 3 2 1

Printed by CPI Cox & Wyman, Reading, Berkshire RG1 8EX

For Frankie, Marcus, Andy Boy, Noodle, Mov, and Franny Jae. My oldest friends and constant source of inspiration.

Hello to everyone in Halla.

It's time once again to rejoin Bobby Pendragon and the Travelers as they track down the evil Saint Dane and try to thwart his next twisted attempt to topple the territories. Since the publication of the last Pendragon adventure, the books have done almost as much traveling as Bobby. As of this writing, Pendragon has been published in seven different languages. I've gotten letters from readers in such far-flung locales as South Africa, Australia, New Zealand, Sri Lanka, Taiwan, Israel, Tokyo, many European countries and, of course, every one of the United States. As exciting as that is for me, it's also interesting to know that no matter how far apart we may live and how different our cultures may be, people everywhere enjoy reading a fun adventure. I'm honored to be able to provide one.

I always like to thank the people who were so important in getting the Pendragon books out to the world. This foreword will be no different. My editor, Julia Richardson, has once again provided invaluable guidance in helping me shape Bobby's latest adventure. Rick Richter, Ellen Krieger, and all the great folks at Simon & Schuster have continued to support the Pendragon books, for which I will always be grateful. Heidi Hellmich has once again done her copyediting magic and turned my writing into something that actually resembles proper English. Debra Sfetsios and Victor Lee have come up with yet another stunning cover. Loor looks great, no? I've got some terrific guys who are always watching out for me when it comes to the business side of things. Richard Curtis, Peter Nelson and his team, and Danny Baror are my own personal acolytes, and I thank them.

Of course, my wife, Evangeline, has once again helped me fashion this latest story. I even have to thank my daughter, Keaton, for allowing me to exist for hours at a time in my own private flume (better known as my office) and not knock on the door too often, wondering where Daddy is. (I don't think she'd understand that Daddy was on Zadaa, matching wits with Saint Dane. She's not even two.)

And of course, my final thank you has to go out to you readers. I've gotten such wonderful letters and warm greetings from everyone. I especially love to meet readers at the various book events I've attended. As much as I love to write these books, it's an extra bonus to hear from those who enjoy them. Thank you all for reading, and thanks for sharing your thoughts with me.

So, is this boring foreword done yet? Yes. Enough preamble. It's time to get back into it. When last we left Bobby, a flume had collapsed. Spader and Gunny were trapped on Eelong; Kasha the Traveler was killed; and Saint Dane was headed for Zadaa, Loor's home territory. Can it get any worse? Is Bobby destined for more trouble? Has Saint Dane hatched another evil plan to destroy a territory?

Do you really have to ask?

Hobey ho, let's go.
D. J. MacHale

ZADAA

It began with a battle.

A nasty one. Then again, is there such a thing as a nice battle? I guess this one seemed especially vicious because it was over something so trivial. At least that's what I thought at the time. At stake was a couple gallons of water. I'm serious. Regular old everyday water. Not exactly the kind of thing you'd expect a group of professional warriors to fight to the death over, but that's not the way it works here on the territory of Zadaa. Water here is more valuable than food, more valuable than treasure. It's even more valuable than life. I know. I've seen people risk theirs to get a few precious drops.

How messed up is that?

Mark, Courtney, it's been a while since I've written a journal to you guys, and for that I apologize. I think after I tell you all that's happened since my last journal, you'll understand why. From the time I arrived here on Zadaa, I haven't had much time to think, let alone kick back and write. I'm doing it now because I'm about to set out on an adventure that was long in coming. I've tried to avoid it, but now I have no choice. Starting tomorrow, life is going to be very different for me. I feel as if I'm closing the first chapter on my life as a Traveler and beginning a new and more dangerous one. I know, that doesn't seem possible, but it's the truth. Before I tell you about it, I need to let you know what happened since I landed back on Zadaa. You'll need to hear it all to understand why I've chosen the path I'm about to take. Maybe writing it down will help me understand it a little better myself.

You won't be surprised to hear that Saint Dane is here. I've already run into him. It wasn't pretty. But more about that later. I also have a good idea of what the turning point is here on Zadaa. I think it has something to do with water . . . or the lack of it. I've no doubt that Saint Dane's evil plan for this territory is somehow tied in to the water trouble they're having. Bottom line is, our quest to stop Saint Dane's plan to crush all of Halla has come to Zadaa. This is our next challenge. And so we go.

I first want to tell you about the battle that happened soon after I arrived. It's important to hear because in many ways it's a small example of the bigger trouble I found on this territory. That, and because one of the warriors involved in the fight was my friend. Loor. The Traveler from Zadaa.

"Keep to yourself, Pendragon," Loor ordered as we strode along the dusty street of Xhaxhu. "Stay in the shadows. Do not look anyone in the eye. It is dangerous for a Rokador to be seen in the city."

"But I'm not a Rokador," I complained.

"Do not argue," Loor said sharply. "Do as I say."

I didn't argue. I knew what she meant. There were two tribes living in this area of Zadaa. The Batu lived above ground in the cities. They were a dark-skinned race, made so because they lived for generations under the hot, desert sun. Loor was a Batu. The other tribe was the Rokador. They lived underground in a labyrinth of tunnels that spread throughout Zadaa. They weren't moles or anything; they were definitely civilized. But as you might guess, living underground didn't do much for their tans. The Rokador were a light-skinned race. So with my white skin and light brown hair, I pretty much looked like a Rokador. And since there was some serious bad blood between the Batu and the Rokador, making myself invisible up here on the surface was a smart idea. To that end, Loor had me wearing heavy, dark clothing that covered my head and arms. It was great for a disguise, not so great for keeping cool. I'm guesstimating that the temperature in Xhaxhu averages about ninety degrees. On a cool day. So I was sweating like a fiend. Or at least a fiend in a sauna wearing a winter coat.

"Can't somebody take your place?" I asked. "I mean, we have more important things to worry about."

Loor looked straight ahead as she strode along. Her jaw set. I'd seen this look before. She had her game face on. I know you guys can picture her. She's hard to forget. I'd grown a few inches since I first met her on Denduron, but she still had me by a solid two inches. Her once almost-waist-length black hair was a bit shorter now, falling to her shoulders. I guess the long hair got in the way when she did her training. As you know, Loor is a warrior. Here on Zadaa they call the warrior class "Ghee." When I first met Loor, she was a warrior-in-training. Since then, she has been elevated to full-fledged warrior status. I'm guessing she was at the head of her class. She's that good. She even looks the part. This girl is totally cut. I'm talking stupid-low body fat. It isn't hard to see this since her light-weight leather armor reveals a lot of skin. Wearing heavy metal armor like the knights of the Round Table wouldn't fly here on searing-hot Zadaa. You'd end up cooking like Spam in the can. Assuming Spam is actually cooked, which I'm not so sure about. But whatever. You get the idea. The warriors here had to be protected, but cool. Unlike me, who had to be wearing a wool-freakin'-blanket.

The muscles in her long arms and legs flexed as she moved down the street, making her look even more formidable. I guess when you're a professional warrior, having an awesome athletic body goes with the territory. So to speak.

"I have no choice but to fight today," Loor finally answered. "I am next in the rotation."

"Rotation?" I snapped. "What are you, a baseball pitcher? Have them change the schedule. Find a relief pitcher. If something happens to you then—"

"If I do not fight," Loor interrupted, "the Ghee commanders will mark me as a coward and banish me to a labor colony in the desert. Or I could get lucky and they would execute me."

"Oh," I said soberly. "Not a whole lot of great choices here."

"Do not worry, Pendragon," she said, finally looking at me. "Our destiny is to stop Saint Dane. I will not let anything stand in our way."

I believed her, but that didn't mean I wasn't going to worry.

"Loor!" came a voice from behind us. Running to catch up was Saangi. I'm not exactly sure what her official title is, but I guess on Second Earth you would call her Loor's squire. You know, one of those young servants who are assigned to knights to take care of their every need. The Ghee warriors of Zadaa operated pretty much like the knights of old, without the Spam-can suits.

"You forgot this!" Saangi said, out of breath. She handed Loor a small, leather container that was about the size of a canteen. In fact that's exactly what it was, a canteen full of water.

"No," Loor said sternly. "I cannot use this."

"But you will need water if the battle is difficult—," Saangi protested.

"Take it back to my home," Loor said firmly. "And do not let anyone see you with it."

When Loor spoke in that serious tone, you didn't mess with her. At least I didn't. I figured Saangi knew better too. The girl's shoulders fell in disappointment. I'm guessing she was around fourteen, only a few years younger than me. She had the dark skin of the Batu, but unlike Loor, her hair was cut tight to her head, like a guy. She wore simple, dark clothes that looked sort of like Loor's, but they were made of cloth rather than leather. Someday she would wear the armor of a Ghee warrior, but until then, her job was to take care of Loor.

Oh yeah, one other thing. Saangi had another job. She was Loor's acolyte. She knew all about the Travelers and our mission to stop Saint Dane. I thought Saangi was kind of young to have that kind of responsibility, but then again, I was only fourteen when I became a Traveler. Still, Saangi seemed more like an eager kid than a future warrior who could help us defeat a world-crushing demon. But that's just me.

"Do not be upset, Saangi," Loor said, taking the edge off her voice. "You were concerned about me and for that I am grateful. But it would not look right for me to be quenching my thirst during a fight over water."

Saangi nodded. "I understand," she said. "But do not begin the battle until I get there!" She turned and ran back the way she had come.

"She is so young," Loor said as we watched her run away. "I wish she did not have to know of the danger we are all in."

"Hey, you and I aren't exactly ancient," I said. "I'd just as soon not know so much either."

Loor gave me a quick look, and continued walking.

"So what exactly is the point of this fight?" I asked, hurrying to keep up.

"It is a contest," Loor answered. "You have seen how precious water is in the city. The situation has become so desperate, it has turned us against one another."

"You mean the Batu against the Rokador?"

"It is worse than that," she answered. "Since the underground rivers have gone dry, the Batu are fighting among themselves in their quest for water. Families guard their small supplies fiercely. It is not uncommon for neighbors to battle one another over a small puddle after a rain shower."

One look around confirmed what Loor was saying. When I first saw Xhaxhu, the city was an amazing, fertile oasis in the middle of the desert. Troughs of fresh, clean water ran along the streets. There were rich palm trees, colorful hanging gardens and even fountains that sprayed water in intricate patterns around the massive statues of stone. But now, the city was dry. Bone dry. The troughs were empty, except for dust. The gardens were gone. The palm trees were dying. Sand from the desert blew through the streets and collected in every corner. Walking through Xhaxhu, I couldn't help but imagine that this is what the cities of ancient Egypt must have looked like when the desert began taking over. Unless something changed, I could imagine the city of Xhaxhu one day being buried in sand, waiting for some future civilization to uncover it.

Loor continued, "It has caused a divide among the Ghee warriors. Half of us remain loyal to our mission. We protect Xhaxhu and the royal family of Zinj."

"And the other half?" I asked.

"They have the same goal, but differ in their methods. The royal family has made it known that they wish to work through this catastrophe peacefully. But there is a growing number of Ghee warriors who feel our only hope of survival is to wage war on the Rokador below and claim whatever water they may be holding. With each passing day, the numbers of this rebellious group grow larger. If this drought continues, I fear there will be war."

"Smells like Saint Dane's kind of party," I said.

"I agree," Loor answered. "He has found a time in our history where we are the most vulnerable. The question is, what is he doing to make it worse?"

"That's always the question," I added. "Tell me about this fight we're going to."

"A well was discovered," Loor answered. "It is not known how much water it contains. It may hold a few feet, or lead to a spring. The dispute is over who will control it. The rebel Ghee warriors want it for themselves, to fortify their strength in preparation for their assault on the Rokador. The Ghee loyal to the royal family wish to have the water distributed to all the people of Xhaxhu."

"So this is a battle between Ghee warriors?"

"It is," Loor answered somberly.

"Which side are you on?" I asked.

"I would like to believe I am on the side of Zadaa," Loor answered. "But in this case I am loyal to the royal family. I do not wish to see a war . . . for many reasons."

"I hear you," I said.

We traveled the rest of the way in silence. Loor needed to get her game on, and I needed to keep a low profile in case a thirsty Ghee warrior saw me and felt like beating up on a Rokador. Loor led me to a city square that was nothing more than a sandy patch of ground surrounded on all sides by towering, sandstone buildings. They reminded me of pictures I'd seen of ancient Mayan temples in Central America.

The buildings rose up like multi-tiered pyramids, finished off with flat tops. Some were taller than others, reaching maybe ten stories high. On all levels were carved statues that I can only guess were famous Batu from the past. Most of them looked like fierce warriors, clutching spears or arrows. It wasn't a real happy-looking bunch.

In the dead center of the square was an ornate fountain. Dry, of course. The fountain had a statue that was a larger-than-life depiction of a Ghee warrior battling a huge beast that looked like a fierce cat . . . with two heads. The beast stood on its hind legs, towering over the warrior with its claws out and ready to slice.

"That monster looks familiar," I said. "But that's impossible."

"It is not impossible because you have seen one before," Loor answered. "It is a zhou beast. That machine on Veelox took the image of the zhou from my memory and—"

"The Reality Bug!" I exclaimed. "I remember! When it burst out of Lifelight, it looked like that thing. You're saying those bad boys are real?"

Before Loor could answer, a trumpet sounded a fanfare. I looked up to see that people were gathering on the tiers of the pyramidlike buildings.

"How come nobody's on the ground?" I asked.

"Because that is the battleground," Loor answered.

"Oh," I said. "I guess I don't want to be here either."

"I would prefer you were nowhere near here," Loor said.

"But I want to see what happens," I said. "I'll be careful."

If she was scared, she didn't show it. After all we'd been through, I can't remember once when Loor was actually afraid. She was incredible. Or incredibly oblivious.

"So . . . , uh, win. Okay?" I said.

"I always do," she said with absolute confidence.

I didn't want to wish her luck because I felt like that would be bad luck. I know, that's dumb, but what can I say? I left Loor and found some stairs up to the first-balcony tier. Climbing the stairs wasn't fun. I had to make sure the dark cloak covered my head and arms. Sweat ran into my eyes, making them sting, but I had to keep it on. Man, it was hot. Did I mention that?

I found a secluded spot in the shade of a towering statue and took up my position to watch events unfold below. Looking down on the square, I got the feeling that we were in an arena. The tiers of the buildings around the square were filling up with spectators to complete the illusion. Either the people of Xhaxhu really cared about how this fight was going to play out, or they had nothing better to do with their time. Either way, there was a pretty decent turnout.

As I looked around at the gathering masses, trying to be invisible, I saw something strange. The more I thought about it, the more intrigued I became. All the people around me were dressed for the hot weather, wearing short, lightweight clothes. I saw several Ghee warriors who stood out in the crowd only because they were wearing black, light armor like Loor's. Everyone else was dressed for hanging out in a blast furnace except for me . . . and one other person.

One tier above me, keeping to the shadow of a statue, was someone else wearing a cloak over his head. I didn't think many people saw him because they were all looking down into the square. I may have been one of the few who actually was in a position to see him. Or her. I couldn't tell which, so I'll refer to him as "he." His cloak was dark, but not black. It looked more like a deep, deep purple. Whoever this mysterious guy was, there were two things I knew about him: One, he didn't want to be seen any more than I did; and two, he was very interested in the battle about to take place. Actually there was one other thing I knew. Unless he was some kind of freak, he had to be as hot as I was. But that only made his being there all the more interesting.

A trumpet fanfare sounded again, and the crowd grew quiet. From two different sides of the square, the contestants entered. Each group had three Ghee warriors who marched in together, their heads held high. Loor was one of them. She was also the only girl. It made me incredibly proud, and more than a little scared. More scary was the fact that they all carried weapons. I had seen war games here on Zadaa a while back. In that battle the contestants used short wooden sticks as weapons to knock colored pegs off their opponents. It was more like a brutal game of capture the flag than real war. Not this time. Here in the dry, dusty square, each warrior had a small shield in one hand, and a short, sharp sword in the other.

Sharp swords meant blood. My heart raced. This was no game.

The two groups of warriors met near the fountain in the center of the square, saluted each other with their swords and stepped back. The crowd cheered its approval. Another Ghee warrior entered the square. He strode to the center and stood between the two trios of warriors. He saluted Loor's group, then the other. He looked up at the crowd and announced: "The challenge has been set. The stakes are clear."

I half expected the guy to shout: "Leeeeet's get ready to rummmmble!" He didn't.

He continued, "To the victor goes the right to control the newly discovered well. The match will follow in the long tradition of the Ghee. Victory shall go to the warrior who cleanly severs two heads."

The crowd cheered. My knees went weak. Did I hear right? Were these guys going to go after one another's heads?

I wanted to scream. I wanted to jump down, grab Loor, and pull her out of there. This was insane! I felt totally, absolutely helpless. As impossible as this sounds, I started to sweat some more.

The Ghee announcer shouted, "To the brave, we salute you!"

He saluted the first trio, then Loor and her team. The crowd cheered again. My stomach twisted. There was every possibility that in a few minutes, Loor would be dead. And for what? A drink of water? The announcer walked quickly out of the killing box. Once he was clear, the two groups of warriors faced each other, and saluted again with their swords.

I wanted to shout out, "Stop!" but that would have been about as stupid as this whole spectacle. The two trios of warriors backed off from each other, while keeping their eyes on their opponents. The crowd quieted. It was eerie. There must have been a thousand people lining the balconies of that square, but for that one moment, all I could hear was the wind from the desert blowing through the arid streets of Xhaxhu.

The trumpet sounded again. The battle was on.

ZADAA

The two trios of warriors faced off against each other in the dry, dusty square. They all looked pretty scary, wearing the black leather armor of the Ghee. They were definitely pros . . . all muscle with short lethal swords and cold eyes fixed on their opponents. I saw no difference between the group loyal to the royal family of Xhaxhu, and the rebels who wanted to start a war with the Rokador. They all just looked like . . . warriors. And Loor's being the only girl among them didn't mean she was at a disadvantage. No way. I'd seen her level guys who towered over her. But when you had six fierce warriors mixing it up with swords, anything could happen.

I stole a quick glance up to the mysterious guy who was watching from above. He was hidden beneath his purple cloak, so I couldn't get a good look at his face. I wondered if he was a Rokador trying to blend in, like I was. Seeing him stand there made me realize that wearing a heavy cloak in this kind of heat probably made us stand out more than if we were walking around with our white skin gleaming in the sun. The truth was, it didn't matter. Nobody cared about us. All eyes were focused down into the square, waiting for the carnage.

The warriors didn't move. I wondered if there was going to be some kind of signal to start the fight. Would there be a whistle? Was a referee going to come in and drop his hand? Or maybe this was more like a quick draw, where the action would begin as soon as somebody twitched. My stomach turned at the thought that I would see these warriors going at it until two of their heads were lopped off. I never even thought I could stomach one of those bullfights where the poor bull was skewered at the end. That was bad enough. The idea of people being decapitated went way past gross and into the land of gruesome. Even worse, the idea that one of them was Loor made me go numb. It was like a dream. A really bad dream.

The two groups stood that way for what seemed like forever. I was dying. When was this going to start? The answer came a moment later. What happened wasn't at all what I expected. In some ways, it was worse.

The silence was torn by a hideous sound such as I had never heard before. It was like an angry screech that came from some vicious animal. In fact, that's exactly what it was. A gasp went up from the crowd when two doors were flung open at the base of one of the buildings, and a black zhou beast charged into the square.

Yikes.

The danger just got dialed up. The beast looked pretty much like the statue in the center of the square. It was a giant cat, way bigger than the klees of Eelong, which were pretty much human-size. If it was up on its hind legs, this thing would be taller than Loor by five feet. Its paws were immense, with six curved claws—I could tell because those lethal claws were out and ready for action. The beast was mostly black, but its sleek fur had shiny spots of red blood oozing from small wounds everywhere. I guessed that somebody must have stabbed at it a bunch of times so it would be PO'd enough to fight, like with a bullfight. It was a logical guess, because this monster definitely wanted a piece of somebody. It leaped from the open doorway, ready to roll. Instantly the door was slammed shut behind it. Whoever was inside didn't want this bad boy to turn around and jump back in, looking for the guy who punched it full of holes. The monster crouched on all fours, looking around for something to chew. It snarled viciously revealing razorlike fangs. My mouth went dry.

Oh yeah, in case you forgot, the zhou beast had two heads, both with equally long, sharp fangs. The two heads acted separately, peering around with keen eyes. I wondered which head was the one that controlled the rest of the body. If one wanted to go right and the other left, well, that would be interesting. This whole event would have been interesting, if Loor hadn't been down there about to be eaten.

The two teams of warriors went into action. They held their swords and shields out defensively. I quickly realized that they weren't interested in fighting one another. This was all about the zhou beast. Two heads had to be severed. That's what the announcer had said. I had to guess that the two heads he was talking about belonged to the zhou thingy. The contest was really about which team would get the heads. At first I was relieved that Loor wasn't in danger of being killed by a fellow Ghee. But it was quickly replaced by the fear she would be killed by a two-headed cat monster. Dead is dead.

The two trios of warriors circled the beast. The monster whipped its heads back and forth, watching them. After a few seconds of this size-up, the beast stopped snarling and crouched low, its tail whipping back and forth like, well, like an angry cat. I wasn't sure if it was afraid, or surrendering, or getting ready to spring.

Loor's team struck first. One warrior had a rope and lassoed the zhou like a rodeo cowboy, snaring one of its heads. The crowd roared its approval. But before Loor or her other teammate could make the next move, the rival team took advantage. One of the warriors leaped onto the back of the zhou and raised his sword, ready to plunge it into the back of the two-headed cat. Bad move. Only one of the zhou's heads was being controlled by Loor's teammate. The other head was free and looking for trouble. Before the warrior could attack, the zhou's free head twisted around at an angle that I didn't think was possible. I guess the warrior on its back didn't think it was possible either, or he wouldn't have been dumb enough to be there. The zhou clamped its mouth around the legs of its tormentor, making the warrior scream in agony. He was so surprised that he didn't even use his sword. The zhou yanked the warrior off its back and started snapping its head back and forth . . . with the warrior's leg still in its mouth, the owner along for the ride.

It was gruesome to see this guy being whipped around like a toy, but I didn't want to miss anything, so I sort of squinted. I know, what a wuss, but my words can't describe how horrible it was. After a few seconds the zhou spit the warrior out, sending him crashing down to the dusty ground. His armor was torn and there was blood everywhere, but he was alive. Loor and her team grabbed the rope and worked together to pull the zhou away from the fallen warrior. The zhou fought back, but Loor and the others managed to drag it far enough away from the injured warrior so that his teammates could run in to rescue him. I thought that was a pretty good show of sportsmanship. They had saved their opponent's life.

As it turned out, the injured guy's teammates weren't as caring. Nobody went to his rescue. They let him lie there, dying. I didn't know which was worse, seeing this guy nearly bitten in half, or knowing that his friends didn't care about saving his life. That told me a lot about the Ghee warriors who favored war against the Rokador. They were cold-blooded . . . just the kind of guys Saint Dane loves to hang with. Note to self: Keep an eye on the rebel Ghee warriors.

Things got worse. The zhou suddenly sprang into the air so quickly that the crowd gasped. I did too. This beast got some serious vertical. It moved so quickly that it took Loor's team by surprise. It yanked the rope away from Loor and one other warrior. The third warrior wasn't so lucky. He got his arm wrapped up in the rope. The zhou whipped its head back, pulling the helpless warrior off his feet. The zhou's next move was to pounce on the fallen Ghee. The poor guy tried to roll away, but he was so tangled in his own rope he couldn't move fast enough. Unlike Loor's team, the rival warriors weren't about to try and save him either. No big surprise.

But Loor tried. Without hesitation she leaped at the zhou, shield first. With one arm she slammed her shield into one head, while slashing at the other with her sword. Both heads reared back in surprise and pain, which gave Loor the time she needed. With one continuous move she spun back, slashing her sword again, severing the rope that tied her fallen friend to the zhou. Their other teammate was able to pull the guy to his feet and get him away before the zhou could come after them again.

Round one went to the zhou beast. Round two went to Loor. But the beast didn't look any worse for the wear, and both Ghee teams were hurting. I wondered what would happen if there was no way they could slay this thing. How would this end? Was this going to be a fight to the death for both sides?

The next move was the beast's. Loor had hurt him. She

had drawn blood. He was ticked. He wanted revenge.

He went after Loor.

Before she realized that she was being attacked, the beast lashed out at her arm, slashing her shoulder. Loor dove away, and dropped her sword. This was bad. All she had left to protect herself was the lame little shield. The beast kept after her. Loor needed help.

"The rope," she ordered her teammates as she rolled away from the two-headed cat. Her team went after the rope as she jumped up and bolted in the other direction. The zhou wasn't fooled. He was right after her. Loor sprinted toward the fallen warrior from the other team. What was she doing? The big zhou leaped into the air. Loor dove to the ground, tucked, rolled, and grabbed the sword from the injured warrior's hand. Yes! She was armed again! The zhou landed, ready to attack. Loor quickly slashed at its front paws. The beast screamed in pain and fell hard, headfirst. Or, headsfirst. Face-plant into the dirt. Or faces-plant.

Loor rolled away, having dodged death once again. But the zhou wasn't finished. Not by far. Loor jumped to her feet, and was headed back to her teammates when one of the rival warriors tackled her. I couldn't believe it! She never saw him coming. The crowd booed, but it didn't stop the warrior. He yanked the sword away from her. I guess he felt it belonged to his team, but c'mon! Before Loor had a chance to react, the rival warrior was scampering back to join his own teammate. I was beginning to hate these guys. Loor was once again without a weapon.

The zhou was getting back to his feet. Loor's teammates were on the other side of the square, holding the rope, ready to help. She wasn't even close to them. She was on her own. The zhou got its wits back, scanned the square with both heads, and spotted Loor. She was out in the open, totally defenseless. The zhou squatted down like a cat ready to pounce. I thought there was nowhere for Loor to go. But I was wrong. Before the beast leaped, Loor sprinted for the center of the square and the statue in the dry fountain.

"Run!" I shouted, like she needed to be reminded.

She made it to the statue of the Ghee warrior battling the zhou and climbed. The crowd was going nuts. Loor had become the favorite. I had no idea what she was going to do up there, except maybe buy a little time. I sure hoped the zhou couldn't climb. If it could, Loor would be trapped, and finished. Her teammates didn't know what to do, and the rival team certainly wasn't going to bail her out. She was climbing up onto a dead end. Dead being the operative word.

She had gotten partway up the statue when I saw someone sprinting across the square. At first I thought it was one of the other warriors, but a quick look showed me that someone else had entered the contest. It was Saangi, Loor's squire. What was she doing? She definitely had a plan, because her head was down and her legs were pumping. She didn't have a weapon, and even if she did, I didn't think she stood a chance against the zhou. One thing was sure. This young girl had guts.

On the other side of the statue, the zhou was crouched and stalking. Either it didn't feel like there was any need to rush, or its paws were too slashed up to run. Whatever. It was closing in on Loor. Whatever Saangi had planned, she had to do it fast. She ran to the spot where Loor had dropped her sword, and scooped it up. Without hesitating, she turned and sprinted for the statue.

"Loor!" she shouted, and threw the sword.

Loor looked in time to see her sword sailing toward her. For a brief second my heart stopped, thinking Loor was about to be impaled by her own sword. I should have known better.

Loor plucked the sword out of the air like a pro because, well, she was a pro. I guess Saangi wasn't so bad either. But this impressive move alone wasn't going to win the battle.

The zhou had decided to throw away caution. It began to charge. The final attack was on. Loor was about to reach the highest point of the statue, which was on top of the stone heads. There was some kind of symbolism here that I didn't bother to analyze. It was pretty clear to me that this statue wasn't tall enough. If the zhou could still jump half as high as I'd seen before, he would nail Loor, sword or not.

But Loor's teammates didn't let her down. Before the big cat made its final leap, they tossed the rope at it, lassoing its leg. The beast's eyes were intent on Loor and didn't see it coming. The two warriors yanked hard, keeping the zhou from leaping. The surprised beast looked down at the rope . . .

And Loor made her move.

She leaped off the statue and onto the back of the zhou. But unlike the rival warrior who had tried this before, Loor's weapon was ready. I think the sword hit its mark before Loor's feet hit its back. The power of her fall drove the sword deep into the back of the zhou, all the way to the handle. It was horrible and strange to see both heads react with surprise and agony. Its body arched up so quickly, it threw Loor off. She landed hard, rolled, then popped up, ready to finish the job.

She was too late. No sooner had she been thrown, than the two rival warriors leaped onto the back of the wounded zhou. Using their swords, they slashed at its dying heads. This time I had to look away. No way I wanted to see this. Luckily the crowd was in an uproar, so I didn't have to hear it either. Half the crowd was cheering because the battle was won, the other half was booing because the true winner, Loor, was not going to come away with the prize. This was all about who got the heads. Loor and her team may have stopped the zhou, but they did not get the heads. A technicality, but those were the rules. I didn't think it was fair, but I was more relieved that Loor had survived.

I stood with my back to the square, not wanting to imagine how gruesome the scene was on the ground. As I stood there, I glanced up to the next level to see how the strange observer with the purple robe was reacting. Whose side was he on? Would he be cheering, or jeering?

I never found out, because he was gone.

ZADAA

Do not move," Saangi ordered. "This will only take longer if you do."

It was the first time I heard anyone give Loor an order. Or maybe I should say, it was the first time I saw Loor obey an order. Saangi may have been her younger aide, but she acted more like a stern, caring mother. Loor sat still, impatiently, while Saangi sewed together the wound in her arm. I'm serious. Needle. Thread. Skin. Gross. It wasn't a deep wound that the zhou beast had cut, but it was serious enough that it needed stitching. To these warrior types, it was no big deal. Loor didn't even wince. But I had to look away, or I would have ralphed right there on the floor of Loor's home. That wouldn't have been cool.

"Does this bother you, Pendragon?" Saangi asked. She knew it did.

"Nah," I lied. "I've seen worse."

Loor and Saangi exchanged glances. They knew I was just trying to be casual. I needed to change the subject or risk being revealed as a full-tilt wussy.

"What happened out there wasn't fair," I said. "You should have won."

"You are correct," Loor said. "It was not fair. Saangi should not have interfered."

I didn't expect that. I looked to Saangi. Saangi didn't react.

"Once she entered the contest, it was over," Loor continued. "Outside interference is not permitted. No matter what happened after that, my team would have lost."

"But she saved your life!" I exclaimed.

"I would have found a way," Loor said calmly.

I didn't argue. Truth was, she probably would have.

"I gotta tell you," I said. "That whole zhou-fight thing seemed a little extreme. How much water did they find in that well?"

"It was dry," Loor said soberly. "Once the well was drained, there was no source below to feed it."

"So six Ghee warriors risked their lives to slaughter a two-headed monster over . . . nothing?"

"The water was an excuse," Loor said. "Tension has been growing within the Ghee. Today the battle was over water. Soon it will be for control of Xhaxhu's future, and Zadaa."

"And maybe Halla," Saangi added, while keeping her eyes locked on her stitching.

"Do you have any idea how Saint Dane fits into this?" I asked.

"Not yet," Loor answered. She looked me right in the eye and added, "That is why you are here."

Right. That's why I was there. Sitting in a hot, dusty apartment in a stone pyramid that housed rival tribal warriors on a desert territory light-years from home, watching my friend being sewn up so we could figure out how to stop a demon from destroying everything that ever was and would be. Yeah, that pretty much summed up the situation. Suddenly the idea of watching skin being stitched didn't seem so bad.

"The Travelers have done well, Pendragon," Loor said. "You have done well. But now the battle has come to my home territory. I do not mean to say that Zadaa has more value than the other territories, but I would be lying if I said it did not hold more importance for me. We will not fail here. Saint Dane will be stopped."

She was right. At least about the Traveler part, anyway. We had done pretty well so far in our mission to stop Saint Dane and his quest to control Halla. Denduron, Cloral, First Earth, and Eelong were all victories. He had tried to turn each of these territories toward chaos, and each time we were able to stop him. Our only failure had been on Veelox. That territory was doomed to crumble because the people chose to live in a virtual fantasy world instead of reality. The Traveler there, Aja Killian, was still doing her best to keep the Lifelight supercomputer running and the people alive. Our only hope for that territory was to defeat Saint Dane. For good. Maybe then we could go back to Veelox and help Aja put the pieces back together.

We were four-and-one, but it wasn't as simple as that. We may have turned Saint Dane back on those other territories, but victory often came at a steep price. I can't help but have the sick feeling that in order to win the battles, Saint Dane has gradually chipped away at our strength. What's that old saying about winning the battle but losing the war? As important as every territory is, this wasn't about any one battle. There's no question that we aren't as strong as we used to be, and the war is still very much on. My uncle Press is dead. So is Vo Spader's father. Osa and Seegen were killed too. Writing it all down like this makes me realize just how many people have made the ultimate sacrifice to stop Saint Dane. I don't know if the feeling I have is sadness, or anger. Probably a little of both. Throw in a little fear for good measure. Never forget the fear.

But that's not all. Spader and Gunny were trapped on Eelong when the flume collapsed. (I don't mean to bring up a sore subject, but if I'm going to do a recap here, I've got to include it all. Sorry.) On Eelong we learned our lesson the hard way that the territories cannot be mixed, and only the Travelers can use the flumes. Not only are two Travelers stuck there, but the collapsing flume killed Kasha, Eelong's Traveler. She was the first Traveler of our generation to die. I hope she was the last. As I'm writing this, I'm looking at the small silver urn that holds Kasha's ashes. One day, I swear, I will return her to Eelong. I'm holding out hope that somehow the flume can be repaired, or another one will be discovered. Not just so I can return the ashes, but to spring Gunny and Spader. I need them. Bad. But we have no control over the flumes. The best I can do is hope.

Each of the Travelers I have met so far have been incredible people. We were each chosen from our home territory to stop Saint Dane and his mad quest. Uncle Press told me that Saint Dane is a Traveler too. If that's so, I wonder what territory he is from? Is it a territory consumed by evil? Is being a violent, murdering, sadist normal for Saint Dane's home? Who knows? Maybe compared to the other people of his territory, he's a *good* guy. How's that for a gruesome thought?

I'm not exactly sure why I'm writing this to you guys. You already know it all. I guess as I'm sitting here, getting ready to begin a new chapter of my life, it helps to look back and take stock. Sometimes I think I've done pretty well. For somebody who still has no idea why he was chosen to be a Traveler, let alone the *lead* Traveler, I can be proud of the way I've helped mess up Saint Dane's evil plans. But there are other times, usually late at night when I can't sleep, that I feel like I'm in way over my head. I've had to make some tough decisions, and they haven't always been the right ones. I've been lucky enough that the other Travelers have picked up the slack when I've messed up. Still, I can't help but fear that one day I'll make a move so wrong, it will blow up in our faces, and we will lose it all to Saint Dane.

It makes for a lot of sleepless nights.

There's so much at stake, it's hard to even imagine. Saint Dane is trying to control the destiny of everything that ever existed, or will exist. *Everything.* I can't even get my mind around the concept of Halla, let alone the idea that someone as evil as Saint Dane wants to bring it all down. Before Uncle Press took me away from home on Second Earth, the biggest responsibility I had was to get my homework done and take out the garbage. Half the time I didn't even get to the garbage. Now I've found myself leading a group of people who are the only force standing in the way of the destruction of all living things. And I'm only sixteen! I think. I've lost all track of time. I guess it goes without saying that I'd rather be home, taking out the garbage.

But that's not the way it was meant to be, or so I've been told. The only way I can keep my head on straight is to not worry about the way I'd like things to be, and deal with the way they are. As overwhelming as it all feels, I have to look forward. But that's tough. I can't help but think about home. And you guys. And wonder what happened to my family. And my dog, Marley. And wish none of this ever happened. But it did. I'm here. Chances are good Saint Dane is too.

And so we go.

"Enough," Loor said sharply to Saangi. "It will heal."

Saangi put down the needle and thread, then slathered a sticky, clear ointment on the stitches. "This will protect the wound and keep it dry," Saangi explained.

"I know what it does," Loor said sharply. I got the feeling that she had been stitched up before. She slid a golden-colored cloth strap around her arm to cover the stitches, and just like that, she was good to go. "Thank you, Saangi," she said sincerely.

"May I speak honestly?" Saangi asked.

"Of course," Loor said.

"Battle lines are being drawn," Saangi said. "But you do not accept them. By trying to understand all sides, you have put yourself in a dangerous position. When the battle begins, by aligning yourself with everyone, you may find you are protected by no one."

Loor nodded thoughtfully. "My loyalty lies with the royal family of Zinj," she said. "I believe they are the best hope for restoring peace. But there is a larger concern, and that is Saint Dane. There is no doubt that he is out there, working to push Zadaa closer to war. Unless we find out how, it won't matter whose side anyone is on, for all of Zadaa will be laid waste."

"But every Ghee is choosing their allegiance—"

"It does not matter," Loor interrupted. "If we are to find Saint Dane, we must be able to speak with all sides. That is why Pendragon and I must leave now."

"I would like to join you," Saangi said.

Loor stood up and stretched her long legs. It was hard to believe she had just been through a ferocious battle and been nearly killed about four times over. For her it was all in a day's work. It was already ancient history. Unbelievable.

"No, stay here," Loor ordered. "We will not be long. Pendragon, come with me."

"You got it," I said, and got to my feet.

"What if you need help?" Saangi complained.

Loor picked up the long, wooden staff that I'd seen her

use so effectively as a weapon, and jammed it into the leather harness on her back.

"You are beginning to sound like a worrisome old woman, Saangi," Loor said. "Pendragon and I are capable of taking care of ourselves."

To be honest, I was kind of hoping Saangi would come along. The more the merrier. But this was Loor's show, so I didn't say anything. Loor walked toward her door, with Saangi right on her heels.

"Pendragon is not a warrior," Saangi protested. "He cannot protect you as I can."

Loor stopped short, and Saangi nearly ran into her.

"Do not make the mistake of underestimating Pendragon," she said firmly. "You do not know him as I do."

I was kind of thinking Saangi was right. I wasn't a warrior. If anybody was expecting me to go all "warrior" and protect Loor if things got nasty, they were counting on the wrong guy. When things got rough, it was usually Loor who pulled *my* butt out of the fire. Saangi whirled and shot me an icy look. She may have only been fourteen, but she was definitely not lacking in the self-confidence department.

"It is my job to serve Loor, as her aide and as her acolyte," Saangi said with authority. "I respect your mission. Please respect mine as well."

"Saangi!" Loor shouted angrily. "Do you realize who you are speaking to?"

"It's okay," I said to Loor. I looked to Saangi and smiled. "I can't tell you not to worry, Saangi, but we're all on the same side here."

Saangi didn't back down. She stared at me a moment more, then stepped out of the way to let me pass.

"I will expect you both back here by nightfall," she said.

I walked past her to join Loor at the door and said, "Yes,

ma'am." I then said to Loor, "Yikes, she's bossier than you are."

Loor didn't think that was funny. She held out the heavy, dark cloak I had worn to the zhou battle. "Put this on," she said sharply. I think she was trying to prove that nobody could beat her in the "bossy" department.

"You're killing me with this, you know?" I said, taking the cloak. I was already wearing the soft, white clothes of the Rokador—a lightweight jacket that crossed over at the waist and tied with a sash, along with simple white pants. And sandals. I hate sandals. To me sandals are for old guys who still think they're hippies, or girls who wear plaid flannel shirts. But I didn't have a choice. As bad as it would have been for a Batu to see a light-skinned guy like me hanging around the city, it would have been worse if I had been wearing Batu clothing. Then they could have accused me of being a spy or something. And for the record, I had my Second Earth boxer shorts on. After I had to go boxerless while wearing the disgusting, rotten rags of Eelong, it felt all sorts of good to be back in boxers and wearing the soft cotton clothing of the Rokador. I would have been nice and comfy . . . if I hadn't had to wear the heavy, hot cloak as disguise.

Did I mention how hot it was on Zadaa?

"Where are we going?" I asked.

"To see what we are up against," Loor answered.

We left Saangi looking teed off, and walked out of the apartment and across the large, central courtyard of the Ghee-warrior compound.

"She's tough," I said.

"She takes her duties seriously," Loor said. "She wishes to be a warrior, but I fear she is too impulsive."

"She had pretty good impulses when she bailed you out of that zhou fight," I teased.

Loor didn't even acknowledge this with a look. All she

said was, "I told you. I would have found another way to defeat the zhou."

"Right," I said.

"You doubt me?" Loor asked.

"Me? Never!" I said with a chuckle. I liked needling Loor, but the truth was, I didn't doubt for a second that she would have found a way to beat that beastie without Saangi's help.

Loor led me across the compound, where we passed several Ghee warriors. Some were exercising, others were in small groups in deep conversation. Though the Ghee were divided, they all still lived in this same compound. I wondered how long this could last. If the conflict got worse, having all these macho types living together could get tense. Or violent. I kept hidden in the cloak. I must have looked like an idiot, walking around in this heat dressed like an Eskimo. But nobody stopped us. I guess nobody wanted to mess with Loor. Or an Eskimo.

She brought me to a horse stable that held some of the most beautiful, powerful horses I had ever seen. These were regular old horses, not like the zenzens of Eelong with their extra leg joint. Loor saddled up two with heavy, leather saddles that were very much like Western saddles at home. We both mounted up and were soon trotting through the streets of Xhaxhu. I was becoming pretty comfortable on horseback. Uncle Press taught me to ride when I was younger back on Second Earth, and I'd had many chances to ride on various territories. I really liked it. Somewhere in the back of my head I felt that when this was all over, if I had the chance to go home, I would get myself a horse.

"You've seen Xhaxhu at its finest," Loor said as we rode side by side. "Now you are seeing the horror of what it has become."

As I mentioned before, the city was dry. But man, "dry" didn't cover it. Some water troughs still had a trickle of precious water running through, but it wasn't near enough to quench the thirst of the hundreds of Batu citizens who knelt by the stone troughs, desperate for the slightest bit of moisture. Some even had their entire bodies inside the troughs to lick at the pathetic trickle. It was pretty sad.

The people of Xhaxhu wore simple, one-piece, short outfits in vibrant colors. There were pinks and bright blues, yellows and oranges, with fancy beadwork around the neck and sleeves. On my first trip here, everything had appeared bright and lively. But now that they didn't have enough water to wash themselves, let alone their clothes, the bright colors had become muted and dingy. That pretty much described the city itself. Dingy. The lush, green palm trees that lined the streets now looked like a fence of dead poles. No music played. There was little conversation or socializing of any kind. The whole city, including its people, seemed as if it was drying up and turning into sand.

"What's the deal?" I asked Loor. "Has it totally stopped raining?"

"That is part of it," she answered. "But we do not rely on rain here in Xhaxhu. We are nourished by the underground rivers of Zadaa. That is where the true problem lies."

"What's happened to them?" I asked.

"That is the question." Loor answered. "The only question that matters. The answer will determine the future of Xhaxhu, and of Zadaa."

"And Halla?" I asked.

Loor shrugged. There still was no proof that Saint Dane had anything to do with any of this, but when you found a territory in trouble, with people suffering and ready for war, chances are Saint Dane was lurking around somewhere.

"So then why did this happen?" I asked.

"I do not know," Loor said. "That is what we must find out."

We trotted to the outer border of Xhaxhu, where there was an immense, stone wall that circled the entire city. I'm talking huge. This wall must have been five or six stories high and made out of giant, truck-size boulders. I didn't want to imagine how much backbreaking work had gone into building it.

"The wall is for protection against invasion," Loor said, reading my mind. "The Batu and Rokador are not the only tribes of Zadaa, but we are the most civilized. There are many tribes in the desert who live like animals and feed on one another."

"You mean they steal stuff from each other to survive?" I asked.

"No, I mean they feed on one another. Many of the tribes of Zadaa . . . are cannibals."

Oh. Nice.

"The Ghee are trained to protect Xhaxhu, which in turn protects the underground of the Rokador. This wall is our first line of defense. It is also protection against the elements. A windstorm could rise up with no warning and pelt the city with sand for hours."

As we trotted through a break in the wall—there was no door—I saw that there were giant sand drifts rising up against the outside of the wall.

"How often does a storm come up?" I asked.

"Often enough," Loor answered. "It can be devastating. I hate to think of how Xhaxhu would handle a storm now, when we are so weak."

I briefly wondered if Saint Dane could possibly cook up a storm, but decided that as powerful as this guy was, he did have his limits. I didn't think he could change the weather. At least, I hoped he couldn't.

Loor led us a few hundred yards away from the walled city to another, smaller wall. It wasn't as tall as the protective wall around Xhaxhu, but it was long. We were at a corner. The wall stretched out for what might have been a mile on either side.

"This is what I want to show you," Loor said. "This is one of the farms where food is grown for the people of Xhaxhu."

A minute later we trotted through an opening in the wall. What I saw inside made my heart sink. Xhaxhu was a big city, with a lot of mouths to feed. I expected to see rows of crops, like on the agriculture barge of Grallion on the territory of Cloral. Well, I didn't. All I saw was sand. Lots of it. We walked our horses toward the middle of the field, their hooves kicking it up. The place looked more like an archeological ruin in Egypt than a farm. The emptiness was eerie.

Loor must have been reading my thoughts, because she said, "The farmers have given up. Without water to irrigate the crops, there is no need to plant, or fertilize, or even to keep back the sand."

"Okay, dumb question," I said. "How important is this farm?"

"There are seven that feed Xhaxhu. The farmers have diverted what little water is still available to three of them. But the food grown on three farms is not even close to being enough. We are dipping deeply into grain reserves. We do not expect they will last long. Reality is that soon, very soon, we will starve."

"I guess that counts as pretty important."

That's when something caught my attention. Several feet in front of us, the sand began to shift. Something was moving beneath it, hidden from sight. A moment later I saw more movement a few feet away. Whatever it was, there were two of them. I glanced at Loor. She didn't look worried, but Loor never looked worried.

"What kind of beasties hang out here in the desert?" I asked nervously.

"You saw the quig-snakes at the gate?" she asked.

"Yeah," I said, not liking where this was going.

"The desert is full of snakes," she said calmly.

Snakes. Snakes are the worst. I was about to kick my horse into gear and get the heck out of there, when I heard something behind us. It sounded like a muffled thump. Innocent enough, but since a second ago there was nothing within a hundred yards of us, any sound could mean trouble . . . especially if there were snakes sneaking around beneath the sand. I whipped a look around, expecting to see a couple of slithering sand snakes about to strike. I was surprised to see that we were no longer alone.

Standing behind us were two white-robed figures. Their heads were completely covered, as if to protect them from the harsh desert sun. Both stood facing us, with their legs apart, each holding a short metal bar that was no doubt, a weapon. I shot a quick look in front again, to see if the snakes were getting any closer.

There were no snakes there, either. Instead I saw two more of these robed figures coming up out of the sand like swimmers rising from the water. These guys looked pretty much like the first two. They got to their feet and held out their weapons, ready.

"Uh," I said to Loor. "Those aren't snakes."

"No," Loor said. "They are Rokador."

Rokador. The enemy of the Batu. Not good.

"They look like they know how to use those weapons," I said.

"They do," Loor answered without taking her eyes off them. "They are Tiggen guards. Like the Ghee, they are warriors."

Oh. Getting worse by the second. These bad boys lived underground, but decided to come to the surface and spring a trap. On us. We were alone, with no chance of getting any help from the Ghee warriors back in Xhaxhu. Another battle was about to begin, only this time, it looked as if I was going to be in the middle of it.

ZADAA

Nobody made a move. Not even Loor. I expected her to tense up, grab her wooden stave, and come out swinging. Instead we all stayed frozen in place. The white-robed figures stood silently, the slight wind snapping at their clothes. Eerie. They were in front of us, and behind. The word "surrounded" came to mind.

"Now what?" I whispered to Loor.

"Stay here," she ordered, and slid off her horse. I didn't know what to think. She wasn't in attack mode. She didn't even look tense. I had a brief thought that maybe there had to be some kind of ground rules set before they started beating up on us with their metal batons. All I could do was sit there and see what came next.

Loor walked boldly up to the two Rokador guys who were directly in front of us. Her weapon was still in its sheath across her back. I figured maybe she was throwing out the white flag, since we were outnumbered and all. But that wasn't like Loor. She'd sooner go down fighting. What happened next wasn't like Loor either. She walked up to one of the guys, threw her arms around him, and hugged him.

Uhhh . . .

She said, "It has been far too long, Bokka."

The Rokador pulled off his hood to reveal a white-skinned guy who stood a few inches taller than Loor. He didn't take off his goggles, so I couldn't get a look at his eyes, but from where I sat, he looked to be our age, maybe a little older, with longish blond hair that whipped around in the wind. I guess I could say he was kind of handsome, too. But I'm no expert in that department.

"I've missed you, Loor," the guy named Bokka said. He spoke with a deep, authoritative voice that you would expect from a warrior. Though I can't really say what it was I expected of anybody who lived his whole life underground.

Loor looked at the guy next to Bokka and said, "Is that you under there, Teek?"

The guy pulled down his hood to reveal another blond guy who was a little shorter than Bokka.

"Hello, Loor," he said with a sheepish smile.

"Pendragon," Loor called. "Please come here."

I didn't move. I think I was still trying to process what was happening. I had been expecting a fight, but instead I discovered that these guys were friends of Loor. If that weren't bizarre enough, Loor had actually hugged the guy named Bokka. Let me write that again, she *hugged* him. I had never seen Loor that affectionate with anybody. Including me.

"It is all right, Pendragon," Loor said. "Please join us."

I took a quick glance back at the Rokador behind us. They stood with their weapons ready. They didn't attack, nor throw off their hoods and join in this warm reunion. They just stood there. Ready. For what, I wasn't sure. I slid off of my horse and took off my black cloak, dropping it to the sand. I figured these guys should see that I looked like a Rokador. Sort of.

Loor put her hand on Bokka's shoulder like he was a bud and said, "Pendragon, this is my oldest friend, Bokka. We have known each other since we were children."

I held out my hand to shake, which made the three other Tiggen guards tense up and lift their metal weapons, ready to rock. I suddenly got the vibe that these guys were like bodyguards. Even Bokka took a step back. I stood there with my hand in the air like a dope, afraid to move.

"It is all right," Loor assured them. "Where Pendragon comes from, that is a sign of friendship."

Bokka relaxed, took my hand, and squeezed. Youch! This guy had a grip! But I wasn't about to squeal. No way.

"Hello, Pendragon," Bokka said. "What tribe do you come from?"

I glanced at Loor, partly because I didn't have an answer, and partly as a plea to get this guy to let go of my poor hand before bones started snapping. Loor reached out and gently eased us apart. For a second I thought my fingers were fused together. I had to work them to get the circulation back. I wouldn't let Bokka see that, though.

"I met Pendragon when I made the journey to the far desert. He is from the tribe known as . . . as . . ." Loor was scrambling. Bokka didn't know about the Travelers. I had to bail her out.

"Yankees," I said. "The Yankees tribe." Hey, what can I say? It was the first thing that came to mind. "It's a strong tribe," I added. "Respected by all . . . except for our mortal enemies, the Sox tribe. They hate us. Especially the Red ones. Cannibals. Nasty characters."

"I haven't heard of these tribes," Bokka said.

"That's okay," I said. "We haven't heard of you either."

"But you're dressed as a Rokador," the guy next to Bokka said. "Why is that?"

"This is Teek," Loor said, changing the subject. I'm happy to say he didn't put out his hand to shake. One bone crusher was enough. "Ask him to show you the scar from when he was bitten by a zhou beast."

"Loor!" Teek said, complaining. "Won't you ever forget that?"

Bokka laughed. Loor chuckled too, and said, "When we were young, a small ceegee bug crept into his bunk while he was asleep. It nipped him and he jumped up shouting 'Zhou! Zhou!' The scar is quite impressive . . . if you look closely enough."

Loor and Bokka chuckled. Teek looked embarrassed, but smiled. "I had been dreaming of a zhou. You would have done the same thing."

Teek wasn't upset. He took the goofing good-naturedly. This was all one big touchy-feely reunion. The whole thing had me off balance. I'm not sure why it struck me as odd at that moment that I could understand these guys and they understood me. Part of the benefit of being a Traveler is that we hear all languages as our own, and others hear us as if we were speaking their language. I guess maybe that still seems like magic. But it always works, so I shouldn't be surprised anymore. Much.

Bokka said, "You did not tell us why you are dressed as a Rokador, Pendragon."

Loor answered for me. "With his white skin, we decided it would be better for him to dress as a Rokador, in case he ran into fierce Tiggen guards, like you."

Bokka nodded. He bought it.

"You have such light skin," Teek said. "Do you live underground too?"

Loor jumped in, trying to get control of the situation before I said something else stupid. She said, "The tribe known as—"

"Yankees," I reminded her.

"Yes, Yankees, lives on the surface in a forest of many trees that block the sun. That is why his skin is lighter than the Batu."

"Yes, it's a forest called the Bronx," I threw in. Why not? It wasn't like he was going to prove me wrong.

"Pendragon is a wise tribe member," Loor continued. "He has traveled here to help us."

Bokka looked me up and down, sizing me up.

"Can you fight?" he asked.

"The idea is to try and solve your problems without fighting," I said.

"If you can do that," Bokka said, "then you have more wisdom than anyone around here . . . from either tribe."

I didn't know how I felt about this guy. I guess I should have been saying that any friend of Loor's was a friend of mine, but if I were being totally honest, I didn't like the way they were being so chummy. Loor and I may not have known each other since we were little kids, but we had been through a whole lot together. You would think that facing death while trying to save everything that exists would have brought us a little closer together than two people who played ring-around-the-rosy when they were kids . . . or whatever it is they play here. Loor treats me like I'm some kind of business partner. That was okay, I didn't think she had more warmth in her than that . . . until I saw her with Bokka. She never let her guard down with me like that. And he was a Rokador! An enemy of the Batu!

"Have you discovered anything?" Loor asked Bokka, changing the subject.

"Nothing," he answered. "Except that the Tiggen guards have been put on alert. The Rokador elite are expecting the Batu to attack at any time."

"But what of the rivers?" Loor asked. "Has there been any explanation from the Rokador elite?"

"Same as always," Bokka answered. "They blame the drought on lack of rain in the north—where the rivers are fed. I have tried my best to find out more, but with no luck."

"Uhh," I interrupted. "What exactly are you talking about?"

Loor explained, "As you know, the Rokador live underground and control the rivers of Zadaa. For generations they have worked with the Batu, channeling the water between the different rivers to ensure it flows to where it is needed most. It is a valuable service that they provide for the Batu."

"But we do more than that," Bokka added. "The Rokador are manufacturers. In our factories we create clothing and weapons and building materials and most everything needed for our own survival . . . and for the Batu's survival as well."

"That is true," Loor said, sounding a little defensive. "In return the Batu grow crops and tend livestock to feed both tribes. We also protect the Rokador from the wild tribes of the desert and the zhou beasts and snakes you've seen. Without the Batu, the Rokador would perish."

"Without the Rokador, the Batu would live like primitives," Teek threw in.

Loor quickly shot back, "We are a warrior race that does not shy from life by cowering beneath the ground."

"You're a crude people with no modern skills," Bokka said quickly. "Look at your ancient weapon, and look at mine." He held up his shiny, steel baton. "This is the product of an advanced race of modern thinkers."

He and Loor exchanged cold looks. They seemed ready to start throwing fists.

"Sandworm!" Loor threw at him.

"Barbarian!" Bokka shot back.

The two glared at each other intensely, then broke out laughing. I'm serious. Loor actually laughed!

"We have argued like this since we were young," Loor said.

"The truth is," Bokka said, "both tribes need each other."

These guys were having a little bit too much fun. I was feeling like an outsider, but I couldn't let that get in the way of our mission.

"So if they need each other so much, why is everybody worried about a war?" I asked.

"There's always been tension," Teek said. "But since the rivers began to run dry, the tension has turned into suspicion, and anger and fear. It has now given way to outright hatred."

Loor said, "The Batu are accusing the Rokador of holding back the water until we are so weakened that they will rise up from their underground home and seize control of Xhaxhu."

"But why would they do that, if everything was going so well?" I asked.

"To put it simply, we are running out of space," Bokka said. "Our way of life is simple. We have always lived below ground. But as our population grows, that is becoming more difficult. The fear among the Rokador is that if we try to venture aboveground, we will be treated as inferiors and forced to live like animals."

"They aren't wrong," Loor said. "Many Batu would treat the Rokador badly. But the royal family of Xhaxhu understands their plight. Our prince, Pelle a Zinj, has made it his goal to convince our people to accept the Rokador as equals."

"But not everybody agrees," I stated.

"That is correct," Loor said. "What is the saying you use? It is a no-win situation. Many of the Batu will not accept the Rokador, and now they fear that the Rokador are holding back the water."

"In return," Bokka said, "the Batu have stopped providing us with food from the surface. We are starving."

"And we are thirsty," Loor said.

"So what's the deal with the water?" I asked. "Are the Rokador holding it back?"

"That's what I'm trying to find out," Bokka answered. "I've heard rumors that there is something dramatic about to happen, but I cannot find out what it might be."

"And with each passing day, the danger of war grows stronger," Loor said somberly.

"So, Pendragon of the Yankees," Bokka said. "Do you still feel as if you can help us prevent this catastrophe?"

I didn't like the way he said that. It was all sorts of smug, as if he knew darn well I had no clue of how to keep these two tribes from killing each other. Unfortunately he was right. I didn't.

"I'll get back to you on that," I said.

"I am torn, Bokka," Loor said. "If the Batu are going to attack, I want to warn you. But then it would mean my own people would be at a disadvantage."

Bokka took both of Loor's arms and held her reassuringly. "I understand," he said. "The only thing we can do is try and stop this from happening. But if it does, I am a Rokador, and you are a Batu. I am a Tiggen, you are a Ghee."

They held eye contact. The grim reality was obvious. These two could very well end up having to fight each other. As much as I wasn't sure about the guy, I wouldn't want that to happen to Loor.

"If you hear anything," Loor said, "please, contact me."

"And the same for you," Bokka said. "Good-bye, Loor. When we meet again, I hope it will be under better conditions . . . as it was when we were young."

Loor nodded sadly.

"I don't know who you are, Pendragon," Bokka said to me. "But if Loor says you can help us, then I do not doubt her."

I nodded. What else could I say to that?

"Good-bye, Loor," Teek said. "And to you, Pendragon."

Bokka took a step backward and flipped up his hood. Teek did the same. Bokka waved to the Tiggen guards behind our horses. I turned to look, but didn't see them. I took a step to my right to get a glimpse of them, but it was too late. They were gone. Vanished into the sand. I turned back around to see that Bokka and Teek had disappeared as well.

"They're like worms," I said to Loor.

"There are tunnels everywhere," Loor said. Without another word Loor strode back to her horse and mounted up. I did the same. We snapped the reins and started back to the city.

"So how is it you got so friendly with a Rokador?" I asked as we trotted along. "I thought the two tribes didn't mingle."

"At one time we did," Loor answered. "Especially the children. Bokka and I were marked at an early age to be trained as warriors. There were two camps, one outside of Xhaxhu and one belowground. Groups would take turns traveling to the other camp. It was a way for us to learn the ways of our tribal neighbors."

"Things have changed," I said.

"Yes they have," Loor said sadly. "That kind of cooperation no longer exists. The royal family of Zinj has been trying to bring our tribes back to the old ways, but prejudices and anger run too deep."

"So, was this Bokka guy your . . . boyfriend?"

Loor thought about the answer. I didn't like that. I wanted her to scoff and say: "Nah! Are you kidding?" But she didn't.

"Under different circumstances, we may have ended up together," she said sadly.

"I guess being from enemy tribes made that tricky," I said.

"Yes," she replied. "And finding out that I was a Traveler did not help either."

Oh. Right. That. So she and Bokka were not meant to be. Awww, too bad. Man, am I being mean or what? I decided to change the subject.

"What about this royal family?" I asked. "Ninja something or other?"

"Zinj is the family name," Loor corrected. "The crowned prince is named Pelle a Zinj. Though he has not yet taken the throne, he has slowly taken on the responsibilities of ruling the Batu. Even the Rokador recognize his wisdom. The king and queen are preparing to hand over the crown very soon."

"Is that good or bad?" I asked.

"It is good," Loor said confidently. "Very good. He will make a wonderful, fair leader. He has dedicated his life to forging a treaty with the Rokador. But I fear it will be in vain. The drought has seen to that."

"Or maybe it was the Rokador who have seen to that," I cautioned. "Like you said, there may be more to this drought than bad weather."

It was a grim journey back to Xhaxhu. I now had a pretty good handle on what the trouble was here on Zadaa, but figuring out something to do about it was a whole nother matter. There seemed to be only two possibilities. One was that Saint Dane was somehow manipulating events. When he disappeared from the celebration at Black Water, he did say he was coming to Zadaa, and he never went to a territory just to hang out. The other possibility might actually be worse. If the rivers had dried up here simply because there was a funky weather thing happening, there was nothing anybody could do about that. The sad truth might be that a war between these two tribes was the way it was meant to be. It would be tragic, but the job of Travelers wasn't to interfere with the normal course of a territory's history. Our only concern was if Saint Dane tried to monkey with things. For Loor's sake, I hoped that wasn't the case. If Saint Dane wasn't involved, then I had no business here. Loor was from Zadaa. She would have to do what she had to do. But I was from Second Earth. I would have to back off. This was going to be a tough call. But I couldn't make it until I found Saint Dane. Or he found me.

We trotted the horses back through the giant opening in the wall of Xhaxhu and went right back to the Ghee stables where the horses were kept. As I think back on what happened next, and I think about it a lot, I can't believe how dumb I was. I guess I have to give Loor some of the blame too, but it was mostly my fault. It was a simple, stupid mistake that could have been easily avoided. But it wasn't. I messed up, and I paid the price.

"Rokador!" a gruff voice screamed.

We had just gotten off our horses. I looked around, wondering what Rokador would have been idiot enough to stroll into the lion's den, the home of the Ghee. There were none to be seen. That's because the person being called out, was me. I was the idiot. I instantly realized my mistake. I had taken off my dark cloak out in the sandy farm. There was so much to get my mind around back there, I had forgotten to put it on again. It was still lying out there in the sand. Loor's mind must have been elsewhere too, for she didn't even notice. So here I was, looking all sorts of gleaming-white, having strolled right into the belly of the beast.

"I will handle this," Loor whispered to me. "Say nothing."

A tall Ghee warrior strode up to us with madness in his eyes. As luck would have it, this guy was bigger than Loor. She stood in his way, saying, "I am taking this Rokador to the superior for questioning—"

The guy didn't stop. He blew past Loor, knocking her out of the way like she was a doll. Whoa. I had never seen that happen before. This day was full of a lot of things I hadn't seen before. I didn't like any of them. As this angry giant strode toward me, I was like a deer caught in the headlights. I backed off, and hit into my horse. There was no place to go. The guy grabbed me by the front of my Rokador jacket and lifted me up until I was on my toes.

"How *dare* you?" he seethed. The guy was out of his mind. That much I could see. "You ride into the Ghee compound? On a Batu horse?"

Loor tried to get between us, saying, "He is my responsibility. I brought him here."

The Ghee warrior looked at Loor and said, "And you will bring him out, when I am finished with him."

The guy held me tighter and dragged me out of the stable and into the light of the compound. By now, several more Ghee warriors had heard the commotion and started to gather. Loor trailed behind, trying to take control.

"What is your division?" Loor demanded. "Who is your commander? This is my prisoner. Your superior will punish you for standing in the way of—"

"Someone quiet her!" the tall Ghee shouted.

Instantly Loor was jumped by two big Ghees. Whatever was going to happen, Loor couldn't stop it. The tall Ghee dragged me to the center of the compound, and threw me to the ground. I landed hard, rolled once, then popped back to my feet ready to, well, I'm not sure what I was ready to do, except run. That wasn't going to happen because we were quickly surrounded by Ghees. I was trapped inside a circle of enemies, with a very big guy facing off against me.

"Never let it be said that the Ghee are unjust," the tall warrior said with a sneer. He walked to one of the other warriors and yanked the guy's wooden stave from the harness on his back. He walked back into the circle and tossed the six-foot stick at me. I caught it, if you could call it that. It was more like I stopped it from hitting me in the head by blocking it with my hands. The weapon fell to the ground. The Ghee warriors laughed.

"L-Look," I said nervously. "I have agreed to speak with your superior and tell them all I know."

The tall Ghee laughed and slowly walked toward me. "That is good to know," he said with a chuckle. "And I will allow you to do that. But first, you must get past me."

The guy suddenly shot forward, grabbed my jacket, and jerked me toward him until we were nose to nose. We were so close I could smell his sour breath. At that instant something triggered in my memory. Smells can do that. It's like there's a direct link from your nose to your memory. It wasn't a happy memory either. I looked into the guy's wild, brown eyes and saw something that made my heart race even faster, if that was possible. We were so close, I was the only one who could see. His eyes changed color. They went from deep brown to lightning white. My mind didn't accept it at first. It was impossible, right? Wrong.

"Welcome to Zadaa, Pendragon," the Ghee warrior whispered. His voice was suddenly calm. Gone was the rage. He was totally in control of himself . . . and me. "Let's put aside all the intrigue this time and show each other how we really feel, shall we?" he said.

In that instant I saw his eyes return to brown as he tossed me down on the ground. I was too stunned to react. The Ghee warrior reached behind his back and pulled out his wooden stave.

"Pick up the weapon!" the warrior bellowed, showing rage once again. Though now I realized it was all a show for the spectators.

Reality had finally settled in. The good news was, I had found Saint Dane.

The bad news was, I had found Saint Dane.

ZADAA

Saint Dane had taken the form of a Ghee warrior. It didn't matter what side he was on. He could have chosen to be with those loyal to the royal family of Zinj, or put in with the rebels who wanted war with the Rokador. Right now, that didn't make a difference. He was a Batu. I looked like a Rokador. We were enemies in the eyes of everyone here . . . and we were about to fight. I shot her a quick glance to see that Loor was being held firm by three of her fellow warriors.

"Loor," I shouted while keeping an eye on Saint Dane. "It's Saint Dane."

Loor gave a quick, surprised look to the tall, dark warrior who had called me out. Saint Dane returned her look, gave her a quick nod, and actually winked at her.

I saw Loor's eyes grow wide. "Who is that Ghee?" she shouted to the other warriors. "I do not know him! He is not one of us! We must summon the commander and—" The Ghees holding her clamped a hand over her mouth. She struggled to get away, but it was hopeless. I was on my own. I looked at Saint Dane. He gave me a quick shrug, as if to say: "Guess you're on your own, pal."

The only choice I had was to reach down and pick up the weapon.

You guys know, I'm not a fighter. Up until that moment I'd managed to survive by luck, and with the help of my fellow Travelers. The one serious fight I'd been in was on Eelong, but that was against a prisoner who was half my size, and so starved and weak that it was a joke. I was now looking up at a warrior who towered over me, with biceps like you'd see in a graphic novel about gladiators. If that weren't bad enough, it was Saint Dane behind all that muscle. My enemy. The demon who was trying to lay waste to Halla. I was scared, obviously. But I was also confused. Why was he doing this? This wasn't his style. For him, fighting was too . . . simple. Unimaginative, even. I had some vague shred of hope that he had another reason for doing this, other than to beat me up. There was a chance this fight would never happen.

"Are you serious?" I asked, trying not to sound as scared as I was. "Isn't fighting beneath you?"

His answer was to lash out with his stave and clock me on the side of my head. It was so fast, and so violent, I wasn't sure if I was more hurt, or shocked. I stumbled, but stayed on my feet. The crowd of Ghees cheered. Saint Dane circled in front of me, relaxed and smiling.

"If there is one thing you should have learned by now, Pendragon," Saint Dane said, "it's to expect the unexpected."

He lashed out with his weapon. I ducked, but it was a fake. He never swung. The Ghees laughed. I backed away. Saint Dane stayed with me.

"Come now, Pendragon," Saint Dane taunted. "Don't you want to hurt me? This is your chance. No pretense. No illusion. Just the two of us."

"Yeah, right," I said. "You can turn yourself into a studly warrior with armor and all. I'm just me. Is that fair?"

Saint Dane laughed. I hated it when he laughed. "Fair?" He chuckled. "What has fair got to do with anything?"

I caught a glimpse of Loor struggling to get away from the Ghees. They held her firm. She couldn't bail me out this time. This was all about me . . . and Saint Dane. I thrust my stave at his gut. He knocked it away as easily as if he was batting a moth. He then cracked me across the back with the other end of his weapon. I stumbled forward. It hurt. He wasn't fooling around.

"Come now, Pendragon," he taunted. "Show a little enthusiasm." He flicked his stave up quickly, catching me on the chin, making me bite my lip. I tasted blood. "Where is your rage? Think of how miserable your life is because of me." He punctuated this with a quick jab that clipped my shoulder. He was playing with me. He was enjoying this. I wasn't.

"Don't you miss your family?" he jeered. "Don't you want revenge for those you've lost? So many have died in your futile crusade. Surely that makes you angry."

He flipped one end of his stave toward me; I actually knocked it away with my weapon and was smart enough to know another blow would quickly follow. He spun away from me and whipped the other end of his weapon backward, like he was paddling a canoe. But I was ready for that one too. I dodged out of the way. It was the third attack I wasn't ready for. Saint Dane spun back around and jabbed at me under-handed, catching me square in the gut. Oof! It hurt, but I was okay. So far. The crowd of Ghees watching didn't matter to me anymore. They were nothing more than a blur on the edges of my vision.

"You can't keep this up." Saint Dane chuckled. "You're going to get hit. Like Kasha did with that rock that crushed her skull."

He was baiting me. He wanted me to attack. I realized if that's what he wanted, it was the one thing I shouldn't do.

"Your uncle couldn't avoid me either. Was there much pain when the bullets tore through his heart? Did he die quickly? I certainly hope not."

That one hit too close to home. I lost it and swung my stave at him in anger. He took a simple step back and danced out of the way. I had swung for the fences and missed, losing my balance and nearly falling over in the process. I sensed that the Ghee warriors were once again laughing, but I didn't care. I had to force myself to get my act together.

That's more like it," said Saint Dane, chuckling. "Rage is such an exhilarating emotion, no?"

He flipped his stave again and clipped me on the knee. I staggered, but I was back in control. At least of my emotions, anyway. I had to be. It was the only chance I had. Saint Dane was making me look bad, but I was beginning to think that making me look foolish was exactly what this fight was about. To embarrass me. To show his power over me. There was no question that if he wanted to, he could knock me silly. But he hadn't. Don't get me wrong, the knocks I was taking hurt, but they weren't serious. I figured I'd be black and blue the next day, but I'd survive. It made my confidence grow. I figured I knew what this fight was about. I decided it was time to fight back.

So I laughed.

"You find this amusing?" Saint Dane asked with a touch of confusion.

"Getting hit, no," I said. "But when you try this hard, all it says is you're getting desperate."

He didn't expect that. He jabbed his stave out at me, but I dodged it.

"Four times," I continued, trying not to let the pain creep

into my voice. "That's how many times you've tried to control a territory, and how many times we've stopped you cold."

He spun around and swung his weapon at me. I ducked. He missed, but it was so close I felt the wind rustle my hair. If he had connected, he would have knocked me into next Tuesday . . . if there was such a thing as Tuesday on Zadaa.

"And Veelox?" he asked. I heard the confidence in his voice waver.

"No biggie," I said cockily. "When you go down for good, we're going back and pull Veelox out too. Aja is working on it right now. Veelox was a draw."

Saint Dane took a step back as if I had physically hit him. I was definitely getting to him. I didn't think it was because of what I was saying. None of it was new news. It was more the way I was saying it, with absolute confidence. It was becoming pretty clear that Saint Dane's plan to embarrass me in this fight, wasn't working. I was slowly getting the upper hand.

"You can beat up on me all you want," I said. "But you can't change the truth. You are losing. I think you know it too. You're getting so desperate that you've resorted to beating me up with a stick. How pathetic is that?"

Saint Dane staggered. Oh yeah, I was hitting him worse than he had hit me.

"You can't even make me feel bad about Uncle Press anymore, because he promised that one day I would see him again. And I believe that. I believe all the Travelers will be together again. I don't know how, but you know what? I think you do. Oh yeah, you know exactly how it's going to happen, and you're getting nervous because that time is getting closer. And when we're all together again, it'll be the end of your sad little quest."

I was hammering him, bad. I saw it in his eyes. He

clutched his stave, wringing it fitfully. It was time to go in for the kill.

"And you know what? The real reason you're going down is because that's the way it was meant to be . . . and there's nothing you can do to change it."

Since the day I learned that I was a Traveler, I had made a lot of mistakes. Some of them small, others not so small. What I had just done with Saint Dane in the Ghee compound on Zadaa was one of the big ones. Saint Dane's plan in picking this fight may have been to embarrass me in front of the Ghees and hurt my confidence, but in that one second, his plan changed. I'm sorry to say that I changed it. What happened next I had brought on myself, with my words. The only good thing I can say about it was that it was fast.

Saint Dane took me apart.

With an angry roar he charged at me, the wooden stave spinning like a helicopter blade. I threw my weapon up to protect myself, but Saint Dane dropped to one knee and kicked up at me with his boot, catching me right in the gut and knocking the air out of my lungs. I doubled over as he stood, driving his knee into my forehead. He was done playing. He wanted to hurt me. To say that I had never taken a beating like this is probably the biggest understatement I have ever made. When his knee hit me, I saw colors. Splotches of green and yellow floated everywhere. My ears rang.

I had a vague understanding that the Ghee warriors were laughing and cheering, but they sounded like they were on the far end of a long tunnel. I turned away to get my balance and cover up, but I wasn't fast enough. A dark flash hit me square on the cheek that must have been Saint Dane's weapon. It spun me around so fast, everything went blurry. I think this is when I dropped my weapon, not that it was doing me any good anyway. I fell to my knees and looked up in time to see Saint Dane winding up and attacking me with his weapon like a lumberjack chopping with a giant axe. The stave came straight down at me.

In that one fleeting instant I realized that this could be the end. It's amazing how many thoughts can race through your head so quickly. In times like this, it's almost like time slows down. It suddenly all seemed so clear. Forget the games. Forget the mystery and the misdirection and the complex plots to turn the territories toward chaos. The only thing standing between Saint Dane and the conquest of Halla were the Travelers, and I was their leader. With me out of the way, he would have a much easier time. Believe it or not, in that one instant I actually wondered what had taken him so long to figure that out.

Saint Dane was trying to kill me.

But I wasn't giving up. I threw my arm up and caught the full brunt of the blow. It didn't even hurt. My battered body was beyond pain at this point. My brain couldn't process it anymore. I deflected the blow from my head, but the force was so strong it knocked me onto my back. Saint Dane leaped at me, ramrodding the end of his weapon into my ribs. Once, twice, again. I knew he must be breaking bones, but I couldn't feel anything anymore. The demon got right into my face.

"Beg me to stop," he hissed angrily. He hit me in the ribs again. I looked into his eyes. They had returned to lightning white . . . and were mad with rage. "Beg me," he demanded. I felt his spittle land on my cheek. His anger had turned to frenzy. There was no plan here. No plot. No trickery. He had lost it.

"*This* is the way it was meant to be, cretin," he growled. "This is what the future holds, for you and your like. That is the promise I made, and I will keep it." He hit me again, but

I was beyond caring. "You will beg for my forgiveness and mercy."

I looked up at him. I can't begin to tell you where I got the strength or the brass to do this, but I smiled and croaked out, "Dude, you are talking to the wrong guy."

He froze. I'm not sure why. Maybe it was because he couldn't believe I had that kind of brass either. At least, that's what I hoped. But the shocked look on his face quickly turned back into a fury that I feared would finally put an end to this beating, and my life. He reared back and let out a howl like a wild animal standing over fallen prey. He looked back down at me and raised his weapon. This was it. End of the line.

"Stop!" I heard a voice call out.

Saint Dane snapped a look to the crowd. He hesitated long enough so that two Ghee warriors had the chance to run in and pull him off me. Somebody had saved me. There was somebody out there who took pity on a poor Rokador. But I didn't recognize the voice. I was flat on my back and barely able to move, but I painfully turned my head to where the command had come from.

Standing in the crowd was a new spectator. He wore a dark purple robe that covered his head. It looked familiar, but I didn't know why. How could I possibly know anybody on Zadaa? I then remembered where I had seen him before. It was at the zhou battle. He was the mysterious guy who was in the tier above me, watching the fight. Whoever this guy was, he was my new best friend. He took a step into the circle, and I was surprised to see that the Ghee warriors backed away from him and knelt down on one knee.

Who was this guy?

He walked up to me and said in a soft, compassionate voice, "This is not what we are about." He then took off the robe to reveal a tall, dark-skinned guy who wore an incredibly ornate, bright red tunic with an elaborate design around the neck. He held out his hand to me and said, "I am Pelle, heir to the throne of Zinj. We will take care of you."

I looked at the guy's hand. For a moment I thought about reaching up for him. After all, he was my new best friend. Instead, everything went black and I passed out.

ZADAA

The first thing I saw was Loor.

I had opened my eyes a crack. Only a crack. That's as far as they'd go. I guess it was because they were swollen from the pummeling I'd gotten. But I didn't have to open them far to recognize Loor. She was sitting close, looking at me. The expression on her face didn't change when I opened my eyes. I think that's because my eyes didn't open far enough to even look like they were open. But I could see her, and she looked fine. And worried.

"How long?" I asked, though I have no idea what it sounded like because my mouth felt about as dry as that sand farm where we met the Tiggen guards. When she heard me croak, Loor snapped to attention and came to my side. She knelt down near my head, which made me realize I was in bed and not still lying in the Ghee compound.

"Pendragon!" she exclaimed. "I was afraid you would never wake up!" There was true feeling in her voice. She sounded worried, relieved, concerned . . . all those good emotions I wasn't sure she actually had in her. At least as they applied to me, anyway. It made me feel much better. Okay, maybe not *much* better since I was a swollen mass of throbbing pain. But I figured I should take the good stuff where I could get it.

"Water?" I asked, and immediately realized I had just asked for the one thing it was probably impossible to give. But I got it. Loor held a cup to my mouth, and I took a sip. It felt good on my lips, and in my mouth, but I coughed when I tried to swallow and blew most of it back out again. What a waste of an eighth of an ounce of liquid gold.

"Oops" was all I could say, lamely.

"Again," Loor ordered and gave me another sip.

I was in more control this time and was able to take a sip and swallow. The water helped to lubricate things a little, so I was able to speak without sounding like Frankenstein's monster.

"How long?" I asked again.

"Since the fight?" Loor asked.

I nodded. It hurt to nod. I was about to find out that doing a lot of things was going to hurt. Including breathing, eating, moving . . . pretty much everything including blinking. Yes, it even hurt to blink.

"You have been asleep for twelve suns," Loor answered.

Twelve suns. The days on Zadaa were around twenty-four hours long, as far as I could tell. That meant I had been unconscious for nearly two weeks, give or take a sun. I think Loor must have seen the surprise on my face because she quickly said, "You were given herbs to help you sleep, and heal."

Oh. So I had been drugged for nearly two weeks. I guessed that was better than being in a coma from having been beaten into mush. I was slowly focusing, which wasn't such a hot thing. My mind was coming around, but that meant I was becoming more aware of the sad and painful shape I was in.

Everything hurt. Everything. Except my toes. My toes were cool. Woo-hoo! I thought of asking for a little bit more of that herb she had mentioned so I could slip back into dreamland, but decided I should stick around in reality for a while. Looking around, I saw that we were in a small room with stone walls. It looked very much like Loor's home in the Ghee pyramid, but there wasn't much in here except for the bed with the grass mattress that I was lying on, a stone chair where Loor had been sitting, and a low table that had some cups on it. Loor must have seen that I was trying to get my bearings because she said, "This is where the Batu care for the sick and injured."

I was in the Batu hospital. It looked straight out of *The Flintstones*. I wondered if some goofy pelican would show up and deliver my medication. I know, dumb thought, but give me a break. I was hurting, and drugged.

"Saint Dane?" I whispered.

"Gone," was Loor's answer. "I asked many of the Ghee if they knew him, but nobody had ever seen him before. I believe Saint Dane turned himself into a Ghee warrior solely to . . . to—"

"To beat me into jelly," I said, putting it bluntly.

"I am ashamed that I could not help you, Pendragon," Loor said, dropping her head in embarrassment.

"Don't be," I croaked. "There was nothing you could do. I know that."

She nodded like she knew it too, but she was definitely feeling bad about the whole thing. Maybe not as bad as I felt just then, but bad just the same.

"We will avenge you," she said with venom. "Of that, I swear."

"Yeah, maybe," I said. "But that might be what he wants. Everything he does is about pushing us into doing things that help him. He may have beat me up just to get you to go after him. We can't fall into that trap."

Loor nodded again, and took my hand. I nearly screamed. It was the same hand I had thrown up to deflect Saint Dane's killer blow. He must have broken bones. But you know, I didn't stop her. It was a rare event when Loor showed me a sign of affection. I wasn't going to let a little thing like searing pain from broken bones stop her. I tried to squeeze her hand back, but I didn't have much of a grip.

"You are being cared for by the finest doctor in Xhaxhu," she assured me.

"Don't they hate Rokadors?" I asked.

"Not when the prince of Zinj himself orders that you be cared for," Loor answered proudly. "There have been two Ghee warriors guarding your room since you arrived. You are safe here."

"I like that guy," I said, stating the obvious. "What's his name again? Payday something-or-other?"

"Pelle a Zinj," she said. "I believe he holds the future of Xhaxhu, and Zadaa, in his hands. He is a man of peace; that is why he stopped the . . . the fight."

"It wasn't a fight," I said. "It was a slaughter."

Loor didn't comment. "You will heal," she said. "And we will return to our mission."

Our mission. Right. That mission had taken a strange turn.

"Saint Dane totally lost it," I said. "He wanted to kill me. It didn't seem like an act or anything. If it weren't for that prince guy, he would have."

"I agree," Loor said. "His rage consumed him."

I pulled my hand away from Loor's. Affection or not, it hurt.

"Maybe that means he's getting desperate," I said. "We

may be closer to beating him than we think."

"If only that were true," Loor lamented.

"There's something else," I said. "When Saint Dane was at his worst, he said something strange. He said that this is what the future holds for me, and those like me. He said it was a promise he made, and he was going to keep it. What kind of promise is that? And who did he make it to?"

Loor frowned. "Saint Dane has always brought pain and suffering. But to know he made someone a promise to do so is . . . troubling."

"Yeah, troubling," I said. "That's one way of putting it. I'd say it's freaking scary. Could there be somebody else out there who Saint Dane answers to?"

We let that question hang in the air. The possibility was far too horrifying to even think about.

"Whatever the answer is," Loor said, "we will not find it until you are well. You must rest. She backed away from me and sat down in the chair.

"Go home," I said. "As long as there are guards outside, I'll be fine."

"Either Saangi or I have been by your side from the time you were brought here," Loor said. "We will be here until you walk out with us."

Wow. Loor and Saangi had been watching over me. That's a strange thing to hear. I hoped I didn't drool in my sleep. I was grateful, of course. But I wasn't sure why they did it. Was it because I was the lead Traveler, and they needed me in the battle against Saint Dane? Or did Loor have deeper feelings than that? As I lay there, watching Loor sitting up straight in the chair, I remembered back to the first time I met her on Denduron. She thought I was useless. It bothered me because nobody likes to be seen as a loser, but I had no idea how to prove her wrong. She was self-confident to the point of arrogance, with the ability to cut through all the junk to see the truth in most any situation. I, on the other hand, was totally freaked out about being yanked away from home. I spent most of my time in a frightened and confused haze. Her confidence gave me strength and clarity. Together we saved Denduron.

I've grown up a lot since then, but in many ways I still feel like the scared kid who left home on the back of Uncle Press's motorcycle. Loor, on the other hand, is a rock. Since Denduron I'd often asked for her help, and she always came through. Now the fight had come to Zadaa. Her home. This time, she needed my help. As I lay on that bed, numb from pain and starting to drift off to sleep again, I swore to myself that no matter what happened from here on, I would not let her down.

I'm not exactly sure how much time I spent in that Batu hospital. If I were to guess, I'd say it was about a month. Medical care on Zadaa wasn't exactly like what we have on Second Earth. There were no thermometers or blood tests or intravenous drips or anything like we have in our hospitals at home. Medicine was limited to some foul-tasting liquids that I had to drink every couple of hours. This guy would come in who I assumed was a doctor. He'd put his hands on my head and on my arm as if he could "sense" what was wrong with me, and then give me a different concoction to choke down. It all seemed so bogus, except for the fact that I gradually began to feel better.

Like I said, at first I couldn't even move. Every part of my body was swollen and sore. Even my face. I had been healing for a month before I even realized this! Rolling over in bed was a major challenge, but this doctor guy kept insisting that I move. He was relentless, saying that the only way I would heal was to move. I wanted to slug him. I think I would have, if I had been able to lift my arms and make a fist, that is. But that wasn't going to happen. If I could have done some damage on the guy with my toes, I would have.

I think I would have argued more with him, if Loor or Saangi hadn't been there watching. I didn't want to look like a wuss in front of them. But man, I was in pain. It was like medieval physical therapy, with the only reward for all the hard work being some drink that made Listerine taste like sniggers. At first he just had me roll over in bed. Then he got me to sit up, then stand. That was a tough one. My legs were so weak they wouldn't even hold my weight at first. But my strength returned pretty quick. I think the only broken bones I had were in my left hand, the one I deflected the weapon with. Maybe a couple of ribs, too. I didn't know for sure because there was no such thing as an X-ray machine. But if pain was any indicator, bones were broken. They had my arm wrapped pretty tight with cloth to keep my wrist from moving. I probably had a concussion, too. That's how bad the headaches were. And the dizziness.

As the days went by, the headaches got less intense and the room stopped spinning. I guess I don't have to say that I had never gone through anything like that before, so it's hard to say how well I was doing. But it seemed to me that after the massive beating I took, I was healing pretty quickly.

The big day finally came that I could walk out of the room and into the corridor. But that was only half of what made it such a big day. The doctor was on my left and Loor on my right, in case I took a header. With all this support, I took my first tentative steps out of the room. I felt like the Tin Woodsman in *The Wizard of Oz* before they oiled him up. Everything was creaky and stiff. But I knew I had to work through it, so I shuffled out. The hallway stretched out to either side of my door, with rooms spaced every few yards . . . just like a hospital at home. Nothing special. But man, I was happy to see something other than the four walls of that room. The next thing I saw were two, huge Ghee guards standing on either side of my door, just as Loor had said.

"Hi, guys," I said, all friendly.

Neither answered or even looked at me. They may have been assigned to protect a Rokador, but they didn't have to like it. I decided not to push it. I took one more step, when suddenly the two guards knelt down on their knees and dropped their heads. For a second I thought they were being all respectful toward me. But then the doctor and Loor did the same thing.

"Uhh, what's the deal?" I asked, confused.

A second later I got my answer. Walking boldly down the corridor toward us was an impressive sight. It was a group of men led by Pelle a Zinj, the crown prince of Xhaxhu. He was wearing the same ornate clothing he had worn on the day he saved me, along with a purple cape that trailed behind. He was followed by a couple of other royal-looking types, along with two Ghee warriors. It was a royal entourage, and I was standing in their way.

"On your knees," one of the Ghee guards growled in a whisper.

I wanted to kneel down, but my body wouldn't let me. So I stood there kind of hunched over and bowed my head. It was the best he was going to get.

Pelle spotted me and broke into a big smile. "You are walking!" he said with a friendly bellow. "I am so happy to see that."

I then realized he was coming to see me!

"Forgive me, I can't kneel," I said while keeping my eyes on the ground.

"There is no need, my friend," Pelle said. "Everyone,

please rise." Everybody else got back to their feet, but kept their heads down in deference to their prince.

"What is your name?" the prince asked me.

"Pendragon," I answered.

"Pendragon," Pelle repeated, as if trying it on for size. "A unique Rokador name."

I shrugged. What was I going to say?

Pelle continued, "Pendragon, I have come here today on behalf of all Batu to apologize for the horrible crime that was committed against you."

I saw the two Ghee guards shoot him a quick look, as if they couldn't believe he was apologizing to a Rokador.

"I know there is tension between our people. That cannot be denied. But seeing the depths to which we have sunk, sickens me. Rest assured that we will hunt down the rogue Ghee who did this to you. He will be punished."

I was a hair away from telling him not to bother. He hadn't seen a Batu beating up on a Rokador, but two Travelers from distant territories going at it. He wasn't going to have a whole lot of luck tracking down Saint Dane. I decided not to set him straight.

"Once you are well, and return to your people, please tell the Rokador elite that I plan on doing everything in my power to resolve our differences, and bring back the balance and mutual trust that the Rokador and Batu have enjoyed for generations. Nothing else has more importance to me. That is a promise."

I didn't want to say anything that would tip him off to the fact that I wasn't a Rokador and didn't know anybody down below, elite or not.

"Thank you your, uh, Your Majesty," I said with bowed head. I glanced to Loor, who gave me a slight nod. "Your Majesty" was the right title.

"I will gladly do as you request," I said, totally winging it. "I believe your sincerity not only because you saved my life, but because you have been so gracious in making sure I have been cared for during my recovery. I am forever in your debt. Thank you."

I figured that was about as generic a reply as I could give. Besides, it was the truth. He did save my life.

"These are difficult times," Pelle said. "Our only hope of survival is by restoring the atmosphere of cooperation, and trust. Our two great tribes will either survive together, or perish separately."

I nodded. Wise words. I hoped there were enough Batu who thought the same way he did.

"Now, I will leave you to rest," Pelle said. "And extend an invitation. The Festival of Azhra is upcoming. I would like to invite you, Pendragon, to be my guest for the celebration."

"I'd be honored, Your Majesty," I answered.

"Wonderful!" he exclaimed. "Now all you must do is mend. Are they treating you well here?"

"No complaints," I said.

"Then best of luck with your recovery." He looked to the doctor and added, "Take care of him."

The doctor bowed and said, "Like he was my own son, Majesty."

Pelle gave me a quick smile and a nod, then turned and hurried off. The Ghee guards, along with Loor and the doctor, did a quick kneel again. Once the royal entourage was gone, everybody stood up. I could feel the dark looks being shot at me by the Ghee warriors.

"I guess I'm going to a festival," I said to Loor.

"You should be honored," she said. "The Festival of Azhra is the most joyous of all days for the Batu. It celebrates the ancient king, Azhra, who fought his way through the desert and tamed this oasis to create a home for the Batu . . . the city of Xhaxhu."

"Sounds like a party," I said. "Now all I have to do is walk."

From that point on my recovery went pretty quickly. Once I started moving, each day I felt a little better. Pain is a weird thing: When you've got it, you know it—but you don't really know the moment it stops. It's kind of like, afterward you realize: "Hey, it doesn't hurt to breathe anymore. Or walk. Or blink." Little by little I was getting back to normal.

Every day Loor or Saangi were by my side. They were my guardian angels. They even slept next to my bed. The doctor was kind enough to bring in a grass mattress for them to sleep on. I kept telling them to go home, but neither listened. To be honest, I'm glad they didn't. Not only did they help with the therapy and exercises, they ran interference for me whenever I ran into another Batu in the hallways. Which was often. The Batu would first act all surprised that a Rokador would dare be in their hospital, like I was bringing in disease or something. Then some would start yelling at me to get out. Loor always stood up to them, saying how I was a guest of Prince Pelle a Zinj. That would instantly make the Batu back off. It also didn't hurt that Loor looked like she was ready to rip their faces off if they messed with me.

That's not to say that every Batu hated my guts. Some were actually nice. I got into a lot of conversations about how they wished things could go back to the old ways, when the Rokador and the Batu lived in harmony. I guess what I was experiencing was the divide between the Batu. Half hated the Rokador and wanted to march down to the underground and annihilate them; the other half wanted peace and a diplomatic resolution.

The one thing they all had in common was the need for water. Food was getting scarce in Xhaxhu. What little they could still grow on the farms had to be spread among many mouths. No one was allowed to bathe, and the latrines that usually had running water, didn't. That meant the waste just sat there. I don't have to tell you that everybody pretty much avoided the latrines, and made their visits short and not very sweet. From what I could tell, the water crises on Zadaa was reaching critical mass, which meant that whatever Saint Dane had in store for the territory was bound to come into play very soon.

The one thing I had plenty of during my stay in the hospital was time. There was a whole lot of lying around going on, especially in the beginning, and I guess I don't have to point out that they didn't have TV on Zadaa. Or radio or an MP3 player or anything else you might use to kill time while doing nothing. I took that time to take stock. I tried to replay everything in my head, from the time I had left home to the moment Saint Dane crushed me in the Ghee compound. After all that thinking, I came to two conclusions. One is the decision I told you about at the beginning of this journal. I'll tell you more about that in a minute. The other is tough for me to write about, but I have to.

Everything I've written in my journals has been the absolute truth as I've seen it. Many things were difficult to write about, either because they were so disturbing, or there were things I had to admit about myself that I wasn't too proud of, but they were always the truth. That's the whole point of the journal, right? That's why I have to write what I'm about to write, as tough as it may be. I'll just write it straight out.

I have feelings for Loor.

There, I said it. I can't say I'm in love with her, I'm not even sure what that means. But as time goes on, I have found myself growing closer to her. It goes way beyond a physical attraction. Loor and I have been through so much together, I feel as though she is one of the only people in all of Halla who can truly understand where my head is. And since the fight, she has cared for me and shown me a side that I didn't imagine existed. For all of her outward toughness, she is an amazingly caring person. She is beginning to remind me of her mother, Osa. I think I understand now more than ever why she is a Traveler. It's not just for her strength, it's for her compassion, which may be the same thing.

I'm not saying this to make you feel bad, Courtney. Or to diminish the great things you've done. I don't even know if I'll ever tell Loor how I really feel. But writing these journals has been the one thing that's kept me sane throughout this ordeal. Writing helps me to keep my thoughts in order and to analyze what has happened. It would be wrong if I stopped writing the whole truth now, and the truth is that my feelings for Loor are growing stronger every day. I'm sorry I had to tell you in a journal this way, but I think it would be worse if I didn't. This doesn't change how I feel about you, Courtney. Or maybe it does. I don't know. This is such a confusing thing. One thing I know for sure, you are one of my very best friends in the world. After reading what I just wrote, I hope you still want to be.

That being said, I had come to another conclusion. This one I had to share with Loor.

The day finally came when I was cleared to leave the hospital. The doctor gave me a final once-over and said he could do no more for me. I was still weak, but that may have been because I was lying around for so long. It was time to move on. I thanked the doctor for all he had done. The guy never spoke much, unless it was about my treatment. I had no idea what side of the Rokador debate he fell on. That's why I was so surprised by what he said when I left that hospital room for the last time.

"I do not know who you are," he said. "I do not believe

you are a Rokador. But I believe you have the power to help us. That is why I am proud to have treated you."

What could I say? All I did was nod and say, "Thank you."

Waiting for me in the hallway were Loor and Saangi. Loor had the dark cloak that I had forgotten out on the farm, the one that had started this whole fiasco in the first place.

"Once you leave here," Loor said. "You will no longer have the protection of Pelle a Zinj."

I put the cloak on gladly, in spite of the heat. I told you how hot it is here, right? The three of us left the hospital and walked through the streets of Xhaxhu, back to Loor's home in the Ghee pyramid. Nobody gave us a second look, I'm happy to say. When we were safely inside, I said to Saangi, "Thank you for everything."

Saangi shrugged and said, "It is my job." She then lightened up for a second and said, "You are very brave, Pendragon. I am glad you have recovered."

I nodded a thanks, then said, "If it's all right with you, I'd like to speak with Loor in private."

Saangi shot a hurt look to Loor. Loor stared back at her, not giving her any sympathy.

"I will be outside," Saangi said. "Call when you need me."

"Thanks, Saangi," I said.

The girl nodded and left.

"You do not need to thank me, Pendragon," Loor said before I could speak.

"I wasn't going to," I said, sounding flip. "It's your job too."

She gave me a confused look. I smiled. "I'm kidding. You know I can't thank you enough."

"What is it you want to say to me?" she asked.

I had practiced these words for weeks. Once I had made my decision, I wanted to make sure that I told Loor in such a way that she knew I was dead serious.

"Sit down, okay?" I said.

Loor sat cross-legged on a floor mat. I paced, getting my thoughts together. This was tough.

"You've known me since I first became a Traveler," I began. "From day one I've survived because the other Travelers were always there to bail me out. You most of all."

"We have all played our part," she said modestly. "You do not give yourself enough credit. You are our heart, Pendragon. Surely you know that."

"Yeah, well, this heart just got pretty banged up," I shot back. "Things have changed, Loor. Saint Dane wanted to kill me."

"I believe he has tried to kill you many times."

"Not like that."

"Dead is dead."

"This was different! Whenever he's thrown something at me, at us, it always turned out to be part of his bigger plan. That's how he's been manipulating us. There was always some other purpose. I think that purpose may have changed. Yeah, we've been in danger before, but I don't think he ever wanted us to die . . . until now."

"You do not think this was also part of some plan?" Loor asked.

"Maybe at first it was," I replied. "But I'm telling you, Loor. He really wanted to beat my brains out. He didn't expect me to walk away from that fight. I told you before, maybe that's a good thing. Maybe we're starting to make him sweat. But whatever the reason, I think being a Traveler just got more dangerous. It's not just about the territories or Halla anymore. I'm beginning to think it's about us, too."

Loor let that ominous thought sink in.

"I do not disagree," she finally said.

"And that's why I need your help more than ever."

"You know I will always be there for you, Pendragon," she said.

"But what about the times when you aren't there? Or you can't help me. You were in the Ghee compound, and I still got hammered."

This hurt Loor. I saw her flinch.

"I'm sorry, but it's the truth," I said. "It wasn't your fault. You can't be two places at once."

"What are we to do?"

This was it. This was the decision I had been wrestling with for weeks. It was something I had been avoiding since the beginning of my adventure, but I no longer had that option. It scared me to death, but not making this move scared me even more.

"Loor," I said. "Teach me how to fight."

Loor gave me a blank stare. I don't think she expected that.

"What's the matter?" I asked. "Don't you think I have the guts for it?"

Loor stood up. This was making her uncomfortable.

"It is not that," she said. "I believe you are the most courageous person I have ever met."

She did?

"Then what's the problem?" I asked. "I'm strong. I'm athletic. I may not be physically back up to speed yet, but it won't be long before—"

"If you die, what will we do?" Loor barked. "I do not doubt that you would make a fine warrior," she continued. "But without you, I do not believe we have any hope of defeating Saint Dane."

This is a weird thing to say, but Loor was scared. I had never, ever seen her frightened before. The idea of going it alone against Saint Dane, without me, terrified her. I actually saw tears forming in her eyes.

"I hear you," I said. "But I'm not asking this because I

want to start running around picking fights. You know me better than that. I need you to give me the skills to defend myself. This war is going to decide the future of all territories, all time, all everything. How stupid would it be to lose that war because I didn't know how to stand up for myself in a simple fight?"

Loor stood staring at the ground.

"Give me the tools to protect myself, Loor. That's all I'm asking."

I said all I wanted to say. The next move was hers. Whatever decision she made, I was prepared to accept it. After a long moment she reached up and wiped a tear from her eye and looked straight at me. Her fear was gone. Her indecision was gone. The Loor I knew was back.

"I will teach you, Pendragon. But I will need help."

I'm writing this journal the night that Loor and I came to that agreement. Tomorrow, my recovery and my life will enter a new phase. I am going to learn the skills I'll need to survive. The skills of a warrior. I have no big illusions. I don't expect to come out of this like some kind of fighting machine. I'm still me. But at the very least, I want to be able to push some of the fear away, and have the confidence that when backed into a corner, I'll stand as good a chance of escaping alive as my opponent.

If that opponent happens to be Saint Dane, so be it.

Try not to worry about me, guys. I've dropped a lot on you in this journal. Please know that my thoughts are always with you. I want to come home. I want to see you both again. But that can't happen until the final play is made in this drama. To make sure I'm around to see that happen, I've got to step it up.

I've got to fight.

Wish me luck.

END JOURNAL #20

● SECOND EARTH ●

Wish me luck.

Mark Dimond dropped the light brown, crusty pages of Bobby's journal from Zadaa onto the floor of his bedroom. He looked around the room. He was alone. Courtney Chetwynde was not there to read with him. It was the first time that this had happened since Bobby's very first journal had arrived. A profound sense of loneliness closed in on him. He had no one to share this latest news with. No one to help him analyze what was happening. No one to keep him from spiraling into a full-on panic attack. He was going to have to suck it up and deal with it on his own.

He really wished that Courtney were there.

In spite of all he had just read about Bobby, his mind went back to Bobby's previous journal. Journal #19. The last one he read with Courtney. It was the journal that explained how badly he and Courtney had messed things up by using the flume to go to Cloral, and Eelong. As acolytes, their job was to protect Bobby's journals and to stay on their home territory and help the Travelers if they visited Second Earth. Their job wasn't to jump into the flume and join in the fight against Saint Dane.

But they had.

They knew it was wrong, but at the time it seemed as if they had no choice. They were the only ones who knew of Saint Dane's plan to use a killer poison from Cloral on the territory of Eelong. If they hadn't gone to Cloral to get the antidote and bring it to Eelong, Saint Dane might have destroyed the territory. Bobby might have died. But by doing it, they weakened the flumes. Acolytes weren't supposed to use the flumes. When they left Eelong for the final time, the flume there collapsed. Not only did it trap Spader and Gunny on Eelong, but it killed the Traveler Kasha. It was all because he and Courtney chose to travel. Things would never be the same.

All these thoughts came rushing back at Mark as he sat in his bedroom, alone, remembering the moment when he and Courtney read the devastating news about Kasha and Spader and Gunny. They had returned from Eelong only an hour before, flush with excitement. They had helped save Eelong. They were heroes who finally got the chance to help Bobby, instead of simply reading his journals. And as a final bonus, they had returned home to find that no time had passed since they had left, so they didn't even have to explain to anyone why they had been gone for over a month. Everything was perfect.

And then Journal #19 had arrived. The journal that would change everything for them. They had taken the journal to the basement of Courtney's house, which is where they read most of Bobby's journals. When they finished reading Journal #19, Mark and Courtney stood staring at nothing for a long time.

Courtney started to cry. Mark had never seen Courtney cry before. It was almost as shocking as the news Bobby had sent. Almost. Mark wanted to comfort her, but he didn't feel all that hot himself.

"I'm sorry," Courtney finally said. "This was all my fault. I talked you into it."

"It w-wasn't," Mark said instantly. "Sure, I didn't want to go at first, but everything you said I agreed with. W-We knew about the poison. We knew Seegen was dead. If we didn't do something, the klees would have destroyed Black Water and Saint Dane would have won Eelong—"

"And Kasha would still be alive," Courtney shouted. "And Spader and Gunny would be helping Bobby on Zadaa right now. Saint Dane played us, Mark. He gave up Eelong to help him win the bigger war, and we made it easy for him."

"N-No!" Mark shouted back, pacing. "We don't know that for sure. Things might have been worse if we didn't help."

Both wanted to believe that, but there was no way to know if it was true or not. Bobby wrote that they shouldn't blame themselves, but Mark and Courtney were having trouble following that advice.

Courtney wiped her eyes and stood up, saying, "You should go home, Mark. Bring the journal to the bank in the morning."

Mark rolled up the parchment paper and tied it with the leather twine.

"Are you okay?" he asked.

Courtney nodded. "Let's let this sink in and talk about it later, okay?"

"Sure," Mark said as he climbed the basement stairs. "I'll see you tomorrow at school, okay?"

Courtney didn't answer.

Mark went to school the next day as usual, though it wasn't easy. He was a very different guy than the day before. That's because in between the two days, he had spent an entire month on Eelong, matching wits with Saint Dane. To everyone at Davis Gregory High, Mark was wallpaper. His claim to fame had always been that he was the best friend of the popular Bobby Pendragon, but it had been two years since Bobby and his family disappeared. People forgot. The disappearance of the Pendragon family was yesterday's news, and without Bobby around, nobody thought twice about Mark Dimond. They had no idea that Mark was taking part in a battle to save everything that ever was or ever will exist. To them, he was a quiet little guy with long, black hair, who ate carrots to improve his vision. He was a member of the prestigious Sci-Clops science club, but that was his only nonschool activity . . . other than fluming to another territory to save a race of cat people from extermination. The most anybody ever spoke about Mark was when they saw him hanging around with Courtney Chetwynde. That's because Courtney was beautiful, smart, athletic, and not even close to being the kind of girl people expected to hang out with a dweeb like Mark. People would whisper. What did she see in him? Of course nobody could know that they were joined by a common bond—their friendship with Bobby and their knowledge that the universe was in danger.

Most of all, Mark and Courtney needed each other to stay sane.

Going to school that next day was one of the toughest things Mark had ever done. He had just taken part in a grand adventure that none of these kids at school could possibly even imagine. Now he had to go to school and act like nothing had happened. But it had. He was a different guy.

And Courtney didn't show up.

He didn't call her at first, figuring she needed time to decompress. But after a few days, she still hadn't come to school. Mark called her cell phone. It was turned off. He went by her house when he knew her parents were at work. Nobody answered the door. He didn't want to have to talk to her parents, but the scary thought started creeping into his head that the Chetwynde's might have disappeared the same way the Pendragons did, so he took the chance and called her at home. He was relieved when Courtney's father answered the phone. Mr. Chetwynde said that Courtney wasn't feeling well and didn't want to talk with anyone. Mark thought the guy sounded tense.

He was glad to hear that nothing bizarro had happened, but he was getting more worried about Courtney by the second. Was she okay? He knew she had been having a tough time of it, even before they hit the flumes. He feared that the realization of how badly they had messed up on Eelong might have pushed her over the edge. Courtney was incredibly proud, maybe too much so, Mark thought. He knew that one of the reasons she had so badly wanted them to jump into the flume was that she was scrambling to prove something to herself, and what better way to do that than save an entire territory?

Mark didn't blame her for convincing him to use the flume. She may have been the one driving the bus, but he was a willing passenger. She didn't twist his arm. Much. Now he feared that after having salvaged her self-confidence by saving Eelong, finding out that it was the wrong thing to do would crush her. He desperately wanted to talk to her, but her parents wouldn't let him. No calls, no visits, no letters. It was like she was a prisoner in her own house. Or a patient.

Courtney hadn't come back to school for the rest of the semester. He asked around and found out that she was having her school work sent to her house. There were lots of rumors that she was sick, but Mark didn't believe them. He knew that her problems were more psychological than physical, not that that was much better. After a while he stopped calling. He figured that he'd wait until he got Bobby's next journal, then he'd somehow get a message to her that it had arrived. He knew that there was no way she could resist finding out what was happening to Bobby.

But no more journals had arrived.

Mark did his best to put Bobby out of his mind and get on with his life. He tried not to think of what a mess they had made of things by jumping into the flume, though he often sat in bed late at night, wide awake, trying to decide what they could have done differently. He never found the answer, which in some ways was comforting. They may have seriously messed up, but after going over every fact, it didn't seem as if they'd had any choice but to do what they'd done. It gave him a small bit of comfort. Very small.

Mark immersed himself in the Sci-Clops science club. But that was difficult too, since his archnemesis, Andy Mitchell, was now a member. Mitchell was an idiot. A thug. A guy who had bullied Mark his whole life. Yet there Mitchell was, a member of the most prestigious science club in the state. At first Mark thought it was a mistake, but the more he saw Mitchell at work, the more he reluctantly had to admit that the goon did have an aptitude for science. Math, in particular. He may have barely been able to write his name with a crayon, or read a stop sign, but Mark saw that Andy Mitchell had an incredible ability to see mathematics on a 3-D level. It was uncanny. Mark figured he was one of those idiot savant types. Heavy on the "idiot." On the one hand he was actually creating chemical compounds that might revolutionize manufacturing, on the other hand he'd go out and extort money from the geeks at school to buy cigarettes.

The only real solace Mark took from this twisted situation was that Andy Mitchell didn't target him for abuse anymore. It was the first time in the history of dorkdom that being the member of a science club actually *saved* someone from getting beaten up.

The rest of the semester passed uneventfully. Meaning, there were no journals from Bobby. However, with only a few weeks left of school before summer vacation, Mark received a letter that changed things once again. It was from Courtney.

> *Dear Mark,*
> > *Hi. I hope you're doing well.*
> > *I shouldn't be avoiding you like this, but as you*

know, I'm pretty much avoiding everything these days. I'm sorry to say this, but most of all I'm avoiding you. I know, it's wrong. But I am so disappointed in myself, seeing you makes me feel even worse. I've let you down. I've let Bobby down. When I start thinking about how I let all the Travelers down, and what that could mean, all I want to do is cry. The idea is too much for me to even think about. I used to believe I could handle anything. Now I can't even handle seeing you, someone I think the world of.

I'm writing you now to tell you that as bad as I feel, I'm getting better. I'm going to be okay, I think. But I'm leaving. My parents want me to go away to summer school. I agree with them, for a change. It's a good idea. I've got to get my act together. Going to a place where nobody knows me sounds like a good thing to do. I'm hoping that in a couple of months I'll have sorted things through enough that I can come back and be the kind of person I know I can be: a better friend to you, a better friend to Bobby, and a better acolyte.

I don't mean to leave you on your own. I'm sorry for that. But I really think for the time being you'll be better off without me. If another journal comes in before I return, I don't want to know. I'll read it when my head is in a better place. Please don't think I don't care. I do. More than I can even tell you. I think that's part of the problem. I've got to get some perspective.

As much as I'm trying to put what happened on Eelong out of my head, the one thought I can't shake is that someday, maybe soon, Saint Dane will set his sights on Second Earth. I believe that when

*that happens, if it happens, we will be needed again.
I want to be ready. It's the one thing that keeps me
focused.*

*I want to say something happy like "have a nice
summer," but that seems so trivial. Please know that
I think about you every day. I'm going to get through
this, and I'm going to come back.*

I know that's the way it was meant to be.

I miss you.

Love,

Courtney

Moments after Mark found this letter in his mailbox and took it to his room to read, his ring began to twitch. He jumped in surprise. Bobby's next journal was on the way in. Mark didn't even have time to process Courtney's message before having to think about news from Bobby.

"Perfect," Mark said to himself sarcastically. "Why does everything always happen at the same time?"

The gray stone in the center of the ring he had received from Loor's mother, Osa, transformed into a brilliant, clear crystal. He took the ring off, placed it on his floor and watched as the familiar delivery process took place. The ring grew to the size of a Frisbee, opening up a conduit to the territories. Light flashed from the hole, bringing with it the haunting musical notes that carried the cargo along.

Mark closed his eyes and waited until the music stopped. Seconds later the ring returned to normal. Lying next to it on the rug was Bobby's next delivery. Journal #20. It was a scroll of parchment paper, tied with a leather twine . . . exactly like #19. In the past Mark would have immediately called Courtney so the two could read the journal together. It was their pact. They would never read the journals alone. The note from Courtney changed all that. Courtney didn't want to read this journal. Mark was on his own. It was an odd feeling. Even scary. As different as Mark and Courtney were, they were always able to bounce ideas off each other to help understand what Bobby's pages contained. Now Mark would have to do it on his own. He would be the only one to know of Bobby's latest adventure. So he read.

◉ SECOND EARTH ◉
(CONTINUED)

The words of Bobby's Journal #20 brought no relief for Mark. The drought problem on Zadaa was bad enough, but Mark was frightened by the fact that Saint Dane tried to flat out kill Bobby. It pained him to hear how his best friend had been hurt so badly, and it put a knot in his stomach to know that Loor was going to teach Bobby how to become a warrior.

As bad as all that was, the idea that Bobby was falling in love with Loor made Mark wince. After learning about what a hard time Courtney was having, he couldn't imagine how she would react to hearing that the guy she had a crush on since they were in the fourth grade was now turning his affections toward somebody else. Nothing that Bobby wrote in his journal was good news. A whole boatload of worry had been dumped on Mark.

The kicker was, he had nobody to share it with.

The only consolation was that Courtney didn't want to know about the journal, which meant he didn't have to tell her that Bobby was falling in love with Loor. He hoped that by the time Courtney returned from summer school, she would be strong enough to handle the news—or at least he'd have time to think of a way to tell her without sending her back off the deep end. No, there was no good news in Bobby's latest journal.

Mark rolled it up, along with Courtney's letter. He brought them both to the National Bank of Stony Brook, where Bobby had opened up and paid for a safe-deposit box in 1937. First Earth. It was the place where Mark kept all of Bobby's journals, holding them for the day that Bobby would need them again, for whatever reason.

He left the bank, ready to explode. There was too much bouncing around in his head. He fought the urge to run to Courtney's house. He needed to talk with somebody, but there was nobody around . . .

Except for Andy Mitchell.

"Hey, Dimond," Andy Mitchell called as Mark walked out of the bank. Mark jumped in surprise. "What are you, some kinda business guy going to the bank?"

"Yeah, that's it," Mark said quickly, keeping his head down. He kept walking. Andy went with him.

"What's your hurry?" Mitchell asked.

"I, uh, I got homework," Mark lied.

"Ahh, homework!" Mitchell scoffed. "The school year's almost over. Take a break. I'll buy you fries at Garden Poultry."

This made Mark stop short. He looked at Mitchell. The thug looked the same, with the greasy spill of blond hair falling in his eyes and the ever-present redness from acne. Still, something was different. Mitchell had never, ever been nice to Mark.

"Why?" Mark asked. "What do you want?"

"Nothing!" Mitchell answered defensively. "Jeez."

Mark stared square at Mitchell, not accepting the answer.

Mitchell buckled. "Okay, maybe something. I want to ask you about that robot you made last year. You know, the one that won the state contest?"

"Yeah, I know which one. What about it?"

"Don't be so twitchy. I was just interested is all. I mean, we're both in Sci-Clops, right?"

Mark had more strange information thrown at him in the last few hours than his brain could accept. First there was Courtney's letter, then Bobby's journal, then here was Andy Mitchell, the hated Andy Mitchell, wanting to talk shop with him. It was almost more than Mark could take. Normally he would blow Andy off and keep walking. But he needed to get his mind off Courtney, and the journal.

"All right," Mark said. "Fries at Garden Poultry."

"Now you're talkin'!"

They started to walk off together, but Mark suddenly stopped and said, "Wait, where did you get the money for fries? Did you steal it?"

"Gimme a break," Mitchell said. "I got a job."

"What job?" Mark asked suspiciously. "Is it legal?"

"You're a piece of work, you know that? I make deliveries for my uncle," Mitchell answered. "He's got a flower store. Is that legal enough for you?"

"You have your driver's license?" Mark asked, surprised.

"Sure, don't you?" Mitchell asked.

Mark didn't. He hadn't even thought about asking his parents for his learner's permit. Could he be any more of a loser?

"Sorry," Mark finally said. "I've got a lot on my mind."

The odd couple walked up Stony Brook Avenue to the Garden Poultry Deli where they picked up a couple of boxes of golden-delicious fries and some sodas. They sat in the pocket park nearby, and Mitchell listened to Mark tell him all about the killer robot he designed that won both the local and state science fairs. It was the project that earned him his invitation to join Sci-Clops. Mitchell listened with interest, which was amazing to Mark. He didn't interrupt. He didn't make fun. He didn't snort and spit. Not once. Mark actually enjoyed telling him about his robot. With all that had been going on, talking about something real like his robot calmed him down. He even forgot for a second who he was talking to . . . that's how desperate he was to get his mind off his problems.

When Mark was finally talked out, Mitchell nodded and said, "I gotta hand it to you, Dimond. You're a freak, but you've got talent."

"Thanks . . . I think," Mark said.

Andy stood up and said, "Maybe someday we'll work together on something. That is, if you don't mind working with somebody you think is a turd."

This threw Mark. It was the first time Mitchell had shown any sign of humility whatsoever.

"Uh, yeah, maybe" was all Mark could get out. "I mean, I don't think you're a turd."

"Yeah, right."

"Thanks for the fries," Mark said.

"Thanks for the story," Mitchell said. "I gotta get to work. See ya."

With that, Mitchell turned and walked out of the park. Mark was left there stunned. It seemed too surreal to be true, but Andy Mitchell had actually just helped him get through a panic attack. Mark chuckled and shook his head and thought, "Life just keeps on getting stranger."

The next few weeks flew by. Mark visited the bank a few times to reread Bobby's latest journal. He tried not to think about Courtney. He figured she'd contact him when she was ready. All Mark could do was hope that Bobby was fully recovered, and that he would avoid Saint Dane.

Mark started a summer job where he assembled and engraved sports trophies. It was better than most dumb summer jobs. At least there was a little bit of creativity involved, and it helped him get his mind off everything else. Mark actually hated summers. He didn't like to do all the things that everybody else did. He didn't like swimming. His family didn't take many fun trips. He didn't like sitting in the sun because his fair skin went from blue-white to raging red with no stopover at tan. But mostly it was because he liked school. Odd as that would seem to most kids, Mark longed for September because for him, summers were boring.

On the weekend of July Fourth, his summer got less boring.

He was working late at the trophy shop, but he didn't mind because they were having a fireworks display in the park at the bottom of Stony Brook Avenue. Mark worked until nearly eight thirty, then stopped off at Garden Poultry for his obligatory box of fries and can of Mountain Dew. With his nutritious dinner in hand, he walked down the Ave to catch the fireworks. Families poured in from everywhere, carrying blankets to stake out their piece of grass and see the show. Mark sat down in the middle of one of the town tennis courts. He didn't like sitting on the grass much, especially with food. He hated battling ants for his fries.

With two huge explosions the fireworks began. Everyone's eyes went skyward to watch the display. Soon after, the traditional "Oohs" and "Aahs" began as each rocket exploded with spectacular sprays of multicolored light. Mark liked fireworks. They were like magic to him. He had no idea how the ancient Chinese could have figured out how to put the right chemicals and explosives together that would erupt in such amazing colors and patterns. He knew it would be easy enough to research and find out how they worked, but he chose not to. He preferred to think of it as magic.

"Excuse me, son," came a voice next to him. "No sparklers in the crowd."

Mark saw a cop standing in front of him. He looked around, wondering who the cop was talking to, but nobody around him was playing with sparklers.

"Did you hear me?" asked the cop, a bit more gruff.

Mark realized the cop was staring right at him.

"Are you talking to me?" Mark asked, confused.

"Don't be smart," the cop snapped. "Kill the sparkler. There are little kids around."

Mark truly didn't know what the guy was talking about. That is, until he felt his ring twitch. He didn't notice it at first because he had been so focused up at fireworks in the sky, but there was a small pyrotechnic display going on right in Mark's hand.

His ring had activated.

It was already growing larger, with shimmering light spewing from the opening, very sparklerlike. The fireworks had been so loud he didn't even hear the music. Mark instantly clamped his hand over the ring.

"S-Sorry, Officer," he stammered. "I'll—uh—I'll get rid of it."

Mark awkwardly got to his feet, but he was in the middle of a crowd on the tennis court. He tried to run off, but ended up either stepping on people, or tripping over their picnic baskets, or generally making a nuisance of himself.

"Excuse me, pardon me, sorry, I'm sorry, oops, sorry," he kept saying as he fought his way through the crowd and off the court. After annoying pretty much everybody along the way, he jumped off the tennis court and ran into the woods. He didn't have to run far. Nobody cared about him. They were all watching the sky. Mark ran behind a tree, dropped his ring to the ground and watched his own personal pyrotechnic display. Unlike the fireworks exploding in the sky, this one actually did have a touch of magic to it.

This display was there to deliver Bobby's next journal.

ZADAA

There's been a tragedy.

There was no warning. No build up. No way we could have been prepared. With everything I've seen, you'd think I'd be used to horrible things happening. Not so. I'm as stunned as ever. Now we've got to pick up the pieces and move on. The only good thing I can say about this, is that it has made our next step pretty clear.

Mark, Courtney, I'm once again writing this journal from Loor's home. We won't be here much longer. Tomorrow we begin a journey. Hopefully, I'm ready for it. Or at least more ready than I was when I wrote to you last.

It's weird. I'm beginning to feel like two different people. I'm still Bobby Pendragon, the guy you know and who wants more than anything to be home and get his real life back. But in many ways, I've changed. I've seen so many things, both horrible and wondrous, that I can't help but think I'm not the same person. I don't like that. I want to be me. But with all that's been going on, the old me wouldn't survive for long. That's why I needed to force myself to change even more. It's all about staying alive. The ironic part is that by forcing myself to be a new person, it feels like I'm killing off the old

Bobby. I hate it, but I don't have a choice. Not if I want to be around long enough to stop Saint Dane.

But right now I need to get my head back to a few weeks ago, so that I can get all that's happened down here in my journal.

Three of us stood facing the flume, deep in Rokador territory beneath the city of Xhaxhu. The rocky tunnel into the territories was quiet now, but wouldn't be for long.

"This is not necessary," Saangi said, annoyed. "I am capable of the job. We do not need more help."

"One day you will be a fine warrior," Loor said to her patiently. "But we need help now. Today."

Without warning, Saangi grabbed the wooden stave she had strapped to her back. She spun it like a baton, dropped to her knee, and expertly whacked me on the back of the legs.

"Ow!" I shouted. "What was that for?"

"My reflexes are far better than his," Saangi said to Loor. "He can learn from me."

I rubbed the back of my stinging legs, then quickly yanked the weapon out of her hands before she could react.

"Gimme that," I scolded. "Sheesh."

Loor gently took the weapon from me. I could see she was smiling slightly.

"You think this is funny?" I asked. "This is tough enough without getting smacked by the good guys. That hurt!"

Loor said, "If you do not wish to be hit, you do not wish to train. Do you wish to train?"

Ouch. Loaded question. To be honest, the idea of getting battered around while training didn't appeal to me. I had finally recovered from most of my injuries. My strength was still low and I was stiff, but most of the injury pain was gone.

The idea of voluntarily getting physically punished didn't exactly appeal to me. I had gotten a lifetime worth of pain from Saint Dane. But you didn't play football without getting knocked around in practice, or box without sparring and taking some punches. If I wanted to learn how to fight, part of that was getting used to being hit. I stopped rubbing my leg.

"I can handle it," I said to Loor defiantly. I looked to Saangi. She had a smug look on her face.

"You will play a part in this, Saangi," Loor said to her squire while giving her back the weapon. "Please be patient."

Saangi took the stave and jammed it into its harness. She stood there with her arms folded, looking all sorts of pouty. Note to self: Watch out for the brat.

That's when the flume came to life.

I heard it before seeing anything. The rock walls shifted every so slightly, groaning like an old man's joints as he worked out stiff kinks. Kind of like how I felt lately. I looked into the tunnel to see a pinpoint of light far in the distance. Someone was headed toward us. The light quickly grew larger as it came closer. I heard the faint jumble of sweet musical notes that always announced a voyage through the flume. A moment later the rocky walls of the round tunnel melted into crystal. Before the incoming light grew so bright that I had to shield my eyes, I could see the star field beyond the clear walls. Though traveling through the flumes had become a common thing, I still had no clue as to how they worked, or who created them. I trusted that one day I would find out, but I usually tried not to think about it too much. There was usually too much going on to stress over the grand cosmic issues I had no control over.

Loor, Saangi, and I stood together, shielding our eyes from the brilliant light show. The music grew loud. The passenger had arrived. A second later the light disappeared, the crystal walls returned to solid rock, and the flume was once again quiet.

Standing before us was a tall, dangerous-looking guy with a sword on his hip. He was wearing heavy leather armor that was much beefier than Loor's. No skin showed on this guy because the territory he had come from wasn't burning hot like Zadaa. I knew, because I had been there. For him to have gotten to the gate, he had to climb a craggy mountain and traverse a vast snowfield to find the hidden cave that held the flume. He was around my age, but much taller than me. He looked every bit like the professional knight that he was.

He also happened to be the Traveler from Denduron.

"Hello, Alder," I said. "Welcome to Zadaa."

"The flume was not at all what I expected," Alder said, sounding a bit shaken. He took a step forward, tripped, and stumbled. Luckily we caught him before he fell at our feet.

"Sorry," Alder said, embarrassed. "I am still shaky from the journey."

"This is the fierce knight you want to help train Pendragon?" Saangi asked with dismay. "He is an oaf."

"He is a Traveler," Loor said sharply. "And you will treat him with respect."

"She is correct, I am an oaf," Alder said sheepishly. "But I am an oaf who can fight." He looked at me and broke out in a warm grin. "Hello, Pendragon. You have changed."

We hugged. It was like getting a bear hug from a, well, from a bear. He was a strong guy. His hair was longish and brown. He wasn't a handsome guy, his features were too . . . big. Big nose, big mouth. Wide-spaced eyes. No, he wasn't a looker. What you saw when you looked into Alder's eyes was sincerity. And honesty. There wasn't a devious bone in his body. What he said, he meant. He was actually more like a big kid than a trained Bedoowan knight. I would trust this guy with my life. Come to think of it, I *had* trusted this guy with my life. I was about to do it again.

"We've both grown up a little," I said.

Alder let go of me and held his arms out for Loor, ready to give her a hug. "Hello, Loor!"

Loor stood stock-still with her arms at her sides. She wasn't the huggy type.

"I am happy to see you, Alder," she said with no emotion.

Alder stood there with his arms out, hugless, looking dumb. "Ummm, right," he said, dropping his arms. "And who is this?" he asked, looking at Saangi.

"My name is Saangi. I am Loor's acolyte. I wrote the note to your acolyte to request that you come here."

"Who is your acolyte?" I asked Alder.

"A Milago," Alder answered. "Her husband was killed by Saint Dane during a Transfer ceremony."

I knew exactly who Alder was talking about. On Denduron the Milago farmers were forced to slave in the mines, digging up a precious, blue mineral called glaze for the ruling class. The Bedoowan. When Saint Dane went to Denduron, he started a brutal practice of choosing a Milago and forcing the miners to dig up his weight in glaze. The Transfer ceremony was where they weighed the poor miner against that day's haul. If they didn't dig up enough, the miner would be killed. I saw a Transfer ceremony where they didn't make quota. The miner was killed. His wife had to watch. I am happy to say that Loor and Alder and I put the mines out of business. We had beaten Saint Dane on Denduron. We were now together again, ready to stop him on Zadaa.

"I hear you have been busy, Pendragon," Alder said. "It seems as if our adventure on Denduron was only the beginning."

"Pretty much," I answered. "I want to hear about what's happening on your territory. I could use some good news."

"You will be pleased," Alder assured me. "The Bedoowan are working with the Milago to rebuild their village that was destroyed when the tak mine exploded."

"Where do the Bedoowan live now that their castle is destroyed?" Loor asked.

Alder laughed and said, "They live in the Milago village! You would not recognize the place, it has grown so!"

"So it's all one big happy family?" I asked.

"It is not perfect," Alder answered. "But it is peaceful. And the Milago are no longer in the mines. The future is bright."

Hearing all this couldn't have made me happier. Denduron had reached its turning point, and we pushed it the right way. But it also made me a little sad, because it reminded me of Uncle Press. I can still picture him standing up on the back of that crude, medieval sled, flying over the snow, heaving spears at the charging quig-bears.

I said, "I want to hear about Rellin, and Queen Kagan and—"

Alder suddenly took a step backward and reached for his leg. With one quick move he grabbed a vicious-looking knife that was strapped to his calf and threw it between Loor and me. We both ducked out of the way in surprise. I spun around to see what he was throwing at and saw something that made my legs go weak.

As I've described before, the huge underground cavern that held the flume was dug from the same light brown sandstone that all of the buildings of Xhaxhu were made from. The way in and out was by climbing up using small holes that were dug into one craggy wall. These handholds led up through a dark cleft in the rock that was barely wide enough for one person to squeeze through. It was a treacherous climb that ended at a trapdoor leading to a storage room used by the Rokador. Alder had thrown his knife toward the wall with the handholds.

His throw was dead solid perfect. Now skewered into the soft sandstone was a snake. A big snake. It must have dropped down, head first, from the cleft in the rock that led to the trapdoor. Alder's knife had drilled through its head. I turned in time to see the rest of its body falling down from above. Dead. It must have been six feet long. Its head stayed in place, pegged to the soft sandstone by Alder's knife.

"Wha—?" Saangi said in stunned awe. She looked to Alder with new respect. "I apologize for doubting you, sir."

Alder shrugged modestly. "I may be a clumsy oaf, but I am also a knight."

I don't like snakes. There's nothing good about snakes. They're quiet, they're sneaky, and they can kill you. Not a whole lot to like there. But this snake was especially nasty. I had run into one on a previous visit to Zadaa.

"Quigs," I said.

"Quigs?" Alder echoed.

"That's what they are on Zadaa," I answered. "On Denduron they're bears. Second Earth, dogs. On Cloral they're sharks. Here they're snakes. Big, nasty snakes."

"Why would they appear now?" Saangi asked, stunned. Gone was the cocky young warrior. She suddenly seemed like a nervous little girl.

"Quigs only show up when Saint Dane doesn't want us using the flumes," I said. "You know what that tells me?"

"What?" Alder asked.

"It means we're doing the right thing," I answered. "Saint Dane is beginning to feel the heat. It's time to get started."

ZADAA

We didn't run into any more quig-snakes on the way up and out of the flume cavern, I'm happy to report. Alder led the way, but without his sword or knife. He had to abandon his Denduron armor and weapons at the flume. Mixing items between territories wasn't allowed. But I guess I don't have to point that out anymore. Saangi fixed him up with a white Rokador tunic since he looked a heck of a lot more like a Rokador than a dark-skinned Batu. She also gave him a silver-rod weapon like the Tiggen guards had carried at the farm above. It was about three feet long with a leather handle on one end that had a loop to go around your wrist.

"What do I do with this?" Alder asked. "It has no blade."

"It is an effective weapon," Loor assured him. "You will see."

We climbed up the footholds, through the trapdoor and stood together in the rock-walled room that the Rokador used to store machine parts. Loor slammed the trapdoor shut that bore the star symbol marking it as a gate to the flume. She covered it with sand, hiding it completely.

"Where to now?" I asked Loor.

"To a place where we will not be disturbed by Batu or Rokador," she answered.

We left the room, following Loor through the twisting tunnel that I had walked through several times before on visits to Zadaa. Shortly we left the smaller tunnel to enter the huge cavern that once held an underground river. When Spader and I were first here, there was a four-story waterfall on one side of the immense cavern that fed a deep, raging river. Now there was only a dribble of water that fell from a rocky mouth into a pathetic trickle of a stream at the bottom of the mostly dry riverbed.

"What happened here?" Alder asked.

"There is a lot to tell," Loor answered. "Later."

Alder accepted that. He was an easy guy.

Loor led us to the opening that was once hidden behind the waterfall, but was now in plain sight. We climbed a few stone stairs, stepped through the portal, and entered a room that held the water-control device I have described to you before. To remind you guys, this thing looked like one of those giant pipe-organs that you see in church. But these pipes ran horizontally, disappearing into the rock wall on either side of the room. There was a platform in front of it that held an amazing array of switches and valves. When I first came here, there was a Rokador engineer on that platform, feverishly working the controls like an expert. I had no idea what the device did, other than knowing it had something to do with controlling the flow of water from the rivers. The guy had maps and diagrams that he referred to while he quickly made adjustments and toggled switches.

Now the platform was empty. A thin layer of sand and dust covered the control board.

"This is one of the many switching stations that the

Rokador engineers use to control the rivers of Zadaa," Loor explained.

"I guess there isn't much to do here anymore," I said sadly.

I heard a booming voice behind me say: "At least for now."

We all turned quickly to see Bokka, the Tiggen guard striding toward us. He was followed by Teek and the other two goons from the farm. At least I assumed they were the same two guys. They didn't drop their hoods last time so I suppose they could be different characters. But it was definitely Bokka. Handsome, confidant Bokka. He didn't wear his goggles down here, so this time I got to see his eyes. They were a unique shade of light green. I had never seen eyes like his before. A quick glance at Teek and the other Tiggen guards revealed that they all had light green eyes. I figured it had something to do with living underground.

Bokka scanned us all in a way that told me he was sizing us up in case there was trouble. His eyes fell on Alder. "And who is this new guest who dresses like a Rokador and carries our weapon?" Bokka asked.

Loor took the lead, saying: "He is from Pendragon's tribe. He, too, has come to help."

"The Yankees tribe?" Bokka asked.

At first I didn't know what the heck he was talking about. I guarantee Alder didn't have a clue either. But he knew enough not to say anything.

"Right," I said, suddenly remembering. "The Yankees tribe. Scourge of the American League."

Nobody had any idea what I was talking about, which was kind of fun.

"Welcome, Alder," Bokka said warmly. "We're honored to have you."

Bokka's friends didn't look all too pleased. They stood there, staring at us like we were the enemy. What a bunch of clones.

"What's with your buddies?" I asked. "Don't they trust us?"

Bokka glanced back to his pals. "Forgive them," he said. "They are Tiggen guards. It is their job to be suspicious of outsiders."

"Then why aren't *you* suspicious of us?" I asked.

"Because Loor tells me I shouldn't be," Bokka said. He looked at Loor and smiled. Loor smiled back and looked down like some freakin' girly-girl. This guy was a little bit too charming for me.

"I understand you had an accident," Teek said to me.

Accident? I could use a lot of words to describe what had happened to me. "Accident" wasn't one of them.

"Yes," I said. "I ran into the club of a Ghee warrior a couple hundred times. But you know, accidents happen."

"I'm sorry to hear you went through so much pain, Pendragon," Bokka said. "But I'm happy to see you've recovered." He sounded like he meant it too. I wanted to not like this guy, but couldn't come up with a good enough reason, other than the fact he had a longtime relationship with Loor and she acted like a girl with a crush whenever she was around him. But that wasn't enough reason not to like him. At least that's what my brain told me. My heart was pushing me the other way.

"This switching station has been closed for quite some time," Loor said.

"Without water it will not reopen," Bokka said somberly. "But I have more disturbing news."

"It gets worse?" I asked.

"There has been a general retreat," Bokka explained. "The Tiggen guards have been ordered back from outlying regions of the underground."

"What does that mean?" I asked.

"It means we are preparing for war," Teek said.

Bokka added, "The fear is that if we are scattered when the Batu attack, we will be slaughtered. Right now all Rokador are gathering in the city of Kidik in anticipation of an attack. We are the last of the Tiggen guard who are spreading the word and rounding up stragglers. The future looks grim."

Nobody said anything for a while. The idea of being on the verge of a war tends to stop conversation.

I finally said, "So what you're saying is that unless there's a huge rainstorm that fills the rivers, it's war."

"The answer to that lies with the Batu," Bokka answered. "The Rokador are simply preparing to defend themselves. We are victims of the drought as well. We have little water and the Batu no longer bring us crops. I understand they barely have enough to feed themselves."

"It is true," Loor said.

"Then the future does indeed look grim," Bokka said.

"What do your leaders say?" I asked. "Can't they bring water from someplace else? I mean, all of Zadaa can't be dry."

"We ask the same thing," Bokka answered. "The elite tell us they have done everything they can. They can't reach out to all of Zadaa. We are at the mercy of the weather, just as the Batu are . . . only we are being blamed for the problem."

He looked at me and asked, "I know you are here to help, Pendragon. I'm not sure how you can do that, unless you have a way to make it rain. Do you?"

The guy wasn't being sarcastic. He really hoped I could do it.

"Afraid not," I said. "The Yankees are good, but not *that* good."

Bokka nodded in acceptance.

"Can you bring us now?" Loor asked.

"Yes, come," Bokka said.

Bokka turned on his heel and walked off quickly, followed by Teek and the other two goons. Loor followed them, and the rest of us went with her.

"Where are we going?" I asked Loor.

"To a safe place away from prying eyes," she answered.

Bokka and his buddies led us through a series of tunnels, each of which looked exactly like the last. They were passageways that were dug right out of the sandstone. Some were barely wide enough for Alder's shoulders; others were as wide as a school corridor with various pieces of equipment and pipes running through them. We passed several wooden doors, all closed. It was amazing to think that these people had created an entire world underground. It wasn't like the fabulous underground of Third Earth. No way. This was all very crude. But there was light. Every few yards I saw small domes imbedded in the wall that gave off a soft, yellow glow. I didn't think they had electricity, so I figured it had to be some kind of phosphorous. The result wasn't exactly bright, but I had no trouble seeing where I was going.

After three turns I wished I had done a Hansel-and-Gretel move by dropping breadcrumbs to mark our route. There was no way I could find my way back. If I got ditched, I'd be lost. We had been walking for about ten minutes when the tunnel opened up into a larger cavern that had several other tunnels leading off it.

"This is called 'the crossroads,'" Loor announced.

The name fit. What stood out most though, was a set of heavy, wooden doors that had to be twenty feet tall.

"What's in there?" I asked.

Bokka looked at us, as if debating whether or not to answer.

"You do not have to tell us, Bokka," Loor said.

Bokka let out a tired breath and said, "No, we're friends. We should be honest with one another. It is a central water-transfer station. This station controls many of the smaller stations, like the one near the waterfall. My team has been assigned to stand guard here." He nodded to Teek and his other pals. They immediately stood in front of the closed doors with their arms folded, looking all sorts of menacing.

"It's okay," I said. "We don't want to go in."

Bokka said, "We're afraid this would be one of the first targets if the Batu attack."

"No offense," I said. "But if a whole bunch of Ghee warriors come charging down here, those guys won't be able to stop them."

"Then they will die trying," Bokka said, staring me right in the eye.

He was totally serious. These guys were willing to die to defend their tribe. It was a weird situation. Bokka and Loor were friends, but technically they were also enemies. If a war did erupt, this would get interesting . . . and not in a good way.

Bokka looked to his pals and announced, "I will return shortly. Teek, you are in command."

Teek gave a quick wave to acknowledge. The others didn't react, no big surprise. We continued on, following Bokka into one of the tunnels off the intersection. We had only gone a few yards when he stopped at another wooden door. I don't know why he chose this one, they all pretty much looked the same to me.

"This is where I leave you," Bokka said to Loor. "You know how to handle this, right?"

"I believe I was the one who taught you," Loor countered.

"Yes, you were." Bokka chuckled. "Among other things."

I didn't want to know what any of those "other" things were.

"You are a good friend, Bokka," Loor said. "I do not know what the future holds for either of us, but please know that you will forever be in my heart."

The two hugged. It was kind of an awkward moment for the rest of us. At least for me, anyway. I looked at Alder and said casually, "So? You getting any trouble from that lousy cannibal Red Sox tribe?"

Alder gave me a blank look. Of course.

"Good-bye, Pendragon," Bokka said. "And good luck." He awkwardly held out his hand to shake, knowing that it was a sign of friendship where I come from. Like I said, I wanted to hate the guy . . . but I didn't. I shook his hand. This time he didn't squeeze so tightly.

"Thanks, Bokka," I said. "Take care of yourself."

Bokka nodded to Alder and Saangi, saying, "Good-bye, friends. When we meet again, I hope it will be under better circumstances." He gave one last look to Loor, then turned and jogged back toward the crossroads.

"So, what's this all about?" I asked Loor.

"We need a secure place for you to train," she answered. "Bokka has provided a way for us to get there without being seen." She opened the wooden door to reveal a room that was like most of the other caverns we had been in, except for one little difference. Sitting in the center of the room was a miniature train. It looked pretty much like a train you'd see at an amusement park. There were four cars in all. The two in the center were open. Each held around ten seats. On either end was an "engine" with two seats. I couldn't tell what powered the thing, but each engine had an enclosed front that I assumed held some sort of motor. The engines actually reminded me of snowmobiles, except they weren't as modern-looking and were covered with a thin layer of sand. The vehicle sat on two rails that were about three feet apart.

"It is like a mine car," Alder said.

"Exactly," Loor answered. "This is how the Rokador travel long distances and remove rock when they are tunneling."

That reminded me of something.

"I heard Bokka talk about Kidik City," I said to Loor. "Does that mean there's an entire city underground?"

"Yes, it is the seat of Rokador power," Loor answered. "I have not seen it for myself. Few Batu have. Please, take a seat."

I put aside my curiosity about how a city could be underground, and boarded the little train with the others. I flashed on going to the Quassy Amusement Park at home when I was a kid. They had this cool miniature train that traveled all around the property, through the woods and over bridges. I suddenly wished I was there instead of somewhere underground on a territory light-years from home that was on the verge of a civil war. Oh well.

"You know how to drive this thing?" I asked.

Loor sat in one of the seats in the engine car and said, "I have been on this tram many times as a child. Bokka and I used to ride it at night, while others slept."

Now I knew what Bokka meant when he asked Loor if she knew how to handle this. I could picture her as a mischievous little girl, sneaking around and hijacking this train for a joyride. Unfortunately I could also picture Bokka doing it with her. I gotta get over this.

With a sudden lurch and screech of wheels on metal track, the little train chugged forward. Seconds later we were out of the cavern room and rolling through a narrow tunnel that wasn't big enough to stand up in. Alder had to bend over or he would have scraped his head along the ceiling. The engine made no sound, which was weird.

"How is it powered?" I asked.

"The Rokador are ingenious," Loor said. "They have created many mechanical wonders."

"But how does it work?" I asked again.

Loor hesitated, then admitted, "I do not know."

That said a lot. Not about Loor, but about the Batu versus the Rokador. From what I'd seen so far, the Rokador were more advanced technologically than the Batu. After all, they had devices that could control the flow of rivers; they worked with metal to create weapons and tiny trains; they somehow brought light to tunnels that were far beneath the surface; and for that matter, they dug tunnels using machinery. The Batu, on the other hand, were a much more primitive tribe. They built these great pyramids and knew how to farm and were pretty good at the warrior business, but the two races seemed as if they were centuries apart on the technology scale. I guess the only real question I had was if the Rokador were such geniuses, why the heck did they live underground like moles?

We rolled along on these tracks for several minutes. Every so often we'd pass through a cavern room, kind of like going by subway stops. I didn't even bother to ask Loor where we were going. I figured I'd find out soon enough. I'd guess that we traveled along for about another ten minutes when the train rolled into another cavern, and stopped.

"We are here," Loor announced.

We all got out, and I asked, "Where is here?"

"This is Mooraj, the camp where Bokka and I trained as children," Loor answered. "All Rokador and Batu youths spent time here as a test to see if they should be groomed as Ghee warriors or Tiggen guards."

Saangi added, "I spent time here as well."

Loor continued, "When tension between the tribes mounted, the Rokador were banned. When the drought came, Mooraj was abandoned."

"The Rokador were banned?" I asked. "How can that be? I thought they controlled the underground?"

"Mooraj is not underground," Loor answered.

She led us to a doorway across the cavern and up a winding set of stone stairs. As we climbed I could feel the air getting warmer. We were leaving the cool underground and heading back up to the baking heat on the surface. We finally emerged to find ourselves in a stone hut that was barely big enough for all four of us to stand in. I guess you could say it was a primitive subway station. Very primitive. There was one doorway, beyond which the light was so bright I had to squint. It now made sense to me why Bokka and his boys wore goggles on the surface. After spending so much time underground, coming out into the sun was pretty rude.

"Your eyes will adjust in a moment," Loor said, as if reading my mind—or seeing that I was squinting like a mole under a spotlight.

After about a minute I said, "Okay, I'm good to go."

"I am as well," Alder added.

"Then welcome to Mooraj," Loor said.

She stepped out into the light. Saangi was right behind her. I was about to follow, when Alder put a hand on my shoulder.

"Are you certain, Pendragon?" he asked.

"About what?"

"You wish to train as a warrior. Is that wise?"

"Only if I want to stay alive," I said.

Alder thought about that a moment, then nodded. We followed the others.

Mooraj wasn't your typical kid camp. I had been to camp. I remember bunk houses and a lake full of canoes and an archery range and tennis courts and horse stables and lots of trees and a swimming pool and a snack bar where you could buy candy and . . . you know. Camp.

Mooraj looked more like a fort in the middle of the desert.

The hut we had come out of was about thirty yards away from the main camp. From where we were, it looked like a six-foot wall surrounded the camp itself. As we walked across the hot sand, Alder pointed off to our left where I saw the tops of the pyramids in the distance.

"The city of Xhaxhu," I said to him. "Where the flume is."

I guessed we were about two miles away. Two miles across a blistering hot desert. Loor was right. We wouldn't be disturbed here. The Batu and Rokador had more important things to worry about.

We entered the camp, and to be honest, it didn't look much different than the abandoned farm we had visited. There were several low buildings against the walls. I guessed they were the barracks where people slept. The center of the compound was wide open. There was some strange apparatus around that looked sort of like playground equipment. You know, jungle gyms and monkey bars and what not. But it didn't look all that inviting. I couldn't imagine little kids playing on this stuff and laughing and having fun. This place looked . . . serious. And there was sand everywhere, building up in the corners and blowing across the center of the compound.

"I'm guessing there's no snack bar" was all I could think of saying.

"We will need provisions," Loor said. "Saangi, you must return to Xhaxhu and bring us food and water."

"That is not fair!" Saangi complained. "You said I was to be part of the training."

"That *is* part of the training," Loor said sharply.

Saangi looked as if she wanted to argue, but a stern look from Loor froze her. She backed off and said, "Very well."

"Go now," Loor said. "Be careful. Make sure you are not followed."

"I know!" Saangi pouted and turned to go back for the subway hut.

"And try to return before the sun goes down," Loor added.

"I will," Saangi assured her.

"Thank you, Saangi," I said.

This made Saangi stop. The young Batu looked at me and said, "I hope you are ready for this, Pendragon."

"Yeah, me too," I said with a chuckle, trying to be light.

She didn't laugh. Oh well, so much for getting her to loosen up. Saangi turned and ran out of the compound.

"Is she okay?" I asked Loor.

"She is restless, and scared," Loor answered.

"Join the club," I replied.

"I would like to know what has been happening here on Zadaa," Alder said. "What is this war the guard spoke of?"

"We must find a place to settle in," Loor said. "Then we can explain everything to you."

Alder nodded. That was fine by him.

Loor asked me, "How do you feel?"

"Nervous," I answered. "But confidant. And a little tired. I haven't been running around so much lately."

"Now you will rest to restore your energy," Loor said. "Tomorrow you will need it."

Gulp.

ZADAA

Fear can be a good thing.

It's the one emotion that always helps you make the right decision. Other emotions can lead you down the wrong path. Anger, jealousy, sadness, bliss—you name it. Good or bad, they take you out of the moment and cloud your thinking so you could easily make a dumb choice. Not so with fear. When you're scared, you pretty much know what you have to do. Usually, it's to get the heck away from whatever it is you're scared of. But that isn't always an option. Fear heightens your senses and makes your thinking so clear, you stand a better chance of beating whatever it is you're afraid of. Whether it's a quig, or a science test, or asking somebody out for a movie. When you're afraid, you're on. I guess you can be so messed up by fear that you freeze up, but short of that, fear can be your friend.

During the time I spent in that blast furnace of a training camp, fear was definitely my friend. It's not that I was afraid of the training, or of getting hurt again, or of anything Loor or Alder would do to me. What I feared was Saint Dane. I knew that if I wasn't able to defend myself, I could be in for another beating like I had gotten at the Ghee compound. If Pelle a Zinj hadn't shown up, I would have died. I'm certain of that. The next time, I might not be so lucky. It was the fear of taking another beating that helped me to keep going. And I needed that help, because what Loor put me through was beyond anything I had expected. I wanted her to teach me a couple of moves, show me how to use one of those wooden weapons to ward off an attack and get in a couple of shots of my own.

What I got instead was a crash course in Warrior Hell, 101.

Loor, Alder, and I made ourselves at home in one of the sandstone bunkhouses that once had been used for young kids who came to Mooraj to be tested. Once inside the hut, it actually reminded me of my bunkhouse at the camp I went to as a kid. There were beds lined up along the walls to make use of every bit of space. But rather than being made from wood, with musty-smelling mattresses, these bunks were low, stone tables with grass mats. The place looked as if it had been abandoned quickly. There were still cups on tables and pieces of clothing scattered around. It was cooler inside too . . . by about a degree and a half. Still, it was a relief to get out of the sun.

We each picked a bed, and I lay down, happy to be horizontal. As I wrote before, I was pretty much healed, but I was totally out of shape from lying around for so long. I was going to have to get my strength back fast to go through Loor's training, and whatever else lay ahead. We took the time to rest and bring Alder up to speed on all that was happening on Zadaa. The drought, the two tribes, the growing tension between the tribes, and the power struggle within the Ghee to either attack the Rokador or stay loyal to the family of Zinj and negotiate peace. Of course, we also told Alder about how Saint Dane went wild and beat me like a piñata, which was pretty much why we were at the camp to train.

Alder listened to everything, nodding in understanding, taking it all in. The only time he reacted with emotion was when I told him that Uncle Press was dead. The news made him wince. Uncle Press had played a huge role in saving Denduron.

"I am sorry" was all he could say.

I nodded. So was I. "So here we sit," I finally said. "You and Loor have the impossible job of teaching me how to defend myself. But more important is figuring out what part Saint Dane is playing here on Zadaa."

"If he has taken the form of a Ghee warrior," Alder said, "he must be trying to convince the Batu to attack the Rokador. Starting wars is what he does best."

"Maybe," I said. "But there's got to be more to it than that. There always is."

"Besides," Loor added. "The rebel Ghee are powerful, but I do not believe they are strong enough to convince the people of Xhaxhu to go against the wishes of the royal family. Pelle a Zinj does not want war. The rebel Ghee may complain and threaten, but they will not go against generations of tradition. They know it would tear the Batu apart."

Alder and I looked at Loor. She didn't realize what she had just said.

"Isn't that exactly the kind of thing Saint Dane would go for?" I asked. "Tearing a powerful tribe apart?"

"Yes," Loor answered coldly. "But our traditions are strong. He may try, but he will fail."

I wasn't so sure about that. Neither was Alder. "Hunger and thirst are powerful weapons," he said quietly.

"Exactly," I agreed. "That's why I think Saint Dane is playing a bigger part in all this. I mean, what's causing all the problems in the first place?"

"The drought?" Loor asked. "Saint Dane has no power over the weather."

"No," I said. "But the bottom line here is lack of water. No drought, no tension, no war."

"Saint Dane must have seen the drought coming. That is why he is here," Loor suggested.

"Maybe," I said. "But Saint Dane doesn't leave things to chance. I think there's something else going on. I have no idea what it might be, but I'll bet I know where to find out."

"Where is that?" Alder asked.

"The underground," I answered. "So far we've only seen the Batu side of this mess. We've got to find out what's happening with the Rokador. They control the rivers of Zadaa. My guess is, if we want to find Saint Dane, we've got to go below and maybe go to that city where the Rokador leaders are. What's it called?"

"Kidik," Loor answered. "That would be dangerous," she said.

"Yup," I shot back. "That's why we're here right now, to make sure we've all got a chance of getting in and out alive."

Loor nodded, thinking this over. She got up and stood in front of me.

"Stand up," she ordered.

I got to my feet slowly. In the short time since we had been lying down, my muscles had already gone stiff. I think I was getting a taste of what it's like to be eighty. I stood in front of Loor, looking into her eyes. She was an inch or two taller than me. I resisted the temptation to go up on my toes. She grabbed my arm, feeling my bicep. With a quick, dismissive "humph," she checked my other arm. She turned me around and felt my lats, then down to my legs, where she clasped my quads, and then my calves. I felt like a horse being examined before being sent to auction. To be honest, I didn't mind it . . . until Loor said, "You are weak."

"Hey, I've been hurt, remember?" I said defensively. "My muscle tone is shot."

"That is true," Loor said dismissively. "But there was not much there to begin with."

I bit my lip. She was the expert, but being told that I was a puny, pathetic specimen didn't do much for my ego. Or confidence.

"Does that mean it's hopeless?" I asked.

"No," she answered with a sigh. "It means you must learn to be clever, because you will never win a fight with force."

Oh.

Not that I really expected it, but once I made the decision, I have to admit that there were a few times I envisioned myself becoming a warrior who was all cut up and fierce looking. I guess that would be a little much to ask for, seeing as we didn't have much time and I had been hurt and— Oh, who am I kidding? I had no chance of coming close to the kind of warrior Loor was. Never did. But I needed to know how to defend myself. So I put my ego aside and took the criticism as constructive.

"What do we do first?" I asked.

"We rest," Loor answered. "Saangi will return soon with our provisions. We will eat, then sleep. Tomorrow morning we will begin."

So far it sounded pretty cake. Saangi returned to Mooraj a few hours later, bringing with her more food than I could have imagined. She had a sack full of bread and fruit and some kind of nutty-tasting cheese that I couldn't get enough of. She also brought a large, leather bag filled with water. Precious water. If we were going to be working out, we needed as much as possible. After we had eaten our fill, I said, "Thank you, Saangi. You're amazing."

"It is my job," she said with a shrug. "I will leave now and bring more."

"No," Loor ordered. "We have plenty for now. I will need you here tomorrow, when the training begins."

Saangi's eyes lit up.

"I will take part?" she asked hopefully.

"Of course," Loor said. "Did I not promise that?"

Suddenly Saangi wasn't so sour anymore. She opened up and told us all about how she collected the fruit and smuggled the water into the underground, all under the noses of the Ghee. I liked Saangi . . . most of the time. Other times she was kind of a loose cannon. As long as things were going her way, she was fine. But if things didn't go the way she liked, she let you know it. I suppose it's okay to be moody, as long as you know when to let it go. I guess what I'm saying is that I didn't entirely trust Saangi. Not that I thought she was against me or anything, but I wasn't convinced that if things got scary, I could count on her.

To be honest, the thought also crossed my mind that she might have been Saint Dane in disguise. I couldn't totally dismiss that possibility, but I couldn't dwell on it. If I started thinking that way, I'd have to look at everybody I met as possibly being Saint Dane, and I'd turn into a paranoid wreck. I had to be trusting, but wary.

"We must sleep now," Loor announced. "We begin first thing in the morning."

"First thing" felt as if it came about two minutes after I lay down to go to sleep. It was pitch dark. I was having a sweet dream about bouncing along on a skimmer on the beautiful, warm waters of Cloral. I hit some waves and got buffeted, but stayed upright, handling the rough motion. That is, until I realized it wasn't a dream. Loor was shaking me awake.

"Get up," she commanded.

I struggled to get up on my elbows, only to see . . . nothing. It was pitch black.

"Morning," I said cheerily. "Isn't it still last night?"

"We must work now, before the sun comes up," Loor explained. "Unless you'd prefer to work during the heat of the day."

I forced myself awake. "No, no, I'm with you. Cool is cool."

"Get dressed," Loor ordered. "Meet us outside."

I heard the sound of Loor walking away. It was time to get my creaky bones up and moving. I figured we'd start out with a little road work like boxers do. Then we'd move on to some tactics and learn about weapons.

We didn't.

I put on my Rokador jacket and sandals, then followed her outside. It was still pitch dark. I couldn't see two feet in front of me and had to stretch my hands out in front for fear of walking into a wall. I found the doorway and stepped outside to ask, "What do we do—"

Whack. I got smacked on the side of the head.

"Hey!" I shouted. "What was that—"

Smack. A shot came from the other side. It was so dark I had no idea who was hitting me, or from where. It didn't hurt. Much. It was more about the surprise.

"A simple game," Loor said.

"Game?" I shouted angrily. "I can't see a thing."

Whack. I got hit on the shoulder.

"Yes, you can," Loor said calmly.

Smack. Whap. I got rocked twice; the second time I fell to the ground.

"No, I can't! Give me a break, it's dark!" I complained.

"Do not get angry," said Saangi's voice. "Anger leads to mistakes."

I jumped back to my feet. It was two-on-one. A minute before, I was happily dreaming about Cloral. Now my adrenaline was spiked as I vainly tried to defend myself against these aggressive ghosts.

"How do I win this game?" I asked.

"The spikes bring reward," Loor said from nowhere.

"Spikes? What spikes?"

Whap. I got hit again. They were using open hands, so I wasn't getting hurt, but it stung getting slapped around like this. I spun around, hands out, hoping to hit something. Anything. All I got was air.

"Control, Pendragon," Alder said calmly . . . just before he hit me in the gut.

Great. Three-on-one. The whole gang was there, taking shots. I was breathing hard and sweating—and already tired.

"Conserve your energy," Loor said, as if she could read my mind.

Smack. Smack. Hands came out of nowhere, hitting me quickly and then disappearing. I glanced up to the sky.

"The sun will not be up for a while," Saangi said.

How did she know what I was thinking?

"You can hear us," Loor said softly. "You can smell us. You can feel the heat of our bodies."

Smack. Whack. Whap. No, I couldn't. Anger gave way to frustration.

"This is stupid," I shouted, and immediately got hit with a barrage of shots that spun me around.

"Feel us," Alder said.

I took a breath. I tried to sense where they might be. I couldn't. Instead I got hit with so many shots that I was nearly rocked off my feet.

"Stop!" I shouted. "You want me back in the hospital?"

There was no answer. No instruction. No comment.

"Time-out, okay?"

No answer.

"C'mon, this is dumb."

Nobody responded.

"Loor? Get serious, all right?"

Still no answer. I still couldn't see a thing. I took a few steps and walked into a wall. Ow! I backed off and fell on my butt.

"This sucks!" I shouted in frustration. I knew they weren't going to hurt me, at least not seriously, but still. Their smacks stung! And not knowing when or where they would come from made it even worse. I couldn't defend myself. I couldn't fight back. I felt totally helpless. And tired. And sore. And angry. I had no idea what this had to do with training as a warrior, but one thing was pretty clear: I was at their mercy, and they weren't going to stop just because I complained.

A quick glance at the horizon showed me that the dark sky was growing lighter. I willed the sun to hurry up so I could see what was going on. I figured that once I could see, at least I'd have a chance to defend myself. I didn't risk standing up again because I was still disoriented. I got on my knees and crawled with my arm out to feel for the wall I had introduced my head to. I felt the rough stone, put my shoulder to it, and cautiously crawled away. I figured if they wanted to smack me around, they were going to have to find me. After crawling a few yards, I came to a doorway. I quickly rolled inside and sat with my back to the wall to catch my breath and wait for light.

I kept glancing out toward the dark compound. My heart raced because I didn't know if another attack would come, or from where. It was torture! I had to force myself to control my breathing. And listen. If I couldn't see them, I thought maybe

I could hear them coming. But the only sound I heard was the distant wail of the desert wind. Eventually I started making out shapes in the Mooraj compound. Light was coming, and with it, relief. I no longer cared that daytime would bring burning heat. Heat was fine, so long as I could see.

A few minutes later it got light enough that I could see something odd in the middle of the compound. A structure had been erected that wasn't there yesterday. There were three sticks, each about six feet long, forming a tepee. Hanging down in the middle of this frame was a small, black bag that I recognized as a canteen. A canteen! Water! I suddenly realized how thirsty I was. I wanted that water. Loor said the spikes brought reward. Were these the spikes? I didn't care. I was too thirsty to care. Without thinking another second, I got to my feet and sprinted for the center of the compound. My eyes were locked on the canteen. My only thought was to get a drink. I was nearly there. I could taste the water. I never thought that this could be a trap. I guess I wasn't thinking clearly. One second I was sprinting for the tepee, the next second I tripped and did a full-on face-plant into the sand. Ouch. I looked back to see that another long stick had been tossed in front of me. That's why my feet got tangled and I ate sand.

Looking up, I saw Loor standing over me, holding still another one of those long sticks. "You have not earned that water," she said coldly.

"This is stupid!" I shouted angrily. "What are you trying to do, kill me?"

Loor stood there, staring at me, holding her long stick like a weapon. I realized that these thin sticks were the exact same size as the wooden weapons the Ghee used, but they were thin and hollow, like bamboo. I also saw that strapped to her elbows and her knees were red, wooden sticks. Spikes.

They were around an inch thick and stuck out about six inches. I remembered seeing these before. When Spader and I came to Zadaa, we saw the Ghee warriors playing a game that was like capture the flag. All the warriors wore these wooden spikes. Instead of beating each other up, the idea was to knock off their opponents spikes, sort of like in flag football. If you lost all your spikes, you were "dead" and had to leave the game.

"Oh, I get it," I said snottily. "I'm supposed to knock off those spikes to get water? Forget it. I don't want to play this game. I asked you to train me to be a warrior, not put me through some kind of initiation."

I moved to get up, but Loor poked me in the chest, knocking me back down.

"Stop it!" I shouted. "I'm done, all right!"

"I cannot give you physical strength, Pendragon," Loor said coldly. "Nor can I give you the skills to fight in the short time we have. Our only hope is to train you to think as a warrior, and to act without thinking."

"What?" I shot back. "That's nothing!"

"No," she said quickly. "It is everything. You have the courage. You have the wisdom. You are agile and quick to react. Those tools are far more useful than physical strength. But they must be developed."

"All I wanted was to learn how to use a weapon," I complained.

Loor tossed her stick aside and said, "Very well. Take one of my spikes and the water is yours."

I slowly got to my feet. Loor was now weaponless, but I wasn't dumb enough to think she couldn't still kick my butt. This wasn't going to be a fight—it was about my grabbing one of those red spikes. How tough could it be? I approached her cautiously. She turned so that she no longer faced me head-on, but was leading with her right shoulder and hip. The wooden spikes now pointed at me, teasingly close. All I had to do was reach out and grab one. I quickly grabbed for her shoulder, but it was a fake and I went for the spike on her knee.

She didn't go for the fake and flicked my hand away as easily as if she were batting away a mosquito. I grabbed at her elbow, she shifted slightly and pushed me forward, nearly knocking me off my feet. I got mad. I dove to the ground, rolled and reached for the spike on her knee. She side-stepped. I didn't come close. I jumped back up and went straight for her, grabbing furiously. She calmly batted me away again and again. And again. It was embarrassing. I felt like a little kid trying to get my hat back from the school bully. Finally, in frustration, I swept the thin bamboo weapon off the ground and swung it at her. I didn't want to hit her, I just wanted her to knock it away so I could go in and grab one of the spikes. I swung, she stepped aside, grabbed the other end, and yanked it down so hard it pulled me off my feet. I let go, but not before being dragged to my knees, out of breath and exhausted.

Loor hadn't even broken a sweat. She leaned down to me and said, "Never make the first move."

"Okay, I get your point," I said. "Now can I have some water?"

Loor walked over to the tepee of sticks and yanked down the black canteen. "When you earn it," she said, and left me kneeling there, beaten.

The worst part was, my ordeal was only beginning.

ZADAA

Two weeks. That's how long I'm guessing we spent at the Mooraj camp. It felt like two decades. It was the most grueling experience of my life, worse than the time I spent in that gar prison on Eelong. There was no rest. Ever. The cruel game was on 24/7—or whatever measure they use to figure time here on Zadaa.

At first the only thing that kept me going was my anger at Loor and Alder and Saangi for the torture they were putting me through. They were relentless. I soon realized why Loor needed Alder's help. They took turns working me over. When they weren't making my life miserable, they were resting up to do it all over again. I didn't have that luxury. I stole sleep where I could, but it wasn't all that restful because I was never sure if one of them would pop up and start working me over again. That's how intense it was. I felt incredibly alone. The only time anyone spoke to me was when they were giving me instructions. There were no time-outs. We didn't hang around at the end of a long day and compare notes over cold drinks. I was on my own.

For me it was all about winning water, and food. If I

didn't earn it, I didn't drink. Or eat. Starvation is a pretty good motivator. It sure makes you focus. Much of each day I spent wandering around Mooraj, looking for where they kept the food. I never found it. The others would be hiding, watching, and planning their next move. Without warning one of them would leap in front of me, and a training battle would follow.

Next up was Alder. He, too, used the hollow bamboo pole rather than the more dangerous, wooden weapon. I guess I should be grateful for something. I had my own pole, taken from the tepee that once held the canteen of water Loor wouldn't let me have.

"Do not face me square-on," Alder coached. "A smaller target is harder to hit."

I attacked, swinging my pole at him. He knocked me away easily, then cracked me on the back of the head.

"You're a pretty big target," I said. "Why can't I hit you?"

"Because you are trying," Alder answered.

"Don't give me that Yoda garbage," I said. "Tell me what to do."

"Relax," Alder instructed. "If you are tense, you will make mistakes. Above all, never make the first move."

"Relax? In a fight?" I lunged at him with the stick straight out like a sword. He easily knocked me away, spun, hit me on the shoulders and then spun back and hit my shins. I felt like I was fighting a swarm of bees. Alder wore the four red spikes, just like Loor. I desperately needed to knock one of them off to get water, but I might as well have been swinging with my eyes closed. I had no chance. What was so amazing was that I was using all my energy to get nowhere, and he was barely moving. After knocking me to my knees one last time, I looked up to see that Alder was gone.

"What's the matter?" I yelled to nobody. "Had enough?"

I got no answer. I didn't know if I was learning anything, but I was definitely losing gas and growing a few dozen black-and-blue marks. My throat felt like sandpaper. I was dizzy with hunger. I needed to score one of those spikes or I wouldn't make it. I got my chance when Saangi appeared on the far side of the compound. She stood holding the black canteen. I didn't want to look too desperate, even though I was. I walked toward her, but slowly. I got about twenty yards away when she held up her hand.

I stopped and called out, "Is it your turn now?"

"I'm here to give you this," she called back, and held up the black canteen.

I could have kissed her, but realized it was probably too good to be true. "What do I have to do for it?" I asked suspiciously.

"Come and get it," Saangi said calmly. "Be sure to watch where you step."

Huh? I looked down to see she had stopped me about a foot from a pit cut into the ground. It was only five feet deep, so I wouldn't have killed myself if I fell in. But it would have hurt. It was a long rectangle that stretched between me and Saangi. I saw that it was around six feet wide, with bars running across every four feet or so.

"What is this?" I called out sarcastically. "A test of my courage?"

"No," Saangi answered. "It is a test of your balance. Make it across and the water is yours."

Oh man. I was supposed to hop from bar to bar. Four feet apart may not seem like much, but the bars looked to be around three inches wide, and there was a drop.

"What if I fall?" I asked.

"Do not," Saangi said.

"Great. Thanks for the tip."

I was scared. But I was thirsty, too. I had to do this. Without taking time to think, I leaped forward, landed on the first bar, lost my balance, and fell to the side.

"Begin again," Saangi commanded.

I went back to the beginning and leaped for the first bar, hit with both feet and pinwheeled my arms until I got my balance.

"Bend your knees, Pendragon," Saangi said calmly.

Oh. Right. I bent down and instantly got my balance. I took a breath and leaped for the next bar, this time keeping my knees bent. I made it! Looking forward, I saw that there were only ten more bars to go. It seemed like a hundred. I leaped for the next one, and hit it off balance. I wobbled back and forth and was ready to bail out to the side, but instead I launched for the next bar. I only got one foot on it . . . and fell through. I caught the bar under my right armpit, making my newly healed ribs burn with pain. But I refused to let go. I hung there for a second, my legs swinging beneath me.

"If you drop off," Saangi said calmly, "you must start over."

I had earned these few bars; I was not about to give them up. Do you know how hard it is to go from hanging below a three-inch-wide bar to getting your feet up on top so you can stand on it? Neither did I. But I found out. I wrapped one leg around the bar and twisted and pulled until I was sitting on it. It gave me a chance to rest, but I still had to get up and get moving.

"Is there a time limit to this?" I asked.

"No," Saangi answered. "You will run out of strength before you run out of time."

"Thanks for the vote of confidence," I said.

I cautiously got one foot up on the bar, put my weight on it, and was able to get my other knee up, and finally, my foot.

I was back on top! Balancing on a three-inch-wide beam wouldn't be all that hard if it were flat on the ground. Keeping your balance while hanging in the air was a whole nother matter.

"Pretend there is no pit," Saangi suggested, reading my mind.

"Easier said than done," I replied.

I decided to change my tactics. Jumping onto a bar and stopping to get my balance wasn't going to work. I had to use momentum. I figured this would either work, or I'd break my head. I bent my knees and leaped forward. I hit the next bar with one foot, but rather than stopping, I kept my forward momentum going. I launched off that foot and leaped for the next bar. And the next and the next. It wasn't graceful, and I was always a breath away from falling, but it worked! I kept going over the last few rungs and with one final lunge I landed on the other side, thrilled to be back on solid ground.

"Yes!" I shouted in victory.

Saangi didn't offer congratulations. I didn't want any. I wanted the canteen. She gave it to me and started walking away.

"What about food?" I asked.

"When you earn it," she said without turning back.

I didn't care. I had water! I sat down and pulled out the leather plug, ready to down the whole canteen. After one gulp of the sweet, delicious liquid, I forced myself to slow down. There was no telling when I'd get more. I didn't want to risk coughing and losing a single drop. Besides, I wanted to enjoy it. So I took my time, and I have to say, it was the sweetest drink I've ever had.

The thrill of victory didn't last long. No sooner did I finish the water than I realized I was still thirsty. And hungry. I knew that in order to survive this ordeal, I was going to have to conserve my energy. Whenever I got the chance, I kept to the shadows or stayed in the barracks. When I wasn't looking for food, that is. Or fighting. And I fought a lot. They all took turns sparring with me, giving me hints, teaching me. Nobody ever got mad or frustrated when I messed up, which was often. They didn't need to yell to make their point. They had a much more effective technique. They hit me. Over and over. I always knew when I messed up because I'd get hit or knocked down. At one point I took off my Rokador jacket to see that I was totally covered with black-and-blue marks. Not pretty.

Loor was the worst. She had no mercy. The two of us would face off again and again. Day after day. Morning and night. After a while I didn't even see her as a person. All I could see were those red spikes sticking out from her elbows and knees. Getting those spikes meant getting food. That's all I cared about.

"Watch my eyes, and my center," Loor would say, pointing to her gut. "In battle the eyes tell what your opponent is thinking; his center tells which way he is going."

Yeah. Whatever. I'd lunge for a stake, and she'd bat me away.

"Never make the first move," she said time and again.

"How can I get one of those stakes if I don't try to get them?" I'd yell in frustration.

She wouldn't answer.

I preferred fighting Saangi. She wasn't as quick as Loor nor as strong as Alder. I took advantage of that. Rather than use my bamboo weapon and try to outduel her, I'd simply jump at her, take a few lumps, and grab a spike. Yes! It didn't take any skill. I didn't care. I was hungry. Saangi was getting angry at me for not following the rules, but hey, tough. This was about survival. If I didn't take advantage of Saangi, I'd have collapsed.

Nights were the worst. I'd try to get some sleep, only to be thrown out of bed and dragged out into the compound for another game of "Let's whack Bobby in the dark." During these fights I tried everything to defend myself and get in some shots of my own, but it was futile. I'd stand there, waiting to get hit. If I heard a sound, I'd flail at it, only to get smacked around and pushed back.

"Never make the first move," Loor would remind me.

"What am I supposed to do?" I complained. "Stand here and take it?"

"Feel us," Alder would say.

Yeah, right.

As the days went on, Saangi was sent out to fight me less and less. Loor must have felt like I was winning too much food from her, without the benefit of improving my skills. But Saangi still played a part. She was the one who gave me the physical challenges, like hopping over the bars of the pit. Mooraj was full of these diabolical playground devices. She would always have a reward, and always make me work for it. Some of the challenges were fairly easy, like moving hand over hand on a frame that looked like monkey bars at a school playground. Other times I had to do simple exercises like push-ups. Did I say simple? They would have been easy in an air-conditioned gym. But in the shape I was in, under the burning sun, they were anything but simple. Other times the challenges were truly difficult, like running a gauntlet of heavy stones that were tied to the ends of ropes. There were about twenty of these painful pendulums. Saangi would get them all swinging in different directions, and I'd have to run through without getting hit. Usually I'd get beaned by one of the heavy stones, and let me tell you, it hurt. Worse, I'd have to start over. But every so often I'd make it through by ducking, dodging, hesitating, and finally diving over the finish line. My reward would sometimes be water; other times it would be fruit or bread.

As time passed I found myself winning more and more of these challenges. The fact was, I was getting stronger. And quicker. Winning some food helped build my strength too. But it was all the exercise that was paying off. I even got to the point where I could run across the pit with the bars every time without falling, no sweat. Well, okay, maybe some sweat. It was hot. I've mentioned that, right?

When I wasn't fighting, I took off my Rokador jacket and went bareback. Slowly my skin started turning brown. I wasn't exactly Batu dark, but I was getting close. I didn't think anybody would mistake me for a Ghee warrior, but I was looking less like a white Rokador every day. And in spite of the daily pounding I was taking, I was feeling better than ever. I think my body got used to getting hit, because the black-and-blue marks went away. I even started to put on a little muscle. I think the weight-lifting regimen that Saangi put me through helped that.

But there was still something missing. Something big. Even though I was becoming more agile and strong, I wasn't doing so well in the fighting department, and after all, that's what this was all about. As I wrote before, what kept me going throughout this ordeal was the fear of facing Saint Dane again. Being in shape and having a nice tan wasn't going to help much in another death match. I was beginning to fear that in spite of all this hard work, I might not be any better off. Then one night I was dragged out of bed for another pitch-dark slap session.

"Feel us," Alder would say.

"I'm trying!" I'd say, waving my arms around like a frantic chicken.

Whack. Whack. Hands would come from nowhere to knock me around.

"How can you do that?" I screamed in frustration. "You can't see me!"

"We see you, Pendragon," Alder said. "Not with our eyes."

"That's stupid!" I shouted.

"Is it?" Saangi said as she smacked me around a few times.

I wanted to cry in frustration, and agony.

"What does this have to do with being a warrior?" I screamed.

"It isn't magic," Loor said. "Fighting is a dance. Every move brings another. If you can sense your opponent, sense his movements, sense his strength and weakness, you will own him."

Right. Use the Force, Luke. I tried to control my breathing. I even closed my eyes. Why not? They weren't doing me any good. I listened. They weren't ghosts. They had to breathe. They had to move. They had to give off heat and smell. As I stood there, trying to use every other sense but sight, I felt something. It was nothing more than a wisp of air on my arm. It lasted a nano-second. It was a slight breeze that came from something moving past. It was small, but I definitely felt it. Without taking a second to analyze, I reacted by sweeping my hand out to where I felt the body might be . . . and slapped somebody on the arm! I was so surprised, I actually said, "Oh! Sorry!"

An instant later, something was dropped at my feet. I didn't see it, but I felt it and jumped back in surprise. I had no idea what it could have been, though I expected it to be some kind of decoy-trick so that when I reached down to grab it, I'd get pummeled again. So I didn't move. Instead, I closed my eyes and tried to sense the others. This is going to sound strange, but after a second, I knew they were already gone. I had felt them. Or should I say, I didn't feel them anymore. I don't know how else to describe it.

After a few more moments, I cautiously knelt down to find out what had been thrown on the ground in front of me. I reached out and instantly felt something familiar, and welcome. It was a canteen full of water. Right next to it was a piece of fruit that felt like a pear. It was a reward. I had done something right. It wasn't just luck, either. I had found my opponent without using my eyes. Had I made a breakthrough? I figured I must have, seeing as I was not only given a reward of food and water, but was then allowed to sleep through the night without getting another beating. It was the first full night's rest I had since my stay at the Batu hospital. Man, I needed it.

I was feeling pretty good about myself, as if I had finally learned something. That was the good news. Bad news was that Loor felt the same way. I had finally shown a hint of promise; therefore she no longer felt the need to show me mercy. What followed on that dry, dusty training ground of Mooraj was the most grueling battle I had been through since my bout with Saint Dane.

This was going to be my final exam, and it wasn't going to be pretty.

ZADAA

"Counter a block with a strike," Loor instructed. "It is when your opponent is the most vulnerable."

I tried. Over and over. I had *been* trying. Loor would swing at me, I'd block it, but when I tried to counter with an attack, she'd quickly back off, or counter that move with a strike of her own and smack me. Hard.

"That's not fair," I shouted. "It's like you know what I'm going to do."

"I do," Loor answered.

"Let's keep going," I said, bearing down.

"The third move is the most important," she explained. "That is the strike that will count."

"I'm trying!" I shouted in frustration.

"Faster!" she commanded.

I tried. I tried. I tried. I failed every time. It was making me crazy. We went at it for hours. My hands were getting raw from squeezing the bamboo pole. I was so thirsty I was nauseous. Still, Loor wouldn't stop, and I wasn't about to give up. Once when she was walking back to get into position, I jumped at her to try and grab one of the spikes. I figured I'd catch her unaware. I didn't. It was like she had eyes in the back of her head. Without turning around, she jammed her pole at me, catching me in the gut, making me double over in pain.

"Never make the first move," she said.

"Yeah, yeah, so you say," I answered, grabbing my sore stomach.

The fight went on. Loor showed no sign of tiring. I showed no sign of making her tired. At one point the two of us stood facing each other, not moving, which was fine by me. I didn't want to get hit again. It was then that I realized something odd. I actually felt pretty good. Physically, I mean. In spite of all the sparring, I still had my breath. Saangi's challenges had helped build my endurance, and the training had taught me to use my energy carefully. Now if I could only get a feel for the fight!

Whack! I got hit from behind. A quick spin showed me that Alder had joined the fun. No sooner did I look at him, than Loor sprang and cracked me across the head.

"Never take your eye off your opponent," she chastised.

"But he was my opponent!" I protested.

"We are both your opponents," Alder said.

The two circled me. "How can I keep my eye on both of you?" I asked.

"Feel us," Alder said.

Great. More Jedi talk. But the truth was, I started to think there was something to it. Loor was on one side, Alder on the other. I looked straight ahead, barely seeing them in my peripheral vision. But I could sense them. I knew where they were.

Alder attacked. I dropped down and rolled away, popping back up and expecting Loor to come from the other side. That's exactly what happened. Loor came in with her stick held high, ready to chop down at me. I was ready. She wasn't fast enough. When she struck, I threw up my weapon and blocked the shot. Yes! But my victory didn't last. A second later Alder cracked me across the head, and I saw stars.

"What was that?" I yelled, jumping up angrily. "I thought it was all about the third move?"

"It was," Loor said. "I made it."

"Exactly!" I countered. "Alder, then me, then you, and I blocked it!"

"Of course you did," Loor said. "Because I made you wait."

She was right. I sensed it at the time, but didn't react. She had come in way too slowly. She was setting me up. She made the third move all right. The important move. The move that set Alder up for the kill. I suddenly felt drained and frustrated. There was too much to learn, and we were taking too long to do it. We needed to be out hunting for Saint Dane, not trying to teach the unteachable. I dropped my shoulders, threw my weapon down, and turned to walk away.

"That's it," I said. "I'm done."

"Pendragon," Loor called.

I didn't stop.

"Pendragon!" she called again.

For the first time since this ordeal began, she sounded angry. I heard it in her voice. I sensed her tension. I felt her coming after me. I kept walking.

"I will not allow you to give up!" she shouted at me.

She had nearly caught up to me. I could sense that she was reaching out to stop me. That's when I made my move. I dropped down, swept my leg, and caught her on the backs of both knees. Loor went down hard. I sprang forward, put my knee to her chin, and leaned down to her.

"Never make the first move," I said.

I reached back and grabbed the red spikes from both her elbows, pulling each one off deliberately, enjoying myself.

Alder laughed. It was as big and boisterous a laugh as I had ever heard from him. He came over and picked me up off Loor like a doll, giving me a hug. Loor got up and stood where she had fallen. I've seen Loor in many fights. Not just in the last few weeks, but against real enemies, when it counted. I had never, ever seen anyone get the better of her. As far as I knew, I was the first. She didn't say anything. She only stood there, staring at me.

"Hey," I said with a shrug. "You're the one who said I had to be clever."

Loor stared me down for a long moment, and then she smiled. In that one instant I felt all the tension melt away. My guess was that she didn't consider this a defeat, but a victory. She had actually managed to teach me something.

"We are done, Pendragon," she said. "There is nothing more we can teach you here."

"Sure there is," I said. "But we can't waste any more time."

"Do not underestimate what you have learned," Loor said. "You have done far better than I expected."

"Seriously?" I asked.

"You are ready, my friend," Alder said.

I glanced between the two of them and added, "You realize I hate you both."

Neither were sure of how to react to that. I smiled and added, "But I'll get over it."

"Saangi!" Loor shouted out. Saangi instantly came running out from one of the buildings to join us. Loor said, "Saangi, please bring the remaining food and water to the sleep area. Pendragon must eat."

Saangi gave me one of her usual sour looks. I expected her to say something like: "Tell him to get it himself." But instead she said, "It would be an honor." She smiled at me and ran off.

Whoa. I didn't expect that.

Alder said, "I will help Saangi." He took off, but not before saying, "I am proud of you, Pendragon."

Loor and I were alone. It was kind of awkward. After having been "enemies" for these few weeks, it was hard to suddenly change my thinking.

"I'm not convinced this did any good," I said. "But thank you for trying."

"You always surprise me, Pendragon," Loor said. "I know how difficult this was for you. You have the courage and the will, but fighting is not in your nature. You did well."

"Well, thanks, but, I'm no warrior."

"That is true," Loor said. "If you meet Saint Dane again, he will not be using toy weapons."

Oh, well. So much for building my confidence. Loor turned it around by stepping up to me, holding my shoulders, and giving me a kiss on the cheek.

"I am proud that you are my lead Traveler," she said.

For once, I didn't know what to say. Really. I was a total mess.

"There is only one task left," she said.

"What's that?" I asked, fearing she had one last diabolical surprise in store.

"We must celebrate," was her answer.

An hour later we were all in the barracks, enjoying a spread of food and water that was greater than anything I had seen in weeks. By Second Earth standards it wasn't exactly Thanksgiving, but having the choice between several fruits and dried meats and loaves of bread was a luxury I wasn't used to. I learned that Saangi had been making daily stealth trips back and forth between Mooraj and Xhaxhu to replenish our supplies.

(I never did find out where she was hiding the stuff.) I figured I had to be careful about eating too much because my stomach had probably shrunk to the size of a walnut. I didn't want to load up and then heave in front of everybody. That would have ruined the party for sure, and wasted a bunch of good food.

It felt like a last meal and a celebration rolled into one. Training was over. We were on the same team again. I knew that we were all thinking about how we would now have to turn our sites toward our real enemy, but after working so hard for so long, we deserved a vacation, even if it was only for a couple of minutes.

"To Pendragon!" Alder said while lifting a canteen to toast.

"To Pendragon!" Loor and Saangi echoed.

"I have one request," Loor said.

"What's that?" I asked.

"You must remain true to who you are," she said. "You have new skills; it does not mean you must use them."

"Believe me," I said, "if I never had to fight again, I'd be a happy guy. All you've done is give me a better shot at surviving. For that, I can't thank you enough. All of you."

I raised my own canteen to them, and we drank a toast. After drinking, Loor pulled something out from beneath one of the bunks.

"You now fight like a Ghee," she said. "With your dark skin, you almost look like a Batu. Almost."

We all chuckled.

She continued, "Therefore, you should dress like one."

Loor handed me the clothes I would be wearing from then on—the lightweight leather armor of a Ghee warrior.

"Are you sure?" I asked with surprise.

"You are not a Rokador," she said. "There is no longer any sense in pretending to be one."

"Thank you, Loor," I said. "I'm honored. I really am."

I took the clothing reverently. With a little help from Saangi, who had to explain exactly how to put it on, I donned the armor of a Ghee. I guess calling it armor is misleading. It was more like black clothing that had leather pads to protect vital areas like the chest, kidneys, and of course, the groin. Always gotta protect the groin. The sleeves and pants were short, but there were extra pads for the forearms that reminded me of the braces I used to wear when street skating. Same with my knees. It was all pretty comfortable, and I could move easily. I even liked the sandals. They had more protection than the open, Rokador variety. And I could keep on my boxers. That was key.

When I was dressed, I stepped back and said, "How do I look?"

Alder smiled and said, "Intimidating."

"Yeah, right," I said sarcastically. But the truth was, wearing this armor made me feel a little more formidable. Who knows? Maybe I had actually come a little closer to my fantasy image of a fierce warrior. Or maybe I was kidding myself.

"You look good," Saangi said. "Nothing like a Ghee, but good."

She was humoring me. That was okay. All I cared about was not looking like a little kid wearing my daddy's armor.

"You will also need this," Loor said.

From under the bunk she pulled out the last piece in the puzzle. It was an official stave, the wooden weapon used by Ghee warriors. It was around six feet long and a few inches thick. It got thicker toward either end so it looked sort of like a long, double-ended club. It was pretty worn, too. This weapon had seen action. The wood was stained dark from sweat, and for all I knew, blood. No question, this weapon had a ton of history. As it turned out, I was absolutely correct.

Loor held the stave out reverently and said, "This was the weapon of my mother, Osa."

My throat clutched. Osa. The Traveler from Zadaa before Loor. The last time I saw her, it was in a battle to defend me. She saved my life, and lost hers. I didn't feel worthy to take her weapon.

"I can't," I said.

"You can," Loor said firmly. "I believe this is the way it was meant to be."

I hesitated, but one look in Loor's eyes told me she truly wanted me to have it. I tentatively reached out and took it. Of course, it was heavier than the bamboo poles I had been fighting with. More important, I felt Osa's spirit in this weapon.

I looked at Loor and said, "I don't know what to say."

"Say you will honor the memory of my mother," Loor said.

"I'll do my best."

Loor nodded. It was a bittersweet moment.

I looked at Alder and said, "By coming here you may have saved my life. I'm really grateful."

"You say that as if I am about to leave," he replied.

"You've done your part," I said. "You should return to Denduron."

Alder picked up the short, metal rod that was the Rokador weapon. With his size and white skin, he still looked very much like a Rokador. There was no sense in dressing him like a Ghee.

"I am a Traveler," Alder said. "That is reason enough. Loor helped us save Denduron; it is time to return the favor."

I looked to Loor. She nodded.

I took Osa's stave and flipped it over my back until it was firmly wedged into the leather harness that Saangi had fitted to me. I'd like to say that I felt all sorts of menacing with my armor and weapon, but after all the grueling training I had been through, the one thing nobody prepared me for was walking around with a big old stick strapped to my back. Talk about awkward! It took me a while to figure out how to position it so I could turn around without whacking somebody. The first time I moved, I nearly beaned Alder.

He laughed and said, "We are on the same side again, remember?"

"Sorry," I said, embarrassed. Yeah, I was a badass warrior all right. I felt more like one of the Three Stooges. "Why didn't you guys teach me how to deal with this?" I said, turning around comically, nearly hitting Loor and Saangi, deliberately. Both ducked out of the way and laughed.

"This is a whole nother skill," I said, laughing. I spun quickly. Alder had to duck or he would have gotten hit. He laughed. "Oops, sorry!" I said, joking. I turned to help him up, nearly hitting Loor and Saangi again. I spun back to them. "Oh, I'm sorry!" I was having fun, for the first time since I could remember. We all were. Even Saangi. To be honest, it wasn't all that funny, but when you don't have much else to laugh about, you take the yuks where you can get them. I spun around the room a few more times, pretending to apologize to one person for nearly hitting them while nearly whacking another one behind me until finally, I hit Alder. He lurched forward, overdoing it. We all laughed. He staggered a few steps, and we all kept laughing until I registered the look on Alder's face. He wasn't laughing. This was no joke.

"Jeez, man, I'm sorry," I said. "Did I really nail you?"

Alder's eyes were wide with shock. He fell to his knee, and turned until we all saw something that made the party stop as quickly as if somebody had flipped off a light switch.

Sticking out of Alder's shoulder was a steel arrow.

The four of us froze. It made no sense. I hadn't seen anything like this on Zadaa before. But Loor had.

"Tiggens!" Loor shouted. "We are being attacked!"

ZADAA

Zing! Another arrow flew through the doorway, whizzed across the room, and imbedded itself into the far wall.

"Down!" Loor shouted.

We all hit the ground. Loor tackled Alder, making sure that he was out of harm's way.

"Is this it?" I asked in a strained whisper. "Has the war begun?"

"No," Saangi answered. "I was in Xhaxhu this morning. There was no plan to attack."

"Then maybe the Rokador are striking first," I said.

"That would be suicide," Loor answered. "And even if they were, why would they attack us out here in the desert?"

Good point. Whoever was attacking, this wasn't about the conflict between the Batu and the Rokador. This was about us. Oh joy.

"I am all right," Alder said, though I could tell he was gritting his teeth in pain. I could see a blossom of red spreading out from the arrow, soaking his white Rokador tunic. "Leave me here," he said. "Take the battle to them."

Loor didn't have to be told twice. She rolled across the

floor toward the back window and crouched up on her feet, ready to go. "Stay with him, Pendragon," she said. A moment later she sprang up and launched herself out the window.

I had to make a quick decision. Was I going to stay here with Alder and hope Loor could protect us? Or was now the time to step up to the plate and use my new skills? I looked at Alder. I think the look in my eyes told him what my decision was.

"You are ready," was all he said, as if to assure me. "Be careful."

"Stay with him, Saangi," I ordered, and rolled for the back window as I had seen Loor do.

"Loor told you to stay here!" Saangi protested.

"And now *I'm* telling *you* to stay here," I shot back. As I stood under that window, I realized that my earlier fight with Loor wasn't my final exam after all. That was only a pop quiz. My true final exam was about to be given now, and this time it wasn't against a friend. Was I ready? It didn't matter. Failing this test would mean death.

I leaped up and hoisted myself out the window. I'd forgotten that Osa's stave was still in the sling on my back. As I went through the opening, I caught one end of the weapon on the window frame. It threw me off balance, and I ended up tumbling down and hitting the ground, back first. This time being clumsy with the weapon wasn't so funny. I didn't have time to feel dumb, though. I quickly jumped up and threw myself against the wall, bracing myself to get hit with one of those steel arrows. A quick look around told me I was alone. I quickly yanked the stave out of the sling and ran to the edge of the building to find Loor.

I got to the corner and cautiously looked around to witness a curious scene. Loor was standing in the middle of the dusty training ground. Facing her were six Tiggen guards, with their goggles on and their heads wrapped. This didn't look like a warm reunion, like when we met those guys on the farm. Everyone here looked tense, with their legs set wide and their weapons ready. Four of them held steel batons. The fifth had a weapon that looked like a medieval crossbow. Only this thing was loaded with a row of steel arrows. Two of them had already been fired. One was sticking out of Alder's shoulder. Stranger still, he had the weapon trained on the back of the last Tiggen guard! It was the only guard I recognized, because he had removed his goggles. It was Bokka, Loor's friend. He stood between Loor and the five others, with a loaded crossbow aimed at his back. I had no idea what was going on, though one thing I was pretty sure of. This was no social call. There was going to be more trouble.

No sooner did I survey the scene, then all hell broke loose. It started with a dark streak flying toward the group. At first I thought it was a bird swooping in, but a quick look showed me that it was Saangi's wooden stave. She had hurled it at the Tiggen guards like a spear. A second later I saw her sprinting toward the group. She hadn't followed my instructions and stayed with Alder. No surprise. Saangi wasn't big on following orders. Then again, I didn't follow Loor's orders either, so I shouldn't criticize. The stave hit the Tiggen with the crossbow, knocking it out of his hands. Instantly Loor attacked. The battle was on. Without taking a second to try and figure out what was happening, I bolted for the group. I had no idea what I was going to do, but I was about to do it.

A quick look told me that Loor was fighting two of the guards. Saangi went after a third. Bokka had turned and tackled the last one, wrestling him for control of his steel baton-weapon. I didn't understand. What had happened that the Tiggens were now against Bokka? There wasn't time to analyze. I went after the leader, who was scrambling to pick up his crossbow. He saw me at the last second, flying in with the stave held high. He didn't have time to pick up the weapon and aim. Instead he grabbed it and threw it at me. I deflected it with no problem, but it gave him time to pull his own steel baton from his belt. I still hadn't seen how the Tiggen guards used this short weapon. It looked pretty solid and would probably hurt if it made contact. I figured that with my longer stave I could keep him far enough away so I wouldn't get hit. I'd only be in trouble if I let him inside. Or so I thought.

I can't say that I flashed back on all the lessons that I had been through over the past few weeks. I didn't. Except for one. Loor taught me to think like a warrior, and act without thinking. She had trained me well. Every move I made from that point on, I did by instinct. If I had taken the time to think, I'd be dead.

I quickly realized that my opponent wasn't all that skilled. He was clumsy, and swung his baton wildly, like a guy with a tennis racket trying to swat a bee. I guess that's why he had the crossbow. He was a better marksman than a fighter. He'd swing at me, I'd knock his shot away, and the following shot, then counter with a blow to the chest, or the head. I kept getting the third shot in. I was winning. It was easy. Fighting Loor and Alder was a lot more difficult than dueling this loser. Of course, I didn't think about that at the time. I just let it fly.

There was only one problem. This was the first real fight I had been in. I was used to sparring against friends with a lightweight bamboo pole. Osa's stave was heavy! I could handle it okay, but I was slower. And I didn't know how much force to put behind it. I think the whole time I was fighting in the training camp, I subconsciously held back, knowing that I was fighting friends. It was more about technique than intent. Here I needed to clobber this guy. But as often as I'd hit him, and it was pretty often, he didn't seem to be affected by it. Now that I think back on this fight, I realize that there is a big difference between sparring, and full-speed fighting. I still didn't quite know how to do it, and it nearly cost me my life.

Loor had already knocked one guy out, and was battling the second. Saangi was holding her own. I figured she only had to last long enough for Loor to dispatch her second opponent before Loor would help her out. One thing was pretty clear: the Ghee were better fighters than the Tiggen guards. It was good to be a Ghee. I also saw that Bokka was wrestling with the last guard and seemed to be in control. It looked as if this fight would be over quickly, and we'd get some answers as to what was going on.

It turned out not to be that easy. Up until that moment, I had easily knocked away every attack my opponent made. It was so effortless, I got cocky. I knew I could beat this guy, so I turned my thoughts to what was going to happen after the fight. It was a near fatal mental lapse. I should have finished him. I didn't. In that quick moment the guy thrust his baton at me. There wasn't much force behind it, but that didn't matter. In that one second I learned what the steel baton weapons were all about. The steel grazed my shoulder, and my arm went numb. I was hit with a jolt of electricity! These steel weapons were stun guns! Suddenly I couldn't use my arm. Osa's stave fell out of my limp hand. I had to quickly react and shift the balance with my other hand, or the Tiggen would have knocked it out of my grasp entirely and I'd have been defenseless.

I could barely control the stave with my one good hand, and there was no way I could counter with an attack. I had all I could do just to keep this guy from jabbing me with that cattle prod again. The guy lunged at me. I backed off, but rather than attack, the guy dove to the ground, away from me. This was a new tactic. What was he doing? He hit the ground, rolled, and scooped up his crossbow. Uh-oh. He rolled into a kneeling position, ready to fire. I was the target. I was dead.

"Pendragon!" came a shout.

It was enough to make my killer hesitate. A silver blur flashed toward him that nailed him square in the head, knocking him down. It was a Rokador baton. A quick look back showed me where it had come from.

Alder had thrown it. He had come out of the safety of the barracks to save my life. But he was hurting. The arrow was still in his shoulder. Blood was spreading. The Tiggen guard that Saangi had been fighting knocked her down, and went after the more dangerous adversary, Alder. He lunged at Alder, smashing his baton across Alder's face. It was a brutal shot, made more so by the fact that Alder took the brunt of the electrical charge. I saw his body stiffen as he fell back.

I flashed back to the moment when the flume was collapsing on Eelong, and the rock fell from above, hitting the head of Kasha, the Traveler. It killed her. I couldn't bear to see this happen to another Traveler. Another friend.

I screamed and sprinted across the sandy yard and tackled Alder's attacker. The guy never saw me coming. I smashed his hand into the ground, making him drop his baton.

"Pendragon!" I heard Saangi yell. I looked up in time to see something that made me freeze like a deer in the headlights. The Tiggen leader that Alder had beaned with his weapon wasn't knocked out. He had recovered his crossbow. It was up on his shoulder. His eye was along the barrel to take aim . . . at me. Loor was still fighting. Bokka was still wrestling. Saangi wasn't close to him. There was nothing to stop this guy from firing, and I was dead square in his sights.

There was nothing I could do, no place to hide. All this guy had to do was pull the trigger and I'd be done. I figured I'd dive away as soon as he fired, but if those lethal little spears were as fast as I'd seen before, I wouldn't stand a chance. I braced myself, ready to dive in either direction. That's when the Tiggen assassin did something I didn't expect. He kept his eye to the barrel of the weapon, but turned away from me. What was he doing? Had he changed his mind?

The answer came a second later. He was no longer interested in me. He had another target in mind. No sooner did he turn the weapon away, than he fired. Once, twice, three times. Rapid fire. As each arrow was released I heard a small snapping sound, and a whoosh as the missiles shot across the training ground toward their target.

Bokka.

Bokka had just thrown the Tiggen he had been wrestling to the ground and was getting to his feet. He never made it. The volley of arrows hit him square in the chest. In his heart. One after the other. The force stood him straight up. He stood there for a second with wide, unbelieving eyes, then fell flat onto his back.

"Bokka!" Loor screamed. With one shot she nailed the Tiggen she had been fighting, and ran for her friend. I didn't know what she planned on doing. He was beyond help before he even hit the ground. My fear was that the assassin would start shooting at Loor. I grabbed the Tiggen baton off the ground and started after the assassin, but he quickly turned and aimed his crossbow at me.

"Do not move," he said with no emotion.

He didn't have to tell me twice. This guy wasn't afraid to shoot. I froze. He motioned with the weapon for me to move toward Loor. I did what I was told. He glanced at Saangi, who also got the message. Both of us warily circled to join Loor. As we walked, the other Tiggen guards slowly got to their feet. They had been beaten up pretty badly, but the guy with the crossbow held all the cards. The other Tiggens limped toward the assassin. I glanced back to Alder, who was lying on his back, not moving. I didn't know if he was dead or alive. His blood was seeping onto the sand, which was actually good news. It meant his heart was still beating. But for how long?

Loor knelt on the sand with Bokka's head in her lap. I remembered the horrible moment when she had done the same with her mother, Osa. It was a cruel twist of fate that Loor now had to see another loved one die the same way. As sad as that was, we had more pressing problems to deal with. Saangi and I joined Loor. I looked back to see the Tiggen guards gather around the assassin, whose weapon was aimed at us. Two words came to mind: firing squad. If the Tiggen guard wanted to kill us, there wasn't a whole lot we could do about it.

"Why?" I asked. "We've done nothing to you."

"Bokka was a traitor," the assassin said. "He deserved to die. We came for him, not you."

The assassin took a step backward, while keeping the weapon on us. The others followed, but kept their eyes on us.

"Do not follow us," he said. "Or you will die along with him."

The other Tiggens turned and jogged off. We didn't move. It wasn't worth it. A moment later they were gone. They probably crawled back into the sand and slithered off like the snakes they were. I was numb. None of this made sense.

"Kidik," Bokka whispered.

He was alive! The poor guy was fighting to stay focused.

"Quiet," Loor said, cradling his head. "We will care for you."

"I know the truth," Bokka wheezed. "I came to tell you. They followed me, to stop me."

This was horrible. Bokka was dying. With his last few breaths he was trying to tell us something that was important enough to be murdered for. With one weak hand, he motioned to his boot.

"What?" I asked.

"Look," he said.

The Tiggen guards didn't wear open sandals like the rest of the Rokador. They wore soft, sand-colored leather boots that reached nearly to their knees. I saw that tucked into his right boot, barely poking out the top, was a folded piece of parchment paper. I pulled it out and unfolded it. It was a map.

"Go to Kidik," Bokka rasped. He was fading fast. "The truth lies beyond the city, out in the center. It is . . . it is . . . a nightmare."

"What is the truth?" Loor asked. I could see that her eyes were tearing up. Her best friend was about to die.

"Find the man," Bokka wheezed. "The stranger." He coughed, gasping for breath.

"What man, Bokka?" I asked. "What is the truth?"

Bokka tried to focus on me, but he was slipping fast. "He says he is from your tribe, Pendragon."

"What?" I shouted in surprise.

"Beyond the city. There is a vehicle waiting to take you there. Find him."

"Who is he, Bokka?"

Bokka coughed. It was painful to watch. I found myself taking a deep breath, as if it would help him breathe. It didn't. He winced, but forced himself to focus. He looked me right in the eye and said, "His name is . . . Saint Dane."

They were the last two words he would ever speak.

ZADAA

The next few hours passed in a blur. We first brought Bokka's body into the barracks and covered him. Loor was amazingly stoic. I couldn't imagine what was going through her head. Her best friend from birth had been killed by his own people. The only way I could relate would be to imagine if something happened to either of you two guys, Mark and Courtney. It was beyond horrible. Bokka died trying to help Loor. To help us. I regretted ever being jealous of the guy. He was a hero. Still, Loor couldn't allow herself time to mourn. We needed to take care of the living, and Alder needed help. Fast. We knew where to get it.

We awkwardly carried the injured Bedoowan knight to the entrance to the underground, and the small train that would take us back to the crossroads. It wasn't easy. Alder was big and heavy. None of us complained. As we traveled along in that miniature train, I hoped that we wouldn't run into the Tiggen assassins. If they thought we were following them, well, let's just say I'm really glad we didn't see them.

We made it through the crossroads without problems, and continued the journey back to Xhaxhu. Luckily we found a cart that we were able to load Alder into so we could push him along. Without that cart it would have taken us twice as long to get back, and every second counted. We had to be careful, though. We didn't want to take the arrow out. Loor said it would only make him bleed more.

Throughout the trip, none of us said anything about Bokka's last words. There would be time for that later. Now it was all about Alder. As we moved quickly through the tunnels, all I could do was stare at him and hope that we wouldn't be losing another Traveler. The thought was too painful to even imagine. Loor had her hand over Alder's heart, as if trying to transmit some kind of cosmic energy into his body to keep him alive. It was sweet, and gut-wrenching at the same time.

Our goal was to get back to the hospital where I had been treated, and hope that the doctor who cared for me would be willing to help. By the time we arrived in Xhaxhu it was night, so we were able to use the darkness for cover as we made our way through the streets to the hospital pyramid. We found our way in and brought Alder to a quiet room, away from suspicious eyes, while Saangi went to find the doctor who had treated me. It didn't take her long. She found him and immediately brought him to the secluded room. When he saw us, his shoulders fell. He did not want the responsibility of caring for another Rokador.

"What is your name?" I asked the doctor.

"Nazsha," the man answered.

I spoke slowly and sincerely, in the hope that whatever abilities of persuasion I had as a Traveler would kick in. If we ever needed them, it was now.

"When you treated me, Nazsha," I said, "you said you thought I could help the Batu. You were right. That's what I'm trying to do. And so is this injured man."

Alder was still unconscious. His white Rokador tunic was

drenched in his own blood. He was alive, but I didn't know for how much longer.

The doctor gave him a quick look and said, "That is the arrow of a Rokador."

"It is," I said.

"And you now wear the armor of a Ghee," he said, confused.

"You were right before," I said. "We aren't Rokador. Without your help, he'll die."

The doctor looked at me. I saw the questions in his eyes. If he didn't believe we were there to help the Batu, at least I hoped he was like the doctors on Second Earth who were supposed to help the sick and injured, no matter what.

"This could bring me trouble," he said.

"Maybe," I replied. "But isn't all of Xhaxhu already in serious trouble?"

The doctor looked back to Alder. I could tell he was debating with himself about what to do.

"Bring him," Nazsha finally ordered.

I'd like to take the credit for convincing the guy to help, but I think it was more because he was the kind of guy who always helped those in need. Loor and I each took one of Alder's arms and carried the big knight through the sandstone corridors to a forgotten area deep within the bowels of the hospital. There, safely away from curious eyes, the doctor went to work. He cut off Alder's blood-soaked clothing and pulled out the arrow, which I couldn't watch. The squishy, sucking sound was bad enough. Alder looked pale, and not just Rokador-pale. It was from the blood loss. Doctor Nazsha cleaned him up and packed the wound with something that looked like leaves dipped in honey. He then went to work with needle and thread to close it up. I guess I don't have to point out that I didn't watch that, either. After he finished sewing, he dressed the wound with some salve and forced Alder to drink a variety of potions, which wasn't easy since Alder was pretty out of it.

"I will continue to administer the medication," the doctor said. "I do not believe the arrow damaged anything vital, but the blood loss may have been too much. The rest is up to your friend. If he lives through the night, he may survive."

"Can we stay here?" I asked.

"If you wish," the doctor asked. "But I cannot protect you if a Ghee discovers you. I am not a brave man. I will help care for your friend, but I am not a warrior."

"You're wrong," I said. "You're a very brave man. Thank you."

The doctor left, with the promise to return frequently.

"I must return to Mooraj," Loor said. "Bokka must be taken care of."

I wanted to argue. It was dangerous to go back through the underground. But if Loor wanted to go, I wasn't about to stop her. She left without saying another word. Saangi stayed with me. I think Loor wanted her there in case there was trouble. Or maybe she wanted to take care of Bokka's body alone. Either way, Saangi and I stayed with Alder. Doctor Nazsha was true to his word. Every few hours he returned to change Alder's dressing and give him more liquid. The guy probably didn't sleep all night. He was a good doctor.

After spending a few hours there watching over Alder, Saangi went out to get some food and water. That was fine, but I didn't have the energy to eat. All I wanted was to be unconscious. I was dog-tired. But as beat as I was, I couldn't knock off. Random thoughts kept bouncing around my head like a foosball game with twelve balls.

There have been many times since I left home that I questioned whether it was a mistake that I had become a Traveler.

Did I say "many times"? How about a few hundred times a day? I wrote to you before about Gunny's theory. He thinks that somebody actually chose the Travelers, though he has no idea who that could be. If it's true, when I meet him the first thing I'm going to ask that guy is: "Why me?" I guess I'd done okay so far, but if I were asked to describe the perfect Traveler, it sure wouldn't be me. As I sat there, trying not to stress over these cosmic questions that had no answers, I heard a familiar voice.

"How is he?"

I looked up to see Loor standing in the doorway.

"The same," I said. "But I think that's a good thing."

Loor walked over to Alder and put a hand on his forehead. I watched her, thinking that when I met that mysterious guy who chose the Travelers, the one question I *wouldn't* have to ask is: "Why Loor?" I knew why Loor. She was strong. She was brave. She was simple, but I mean that in a good way. She didn't overanalyze everything the way I did. Right and wrong were as easy for her to pick out as left and right. All the Travelers are special in some way, but I have to say that Loor is our backbone. If we lost her, we'd be done. I know I would. I actually thought ahead to a time in the future when this battle with Saint Dane would be over. Would I ever see Loor again? Would I continue to ride the flumes? Would she come to Second Earth? I couldn't imagine life without her being part of it. How that might work was a whole nother problem for another day. I already had too many balls bouncing around the foosball table in my brain to worry about that.

She left Alder and walked over to me. "Bokka is at rest," she said before I had the chance to ask her. "I honored him in the traditional way."

I knew what that meant. She had cremated Bokka's body,

the same as we did with Kasha. I couldn't begin to imagine how tough that was. I didn't want to.

"I'm sorry, Loor" was all I could say. "I wish I knew him better."

"In many ways he was like you," she said. "He believed that good could be found in everyone. That was what I liked most about him."

I nodded.

"Pendragon?" came a raspy voice.

It was Alder. He was awake! Loor and I hurried to the bed to see that his eyes were open. They were unfocused and glassy, but open. I wasn't sure if that was from the blood loss, or the wacky mind-numbing medicines the doctor had been pumping into him.

"Water," he croaked.

I grabbed a cup and brought it to his lips. Alder raised his head to take a few sips, then dropped back down as if the effort were too much.

"Weak," he whispered.

"I hear you," I said. "But you're gonna be okay."

At that moment Doctor Nazsha entered, along with Saangi.

"He's awake!" I announced.

The doctor went right to Alder and did a quick exam.

"I am amazed," Nazsha said. "His wounds are healing." He looked at me and added, "You and your friend have remarkable recuperative powers."

We did? When I was in that hospital it sure felt like my recovery took a long time. But then again, I'd never had my entire body pummeled and broken before, so I didn't have any frame of reference.

The doctor continued, "If there is no infection, I believe he will be fine."

Relief? Yeah, that's an understatement. Even Saangi smiled. More surprising than that, Loor hugged me. Loor. Cold, professional Loor. I didn't know if this meant she was warming up, or she was totally relieved that she wouldn't have to witness the deaths of two friends. It didn't matter. I hugged her back.

Alder rasped, "I feel as weak as a baby."

Loor said, "Not for long. You are stronger than any Ghee."

The doctor said, "It will take time before you will be well enough to move. I will care for you until then."

Alder nodded and fell back to sleep. Lucky him.

"Thanks, Doctor," I said. "You did a good thing here."

Nazsha nodded and said, "I trust you will be as successful in your quest." He left. The pressure was off. Alder would live. Knowing that, my mind instantly went to the challenge ahead.

"I know this is tough to talk about," I began. "But we have to. Bokka died trying to give us information. Something is going on with the Rokador. It was so important that he was killed by his own people to stop him from telling us."

"He said it was a nightmare," Saangi added.

"Right, nightmare," I said. "Remind you of anyone?"

"Saint Dane," Loor said.

"Yeah, Saint Dane," I echoed. "Tell me about Kidik. It's a city, right?"

"It is the seat of Rokador power," Loor explained. "Not many Batu have been there. I have never seen it myself."

I took Bokka's map from where I was keeping it, inside the chest piece of my Ghee armor. I unfolded the parchment to see that it looked like a crude road map. But rather than roads, this map showed tunnels. Hundreds of them. Some wider than others. It was pretty extensive, too. Imagine looking at a road map with no markings other than the roads. No landmarks, no mountains, and certainly no rest stops with a McDonald's. The route to Kidik was traced in red.

"Bokka has shown us the way," I said. "He said we'd find the truth at the center, beyond Kidik. Do you know what that is?"

"No," Loor said.

I looked to Saangi. She shrugged.

"Well," I said, "I think we have to go find out."

"We are going to Kidik?" Saangi asked, eagerly.

"Not you," Loor answered. Saangi wanted to argue, but Loor cut her off fast. "Stop!" she commanded. "That is my decision. You must remain here to care for Alder. When he is well enough to move, you must bring him to the flume and send him home."

"Uh, but don't use the flume yourself," I added, just in case.

"But Loor—"

"That is final!" Loor said. She meant it. Saangi realized it and backed off.

"Let's go now," I said. "I'm ready."

"Not just yet," Loor said. "Tonight is the Festival of Azhra, remember? You have been personally invited to attend by Pelle a Zinj. I believe we should go."

"What?" I shouted. "We finally have a hint that might lead us to Saint Dane and you want to go to a party? Bokka died to give us this information. We have to go!"

"I agree," Loor said. "But I believe the one person who will determine whether or not the Batu go to war with the Rokador is Pelle a Zinj. The royal family always makes a ceremonial presentation and a speech to the city at the festival. I believe it would be wise for us to hear what he has to say."

I couldn't argue with that. If Pelle a Zinj was going to make a big speech to the whole city, he wasn't going to be talking about sports. Loor was right. This speech might tell us if war was near.

"Okay," I said, reluctantly. "I guess whatever is down there can wait a day."

Loor said, "Saangi, I know you are disappointed, but Alder is a Traveler, and a friend. We need him, and he needs you. You must stay with him until he is well enough to move."

"I understand," Saangi said. "Forgive me for arguing."

Loor smiled and said, "I would have been surprised if you did not."

I was happy that Loor had ordered Saangi to stay, and not just because Alder needed her help. I wouldn't say anything, but after being fooled so many times on the other territories, I wasn't a hundred percent sure that Saangi wasn't actually Saint Dane in disguise. I didn't think she was, but there were a lot of other people I never suspected either. I wasn't to the point where I was paranoid about everybody. That would have made me nuts. But I'm to the point where if somebody gets too close, I get suspicious. For those reasons, it was better that Loor and I traveled to Kidik alone.

She and I left the hospital, doing our best to keep clear of people. At least I didn't have to hide under the heavy, dark robe anymore. Between my darkened skin and my Ghee warrior clothes, I fit right in. Sort of. I still wore a small hood over my head. Tan or no, I didn't have the features of a Batu.

The sun was beginning to rise over Xhaxhu. Loor and I went back to her home in the Ghee warrior complex and made the really smart decision to get some sleep. The festival wouldn't begin until sunset and there was no telling when we'd get another chance to rest. Now that our path was set, and Alder was healing, I was actually able to conk out and get some much-needed sleep. I lay down on a grass mat in front of Loor's fireplace and drifted off instantly. No thinking. No dreaming. No foosball. I don't think I moved for hours. The rest of the day I was comatose, enjoying a deep, healing sleep that was long in coming.

The next thing I knew, Loor was kneeling by me, gently nudging me awake.

"It is time to prepare," she said.

"Prepare what?" I asked. "Are we supposed to bring dip or something to this party?"

"First we must eat," she said. On the floor next to me was a tray of fruit and bread and a cup of precious water. "After we eat, you will wear this." She held up a white Rokador jacket and pants. It was pretty much like the other Rokador clothes I had worn, but the collar and sleeves had some kind of gold-braid design around them.

"Rokador dress-up clothes?" I asked.

"They wear this on special occasions," Loor confirmed.

"What about my Ghee armor?" I asked.

"Nobody wears armor to this festival," Loor said. "And you must act as a Rokador. Remember, Pelle a Zinj believes you are one, and you are his guest."

"Right," I said, sitting up. "I hope he doesn't ask where I got the tan."

"He may not even know you are there," Loor said. "This is just a precaution. Now I must prepare."

Loor left me and went into the other room of her home. I figured she had already eaten, so I ate my fill of the delicious fruit and bread, washing it all down with the water. Once I was full, I got up and reluctantly took off my Ghee armor clothes. I hoped I could figure out how to put it all back on again. I then slipped on the soft white pants and jacket of the Rokador. This material felt finer than what I had been wearing before. These were definitely "dress-up" clothes. I also put on another pair of the open sandals. I hated those. Have I mentioned that?

I stood up straight, stretched out the kinks, and called out, "Are you ready?"

"I am," Loor said.

I turned to see Loor standing in the doorway to the next room. I gasped. Yes, I actually gasped, I'm embarrassed to say. I couldn't help it. The surprise was too much. Loor stood there looking absolutely gorgeous. In the past I had seen her wear the leather clothes of the Milago peasants, the jumpsuit of a Lifelight jumper, the leather armor of a Ghee warrior, and even the jeans and T-shirt of Second Earth. But nothing I had seen before had prepared me for this.

She looked like a princess.

Gone was the black armor. Loor wore a short, deep red tunic that hugged her incredible, athletic body. Unlike the armor, this dress was soft and very feminine. There were ornate tapestrylike designs around the neck and the bottom of the short skirt. She wore lightweight sandals, with leather straps crisscrossing up to her knees. The sleeves were short, and on each bicep she wore a colorful, beaded strap. Around her neck was a necklace of blue crystal stones that reminded me of the glaze from Denduron. As breathtaking as the whole outfit was, what really stood out for me was her hair. Loor always had her hair tied back practically, so it wouldn't get in the way. Now her long dark hair was totally loose and combed out. Her hair was so black and shiny, it sparkled with light from the fireplace. Around her forehead she wore a simple headpiece that looked as if it were made from pearls. There was an ornate piece in the center, with two drapes of pearls coming down across either side of her forehead.

In a word, she was stunning.

I said, "Uhh." That's it. "Uhh." Smooth, huh?

"How do I look?" Loor asked.

"Beautiful," I said. Though "beautiful" was a totally

inadequate word. Given time I could think of a few thousand others that would work much better.

"I do not often dress like this," she said, walking into the room. "But there are times when conflict must be put aside. The Festival of Azhra is one of them."

When she walked, I expected her to move like a guy dressed up like a girl. She didn't. Loor had a way of moving that was solid, but at the same time, graceful. It's like she sort of . . . flowed.

"You are staring at me, Pendragon," she said. "Is something wrong?"

"Wrong?" I laughed. "Things are about as right as they can get. You look great."

She gave me a small smile. "As do you," she said. She was being polite. I looked like me with a tan and a goofy bathrobe. With sandals.

"We should go," she said. "We do not want to miss anything."

The Festival of Azhra was pretty much like big celebrations back on Second Earth. Loor explained that a parade would wind its way through the streets of Xhaxhu, ending at the palace of Zinj. Once the parade ended, all the citizens of Xhaxhu would gather in the square in front of the palace for the traditional greeting and speech given by a member of the royal family. It was all followed by families returning to their homes and big feasts that lasted through the rest of the night. It sounded like fun. I wondered what kind of vibe there would be, seeing as the city was gripped by a drought and on the verge of war. I didn't imagine there would be much feasting, either.

I was thrilled to discover that at least for a night, the people of Xhaxhu forgot about their troubles. Loor and I walked through the streets as people flooded out of their homes, headed for the parade route. Everyone was dressed in their colorful best and ready to party. Even seeing a Rokador, me, didn't seem to bother them. This was a night of celebration. They'd have plenty of time for hatred tomorrow.

Loor and I arrived at the parade route in the village square where she had fought the zhou beast. Spectators packed the upper levels of the pyramids to get a look down at the show. The parade was made up of groups of dancers wearing rainbow colors doing traditional dances, bands playing flutelike instruments and leather skin drums, and colorful, giant animals made out of paper. I saw a dozen paper zhou beasts, in every color of the rainbow, along with giant snakes that had giant fangs. The marchers in front of them pretended to be battling them with paper spears. Loor explained how this represented the dangerous journey of Azhra through the desert.

It was a long parade too, with many musicians and marchers. The parade entered the square, wound around the statue of the Ghee battling the zhou beast, and continued out the opposite side. From above, happy spectators cheered and rained down colorful confetti. It was like New Year's Eve, Mardi Gras, Chinese New Year, and a Thanksgiving Day parade all rolled into one.

I looked to Loor. My heart went out to her. Only hours before her best friend had been killed. Here at the parade, it seemed as if she was able to forget that for a brief moment and enjoy the spectacle with the eyes of an innocent child. I was glad to see that she could relax. At least for a short time. I didn't hate it either. We both needed it.

"Is it like this every year?" I asked.

"Yes," she said. "But this seems particularly festive. Maybe it is a way of releasing the tension."

I'm sure she was right. These people needed a break. This festival came at a perfect time.

"We should go to the palace," Loor said.

She grabbed my hand and pulled me onto the parade route. We jogged through the marchers and dancers, musicians and floats. Many of the dancers met me and put a wreath of paper flowers around my neck. I thought it was interesting that they would do this to a Rokador. It made me realize that these were good people and not mindless, drum-beating vigilantes who wanted nothing more than to crush the Rokador. These were ordinary people, just trying to get by. But survival is a strong instinct. Before that night, I felt as if the Batu were the aggressors who wanted to strike out at the only enemy they could target. The Rokador. That may have been true, but this festival made them feel human. More than ever, I truly hoped this war could be avoided.

On that mad dash through the parade, I also saw the more human face of Loor. She laughed and danced with the musicians as they continually stopped her and gave her flowers. Up until then I had mostly seen her warrior side. Seeing the real Loor made my feelings for her even stronger, if that was possible. This may be weird to say under the circumstances, but for a few minutes there I kind of felt as if we were on a date. At one point we were stopped at an intersection while a thirty-foot-long red snake wound its way in front of us. I pulled Loor back because she was about to walk right into it. She looked at me and laughed. Her face absolutely lit up. She was beautiful. The two of us stood there for a moment, looking at each other. All I wanted to do was kiss her. I moved in slightly, expecting her to back off. She didn't. I think she wanted to kiss me, too. It was perfect. The confetti fell down around us like colorful snow. Music was everywhere; Batu revelers surrounded us, singing and dancing. But for that moment it felt like the two of us were alone. In many ways we were. We were so different than everybody else there. Nobody knew what we knew or had seen the things we'd seen. Loor and I were forever joined, not only in the battle against Saint Dane, but in the bond that was created by the fact that we owed our lives to each other. It was a magical moment that my words can't begin to describe.

I didn't kiss her. I'm not sure why I stopped. Maybe I didn't want to risk the rejection. Or to move our relationship into uncharted water. Even though my feelings for her were stronger than ever, we had work to do. We couldn't let anything stand in the way of that. If we were meant to be together, we would be. But not until our job was done. So I backed off. I'm not sure if the look on her face was disappointment, or relief. Either way, the moment had passed and we moved on.

She led me through the insane party to another large square and the royal palace of Zinj. The building was breathtaking. Where all the other pyramids of Xhaxhu were made from brown sandstone, the palace was pure white. I don't know if it was made of marble or what, but it stood out among the brown buildings like a brilliant, magical castle. Everything about the palace was white. The stone stairs leading to the immense front doors, the many giant statues that lined both sides of these stairs, even the elaborate fountain on the roof. It was carved to look like a beautiful oasis full of palm trees and flowers. For the occasion the fountain was actually working. Water jetted up in several places to form intricate patterns that danced across one another. It gave me a brief reminder of what Xhaxhu was like before the drought.

"Here!" Loor declared. "I come to this spot for every celebration."

She positioned us on a series of steps that led up to the building right next to the palace. From there we had a perfect view of the palace. Halfway up the palace stairs, a platform was erected that I figured would be where Pelle a Zinj would make his speech. It was draped with purple cloth, making it look very regal. On the platform were two heavy, stone chairs that looked like thrones. Tonight the people of Xhaxhu would hear about their future from the one they trusted the most. I felt as if we were in the right spot at the right time.

The square below us was full of people awaiting the parade and the speech. When the parade arrived, thousands more revelers came with them. Soon the square was packed to capacity. There was cheering and music and general joyous mayhem. These guys really knew how to throw a party!

"Look," Loor said, pointing to the palace.

I had been so interested in the parade, I hadn't notice that the royal platform was now occupied. Two people sat in the thrones—a man and a woman who looked to be in their sixties. They wore elaborate, purple robes with colorful, beaded collars. Both had on golden crowns. They weren't big and goofy looking either. They were actually pretty simple.

"The king and queen," Loor said, though I pretty much had that figured out on my own.

Joining the two on the stage was a familiar face—Pelle a Zinj. He, too, wore a purple robe, but it was nowhere near as elaborate as his parents'. Same with his crown. It was barely a small circle of gold. It looked more like a halo than a regal crown. Pelle stood at the front of the platform, looking down on the festivities with a huge smile. As tough as it must have been to have the responsibility of ruling an entire tribe, there had to be some good times too. This was one of them. As Loor put it, he and his family were the voices of reason. They did not want war with the Rokador. I knew our paths would have to cross. He could very well be our best ally against Saint Dane here on Zadaa.

Behind him, protecting the platform, was a group of

around seven Ghee warriors. These guys really stood out because they were wearing the black armor. They looked like the Secret Service in charge of guarding the boss. All they needed were shades and earpieces. Nobody was going to mess with the royal family with those goons standing guard.

Pelle's gaze rose from the parade below to look out over the crowd. He had this great smile on his face that showed how much he loved his city, and his people. His gaze wandered across, and fell on me. I expected his smile to fall when he saw this somewhat tan Rokador intruding on his party. Instead his smile grew even bigger. He waved to me and touched his heart as if to say: "I am glad you are here." I did the same. It was an awesome experience, like I had just been acknowledged by the president or something. That wasn't the end of it. Pelle whispered something to his Ghee bodyguards, and pointed to me. Uh-oh. Was this all some cruel joke? Was he going to have his bouncers throw me out? The guards scowled and shook their heads. Whatever Pelle told them, they weren't happy about it.

"What is happening?" Loor asked.

A moment later we had our answer. Pelle walked down off the platform and made his way through the crowd toward us! This guy truly was a man of the people. He didn't stand on ceremony. He put on a disguise so he could watch the warriors battle in the square, he visited his subjects in the hospital, and he didn't mind coming down from his pedestal to visit with a common person. An enemy Rokador, no less. Me.

"Pelle is coming to see us!" I said, barely believing it.

Pelle had trouble getting through the crowd. Everybody wanted to touch him or his robe. He smiled at everyone and touched as many as he could, kind of like the Zadaa version of a politician. If there was a baby held up, he probably would have kissed it. Two of the Ghee guards followed close behind, looking tense. They weren't happy about this spontaneous visit. The others stayed behind with the king and queen. None of them were armed. That was the rule of the festival. They looked pretty scary just the same.

"What do we do?" I asked nervously.

"Be sure to bow," Loor said. "Call him 'Your Majesty' and let him do the talking."

"But this is our chance," I said. "He's the big boss. If we can get in good with him, it might help us deal with Saint Dane."

Pelle was getting closer. Whatever plan we were going to come up with, we had to do it fast.

"We cannot be too forward," Loor cautioned. "Be polite. That will impress him. He will remember that, if we need to call upon him in the future."

"Got it. Impress. Polite. I can do that."

The crowd on the stairs next to us parted as the prince of Xhaxhu approached.

"Pendragon, my friend! You are well!" he said with a big, warm smile.

Unbelievable. He even remembered my name.

"I am so happy," he continued. "And you have gotten some color! If I didn't know better, I would have mistaken you for a Batu."

"I am healthy once again, thanks to your kindness, Your Majesty," I said while bowing deeply. Loor bowed too.

"Please," he said. "It is I who should be grateful to you."

"I do not understand, Your Majesty," I said.

"Now that you are healthy, I trust you will keep your promise to return to your people and explain that as long as I am ruler of Xhaxhu, there will be no war."

Oops. I had forgotten about that.

"Of course, Your Majesty," I said, bowing again. "I remained here in Xhaxhu so that I may accept your generous invitation to the greatest festival I have ever seen. Tomorrow I will return to pass along your message."

"Wonderful," Pelle exclaimed. "Our people need each other. I am confidant that once this horrible drought is over, and it will be, we can bring back the atmosphere of mutual respect we both deserve."

"You are a wise ruler," I said. "However, there is one thing."

I sensed Loor glancing at me, worried that I might say something stupid. I was about to take a risk, but this was a golden opportunity to forge an alliance. I couldn't let it pass.

"What is that, my friend?" he asked.

"There are those who do not wish for peace," I said. "For them, I fear the drought is simply an excuse to spread hatred among the tribes."

Pelle sighed and said, "I agree. But do not fear. The rebel Ghee may wave their weapons and bellow loudly, but their numbers are small. I trust that once the drought is over, their voice will no longer be heard in the city of—"

Pelle suddenly stopped speaking. Just like that. In mid-sentence. The expression on his face didn't change. He simply . . . stopped talking. Everybody around us stood there awkwardly, not sure about what was going on.

"Majesty?" I asked.

A second later Pelle fell to his knees. The crowd gasped and backed off. A thin line of blood trickled from his lips. As the raucous festival continued around us, the small group of people around Pelle a Zinj stood statue still, frozen in shock. The prince fell forward, flat on his face.

Sticking out of his back was the handle of a thick knife. My brain locked. It was almost an exact copy of what had happened to Alder, except for one thing. Pelle was dead. Nobody moved. Reality hadn't hit. From the time Pelle stopped talking until total chaos broke out was probably only five seconds, but time slowed down for those few moments. It was an unreal sensation . . . that got very real, very fast.

"Death to the Batu!" shouted a Rokador who had been standing directly behind Pelle. It was a guy I had never seen before, wearing a long, yellow tunic. Splattered across the front was a wash of blood. Pelle's blood. This guy was the killer. He had made his way up behind the unprotected prince and stabbed him in the back. I wondered if it was Saint Dane, but realized that it couldn't be. Saint Dane never did his own dirty work.

"The Rokador will prevail!" the killer shouted, pointing at me. His eyes were crazed. A Ghee guard tackled the guy, the other fell to his knees to protect Pelle. He needn't have bothered. The crown prince of Xhaxhu was dead. The people around us began to scream and scatter. But the festival was so loud, few of the thousands in this square realized what was happening. On the royal platform, the king and queen glanced over curiously, unaware that their son had just been murdered. The remaining Ghee warriors closed around them protectively forming a shield against the masses.

Loor grabbed my arm and pulled me away. We started up the stairs, only to see a stream of Ghee warriors, in armor, flooding out of a building and pushing their way through the crowd to get to Pelle. They were armed and ready to go. Their dark black armor stood out ominously from the brightly colored tunics of the revelers.

"Not that way," I said.

"Rokador!" one of the Ghee guards shouted at me. "Do not move!"

In that one second my mind flashed forward to what was about to happen. I was a Rokador who stood only a few feet away from the beloved Batu prince when he was murdered . . . by another Rokador. Emotions were running high. They might throw me in prison just for being there. Or think I had something to do with it. Or worse, they might tear me apart right then and there out of anger. We had to get gone while everybody was still in shock. There was a small window; we had to take it.

Loor always said, "Never make the first move." I didn't. The Ghee guard lunged at me. I was ready to defend myself, but Loor did the honors. With his attention focused on me, Loor got in both the second *and* the third shots. With a quick blur of fists, she hammered the guy and swept his legs out, sending him crashing to the stairs. She may have looked like a beautiful princess, but she was still a Ghee warrior.

"Hurry," she ordered, and forced her way down the stairs, through the crowd. I was right after her, but before leaving I took one last look at the murder scene. The Batu killer was ranting: "Death to Xhaxhu! Freedom for the Rokador!" He was out of control. The Ghee guard needed help to control this guy, and he got it. The other Ghees arrived from above. Three descended on the killer, burying him in a wave of black armor. The others went right to their fallen prince.

"Pendragon!" Loor called.

I was about to follow her when I saw something that hit me like a punch in the gut. Several Ghee warriors were lifting the body of Pelle a Zinj to get him off the steps. They were all focused on their fallen leader. All but one. This one guy looked away from Pelle, and right at me. I knew who it was. It was the same Ghee who nearly beat me to death in the warrior compound. It was Saint Dane. He gave me a small smile and a wink.

I felt the blood drain from my head. I nearly passed out right there. I probably would have if Loor hadn't yanked my arm and pulled me away from the scene. We fought our way through the dense crowd of joyous Batu who still didn't know that their lousy lives were about to get a lot lousier. The parade continued, the music played, the cheering echoed off the pyramids. It wouldn't last long. As the saying goes, this was their last hurrah. Loor and I pushed our way through the crowd and moved back along the parade route to get to her home. It was surreal. We didn't say a word to each other along the way. I was on autopilot. I don't even remember much of the trip. That's because my mind was racing ahead, wondering what would come next. As we ran, an idea began to take shape. The more I thought about it, the more I felt sure I was right.

It wasn't a happy thought.

We finally got out of the crowd and stood together in the entryway of a pyramid trying to catch our breaths. Loor was so wired, she paced like an angry cat. I knew that when I told her what I was thinking, she'd become even angrier.

"That was it," I said softly.

"That was what?" she asked, her eyes wide and wild. "The end of our chance for peace? The death of the lone voice of reason? The destruction of Xhaxhu? Tell me something I do not know, Pendragon."

"Saint Dane was there," I told her.

Loor shot me a surprised look. "Are you certain?" she asked.

"How could I forget?" I said. "He took the form of a Ghee warrior. The one who nearly beat me to death. I don't think I could mistake that."

"So he had something to do with Pelle's death?"

"Probably," I said. "He might have snuck that Rokador near the palace, or given him the knife, or talked him into assassinating Pelle for all I know."

"Without Pelle, the chances for war just became greater."

"Especially because he was killed by a Rokador," I added. "Revenge is going to get people's blood boiling. But there's more. I think this was it."

"You said that before," Loor barked. "What do you mean?"

My stomach turned over. I felt sick. I knew I was right, and it was killing me.

"This was the turning point," I said flatly. "The turning point for Zadaa."

Loor gave me a blank stare. Maybe her mind didn't want to accept it. "Why do you say that?" she finally said, though much softer.

"Because if we hadn't been there, Pelle would still be alive," I answered. "He was safely on that platform, protected by his guards. There was no way that assassin would have gotten to him. But he came into the crowd to see us. We changed the equation. The turning point on Zadaa just got pushed the wrong way, and we helped push it."

This is where I'm ending my journal, guys. I'm going to send it to you through my ring right now. Tomorrow Loor and I leave for the underground. Our goal is to get to Kidik and learn the truth that Bokka died trying to tell us. We have no choice. Saint Dane is waiting. This would be a dangerous trip under any circumstances, but now the clock is ticking. Pelle a Zinj is dead. That's the tragedy I referred to at the beginning of this journal. With his murder, there's no doubt that the Batu will attack the Rokador. The only question is, when?

Be well. Be safe. The next time I send you a journal, it will probably be from far below the surface of Zadaa.

And so we go.

END JOURNAL #21

◦ SECOND EARTH ◦

Courtney Chetwynde felt as if she were drowning.

If there was one word that could be used to describe Courtney, it would be "controlled." Courtney was always in control because she had the tools to do it. She was smart and pretty and athletic and funny, and pretty much all the things that lesser human beings could only aspire to. Courtney had the whole package. Things always went her way because she made *sure* they went her way. She was a force of nature. In school, with sports, with boys, even with her parents. Courtney had it all.

Until she lost it all.

It wasn't as dramatic a change as what happened to Bobby Pendragon. She wasn't plucked out of her perfect life, flumed across time and space and given the responsibility of saving all existence. What happened to Courtney was, in some ways, worse. Bobby left his normal life behind. Courtney stayed home and had her normal life turned inside out. And it had nothing to do with her relationship with Bobby, and becoming an acolyte with Mark Dimond. At least not at first.

Courtney defined herself as an athlete, but for some unexplainable reason, she was no longer competitive. It wasn't for lack of trying, either. One day she woke up to find she wasn't as good as she had been her whole life. Or looking at it another way, everybody suddenly had gotten a lot better than she was. Failing at sports was like the first piece of yarn that works loose in a sweater. Once you start pulling on it, the whole sweater unravels.

Courtney's life unraveled.

She became so obsessed with her failures on the field, she let it affect school. Her grades took a serious nosedive. That made her parents unhappy and caused all sorts of tension at home. All this turmoil and failure made the once happy and friendly Courtney not so much fun to be around. Her friends stopped calling. But that was okay with her. She wasn't calling them, either. Courtney went from outgoing, to withdrawn. From friendly, to bitter. From being Courtney, to being a hazy shadow of Courtney.

Her only release was her relationship with Mark, and their responsibility of being the acolytes for Bobby Pendragon. In comparison to the troubles facing Bobby and Halla, her own problems seemed petty. Perspective was good. Bobby's journals gave her that perspective. But as time went on, reading about Bobby's adventures made her feel almost too small. Insignificant, even. She and Bobby had always been friendly rivals. More times than not, she would get the better of him. But now, Bobby was battling to save humanity, while Courtney was left to battle her own inner demons. And she was losing. Every time she turned around, her ego took another beating.

That's why, when the opportunity presented itself to help Bobby, she jumped at it. Courtney would never admit it, but when she and Mark entered the flume to help save Eelong, she was also trying to save herself. She saw this as a chance to get back her self-confidence and prove to everyone that she hadn't changed. Most of all she needed to prove it to herself.

When Courtney and Mark left Second Earth, they definitely

rose to the occasion. If they hadn't stepped in, Eelong would have been doomed. Worse, Bobby might have died. Their adventure on Eelong was everything Courtney hoped it would be. They were heroes. Her self-doubt disappeared. She had proven to herself that she was every bit the force of nature she had always been. Balance had been restored.

And then it all came crumbling down. Literally. Acolytes were not supposed to use the flumes. She knew that. Bobby knew that. Everybody knew that. But they used them anyway. The result? The flume on Eelong collapsed, killing a Traveler and stranding Gunny and Spader. The horrifying truth was that Saint Dane's plan all along had been to get them to use the flumes. He didn't care about Eelong. He cared about tearing the Travelers apart, and Courtney was quick to oblige. For a brief, glorious month, when she and Mark were on Eelong, Courtney felt as if she were back in control. She was wrong. Saint Dane was pulling her strings all along. Courtney went from feeling as if she were invincible, to being crushed by the guilt of her part in bringing about the death of a Traveler and hurting Bobby's chances of defeating Saint Dane.

That's why she felt as if she were drowning.

She went into a depression. She could barely get out of bed. Sleep was good. At least while asleep there was a chance of having a happy dream. Being awake felt more like a nightmare. Her parents took her to a therapist, but it didn't do much good. She tried to explain to the doctor how she had such high expectations of herself, and it killed her to fall short. But saying it like that made it all seem so trivial. The problem was, Courtney couldn't be fully honest with him. She couldn't tell him about Bobby, and the flumes and Saint Dane and how her arrogance may have doomed all of humanity. But she wanted to, and then scream at the doctor: "Don't you think you'd be a little depressed if you had to deal with that?" She didn't, because she knew where that would lead. The therapist wouldn't consider her depressed anymore. He'd move her into the "crazy" category. That's why she mostly kept quiet during therapy. It was frustrating for both of them.

This went on for months. Tension at home was unbearable. Her parents tried to help, but they didn't understand. Their efforts usually led to more arguments. Then they'd argue about having so many arguments. Like with the therapist, Courtney wasn't able to fully explain what was going on to them. The sweater of Courtney's life was almost completely unraveled.

It was during a particularly gruesome argument when, out of total frustration, her mother threw up her hands and said, "I can't help you. I wish I knew somebody who could!" Her mother stormed out of Courtney's bedroom, not realizing that those words had struck a chord. It was a small realization, but an important one. Courtney quickly flipped through her memory, wondering if there actually was somebody out there she felt could help. She came up with someone. The more she thought about it, the more she felt sure this was the only person who could help her get her life back together.

Courtney needed to help herself.

It was one of the greatest challenges she could imagine. It wasn't about games or grades or even about saving Halla. It was about saving Courtney. Thinking this way actually made her smile. There was a rumbling. It was faint, but it was there. It was a far-off whisper that told her after all she had been through, after having her spirit crushed, after losing her entire sense of worth, there was a slight glimmer of hope. This rumbling made her realize that somewhere down deep, she wanted the challenge. She needed the challenge. Even in failure, she had never backed down from any test. Any hurdle. Any opponent. She was actually getting excited, and it felt good. It made her realize that the drive was still there. It was buried pretty deep, but it was there. It made her feel as if maybe there was a little bit of Courtney left, and she wanted to bring her back.

It was that realization that led her to be riding in the back-seat of her parents' car, driving along a winding country road through the Berkshire Mountains of Massachusetts. She was going to summer school. Sleepaway school. Courtney felt that if she were going to reclaim her own spirit, she was going to have to do it away from all things that were familiar. It meant getting away from home, her parents, Stony Brook and her friends, and most painfully, Mark Dimond. She no longer felt worthy of being an acolyte. Walking away from that was the toughest decision she had to make. She was worried to death about what was happening with Bobby and the Travelers. But she felt certain that if she wanted to get her head back on straight, she had to start from scratch to find out who she was. Six weeks of sum-mer school where nobody knew her seemed like a pretty good way to start.

"Look out!" Mr. Chetwynde screamed. He turned the wheel hard, careening off the road to avoid a near collision with an oncoming car that had drifted into their lane.

Mrs. Chetwynde screamed. Courtney whipped around to get a look at the car. It was an old-fashioned, jet-black sedan with shiny chrome bumpers that probably rolled out of the show-room in 1950. Mr. Chetwynde kept control of the car and got them back on the road. The only damage was to their nerves.

"What is wrong with that guy?" Mrs. Chetwynde said, her eyes wide. "He's a menace!"

"Must be an old geezer," Courtney said. "That car is ancient. It doesn't even have plates."

"Somebody should yank his license!" Mr. Chetwynde said, his heart racing.

"Yeah, Dad," Courtney said. "Let's go get him. Citizen's arrest."

Mr. Chetwynde turned around to give Courtney a look . . . and laughed. Courtney laughed too. So did Mrs. Chetwynde. It felt good. There hadn't been a whole lot of laughing with the Chetwyndes lately.

A few minutes later they arrived at the Stansfield Academy. Courtney's home for the next six weeks. It was a private school, K-12, that had been around since the dark ages. It looked it too. The buildings were brick and covered with leafy vines. There was a grassy campus with huge shade trees that Courtney could envision herself lying under to read and do homework. Kids were everywhere. Some were arriving with suitcases. Others were playing catch with various footballs, baseballs, and Frisbees. Courtney thought it was a pretty place, in a boring New England kind of way. That was okay. She wasn't there for excitement.

The Chetwyndes' picked the place out of a catalog. During the school year it was the last kind of place Courtney would be caught dead in. It was an elite private school where the boys wore boring blue blazers and the girls wore . . . boring blue blazers. But things were much more relaxed during summer session. There were kids from all walks of life, not just the snooty types. After walking across the campus, Courtney's first impression was that they had picked the right place.

"Heads up!" A soccer ball game flying by, nearly hitting Mr. Chetwynde. Courtney caught it without thinking. A guy came jogging up to get it.

"Sorry," he said.

"No problem," Courtney said, tossing him the ball. Courtney sized him up quickly. Cute, athletic, polite, cute. He was nearly six feet tall, with short, wavy blond hair and dazzling gray eyes.

"That was a good catch," the guy said. "You play?"

Courtney had to think about that answer. Did she play? She could probably dribble rings around this pretty boy. Then again, maybe she couldn't. She didn't want to have to find out.

"No," she said. "I'm not much for sports."

Courtney's parents both gave her a quick look, but chose not to comment.

The guy backed away, saying, "You don't know what you're missing. Play with us sometime."

He turned and jogged back to his group of friends who were playing in the pickup game. Courtney watched him go, checking out his muscular legs. A second later she felt the stares of her parents. She looked at them to see they were holding back smiles.

"What?" she said. "I'm not here to play soccer."

"Neither is he," Mr. Chetwynde said with a chuckle.

"Oh, please," Courtney said playfully, and kept walking.

The Chetwyndes spent the next few hours getting Courtney settled. They picked up her registration materials and class schedule. They got a tour of the dining hall, the swimming pool, the game room, the student lounge, the buildings where her classes would be, and finally, her dorm. Courtney caught a huge break and didn't have to share her dorm room with anybody. It's not that she didn't want to meet anybody, but after having spent the better part of the last few months in bed with the covers over her head, Courtney was grateful that she could return to being social on her own terms. So far it was all good.

After spending several hours at Stansfield, any doubt that Courtney had about this being a good idea had vaporized. She was happy to be there. Her mom helped her unpack while her dad brought up the small refrigerator they had rented for the term. Finally, after taking care of all there was to take care of, it was time for her parents to leave. There was an awkward moment, for all sorts of reasons. Courtney had never been away from home for that long before—at least as far as her parents knew. They didn't know about her journey to Eelong. Beyond that, their relationship had been pretty rocky over the past year. It made saying good-bye difficult.

"I'm glad you're here," Mrs. Chetwynde said. "I mean, not that I don't want you home, but I think it's better that you're here instead of . . . Oh, this is coming out all wrong."

Courtney broke the tension by giving her mother a hug. "I know what you mean, Mom," she said. "This is a good thing. But I miss you already."

"Really?" Mr. Chetwynde asked, surprised.

"Well, no, but I'm pretty sure I will real soon," Courtney said.

The three had another laugh over that. Courtney hugged her dad.

"You know how much we love you," he said. "And we'll always be there for you."

"I know, Dad," Courtney said. "I love you too."

"Call us," Mrs. Chetwynde said. "We'll send you a care package. And maybe you can come home some weekend."

"Mom, it's only six weeks. I'm not moving out."

"I know, honey," Mrs. Chetwynde gave Courtney another hug while brushing back tears. "I'm so proud of you for doing this."

"Thanks," Courtney said. "Now go."

After one last round of hugs, the Chetwynde's left and Courtney was alone. She looked around the room that was going to be her home for the next few weeks. The dorm was ancient. She wondered how many kids had said good-bye to their parents on this very spot. She suddenly missed her folks, for real. She went over to the window and caught a glimpse of them as they left the dorm and walked across the grass toward the car. She also caught a glimpse of something else.

Parked along the roadway, not far from the dorm, was the black sedan that had nearly run them off the road. There was no mistaking it. Courtney looked to see if her dad had seen it. She wouldn't put it past him to actually go over there and make a citizen's arrest. Or at least tell the guy off. But her parents kept walking.

The mystery of who owned the ancient car that nearly ran them off the road would remain a mystery.

For a while.

◉ SECOND EARTH ◉
(CONTINUED)

Courtney's summer at Stansfield started out to be exactly what she needed. Nobody knew her. Nobody expected anything from her. People didn't whisper behind her back, "That used to be Courtney Chetwynde." She had no reputation, good or bad. Nobody knew that she may have helped a demon in his quest to destroy all of humanity. She wasn't about to tell anybody either. For Courtney it was like starting over fresh.

She took three classes. Classic literature, algebra-trig, and drawing. She had discovered that she had a talent for sketching, so she figured it would be a fun thing to do. Certainly more fun than algebra-trig. Courtney found that she had no problem getting up and going to class. She looked forward to it. She ate her meals in the dining hall and started hanging with a group of girls from New York. They were giggly and more interested in checking out the boys than finding out about Courtney, which was fine by her. These girls pretty much had only two subjects they could talk about. Boys and themselves. If Courtney tried to change the subject to something she may have read in the newspaper, or learned in class, the girls would look at her blankly, take a beat, and jump right back in, talking about how cute a particular teacher was, or about how the humidity was destroying their hair.

It was all so mindless and trivial to Courtney . . . she loved it.

She spent hours sitting under the shady trees, reading. Or sweating over math problems. In the afternoons there was always a pickup soccer game going on. The guy who nearly beaned her dad played every day. Courtney thought he was pretty good, too. He was probably a high-school varsity player at home, she thought. She felt sure she could beat him one on one, but had to force that thought out of her head. She wasn't there to compete.

The other thought she had trouble forcing out of her head was that this guy was pretty cute. Thinking this way made her feel like she was cheating on Bobby. Though they were light-years apart, literally, she and Bobby were supposed to be together. If it weren't for that silly little thing of his having to leave home to save Halla, they'd be together right now. But it had been nearly two years since she admitted her feelings to Bobby. Two years since he told her he liked her too. A lot had happened in that time. She wasn't even sure if Bobby still felt the same way. Still, she thought it would be wrong to start a relationship with somebody new, without telling Bobby. So she tried not to look at this blond guy who played soccer everyday between 3:00 and 4:15. But that didn't stop her from making sure she sat down under the big maple tree near the lawn where they played . . . every day between 3:00 and 4:15.

Making things more difficult, she started seeing this guy around campus. They didn't have any classes together, but he was often in the cafeteria around the same time she always ate. A couple of times they even made eye contact, but he never seemed to show any recognition that she was the one whose father he nearly beaned. He didn't show any interest at all. She even saw him in the library at night. She would go there to study, just to be around people. One night she was walking through the stacks, looking for some obscure book on Jack

London that she needed for research, when she saw the guy sitting at the end of the aisle, on the floor, immersed in a book. He wore these round, wire-rimmed glasses to read, which she thought were sweet. When playing soccer and joking with friends, he always seemed so perfectly put together and confident. Seeing that he wore glasses gave him a slight bit of imperfection that, if she were forced to admit it, made him even more appealing.

In all, the first few weeks at Stansfield were proving to be exactly what Courtney needed. She was feeling human again. She proved to herself that she could function. She was beginning to heal.

There was only one odd note about her time at Stansfield up till then. It was the car. The black car. This old auto always seemed to turn up at the strangest times. If not for the near-miss accident with her parents, this jalopy would never have been on her radar. But now she would see it parked outside the building where she had classes. It was often parked outside her dorm. She'd look out at night and see it sitting there, its chrome bumper gleaming under the streetlight. The shape of the bumper made Courtney feel as if this odd car were actually smiling. Creepy. Courtney rode her bike around campus and many times she would get the feeling that she was being followed and she would quickly glance over her shoulder. Usually nothing was there. But more than once she caught a fleeting glimpse of the car as it turned off the street behind her. She figured it must belong to one of the teachers and asked the girls she hung out with if they knew whose it was. None of them could even remember seeing the car, let alone knowing who it belonged to.

One night she was leaving the library after hours of reading. She was tired and wanted nothing more than to hit the pillow. It was late. The campus was empty. She always walked the same route back to her dorm. There was a shortcut through a narrow alley that ran between the gym and the auditorium. It was barely wide enough for one car. As she had done many nights before, she turned into this corridor without thinking. She was nearly to the far side, when she was suddenly blinded by headlights. A car was parked on the far end, facing her, its engine revving. Courtney stopped. The hairs went up on the back of her neck. What was this guy doing? The answer came fast. The car's engine roared, and it peeled forward into the alley, headed right for Courtney. She was trapped. The alley wasn't wide enough to move to the side so the car could pass. If it kept coming, she'd get hit.

It kept coming.

Didn't the driver see her? Courtney turned and ran. She hadn't done anything remotely athletic for months, but old habits die hard. She dug in, pumped her arms, and used her long legs. In no time she was sprinting out of that alley, with the headlights burning her from behind. It was going to be close. She never turned around to see if the car was closing. Why bother? It would only slow her down. She reached the far end and cut sharply to her right, getting out of the mouth of the alley. A second later the car burst out and onto the road.

Yes, it was the black sedan. The car bounced onto the main road, skidded into a turn, and gunned off into the night. Courtney ran out toward the street, trying to get a look at the driver.

"What is wrong with you!" she screamed.

The car didn't stop. It spun around a corner and was gone. Courtney stood there, breathing hard. She was now convinced that the car didn't belong to a teacher, but to a jerky student who thought it was funny to harass people.

"Hey!" came a voice from behind her. Courtney turned to see the blond soccer guy jogging up from the alley. "Are you okay?"

"Did you see that?" Courtney asked, still out of breath.

"Yeah, he nearly ran you over," the guy said. "We should report him to the campus police."

Courtney thought about that. She glanced back to where the car had disappeared, and said, "Nah, what good'll that do?"

"It might stop him from killing somebody," the guy said. "Come on, it's not like there's a lot of cars like that around. They'll get him."

"Forget it," Courtney said. "It'll just be my word against his."

"Well, no it won't," the guy said. "You've got a witness. Me."

Courtney wanted to talk to this guy, but not under those circumstances. She was too fired up and upset about the near accident. So she backed away from him, headed for her dorm.

"Thanks, but it's not worth it," she said. "I'll see you."

She turned and hurried off.

"Whatever," the guy called after her. "If you change your mind . . ."

Courtney waved, and kept going. She wasn't entirely sure why she bailed on the guy. He wanted to help her. He was being nice. It was the perfect opportunity to find out more about him. Still, she was too flustered by the near miss. She didn't feel as if she were herself. As she walked back to the dorm and calmed down, she kicked herself for not talking more with him. She hoped she'd get another chance.

She did. The next afternoon she went to her usual tree near the lawn where the soccer game was under way. She was about to sit down when she heard a familiar "Heads!"

She turned and saw a soccer ball flying her way. Without thinking, she expertly trapped it with her body, got it under control with her knee, then kicked it back toward the field. All effortlessly.

The kid with the blond wavy hair came running after the ball. He stopped short when he saw Courtney's kick.

"Whoa, I thought you didn't play?" he asked, dumbfounded.

"Oh?" Courtney said, teasing. "I didn't think you remembered me."

The guy walked up to her and smiled. "Sure. Aren't you the girl who was nearly roadkill?"

"Nice," Courtney said with mock sarcasm. "That's a great way to be remembered."

"There was that, and the fact that I nearly took your father out the day you showed up."

"Ahhh," Courtney said, teasing. "So you do remember."

"Of course I do," the guy said. "I thought you were avoiding me. It took a near fatal accident to get you to slow down enough to talk."

Courtney looked around and said, "Well, I'm not about to get run over now, and I'm talking."

"Then let's introduce ourselves," he said, and stuck out his hand to shake. "My name's Whitney. Whitney Wilcox."

"Whitney Wilcox?" Courtney said, laughing. "That's a joke, right? You took it from some bad soap opera."

"Well, no," he said, laughing. "That's really my name. What's yours?"

"Courtney Chetwynde."

"Oh, and that's not a bad soap-opera name?"

"Guilty," Courtney said while taking his hand to shake. "Hello, Wilney."

"It's Whitney. Wilcox."

The two were laughing at the silly exchange.

"I don't know if I should believe you, Corwind," Whitney said.

"Courtney. About what?"

"Well, you said you didn't play soccer, but from what I saw, you're obviously pretty good."

Courtney looked down, saying, "Yeah, well, I'm over it."

"You can't get over soccer!" Whitney said. "Let's play."

Courtney was tempted. Really tempted. But she felt her competitive juices starting to rise, and fought it. She sat down under the tree.

"Thanks," she said. "Maybe another time."

"Whatever," Whitney said, backing toward the field. "See you at dinner?"

"Uh, sure," Courtney said, and pretended to start reading.

Whitney jogged back to the field. Courtney stole a look at him just as Whitney looked back at her. Busted. Courtney blushed and went back to reading. She had no idea what had just happened. Did they just make a date for dinner?

When Courtney went to the cafeteria that night, her palms were sweating. She did all she could to look casual as she went through the food line while stealing glances out to the tables to see if Whitney was already there. She really hoped he wasn't. Not because she didn't want to eat with him, but she didn't want to be the one to go over and sit with him if he was already eating. She wanted him to come to her. That's why she showed up ten minutes earlier than usual, to make sure she was sitting before he got there. She left the food line with her tray, and the only thing she did differently was to sit at a table alone, instead of the usual table with the giggling girls. She didn't want them to get a crack at Whitney before she figured out what was going on between them. She had a fleeting thought about Bobby, but forced it out of her mind. She told herself this was just dinner. Nothing more.

"Hey, Corwind!" came a voice from across the cafeteria. It was Whitney. He was already there. Courtney hadn't seen him. He got up from the table with his tray and joined her. "You dodging me again?" he asked with a smile.

"I didn't see you. Have a seat . . . unless you'd rather eat with your friends."

"Nah, all those guys talk about is girls and the Red Sox."

"I'm a girl," Courtney said.

"Oh, right," Whitney said playfully. "You like the Red Sox?"

"I've been a Yankees fan since birth," Courtney replied.

"I knew I liked you," Whitney said with a beaming smile.

The two had a fun dinner together. The very next night, they had another fun dinner together. They did the same the next night and the one after that. Courtney wasn't exactly sure what was happening. She liked Whitney, that much was obvious. But it was more than just a physical attraction. Whitney seemed to think the same way she did. They had the same sense of humor. They were both into sports. They both liked to poke fun at each other. It was fun and funny. Courtney learned that he came from a suburb of Hartford. He longed to travel and see other cultures. He was good in school and in sports, but he was beginning to feel the pressure of high expectations—from others and from himself. Courtney felt as if Whitney were describing her. He was as driven to succeed as she was. He even had a girlfriend back home, but he wasn't sure where the relationship was going.

Of course, she couldn't confide in him about Bobby and Saint Dane, but she didn't feel the need to. They were connecting on such a basic level, they were able to share ideas and feelings without having to discuss specific events. It was the best kind of therapy she could have gotten—way better than the doctor who made her sit in his stuffy office as he pulled on his eyebrows and took notes that she thought were probably just doodles.

Courtney and Whitney started spending much of their free time together. He even got her into one of his soccer games. As reluctant as Courtney was at first, she found that she actually had fun. It was the first time she had fun playing soccer since she was in grade school. There was no pressure, no drive to win at all costs, just the pure joy of doing something she loved. For Courtney, Whitney was giving her an incredible gift. He was teaching her how to be herself again.

She thought it ironic that what brought them together was the near miss by the mysterious black sedan. A few times when she and Whitney walked past the parked car, Courtney made sure that Whitney didn't see it. She didn't want him to try and convince her to report the driver. With only a few weeks left of summer school, she didn't want to deal with the police over something that was probably an accident. Accidents happened. So did near accidents.

She continued to catch glimpses of the dark car from the corner of her eye, but she no longer cared. There were no more near misses. The thought did occur to her that maybe the reason for that was because she was always with Whitney. If somebody was targeting her, they'd have to target both of them. They didn't. Whitney was like her protector. But Courtney didn't want to think of it that way. She didn't want to believe that somebody was out there lying in wait to "get" her. She didn't want to let anything stand in the way of having fun with Whitney, and the absolute, total joy of becoming Courtney again.

"Big night tonight," Whitney exclaimed as he met Courtney one day after her literature class.

"What's going on?" she asked. Courtney thought that Whitney seemed a little nervous.

"Well, uh, a bunch of us are going into town," he said. "Technically, we're not supposed to leave campus. But we're all feeling a little caged in, and we thought it would be cool to hit this place called the 'Pizza Palace.' It's supposed to be decent. Do, uh, do you want to come?"

"Whitney!" Courtney teased. "Are you asking me out on a date?"

"Uh, well, yeah, I guess I am," Whitney said nervously.

Courtney smiled. She realized that Whitney was nervous because he had never actually, officially asked her out. Up until this point, all they had done was hang out as friends. They might as well have been two guys, or two girls. But this was different. This was a girl/guy thing. There could potentially be kissing involved. Courtney wanted to go in a bad way.

"What time?" she asked.

Whitney looked visibly relieved. "Six o'clock," he said. "A friend of mine has a car. We'll pick you up."

Courtney's shoulders fell. "I've got art class until seven," she said.

"Ditch!" Whitney said.

"I can't. There's a guest artist coming, and it's a pretty big deal. But I can meet you later. Town is what? Two, three miles away? I can ride my bike after class. It'll still be light. Then we'll put the bike in the trunk of the car on the way back."

"Awesome," Whitney said. "The place is called—"

"I know, the Pizza Palace," Courtney interrupted. "You just told me."

"Oh, right." Whitney laughed. "You can't miss it. There's only one pizza place in that dinky town."

"Can't wait," Courtney said. She meant it. She was so excited, she wanted to dance. Or sing. But since doing either would be totally out of character and uncool, she did the next best thing.

She called Mark.

Mark Dimond was busy at work. He was engraving a huge, silver cup for a local boating race, and he was so nervous about it, his hands were shaking. In the engraving biz, shaky hands were not a good thing. Mostly he engraved brass plates that went on plaques and trophies. If he messed one up, no big deal. The plates were cheap. But this silver cup was worth more than he was going to earn all summer. One slip and he'd have to change his name and move to another state. Mark's palms were sweating. He was about to touch the cutting edge of the engraving tool to the silver surface . . . when the cell phone in his pocket rang.

The surprise made him jump. Luckily he hadn't started engraving yet. If the call had come a second later, there would have been a deep gouge slashed across the Stony Brook Yacht Club logo. He took a deep, relieved breath, then wondered why there was an electronic waltz coming from his pants. Mark never got calls on his cell phone. He only had it for emergencies and to tell the time. Incoming calls were an alien experience. The phone had to ring again before he realized what it was. He dug the phone out of his pocket and flipped it open.

"Hello?"

"Hey. It's Courtney."

"C-Courtney?" The surprise of hearing Courtney's voice was even greater than the surprise of having the cell phone ring at all. "Chetwynde?"

"Well, duh. How many Courtney's do you know who have your cell number?" Courtney asked, laughing.

"Man, it's good to hear your voice. Where are you?"

"I'm at school in the Berkshires. A place called Stansfield. I've been here for about a month."

Mark said, "Right! Summer school! That sounds like, well, something *I'd* do." They both laughed.

"Actually, it's pretty sweet," Courtney said. "I'm only taking three courses, and one of 'em is art. Algebra-trig is a drag, though."

"You're taking algebra-trig?" Mark laughed. "Need some help?"

"Yes!" Courtney said quickly, laughing. Mark laughed too. It felt good.

"So, uh, how are you?" Mark asked tentatively. It was a simple question. Both knew how far-reaching it was.

"I'm okay. Seriously. That's why I'm calling. We've got a ton to talk about, but not till I see you again. I just wanted to tell you that coming up here has been great. I'm really getting my head back together."

"I'm really glad to hear that, Courtney."

"I haven't been thinking too much about, you know, stuff. And that's good."

Mark didn't respond. He knew what she meant.

"This is kind of weird to say," Courtney continued. "But I met somebody."

"Of course you did," Mark said. "I didn't think you were there alone."

Courtney chuckled. "No, dope. I'm talking about a guy."

"Oh," Mark said. "You mean like, a guy?"

"Yeah, a guy. His name's Whitney."

"Whitney? That sounds like a bad soap-opera name."

Courtney laughed. "It's worse. His name is Whitney Wilcox."

"You're kidding, right?"

"Unfortunately, no. But he's cool. We've, uh, we've got a date tonight. I'm riding to meet him for pizza."

Mark wasn't sure of how to react. It was weird to hear that Courtney liked somebody other than Bobby, but after reading that Bobby had feelings for Loor, maybe it was all for the best. Of course, he couldn't tell Courtney that, for all sorts of reasons.

Courtney said, "I wanted to tell you about him. I'm not really sure why."

"I'm glad you did," Mark said.

There was a long pause, then Courtney said, "Do you hate me?"

"Hate you? No! No way!" he said quickly. "I think it's great you met a guy."

"Not just that," Courtney said. "About . . . everything."

"I don't hate you, Courtney," Mark said. "C'mon. Give me a break."

"Seriously?"

"Yes! There's a lot going on. We've got to do what we've got to do."

"Thanks. I needed to hear you say that." There was another long pause, and then Courtney said, "I'm sorry for taking off on you. That wasn't cool."

"It's okay. I'm okay."

"Still, I'm not proud of myself. But if you saw the shape I was in, you'd know I did the right thing."

"I already know it," Mark said. "I can tell by your voice. I can't wait to talk to you in person."

Mark knew a question was out there that hadn't been asked. He really hoped she wouldn't ask it.

She did.

"So, uh, has anything—"

"No," Mark said quickly. He knew she was going to ask if Bobby had sent a new journal. He didn't want to tell her. If she was working hard to put her head on straight, the last thing she needed to hear was that Bobby was about to step into the middle of a tribal war and had fallen in love with Loor—even if she did meet a new guy. He knew he'd eventually have to spill the news, but this wasn't the time.

"N-Nothing new," Mark added, and winced, wishing he had stopped at "no." He felt sure Courtney would pick up on his nervous stutter.

"Oh, okay," Courtney said.

Mark sensed her hesitation. There was something in the way she said it that made him realize, she knew.

"When are you coming home?" he asked, desperate to change the subject.

"In a couple of weeks. We'll talk then, okay?"

"I can't wait to see you," Mark said, relieved that she didn't press him about the journals.

"I miss you, Mark. Even though you're a dork and all."

"Gee, thanks," Mark said, laughing.

"We'll get some fries at Garden Poultry and catch up, okay?"

"It's a date. Bye, Courtney. Take care of yourself."

"Later, gator!"

The phone went dead. Mark smiled. "Later, gator?" He thought Courtney sounded great. And happy. Just like the old Courtney. As weird as it was to think that she liked somebody besides Bobby, this new guy seemed to be helping her heal. That was a good thing. He hated having to carry the weight of Bobby's journals on his own, but if it meant getting Courtney better, it was worth it. He flipped the phone shut and jammed it back into his pocket with the feeling that things were definitely looking up. Now if he could only tackle this stupid silver bowl.

His phone rang again.

What was going on? Why was he suddenly so popular? He dug the phone back out and flipped it open, saying, "Courtney?"

"Courtney?" the deep guy-voice mimicked. "Do I sound like a Courtney?"

"Mitchell?" Mark asked in disbelief. "How did you get this number?"

"Who cares? From Sci-Clops. We're both members, remember?"

"Oh, yeah. What do you want?"

"I'm in trouble, Dimond," Mitchell said. "I need your help. Now."

◉ SECOND EARTH ◉
(CONTINUED)

Mrs. Dimond, Mark's mother, gave Mark a ride to a lonely, country lane in Stony Brook that Mark knew well. It used to be part of his paper route. There, at the corner of Riversville Road and Carroll Street, they found what they were looking for. It was a beat-up, seventies-looking station wagon with fake wood paneling. Leaning against the hood, smoking a cigarette, was Andy Mitchell. When he saw the Dimonds' car approach, he quickly stubbed out the smoke.

Mrs. Dimond stared at Mitchell like he was a walking disease and said to Mark, "Are you sure you're going to be okay?" To her, this guy looked like bad news. Mrs. Dimond was a smart lady.

"Yeah, he's a friend. He's in Sci-Clops," Mark said.

"That hoodlum is in Sci-Clops?" Mrs. Dimond asked incredulously.

"Believe it or not," Mark answered with a smile. "Thanks, Mom. He'll give me a ride home."

Mark got out of the car, opened the rear door, and pulled out a full can of gasoline. Andy's big problem was that he had run out of gas.

"Thanks, lady!" Andy called, sounding as polite as could be. "You saved my life."

Mrs. Dimond waved and smiled, then turned the wheel and drove off, but not before giving Mark a final, concerned look that said: "Are you sure about this?" Mark waved as if to say, "Don't worry."

"Thanks, Dimond," Mitchell said as he took the gas can from Mark. "Really. Thanks."

It sounded to Mark as if he meant it too. Mitchell went to the rear of his beater and started funneling the gas into the tank.

"How could you run out of gas?" Mark asked.

"The gauge is busted," Mitchell said. "Whenever I fill it up, I zero out the trip odometer to tell me how many miles I go so I know when to fill up again."

"So what happened?"

"The trip odometer's busted too. Piece of garbage car."

Mark had to keep himself from laughing. Mitchell truly was an idiot.

"I got this call to make a real important delivery. Big rush. I picked up the flowers, got here, and chug chug chug. Dead. You really saved me, man."

"What's so important about the delivery?" Mark asked.

"Huge client," Mitchell answered. "Big-shot corporate guys. They're having a meeting tonight at seven o'clock, and they ordered a bunch of flowers for the tables. Last minute. Those guys don't care. Money talks, you know? But if I don't get 'em there in time, we'll never get another order. Those guys don't fool around. One mistake and you're gone. My uncle is the same way. If I don't deliver, I'll be gone too. And I need this job."

"So why didn't you call your uncle for help?" Mark asked.

"Yeah, sure," Mitchell replied sarcastically. "So he'd know how bad a screwup I am? I may not be smart, but I ain't dumb."

That surprised Mark. Hearing Andy Mitchell call himself a screwup was out of character. This was turning out to be a day full of surprises. Mitchell emptied the can and put the cap back on.

"Time?" Mitchell asked.

Mark checked his cell phone. "Six-oh-five," he announced. "Plenty of time."

"Let's go!" Mitchell said, and jumped into the car. He truly had to jump because the driver's door wouldn't open. He had to slither in through the window.

The meeting was taking place not far from where Andy broke down, at a posh country club. As Mitchell drove, Mark sat in the passenger seat thinking two things. One was that he couldn't believe he had come to the rescue of his archnemesis. The other was that he feared the sticky, vinyl car seat was infested with Andy bacteria. The only reason he didn't gag at the putrid car stench was because the sweet smell from the flower arrangements in the back masked the vile odor. He feared what would happen after they made the delivery and the flowers were gone. It was going to be a long ride home.

"So, why me?" Mark asked.

"Why you what?" Mitchell asked back.

"Why did you call me for help?"

"Sci-Clops," Mitchell answered. "We gotta stick together, right?"

"Well, no," Mark said. "It's a science club, not the Boy Scouts. Why did you call me? You hate me."

Mitchell didn't answer right away. At first Mark thought the imbecile had forgotten the question.

"I don't exactly have a load of friends," Mitchell finally said. "I know, hard to believe, but it's true."

"Not so hard to believe," Mark said.

Mitchell shot him a glance, but didn't fire a shot back. Instead he shrugged. "Okay, I had that coming. I've given you a hard time."

"Hard time?" Mark said, incredulous. "You've bullied me for years. You've hit me. You've stolen my lunch money more times than I can count. You've hit me. You've robbed my house. You've hit me. Need I go on?"

"Guilty, guilty, guilty, all right? What do you want me to say?"

"I don't want you to say anything. You're a jerk. End of story." Mark was feeling bold. He no longer feared Andy Mitchell. That stopped a while ago. His fear turned to pity when he realized that the guy was such a lamebrain. But lately, after seeing what a brilliant mathematical mind he had, Mark actually found himself envying Andy. It was all so twisted and weird.

"If it makes you feel any better, you aren't the only one I stepped on," Mitchell said.

"Oh, good, now I can rest easy," Mark said, dripping sarcasm.

"Hey, you asked, I'm tellin'."

"Sorry, go ahead."

"I ain't the sharpest tool in the deck, in case you hadn't noticed," Mitchell continued.

"I noticed," Mark said, rolling his eyes. Mitchell couldn't even get the figure of speech right.

"But that only has to do with words and talking and whatnot. The thing is, with numbers I'm pretty good."

Mark didn't argue. He'd seen Andy at work. With numbers he was better than pretty good.

"That didn't go down so well when I was a little kid. It was like, how do you say it, I had the worst of both worlds. Half the guys gave me a hard time because I sounded like an idiot. The other half gave me grief for being a brain. I was too smart to hang with the tough kids and too dumb to hang with the geeks. That works on you after a while, you know? Not fittin' in anywhere."

Mark knew. He was an old pro at not fitting in.

So I guess I kind of built up this, I don't know, this shell. I didn't let nobody in; didn't put myself out there in case I might get whacked; and didn't take nothing from nobody. It's not like I had a choice. It was either that, or hide under my bed. But it was tough. I was angry all the time. I guess I took it out on a lot of people, including you."

"Especially me."

"Yeah, whatever. But then I got hooked up with the university and they actually liked that I had some good ideas. They encouraged me, you know? I wasn't used to that. That got me to join Sci-Clops and—hey, I don't mean to get all girly on you, but for the first time I'm starting to be happy with the way things are going. Most of the time, anyway."

Mark didn't comment. For a second he thought Andy might cry. It was a strange feeling. For the first time, ever, he was looking at Andy Mitchell as a human being, not a cartoon bully. He wasn't entirely sure he liked it. Life was already weird enough. Having Andy Mitchell turn into a good guy just put things another notch higher on the surreal meter. Thankfully the conversation ended, because they had arrived at the Burning Hill Country Club.

"We're here!" Mark announced to break the tension.

Andy pulled the car up to the wide, flagstone front entrance and rolled to a stop.

"Looks kind of quiet," Mark observed.

"And dark," Andy said. "What time is it?"

"Six thirty," Mark answered. "There has to be somebody here if the meeting is in half an hour."

Mark and Andy got out of the car and walked up the few steps to the front door. Mitchell tried the knob. It was locked.

"What the hell?" Mitchell said, confused.

Mark looked inside the glass pane in the door and said, "There's a board in there with the schedule. What's the name of the company?"

Mitchell pulled a piece of paper from his pocket, unfolded it, and read, "Praxis Associates."

"There it is," Mark announced. "Praxis Associates. Seven o'clock."

"Exactly!" Mitchell said. "Half an hour from now."

Mark looked inside again and said, "Uh, actually, it's twelve and a half hours from now."

"Say what?" Mitchell shouted.

Mark said, "The sign says it's a breakfast meeting."

Mitchell quickly looked back at the packing slip. He reread it and yelled, "No way! It says right here. Praxis Associates. Seven A."

Mark took the paper and read it. "Yeah, seven A, as in seven A.M. The meeting is tomorrow morning."

Mitchell stared at the page blankly. He then sprang back to the door and looked inside. "There's gotta be a mistake."

Mark said, "Well, yeah. There was."

Mitchell banged his head against the glass, finally accepting that the mistake was his.

"Will the flowers keep?" Mark asked.

"Yeah," Mitchell said, sounding beaten. "I am such an idiot. C'mon, I'll drive you home."

The two didn't say much on the way back toward town. Mitchell was too embarrassed and Mark was too cool to make him feel any dumber. When they got to Mark's house, Mark hopped out of the car and grabbed the gas can.

"It's been . . . interesting," he said.

"Listen, Dimond," Mitchell said. "Thanks. I know how you feel about me, that only makes it all the cooler that you helped me out."

"Hey, we Sci-Clops types have to stick together, right?"

Mitchell laughed. "Yeah, sure. I owe you one. I mean that. If you ever need anything, all you gotta do is ask."

"Sure, uh, Andy. Good night."

"G'night."

Mitchell hit the gas, the car belched once and rolled off,

leaving Mark standing alone on the sidewalk in front of his house. It was a strange ending to a strange day. Mark couldn't help but wonder what the next chapter in the strange saga of Andy Mitchell would be.

For Courtney, she felt as if her day was just beginning. Ever since Whitney had asked her to go into town, she counted the minutes until seven o'clock. The rest of the day crept by slowly. It seemed like an eternity until she finally made it to art class. She sat there, listening to the guest speaker talk about the challenge of sketching the human hand. With Courtney's head being where it was, the lecture seemed about as interesting as algebra-trig. Still, she had made a commitment to this class. She wasn't going to blow it off. Though she might as well have. Her mind wasn't on sketching. It was on Whitney, and what the rest of the night might hold.

When seven o'clock finally came, most of the students stuck around to talk to the artist and pick his brain. Not Courtney. She was out the door before the echo from the bell had died. To save time, she had ridden her bike to class. It meant bringing her backpack and books into town, but she figured that was better than taking the time to go all the way back to her dorm to drop them off. That would have wasted precious minutes. She quickly unlocked her Tech road bike from the rack, tightened up her backpack, and began pedaling for the main road, and town.

Stansfield Academy was in a rural area of the Berkshires, a few miles outside the small town of Derby Falls. Courtney knew that from when she'd first visited Stansfield with her parents. The road between Stansfield and Derby Falls was a beautiful, winding country lane that snaked up along one ridge of the mountain, through a dense pine forest and then down the other side and into town. As much as she focused on getting to town as quickly as her legs would bring her, it was hard for her not to notice how beautiful the mountains were.

The sun was on the way down, creating long pine-tree shadows across the road. The amber rays sparkled through the trees as Courtney rode, making her feel as if she were riding through the beams of a strobe light. She passed a rolling meadow where black-and-white dairy cows grazed. There were a few farm stands along the way, where you could buy corn on the cob and tomatoes that had been picked that day. They were closing up for the night. The birds were out now. It was time for them to feed. Courtney could hear them twittering in the trees. She even saw a few fireflies spark in the woods. It was a truly idyllic ride. Courtney promised herself that she would make this trip again, maybe on a Sunday when she wasn't in such a hurry. And maybe she could convince Whitney to come with her. Things were about as right for Courtney as they could be.

The road inclined quickly as it brought her up into the mountain. She was in shape, but still, a steep climb is a steep climb. It was no problem, but she worried that she'd be all sweaty for her date. Lugging the heavy books along suddenly seemed like a bad idea. But there was no turning back now. She had to gut it out, sweat and all.

The road got even steeper and wound sharply to the left. Courtney didn't remember it being so steep, though the last time she made this trip it was in a car. Roads never seemed as steep in the car as they did when you were riding or running. She rounded the bend and saw that the road continued to bend around the mountain. She couldn't see how much farther it was to the crest, but she knew it must be just around the curve ahead.

That's when she heard the car.

It was faint at first. She was breathing so hard that she couldn't make it out right away. But the sound quickly grew louder. There was no doubt. A car was coming up behind her. Fast. She glanced back, but there was nothing to see except the bend she had just come around. The oncoming car hadn't gotten there yet. In a few seconds it would scream around the corner and be right behind her. The road was pretty narrow, and she thought about getting off and moving to the side for safety. But the idea of having to start up again on this steep hill wasn't a happy one. She did a quick calculation and figured the car would see her in plenty of time to move over. She stood up and pumped harder, hoping to get to the top of the rise before the car.

Behind her, the car rounded the curve. The engine was working so hard it sounded as if it were roaring. A quick, scary thought came to her. Could it be the mysterious black sedan? She hadn't thought about that strange car for days. Her heart raced, faster than it had from the climb. All she wanted to do was get around the next corner and see the top of the rise.

The roar of the car grew louder. She decided to jump off her bike, but a quick look to the side showed her that the shoulder was too narrow. There was a steep drop-off. If she dismounted now, there would be no place to go. If this car wanted to run her down, it had found the perfect place to do it.

Seconds later the car was on her. Courtney closed her eyes, bracing herself to get hit. She gritted her teeth, tightened up, and . . . the car roared past. It was so close she felt the breeze as it sped by. She opened her eyes and saw that it was a minivan full of little kids being driven by a mom. The woman tried to move over to get clear of Courtney, but there was just so far she could go without going into the oncoming lane, with a blind curve ahead. If the van was in that lane and a car came from the other direction, *boom*.

Courtney looked up to see the little kids pressing their faces against the rear window, waving at her. Courtney smiled and waved back. She was exhausted, but relieved. She laughed at herself for being so paranoid. Black sedan, yeah, right. Now all she had to do was get to the top of the rise and the torture would be over. The minivan had disappeared around the corner. Courtney put her head down and stood up on the pedals to dig in for the final push. The roar of the minivan echoed off the side of the mountain.

That's why she didn't hear the car that was coming the other way.

Courtney downshifted, pumped her legs, and looked ahead in time to see the spooky black sedan screaming around the corner, headed directly for her. This driver wasn't worried about being in the wrong lane. The car had crossed the center line and was charging right for Courtney. There was only one thing she could do: bail out. Courtney threw the bike and dove to her right. The black sedan hit the bike's front tire before Courtney was completely clear. She heard the screech of brakes and the shrieking sound of the tires skidding on the road. The driver didn't mind hitting Courtney, but wasn't prepared to crash over the edge while doing it.

The force from the impact twisted Courtney around so quickly and violently that she had no hope of making a controlled fall. The weight from the books on her back made it even worse. They acted like a counterweight, twisting her around with even more force. Before she hit the ground, Courtney had one brief thought: "Why didn't I wear my helmet?"

Her shoulder hit a tree. The force snapped her head back. She fell to the ground and hit hard on her other shoulder. The pitch was so steep that she kept moving, tumbling head over butt over arms over legs. She was an out-of-control rag doll, slamming into trees and boulders on the way down. Finally, with a rude thud, she slammed into one last tree and stopped. A second later, just to add insult to injury, the bike landed on her legs.

Courtney was in shock. She had no idea how badly she was hurt, or if she was bleeding or if she was even going to live. There wasn't any pain. It was like being in a dream, half asleep, but unable to move. She opened her eyes to see she had fallen far from the road. Even if she could move, there was no way she would be able to crawl up the steep hill. Worse, she feared that she had fallen so far that nobody would see her lying there, and night was coming on. She moved her eyes slightly to get a better look at where she had fallen, and saw something that made her catch her breath.

Parked on the edge of the road was the black sedan. The sun was long gone, so its headlights were on. Behind the gleaming beams, the chrome bumper grinned at her. The driver's door opened. She was finally going to see the monster who had run her off the road. Who could it possibly be? The driver walked to the front of the car so he could be seen in the headlights. It was like he wanted Courtney to see him. At first Courtney didn't understand what she was seeing. It didn't make sense. Standing on the edge of the road, looking down at her . . . was Whitney.

The cute, wavy-haired blond athlete stood in the lights of the black sedan with his hands on his hips, staring at Courtney. Courtney felt hope. It was Whitney! This was all an accident! She realized the car must belong to one of his friends. He must have been worried about her and taken the car himself to go back to school and get her. This was nothing more than a horrible, ironic accident. It had to be. She was saved. She wasn't going to have to spend the night in the forest. Courtney was sure that everything was going to be fine—until Whitney spoke.

"I give, and I take away," Whitney said with an arrogant air. "You people of Second Earth are so easily controlled. I was hoping this would be more of a challenge but, alas. It was not meant to be. I'll send your love to Pendragon . . . Corwind."

With that, Whitney laughed. It was a horrible, screeching laugh that froze Courtney's soul. What she saw next did the same to her mind. Whitney's body turned into a liquid shadow. It hovered in the air, changing shape until he became a huge black bird. With a quick flap of its wings, the bird lifted off from the ground and flew into the Berkshires, leaving Courtney to die.

Courtney was spiraling into oblivion. Soon she would be unconscious. It was over. She had lost. It was the most important challenge of her life, and Courtney had lost.

Courtney didn't like to lose. It was the one thing that stayed constant throughout her torment and trouble. As bad as things got, she never accepted defeat. That simply wasn't in her nature. As she lay in that forest, broken and barely conscious, she willed her hand to move. An inch. Two inches. She knew that if she had fallen the wrong way and her hand was pinned under her, her desperate move would be futile. But she hadn't. She was able to walk her hand along, pulling it forward with crawling fingers, until she grasped the cell phone clipped to her belt. Miraculously it hadn't been torn off in the fall. Courtney couldn't see it, but she could feel the buttons. The chances of dialing a number, even 911, were impossible. She was losing consciousness, fast. She had to fight it. Her best chance was to use speed-dial. She felt the buttons until she found what she thought was the number 1. She hit it, while using every bit of concentration and willpower she possessed to stay conscious.

Mark Dimond finished dinner, washed the dishes, and dragged himself up to his room. His plan was to surf the Net for a while, catch a show on *Comedy Central,* and crash. No sooner did Mark get to his room than he realized his night was going to be very different from what he expected.

His ring started to twitch.

Suddenly he wasn't so tired anymore. A quick jolt of adrenaline will do that. Mark quickly closed his door, locked it, and put his ring on the floor. The light show was beginning. In a few moments Bobby's next journal would arrive. He knew there would be no *Comedy Central* that night. It was time to go back to Zadaa.

Mark didn't realize that on his desk, another message was waiting for him. His cell phone was flashing. But he never checked that phone because nobody ever called him. With a new journal coming in, there was even less chance of him checking it. His attention was on his ring and the incoming journal. If he had looked at his phone he would have seen a two-word message flashing over and over.

MESSAGE WAITING.

But he didn't look.

ZADAA

War.

It's such a small, innocent word that's used to describe something that isn't small or innocent. Why is that? Shouldn't war at least be a "four letter word"? Whatever. I'm sitting here, deep underground in Rokador territory, waiting for it all to begin. Or end, depending on how you look at it. Everything we feared would happen is going to happen. The Batu are about to attack. The assassination of Pelle a Zinj pretty much cemented that. Whatever chance there was of finding peace between the tribes has died along with Pelle. The only question left is how soon the fireworks will start.

We know a lot more about what's going on now. None of it is good. We now know what Saint Dane has been up to here on Zadaa. All of it. He had a hand in engineering the assassination, as I figured he did. If Pelle had lived, there was a good chance he would have stopped the war. But that wouldn't have worked into Saint Dane's plan. He needed Pelle gone, and he got an impressionable Rokador to do it for him. As usual. He never does the dirty work himself. It's always about getting the people of the territory to hurt themselves.

But that was only the beginning of his plan to topple Zadaa. As I write this journal to you guys, I'm afraid he's going to win here. I don't see how we can stop it. The events that are about to take place will change the course of Zadaa forever. It won't be for the better, that much I can guarantee.

I'm going to tell you everything that's happened since Pelle was killed. These are the events that have led Zadaa to the brink of disaster. As I sit here, so far belowground, I can't help but wonder if I will ever see the sun again. Any sun.

There is a huge irony here too. By manipulating events so that Pelle was killed, Saint Dane put the tribes on a path to war. However, the trigger was pulled by an event that was totally out of his control.

It began to rain.

"Keep moving," Loor ordered as we ran against the festive crowd that continued to follow the parade toward the palace of Zinj. These people had no idea that their joy would soon turn to anguish. They were about to discover that their beloved prince had been killed. It was a sad feeling, knowing that these happy, jubilant people would soon be crushed.

Suddenly the crowd stopped moving. A moment before, they had been pushing to get to the palace. The streets were so dense with people, we could barely work our way through. Now the mass of humanity had stopped. Oddly, one by one, they looked toward the sky. The raucous music and laughter of the festival died. An eerie quiet fell over the masses. Loor and I were so focused on getting through, we didn't stop to question what was happening. That changed the instant we heard someone yell: "Look!"

We stopped short, looked at each other, then to the sky. The surprise wasn't what we saw, but what we *didn't* see.

There were no stars.

"Is it possible?" I asked in awe.

Loor answered in two whispered words. "Rain clouds."

A moment later the skies opened up. It wasn't just rain, it was a storm. A deluge. There was an odd moment where the crowd stood there, not reacting. I don't think anybody could believe it. But that didn't last. A cheer went up, then another, and another. The excitement spread and in seconds, the crowd went nuts. Their wild, festive dancing for the parade was just a warm-up. Lightning flashed through the sky, followed by a boom of thunder that rocked the ground. The people ate it up. They hugged, they cheered, everybody was everybody's friend. I got grabbed and kissed by a couple of Batu women. These people were celebrating as if their long, horrible nightmare was finally over.

"Is that it?" I screamed to Loor over the crowd. "Does it all end this easily?"

Loor started to answer, but realized we couldn't hear each other. She waved for me to follow, and we left the crowd to find a quiet place where we could talk.

"I do not know," Loor answered. "I suppose it depends on how much rain falls."

"This is incredible!" I said, and stepped out of the doorway to feel the healing rain on my face. "Wouldn't it be awesome if all it took to beat Saint Dane was for the weather to change?"

Loor didn't look so optimistic. "Do not forget that Pelle a Zinj has been assassinated. By a Rokador. That will not help Batu-Rokador relations, even if the drought is over."

"Right," I said soberly. "Saint Dane could have set up that murder to make sure there would be a war even if the drought ended."

"There is much we do not know," Loor said. "I will go to the Ghee command to see what their thinking is."

"I don't suppose it would be cool if I went with you," I said.

"No. Go to Alder. I will return as soon as I learn more."

Before we split up, I took a long look at her. It didn't matter that she was soaking wet, she still looked amazing. Maybe more so because the rain made her hair glisten and her eyes sparkle. I wanted to hold that image in my head.

"What is wrong?" Loor asked.

I almost said, "I think you're beautiful." I didn't. It wasn't the right time. Who knew if that time would ever come?

"Nothing," I answered. "Be careful."

"And you," Loor said.

She leaped out of the doorway and sprinted off through the rain. Her long strides took her away quickly as she splashed through the newly formed puddles. The sick thought suddenly hit me that I wasn't sure if I could find my way back to the hospital. That would have been a totally stupid move. As it turned out, I only took a few wrong turns before getting there. I was also able to make my way down deep into the bowels of the building and easily find the room where Alder was recovering. When I arrived, I saw that he was still sleeping. Saangi was sitting by his side. When she saw me, her face lit up.

"Is it true?" she asked. "Is it raining?"

"You tell me," I said, holding out my wet arms.

Saangi touched my wet sleeve as if it had been dipped in gold. She squeezed the material until water dribbled out, then touched her wet finger to her lips. She smiled. It was the bright, happy smile of a young girl, something I hadn't seen in Saangi since I met her.

"Does this mean there will be no war?" she asked.

That was the big question. I hated to have to be the one to tell her the bad news about Pelle, but I had to. When I told her what had happened, her smile quickly fell. Her short moment of freedom from worry was over.

"The rain does not matter," she said coldly. "Hatred cannot be washed away. I fear there will still be a war."

"That's what Loor's trying to find out," I said.

I checked on Alder and saw he was sleeping peacefully.

"Doctor Nazsha believes he will fully recover," Saangi said. "What do we do now?"

I sat down on one of the hard, stone chairs and said, "We wait for Loor."

I closed my eyes. I didn't want to talk anymore. If we had to wait, I figured I might as well take advantage and get some sleep. If there's one thing that I learned as a Traveler, it was to steal naps when I could. It didn't matter what time of the day it was, or how long I had. Even a few minutes helped. I closed my eyes and tried to shut down my mind. It worked. I have no idea how long I was out. It could have been a few minutes, or a couple of hours. It didn't matter. However long I was out, my peaceful rest was instantly shattered when I opened my eyes to a sobering sight. Standing in the doorway was the answer to the question of whether or not the rainstorm was going to wash away the war. It was Loor. She didn't have to say anything. She simply stood there. But seeing her, I knew.

She was back in her armor.

Gone was the beautiful red dress and open sandals. Gone too was her jewelry and decorative armbands. Her hair was tied back tight, and her wooden stave was lashed to her back. She was once again dressed to kill. Literally.

"Get ready," she said to me, and held out a pile of black clothing. It was my Ghee armor. The party was officially over. I quickly dressed while we talked.

"What did you find out?" Saangi asked.

Loor looked troubled. "The rain has come from the north. Scouts have been tracking it for hours. It is a very big storm, big enough to begin the process of ending the drought."

"Why do you say that like it's bad news?" I asked.

"Because the water is disappearing," Loor answered. "Yes, the troughs in the city are collecting a small amount, but that won't last. There is still nothing coming from the rivers below. With all the rain that has fallen in the north, there should be some sign that the water is rising and the rivers are returning. There is not. They are as dry as they were yesterday."

"So, you think that's proof that the Rokador are holding it back?" I asked.

"It doesn't matter what I think," Loor said. "It is what the Ghee commanders are saying. This is the justification they were looking for. And now that Pelle a Zinj is dead, there is no one to stop them."

"Whoa, wait," I said. "It's one rainstorm! That's not enough proof."

"There is more," Loor said. "The Rokador ambassador to Xhaxhu has disappeared. He was last seen heading underground, along with his staff. Why would he leave? Especially now, when the Batu are saying the assassination was a Rokador plot. It would be his duty to defend the Rokador against those charges."

Saangi said, "Unless he has no defense."

I said, "Okay, I admit, that looks bad. But the Ghee have to cool off. This rain might keep coming and—"

"You do not have to convince me, Pendragon," Loor said. "I am not the one preparing to march into the underground."

My mouth went dry. Saangi shot Loor a look.

"Say that again?" I said.

"The rebels have taken control. Ghees who were loyal to Pelle now believe that war is the only answer. They are preparing to launch their attack."

We all stood there, letting that ominous concept sink in.

Those who wanted war because they blamed the Rokador for the drought now had their proof. Those who stood behind the royal family now had their reason as well. Revenge. The two sides had come together. There was going to be a war.

"How much time?" I asked.

"I do not know," Loor said. "Maybe a few suns. They are smart. They will not launch this war until they are fully prepared."

"What about you?" I asked. "Aren't you supposed to be with the Ghee?"

"I am now a deserter," Loor said with no emotion. "If found, they will hang me."

I felt dizzy. Things were happening a little too fast.

"Do you still think we should go to Kidik?" I asked.

"Now more than ever," Loor said. "We need to know what Bokka found."

"Do you think he discovered that the Rokador are holding back the water?" I asked.

Loor thought for a moment, and then said, "Since the beginning of the drought, I have held out hope that the Rokador would not deliberately try to harm the Batu. I still believe they would never do something so foolish, unless there were other forces at work."

"Other forces like . . . Saint Dane?" I asked.

Loor nodded and said, "If it is true and the Rokador have been holding back the water, I believe that Saint Dane has somehow convinced them to do so."

It was so simple. If the Rokador had the power to hold back the water, then it made all sorts of sense that somehow, some way Saint Dane had wormed his way into their confidence and convinced them to do it. That's how he operated. He tricked people of the territories into making bad decisions. And unless Bokka's dying words referred to somebody else named Saint Dane, then the evil demon was down there. It was now more clear than ever that if we had any hope of stopping this war, we had to go to Kidik.

"What about my stave?" I asked.

Loor reached outside the doorway and retrieved my familiar, worn stave. Osa's stave. She hadn't forgotten to bring it. I felt its weight, flipped it over my shoulder and into the harness. I was ready to go.

"This is gonna be tough," I said. "A Ghee and a half aren't going to be welcomed by the Rokador with flowers and songs."

"We will reach Kidik," Loor said confidently. "Have faith. You have learned from the best."

I had to smile. Loor's confidence was infectious. It was starting to rub off on me a little too.

Saangi said, "I will say again, I should come with you."

Loor actually softened and said, "Saangi, I wish you could. I truly do. But Alder is in danger here. As soon as he is able to move, you must get him back to the flume. The battle against Saint Dane is not about Zadaa. It is about Halla. Alder must be kept safe."

Saangi nodded. She hated to, but she nodded.

"It has been an honor to serve you," Saangi said to Loor.

"You have my eternal thanks," Loor responded.

"Whoa, time out," I said. "Don't go saying that like you're never gonna see each other again. We'll be back."

I thought I caught a small tear forming in Saangi's eye. Truth was, she might not see Loor again. Not if we got caught in the middle of this war. My words didn't comfort her in the slightest. They sounded kind of hollow to me, too.

"Pendragon," Saangi said, "I may be short in my manner, but I want you to know that I believe in you. If there is a chance of stopping this war, you and Loor will find it."

"Thanks for that, Saangi," I said. "And for everything."

I gave Alder a quick touch on the shoulder. I didn't want to wake him. He needed the sleep. I wished he were coming with us.

"Let's go," I said.

We were soon jogging through the dark, rainy streets of Xhaxhu, headed for the building that would lead us down into the depths of the Rokador tunnel system, near the flume. It was a familiar route. Loor didn't have to direct me. We found the building, entered the doorway, and descended down the spiraling ramp that brought us into the underground. Once we were below, the concept of day and night went away. The lighting was always the same. The domes embedded in the walls gave off the same, soft yellow light whether it was midday or midnight. We didn't stop to talk until we had walked through the abandoned water-control station, and emerged into the vast chamber that used to hold the raging river. Even with all the rain, there was only a small bit of water trickling along the dry riverbed. I had to admit, this looked bad for the Rokador. I was now convinced that they really were playing games with the water.

"Do we have a plan?" I asked Loor.

She took out the map that Bokka had given us. I took another look at the complicated labyrinth of tunnels and the route marked in red.

"What are those?" I asked, pointing to several unique sketches that showed up every so often along the route. They were all different. Some were slashes across the tunnels. Others showed what looked like small structures off to the side.

"I do not know," Loor answered. "But we will find out."

"Which way?" I asked.

"Bokka's route begins at the crossroads," she said. "We

must go through those large doors to begin our journey."

"So right off the bat, we've got to go through a team of Tiggen guards who were assigned to make sure nobody goes through those doors because there is a major water transfer-control machine on the other side?"

"Yes."

"Just checking."

We started off, retracing the route that Bokka had led us on when we first went to the crossroads. I got confused pretty quickly. There were many turns and options. But Loor knew where she was going. I followed as if I did too.

"If we meet with resistance," Loor said, "listen for my commands."

"No problem, you're the pro," I said.

I was actually feeling pretty confident. When we were attacked by the Tiggen guards before, I did all right. I was getting more used to Osa's stave, so I felt sure I could put a little more "oomph" behind it this time. On the other hand, there wasn't much we could do to defend ourselves if that assassin were there and he started shooting those steel arrows. We had to watch out for that dude. In a few minutes we arrived at the final tunnel that opened out into the large cavern called the crossroads. My heart sank when I saw that there were three Tiggen guards in front of the door. The road to Kidik was through those guys, and the doors they were guarding. The only good news was that the guy with the crossbow was nowhere to be seen.

"They are not alert," Loor whispered.

"How do you know that?" I whispered back.

"From the way they are standing," she answered. "Either they have been on duty for a long time, or they do not believe they will be attacked. Possibly both."

"Tell me what to do," I said.

"Fight," she said, and took off running for the guards.

Just like that. No plan. No sneaking around. No coordination. No signals. Just an all-out, frontal attack. I pulled out my stave and followed.

I shouldn't have doubted Loor. She actually did have a plan, and it was the only one possible. The crossroads was a large, empty cavern with nothing but the two huge wooden doors that were being guarded, and a number of tunnels that led off to other points. The tunnel we had come out of was directly across from the wooden doors. There was nowhere to hide. No place to sneak and get closer without being seen. Loor made the only choice possible. She ran quickly and silently for the guards. If she was right, and they were not alert, we'd get pretty close before they even realized what was happening. If she was wrong, well, ouch.

Loor was right. She moved so quickly and so quietly that she was nearly on the first guard before he knew it. He never even got the chance to go for his weapon before Loor swung her stave. She knocked him to the ground with one shot, out cold. The other guards were just as slow to react. Loor targeted the next guy while I took the third. Neither of them even reacted to their buddy getting beaned. I figured my guy would pull out his steel baton and wait until I got close enough so he could dig it into my ribs and zap me. I didn't give him the chance. Just before I reached him, I dropped to the ground and swung my stave at ankle level. I was hoping to get him to reach down to protect himself, but it turned out even better. The stave hit his ankles and the guy toppled. He was on his back before I finished the swing. I brought the stave back, ready to drill the guy when I heard, "Pendragon, stop!"

It was Loor. I froze, but kept my eye on the Tiggen guard. I didn't want him to pull a sneak attack when I was looking away. I had learned my lesson, over and over again, that I had to keep my eye on my opponent. As I stood there with my stave raised and ready to strike, I saw something odd. The Tiggen guard still hadn't moved. As he lay on his back, he didn't even turn to look up at me. I figured he might have hit his head on the way down and been knocked senseless.

"Relax, Pendragon," Loor said calmly. "They will not give us trouble."

A closer look at my opponent revealed something eerie. His face looked frozen. Almost . . . dead. My heart raced. Had I killed the guy? There was no way. All I did was sweep out his feet. Loor walked over to the guy, reached down, and yanked back the white hood that covered his head.

"Dummies!" I exclaimed.

His face was a cloth mask. A quick look back showed me that all the guards were fake. They had been propped up to look as if they were guarding the doors. From a distance, the effect was pretty good. Now I knew how we got so close without them reacting. The word that came to mind was "scarecrows."

"I do not understand," Loor said. "Why would they no longer have real guards protecting such a valuable piece of machinery? Did Bokka not say they feared the first attack would be here?"

"I don't know," I said. "But we can find out."

I walked up to the large wooden doors. There was a heavy lock on the handle, but it was no match for Osa's stave. With two quick whacks I knocked it open.

"Let's see what's so important in here," I said as I grabbed the handle and pulled the door open. It was heavy. No big surprise since the door had to be twenty feet high and made out of wood that looked to be four inches thick. But it swung easily on its hinges. I was about to peek inside when Loor pulled me back.

"Careful," she said.

She took the lead. It didn't hurt my ego. Whatever nastiness might be waiting on the other side, she was better equipped to deal with it than I was. I grabbed my stave, exhaled, and took my first step onto the map, and into the fire.

ZADAA

What we saw beyond the door made no sense. Like Bokka said, there was another one of those water-control machines. And it was awesome. It had to be four times the size of the one back at the waterfall-that-was-no-longer-a-waterfall. The pipes that passed through this monster had to be six feet wide. There was no doubt that this was a major piece of machinery.

But it was shut down. And the cavern that held it was empty. There wasn't a Rokador in sight.

"Strange," I said. "I thought they were all sorts of worried about the Batu getting control of this."

I walked to the monstrous device to get a better look. The gauges all registered zero. It made no sound. I touched it. It was as still as a rock. Stranger still, there had to be several dozen valve controls, but all of the knobs and levers were gone. All that was left were small stems where the levers used to be. I ran my finger across several of the gauges, wiping a clear path through a thick layer of dust.

"This thing hasn't been used in a long time," I said.

"There has not been water in a long time," Loor commented.

"So why were they guarding it yesterday?" I asked. "And why did Bokka tell you this was such an important piece of machinery?"

Loor didn't know any more than I did. I took a look past the machine to see that this cavern narrowed down into a small tunnel that led deeper into the underground.

"I guess that's the Yellow Brick Road," I said.

"The what?" Loor asked.

"The way to Kidik." Note to self: Stop making clever Second Earth references.

Loor glanced at the map and said, "Here. The first of the strange markings."

She showed me the map. I could see the big cavern with the monster water-control device. There might as well have been a note saying: YOU ARE HERE. I could also see on the map where the cavern narrowed down to a small tunnel opening, just as it was in front of us. The odd thing was that on the map there were three X's across the mouth of the smaller tunnel.

"Any idea what it means?" I asked.

Loor shook her head. We kept our weapons ready and began our journey to Kidik, the capital city of the Rokador world. We walked quickly to the far end of the cavern, stopping just short of the opening to the smaller tunnel. After a quick look around I announced, "No X's here." I took a step through the opening. The instant I broke the plane, I heard a rumbling sound. I had triggered something.

"C'mon!" I shouted, and leaped through.

Loor didn't hesitate and jumped after me. Her quick reaction saved her life. The instant she entered the tunnel, a series of steel spikes shot down like spears from above, closing off the opening. If Loor had been a hair slower, she would have been skewered. We stood together, holding each other, breathing hard. The opening to the tunnel was now cut off by the spikes that had become vertical bars.

"Good news—bad news," I said. "The route to Kidik may be booby-trapped."

"Booby-trapped?" Loor said, confused.

"Full of dangerous surprises like that," I said. "If we make a wrong move, it could hurt."

"And what is the good news?" she asked.

"Bokka's map will save us," I answered. "I'll bet these odd markings on the map show where the traps are."

We both took another look at the map. Those strange markings now took on a whole new importance . . . and there were a bunch of them between us and Kidik.

"This may show us where they are, but not what to expect," she pointed out.

"Yeah," I said. "This is going to be interesting."

We weren't doing any good standing there staring at a map, so we continued on. The map led us through many different-size tunnels and caverns. The more I saw, the more amazed I became at how the Rokador had burrowed out an entire civilization underground.

"Are these tunnels natural?" I asked. "Or did the Rokador dig them?"

"Both," Loor said. "I believe the larger caverns are natural, but the adjoining tunnels were created by the Rokador."

"But how? This is, like, solid rock."

"The history of the Rokador is best told by a Rokador," Loor said. "But I am familiar with the dygos."

"The huh?"

"Dygos," Loor repeated. "Tunneling machines. We will see them on our journey."

I decided not to ask any more questions until I had a visual aid. Besides, I was too stressed about running into another booby trap. Fear beats out curiosity any day. Walking through this labyrinth of underground tunnels was strange in that it didn't feel all that claustrophobic. Sure, some of the rocky tunnels were narrow, but they often opened up into caverns where the ceilings were as lofty as a cathedral. And there were lights everywhere. It didn't feel anything like we were traveling deeper and deeper underground. To be honest, I tried not to think about that. I couldn't imagine living down here under multiple tons of rock, unless you were an ant.

The thing we didn't find was people. Not a single living soul. We passed hundreds of different rooms that were full of equipment. Some looked like living spaces with cots and furniture. Others were stacked with boxes and tools. There had been people here once, and not long ago, either. The word that kept coming to mind was "abandoned."

Every so often the route would take us through a less developed area, where there would be a marking on the map, and another booby trap. One time Loor took a step and felt the ground rumble. She leaped forward and I jumped back a second before the floor caved in, leaving a gaping black hole that dropped down to nowhere. We found ourselves on opposite sides of a hole that went from wall to wall. Unfortunately for me, I was on the wrong side, with no way to get across.

"There," Loor said, pointing.

I saw a thin lip of stone floor that hadn't fallen. It was no wider than a brick and sticking out from the wall along one side of the hole.

"You want me to walk across on that?" I asked in horror.

"Unless you can leap over," Loor said.

I couldn't. It was a thirty-foot jump. I had to go the lip route. Swell. Facing the wall, I tentatively put my right toe onto it and pressed down to see if it would crumble. It didn't.

Still, this was going to be tough, even if the lip held. It was only a few inches wide. Gulp. I had to press my chest against the rock wall, with nothing to grab on to, and slide my feet along. It kind of reminded me of the training pit back at Mooraj. Only with this pit, if you fell, you died. I moved my right foot first, then brought my left foot up to it. There was no way I could cross them over. I would have lost my balance for sure. I kept the palms of my hands flat against the rock, carefully feeling for any little crag that I could hang on to with my fingers. My left cheek was pressed flat and I stayed up on my toes—anything to keep my center of gravity forward.

I tried not to think about how my butt was dangling out over oblivion. My entire being was focused on keeping my weight against the wall. I crept along like this, moving slowly, but moving. The lip held, and I was getting closer to safety. It wasn't until I was almost to the far side that my luck ran out. The wall bowed out ever so slightly. It wasn't much, but it was enough so that I had to move my center of balance back to get around. Bad move. I felt my weight shift toward oblivion. I grabbed for the wall, but my fingers brushed over the rock face uselessly. I was going down.

I didn't get far. Something hit me on the back. Hard. I carefully peeked to my right and saw that I was close enough to the far side that Loor was able to reach out with her stave and pin me to the wall.

"Ouch," I said. I didn't mean it. She had saved my life. Again.

"Keep moving," she commanded.

Having her hold me against the wall gave me confidence. I quickly got my feet shuffling again, and a few seconds later I was on the far side.

"Thank you," I said. That hardly covered it, but what

else could I say? Saving each other's lives was getting pretty common. Loor didn't need to be thanked. She was already on to the next challenge. How strange is that? I could very easily have died just then. But I didn't, so we had to move on like it was no biggie. That is what my twisted life has become. I shouldn't complain. At least I'm still around to write about it.

"It seems as though the Rokador abandoned these tunnels and set these traps to stop those who would follow," Loor said.

"Yeah, us," I said.

"Or the attacking Batu," Loor said. "The Rokador are not warriors. In battle the Ghee will destroy them."

"What about the Tiggen guards?" I asked.

"Bokka would not agree with me, but they are no match for the Ghee. Even if they were, they do not have the numbers we do. If they hope to win a war against the Batu, they will have to do it with cunning, not force."

I agreed with her. From what I saw, the Tiggen guards weren't the fighters that the Ghee were. Heck, even I held my own against them. How pathetic is that?

"These traps are a pain for us," I said. "But they won't stop an army."

"Not from what we have seen so far," Loor said. "We should continue."

I was right about the map. It showed the location of every booby trap. Without it, we would have been history. Thank you, Bokka. But the markings only showed us where the booby traps were, not how to prevent them from springing. We were nearly skewered about a dozen times over. Rocks crashed down in miniavalanches. One time the ground started to churn below our feet to reveal the sharp teeth of grinding gears that nearly turned us into hamburger. It was like making our way through a medieval video game full of pit-falls and surprises. Only this was no game.

There was something else we saw along the way that I should mention. Whenever we reached one of the larger caverns, on either wall there would be these huge, round metal plates sunk into the rock. They each had to be about thirty feet in diameter. When we saw the first one, I stopped to examine it.

"I do not know what it is," Loor said before I had the chance to ask. "I have never come this far into Rokador territory."

I couldn't help but wonder what they were, and if they might give us trouble. They weren't on the booby trap map, so chances were they were safe. After passing hundreds of these giant disks, I didn't know any more about them than after I'd seen the first one. Though my curiosity was still tweaked, the main thing was that they didn't do us any harm, so I had to ignore them.

We continued walking cautiously for a couple of hours. There's no way to tell how far we had traveled, since we had to stop often to find ways around the booby traps. The map was really accurate. It showed every intersection, tunnel, and cavern exactly as we were seeing it. At one point we rounded a corner and came upon yet another bizarre sight. It was sitting to the side of a larger cavern, looking totally out of place. It was a giant, silver ball. I was so surprised by seeing this thing, I actually took a step back. It didn't faze Loor, though.

"That," she said, "is a dygo."

Dygo? Oh, right. The tunneling machine. Very cool. I took a closer look at this odd device to see that the silver sphere was actually a passenger cab. It wasn't much bigger than a golf cart. It looked like it could hold two people, with a clear window that wrapped halfway around. The giant silver ball rested on treads, like a tractor. This thing could move forward, back, or turn in place. But the most amazing thing was the gizmo attached to the outside. It was a six-foot-long drilling device. It was shaped like one of those old-fashioned megaphones—as wide as the sphere at its base and narrowing down to a hollow point that was about a foot across. Along the body of the drill were dozens of rings with various gnarly looking cutting devices. The circular tip had inch-wide teeth that looked like they could drill through pretty much anything.

"That's how they dig the tunnels?" I asked.

"Yes, though it is one of the smaller vehicles."

I took a step closer to admire this silver tractor, drill, rock eater, whatever. "I figured they needed something more than shovels to create the underground, but this thing is . . . is . . . just killer."

"Bokka and I used to race dygos through the caverns," Loor said.

"They let you do that?"

"No."

Oh. Those wacky kids.

"So you can drive this thing?" I asked.

Loor smiled mischievously, as if remembering some taboo joyrides. "They are quite fast."

"So let's jump in and drive to Kidik," I said. "If it can drill through rock, it'll definitely protect us against the traps."

"Unless the trap is another bottomless pit," Loor said.

"Oh, yeah." I'd forgotten about that.

We had done all right getting by the booby traps up until that point, so it made sense not to mess with success. We left the cavern with the strange vehicle and continued our journey. Along the way I noticed more dygos. Some were parked in dark caves off to the side. Others were lined up in larger caverns, waiting for the next big project. I was getting very curious about the Rokador. In many ways they were incredibly advanced technologically. Yet they chose to live like moles. I hoped that someday I'd learn more about them—hopefully before they were annihilated by an army of Ghee warriors.

"We are getting close," Loor finally announced.

I took the parchment and saw that we were only a few turns away from the top of the map. The markings showed that the final tunnel led to an area with no detail. That had to be Kidik. My excitement started to build. Not only were we nearing the end of a dangerous journey, I was dying to see what an underground city would look like here on Zadaa. I tried not to think about the fact that we would be going from the frying pan into the fire. We were Batu. At least Loor was. I was kind of an honorary Batu. Bottom line was, we were the enemy. There was every possibility that the Rokador would capture us and lock us away. Or worse.

"Let's rest a minute," I suggested.

We double-checked the map to make sure there weren't any land mines around, and sat down.

"There's something we need to talk about," I said to Loor.

"What is that?" she asked.

I had been bothered about something since we decided to leave for Kidik. It was a problem I didn't know how to handle. Now that we were on the verge of arriving at our destination, it was time that I shared my concern with Loor. "We still have no proof that Saint Dane is controlling events down here," I said.

"But he was there when Pelle a Zinj was assassinated," Loor argued. "And Bokka said he is down here—"

"Yeah, I know, but we still don't know what he's up to. We're only guessing. Maybe he's just hanging around, observing."

"What are you saying, Pendragon?" Loor asked.

"We came down here thinking that we've got to stop the war," I answered. "I have no idea how we're going to do that, but it's why we're here. What are we going to do if we find out that Saint Dane hasn't influenced events after all, and the war between the Batu and the Rokador is the way it was meant to be? What do we do then?"

This truly was a dilemma. If Saint Dane wasn't controlling events, then the Travelers had no business being here and monkeying around. We're not supposed to mess with the natural course of a territory. That's not our job. We already screwed things up by putting Pelle a Zinj in a position to be killed.

Loor said, "I believe the real question is, am I here to do the work of a loyal Batu, or a Traveler? As a Traveler, I must do all I can to stop Saint Dane. But as a Batu, I must be loyal to my tribe."

"Right, which means you might suddenly have to go from somebody who wants to stop the war, to being the first warrior who has to fight it."

Loor looked at the ground, thinking. As we sat in that cavern, only a few yards away from Kidik City, we truly didn't know if Loor was there as a peacekeeper or an invader.

"That is our first challenge," she finally said. "We must learn what Saint Dane has been doing. Once we know that, we will decide how to proceed."

She was right. Until we found Saint Dane, we wouldn't know what to do. I took a tired breath and asked, "Is this Traveler stuff ever going to get easier?"

"I do not believe so," Loor answered.

We continued on through the last portion of the tunnel. Up ahead I saw that the stone corridor turned sharply to the right, just as the map showed. My heart raced. Around that corner was our destination. Kidik. I was excited about what we would find . . . and scared to death.

"You ready for this?" I asked.

"Do you need to ask?" Loor shot back.

I gave her a smile, and we continued on. We reached the corner, made the turn, and came face-to-face with . . . a dead end.

There was no Kidik.

ZADAA

Loor and I stood staring at a huge, blank wall of rock where there was supposed to be a city.

"No way," I said.

It was the end of the line. There wasn't any way around it. Literally. The tunnel opened up into a large cavern, but instead of a city, there was nothing but a vast wall of rock. There were no tunnels. No doorways. No hidden passageways. We had come to the end of the map, but there was no Kidik.

"This doesn't make sense," I said, looking at the map. "Did Bokka send us on a totally useless trip?"

"No," Loor said defensively. "Why would he do that?"

"I don't know. Maybe, maybe . . ." A thought hit me. "Maybe we didn't get this map from Bokka after all."

"You were there, Pendragon," Loor said impatiently. "You took it out of his boot."

"Yeah, but was it really Bokka? Maybe Saint Dane turned himself into Bokka to get us this map!"

Loor dismissed it, saying, "Then Saint Dane's ashes are now scattered across the desert."

Oh. Right. Bokka died. Maybe I was getting a little too

paranoid about Saint Dane turning up in various disguises. "Okay, so it was Bokka," I said. "Then why did he send us into a dead end?"

Loor stared at the blank wall, looking to find some clue that would make sense of this.

She found it.

"Look!" she said, pointing to where the rock wall met the ceiling.

I looked. I didn't see a thing. "Look at what?" I asked.

"Look to where the wall in front of us meets the side of the cavern."

I looked. Nothing. "I'm still not getting it," I said.

"Look at the color of the rock," she explained. "The wall is different from the ceiling, and the side. That is not natural."

A closer look told me she was right. The ceiling and side walls were a different brown color than the wall. The dead end wall was ever so slightly darker.

"So what?" I asked.

"That is not natural, Pendragon," Loor said. "I believe this wall in front of us was constructed."

"Constructed?" I shot back. "You can't just build a huge wall of rock."

"The Rokador can," Loor said confidently. "How can you doubt that, after seeing the world they have built? I believe this is another attempt to stop the Batu attack."

I took a step back and tried to imagine the wall not being there. Now that I was thinking that way, it did seem like where the wall met the sides and the ceiling, and even the ground, was a little bit too perfect and precise.

"Okay," I said. "Maybe they sealed off the cavern. It's still a wall of rock and we're still stuck."

Loor smiled and said, "Maybe not."

"It's a stone wall, Loor," I said impatiently. "Whether it

was made by the Rokador or not, we can't get through—"
The words were barely out of my mouth when the lightbulb
went on. I realized what she was talking about. "Are you serious?" I asked. "Do you really know how to use those things?"

Her answer was to take off running back the way we had
come. Not knowing what else to do, I followed. Loor led me
past the open area where we had stopped to talk, through
another section of tunnel, and back to a larger cavern that
had two sizable passageways off to either side. When I looked
down one of these passageways, I saw something hidden in
the shadows. It was the silver shell of a dygo.

"Wait here," she said, and ran to it.

A few seconds later I heard what sounded like an engine
starting up. But it was like no engine I was familiar with. It
was a deep, growling buzz. A moment later the silver sphere
came rolling out of the shadows. The giant ball rolled on
treads. It moved to the center of the cavern with the giant
drill bit positioned to the rear. It stopped, Loor lifted up a
side hatch, popped her head out, and said, "Would you like
a ride?"

"Oh, I am loving this!" I said.

She leaned back so I could get in. I stepped up on the
tread and slid past her to enter the small vehicle. I had never
been in a space capsule, but I imagined this was kind of the
same thing. It was pretty cramped inside. There were two
hard seats, side by side. In front was a window for both seats
that was only about a foot high. It wrapped halfway around
the sphere to give a little bit of a sideways view. There was no
way to see behind us. The controls were in front of the left-
hand seat. Loor's seat. The instrument console had a few
switches, along with a round glass ball that looked like one of
those compass things people sometimes put on the dash-
boards of their cars. There were two joysticks in front of the

driver's seat. It didn't look all that complicated, but I was just as happy to know that Loor had driven one before. She sat in her seat and pulled the hatch shut. It closed with a solid *thunk*.

"The shell is thick," she said. "It can withstand tons of pressure."

"Good to know," I said. "Let's not test it. What about air?"

"There are vents to the rear," she explained while toggling a switch to the left of her controls. "They can be opened and shut, depending on what kind of material is being tunneled through. When they are shut, there is enough air inside to last several minutes."

"Let's keep them open," I suggested.

Loor grabbed the two joysticks and gave me a quick demo. She manipulated the sticks and the sphere instantly responded, moving quickly and smoothly to the right, then the left, up, and down. Our seats swiveled and rotated on yokes, so we were always upright. She cranked one stick one way and one the other, and we did a complete three-sixty. I noticed that the glass ball on the control panel always stayed in one position. I guessed this was the device that told you which way was up.

"The sphere moves in every direction," she said. "As does the drill."

She twisted the grip on top of the joystick, and the drill came over the top and settled in front of us. Since the huge drill was hollow, it was possible to see all the way through to the front and ahead of us. Loor moved it to the left, to the right, up, and down, demonstrating how it had complete maneuverability.

"So, this thing can drill any way but straight down?" I asked.

"It can do that too," she said. "The treads move to the side and raise the vehicle up to allow the drill to face downward. It is quite ingenious."

"The Rokador are pretty smart people," I said.

"With machinery, yes," she said, sounding a touch insulted. "There is much they are not as capable of."

Meow. Loor's competitive nature was showing itself. But this wasn't the time to start a debate about which tribe was better, so I didn't press. Loor positioned the drill so it was directly in front of us, pushed her foot down on a floor pedal, and we moved forward. The ride was pretty smooth. I guess the treads softened out all of the bumps. Loor was pretty capable, too, steering the vehicle like a pro. It was a good thing the dygo was so small because we had to travel through some narrow passages to get back to the dead end. In no time we were looking at the blank wall of rock where the map, and our trip, had ended.

"What if we're wrong and there's nothing but rock?" I asked.

"Then it means Bokka has betrayed me," Loor said. "I do not believe that is an option."

"Let's go," I said.

Loor toggled a switch on the control panel. The massive drill whined to life and the cutting rings began to spin. She pushed the joystick forward, and the dygo rolled ahead. The tip of the drill touched the wall, and cut through it as if it were cotton candy.

"Whoa," I said, totally impressed. "No problem."

It was amazing. The spinning rings were designed so that they not only cut into the rock, but pulled the material back and away, pulverizing it. The rock that was within the hollow drill bit was chewed up and spit out as easily as if we were shredding paper into confetti. The dygo vibrated slightly as it cut, but it was pretty minor considering we were boring through solid rock. It wasn't very loud, either. I guessed that was because we were sealed inside this thick sphere and insulated from the outside noise.

"Are the vents open for air?" I asked.

"Yes," Loor answered, but kept her attention straight ahead.

"How thick do you think the wall is?" I asked.

Loor didn't have to answer. A few seconds after we started drilling, I saw light come through the hollow tip of the drill. The wall couldn't have been any more than a few feet thick. The drill kept grinding, though. We needed to make the hole large enough for us to move the dygo through. Moments later I felt the shuddering come to a stop. We were through. Loor stopped the drill, turned to me, and announced, "*Now* we can see Kidik."

ZADAA

Loor powered down the dygo and cracked open the heavy hatch. The first thing I noticed was the sound. We had been in closed tunnels for the last couple of hours, where the echoes from our footsteps bounced back at us. Here on the far side of the wall I heard something that didn't make sense at first because we were underground. But there was no mistaking it. I heard wind. Wherever we were, it *sounded* bigger. Loor crawled out of the sphere. I followed and took a quick look back at the wall to see we had cut a perfectly round hole.

"Wow," was all I could say. "That is just flat awesome."

"Pendragon, look," Loor said.

I glanced over to see she was staring up at a building. Yes, a building. It looked like one of those pueblo structures that you see built into the cliffs of the Southwest on Second Earth. The structure must have been four stories high, with window openings and doorways and even balconies. All I could do was stare and think how impossible it was that we were underground. Several yards across from it was a similar building that was also built into the rock. The two stood together, like sentries guarding an entrance. Beyond them the rocky walls formed a slot canyon that wound its way into parts unknown. I felt sure this was the entrance to Kidik. The two of us stood there for a moment, knowing that we were about to face a whole new danger.

"You said that the Rokador had no chance of defeating the Batu, unless they were cunning," I said.

"I did."

"The tunnels were abandoned," I continued. "The Rokador have retreated, but they have to be somewhere. Is it possible that the entire Rokador tribe is in Kidik, preparing for the attack?"

Loor glanced at the two buildings that guarded the entrance to the city. She had a dark look on her face. She didn't have to answer. I knew she was thinking the same thing. The two of us might be stepping into a city that was preparing for war . . . against us. Loor pulled her stave from her harness. I did the same.

"Be careful," Loor said.

"Is that possible?" I asked.

Loor ran quickly to the building on our left. She didn't go in, but crept along the wall, headed toward the city. Smart move. We needed to be cautious. Walking down the center of the street might have been suicide. I hugged the wall behind her. I remembered back to what I learned during those long nights in the training compound when I got whacked around in the dark. My senses were on alert, tuned for anything that might foreshadow an attack. If a steel arrow came flying at us, I wanted to hear it hiss through the air. If a team of Tiggen guards charged, I wanted to smell their sweat. I had no clue if I was capable of that, but I had to try.

We quietly crept past the two buildings and along the rocky wall. The narrow canyon bent to the left. Loor slid ahead boldly, with me right behind. As we moved, I heard the same, strange sound that I heard when we first broke through the wall. It sounded like wind. It was spooky, actually, because it was more like a deep moan. I listened to this sound, trying to place it. It was then that I realized something was missing. There should have been another sound, but there wasn't. We should have heard the sounds of a city, with people. We didn't. All I could hear was that distant, spooky moan. I was beginning to think that Kidik was still a long way off, until we turned the corner.

I caught my breath. We had arrived.

We stood at the edge of an incredible city that was carved completely out of rock. The slot canyon we had come through opened up into an enormous cavern where the sides stretched high above us on either side. There was no sky, only a vast ceiling of rock. There were thousands of structures built on top of one another. The city didn't cover all that much ground, but the buildings rose up on either side of us, all connected by roads and pathways that snaked up and around on hundreds of levels. None of the individual buildings was very big. The tallest of them was maybe four stories. But there were thousands of them, all seemingly piled on top of one another and crammed in together. Like the two buildings we had first seen, they reminded me of Southwest pueblos. There were windows, but no glass panes. The doorways were open as well. I saw carved staircases leading up from the road on both sides and into the honeycomb of buildings. The effect was so vast, so complex, so impossible, I forgot for a second that we were stepping into enemy territory.

"It is empty," Loor declared.

I was so awed by the spectacle, it hadn't hit me. She was right. Like the tunnels we had come through, there wasn't a single, solitary Rokador to be seen. Anywhere.

"This is impossible," I said. "They can't abandon an entire city!"

"What do your eyes tell you?" Loor asked.

I glanced around, listened, and said, "Okay, maybe they can."

We continued to walk, still cautious. There were about eight million places for somebody to be hiding, waiting for the first arrival of the Batu. We stayed close to the walls on one side of the street, just in case.

"Where is everybody?" I asked. "Obviously they're not all here getting ready to ambush the Batu."

"I believe when we find that answer, we will have the truth that Bokka spoke of," Loor said.

"He said that the truth was on the far side of the city, to the center," I said.

"He also said that it was a nightmare," Loor added.

"Yeah, swell," I said. "Let's keep moving. Can't wait to see the nightmare."

As we walked I couldn't help but wonder, again, what the Rokador were all about. They were definitely advanced technologically. Still, they not only chose to live underground, they carved primitive buildings out of stone that were barely more advanced than caves. It was a weird balance. They had no glass in their windows, yet they had streetlights on every level of the city. They built incredible machines that could drill through rock, but you had to climb old fashioned stairs to get from one level to the next. They figured out how to generate power, but didn't use it to create any kind of modern convenience beyond what was absolutely necessary. It seemed like they could have so much more, but chose not to. What a weird, freakin' bunch.

I tried to put myself in Saint Dane's place. What could I tempt these people with? What could I tell them they would gain by fighting the Batu? Bokka said their population was growing and they were running out of space. You sure couldn't prove that by what we had seen on our journey, because we saw nobody. No-body. The more I learned about the Rokador, the more of a mystery they became. Nothing was more mysterious than this complex, deserted city.

Loor and I kept sharp, watching everything, expecting an attack. The only sound we heard besides our own footsteps was the haunting, groaning sound that grew louder as we moved through the city. It was beginning to feel as if the place were haunted. The moaning sound grew louder by the second. We were approaching what looked like a dead end. We had been walking for ten minutes, so I'd say the city was about a half mile across. Looking ahead, all I saw was rock. It seemed as if the main street of Kidik was going to end at a blank wall that stretched up to the vast ceiling above.

I couldn't have been more wrong.

The roadway rose slightly. When we reached the crest of the hill and looked down the other side, we saw that there was definitely a wall at the end of the street. Now that we were looking down on it, we could see that at the base there was an entrance to a wide tunnel. As we got closer we saw this opening was at the top of a flight of stone stairs that led down. Both the opening and the stairs were wide—I'd say about fifty yards across. The moaning sound was pretty loud now. Whatever was making it was at the bottom of those stairs.

"We've got to keep going," I said.

We started down. The stairs were steep and long. Looking to either side, I saw that every thirty feet or so a flat ramp was carved into the stairs that was about ten feet wide. I figured this is where the dygos went up and down so they wouldn't chew up the stairs.

"What is that sound?" I asked. "It's making me crazy."

Loor shrugged. She didn't have any more of a clue than I

did. As we descended the steps it got cooler. Soon we were hit with a stiff breeze. Whatever was making this breeze had to be causing the howl, too. But what was it?

Loor saw it first. She was several steps farther down than I was, nearing the bottom of the stairs. The ceiling of the tunnel was dropping down on the same angle as the stairs, preventing us from seeing directly ahead until we were almost at the bottom. When Loor dropped below the ceiling, she was able to see what lay ahead. It was a large, empty cavern with a stone floor. Nothing all that out of the ordinary, at least for the underground world of the Rokador, anyway. She stepped down onto the stone floor, and looked to her right. What happened then was something that I never thought possible. On an adventure full of surprises, this one ranked right up there near the top.

Loor froze . . . and dropped her stave.

Uh-oh. Whatever she was looking at had shocked her so badly that she dropped her weapon. Let me write that again. Loor was so shocked, she dropped her weapon. Loor. I don't have to tell you how wrong that was. I hesitated a second. If something out there was so incredible that it could make Loor drop her weapon in shock, I wasn't so sure I wanted to see it. Of course, I had to. I grasped my stave tighter, in case I had the same reaction. Slowly I continued down. To be honest, I kind of squinted. I could still see, but somehow squinting made it easier to take, like I was in control. I used to do that in horror movies. I wouldn't fully close my eyes, I'd just squint. That way, if something icky jumped out, I could close them quick.

But no amount of squinting helped prepare me for what I saw when I hit the bottom of the stairs and turned to my right. I discovered what was making the moaning sound. It was wind. The mystery was solved, though a much bigger mystery had taken its place. What we saw was impossible, yet real—as real as the desert sand on the surface, miles above. Stretched out before us, as far as could be seen, was an ocean. An honest-to-god, underground ocean. The moaning wind slashed across the surface, kicking up whitecaps. I could feel moist air hitting me in the face. The sight was so impossible and so wrong, I'm surprised I didn't drop my weapon too.

I walked to Loor, and without taking my eyes off the water, I said, "Now there's something you don't see every day."

Loor couldn't speak. It was like her brain wouldn't accept it. But it was no illusion. A forty-yard-span of stone floor stretched between us and the water. I left the cavern at the base of the stairs, passed under an archway, and walked across the deck to the edge of the water. There was something I had to know. I got down on my belly, and scooped up a handful of water. Touching it to my lips, I instantly realized that somebody somewhere had some serious questions to answer. This was freshwater. It was drinkable. I had no idea how deep it was, but the surface was vast. I had no doubt that there was enough water here to feed the rivers of Zadaa and end the drought.

Loor walked up behind me. "Someone will pay for this," she said while staring out over the water. "My people are starving and there is enough water here to . . ." She didn't finish the sentence, that's how ticked she was. She gazed from right to left and said, "There." She was pointing to the right of us, where I saw that tied to the stone deck, bobbing in the water, was a small boat.

"Bokka said a vehicle was waiting to take us to the center," I said. "Do you think—"

Loor's answer was to walk quickly toward the boat. I followed. Without another word we boarded. It was about the size of a rowboat and made out of the same silver steel as the dygo. There was nothing sleek or modern about it, though. It looked to have been hammered out of sheet metal into a shape that was kind of like a Boston whaler with two bows. One end had a tiller, which made it the stern. Loor went right to work. There was a small control panel in the stern that reminded me of the instrument panel in the dygo. Loor toggled a switch, and I heard an engine start up with a low growl.

"Can you handle this thing?" I asked.

With one quick move she tossed the line back on the deck and gunned the engine. That meant yes. I sat down in the bow quickly, and not a second too soon. If I had been standing, I would have toppled. Loor kicked the throttle open and in no time we were bouncing across the waves. This wasn't a pleasant skimmer ride, like on Cloral. This was more like being in a small boat on the choppy Long Island Sound at home. It was dark, too. Once we got away from Kidik, there were no lights to guide our way. Of course, there was no moon or stars above either. Only the rock ceiling. I glanced back to Kidik and saw a giant wall of stone. At the base was the opening that led to the cavern at the bottom of the stairs we had just come through. The platform and cavern were lit up, but this light wasn't anywhere near powerful enough to help us see farther out over the dark ocean. I tried to memorize where this opening was, since we would have to come back this way. At least I hoped we'd be coming back.

Loor was focused. Her jaw set. She had been hit with a lot over the past few hours. I had no idea how close to the edge she was. I figured the best thing to do was try and diffuse her anger.

"Yeah, it sucks," I said. "Bokka is dead, and it looks like the Rokador have been hoarding water from the Batu. But we gotta stay focused. There's more to come, I guarantee it. I need to know you're with me."

That was pretty harsh. Basically I'd just told Loor I was worried that she'd let her emotions take over to the point where she'd do something dumb. Spader had done that, more than once, and it cost us. I couldn't allow Loor to do the same thing.

"This has become personal, Pendragon," Loor said. "My best friend is dead, and my people are starving. If this is the work of Saint Dane, he will suffer for it."

I felt the anger in her voice. We had reached a crossroads. I couldn't blow this. It was my job.

"You're not the only one who's lost friends and family," I said just as firmly. "Yours isn't the only territory in trouble. We've come too far to let Saint Dane goad us into doing something stupid. We've all made mistakes. Big ones, and we've paid for them. I will not let you do it too. Not here. Take a breath and get your head back in the game!"

My eyes stayed locked on hers. I wasn't about to blink. Loor was supremely confident in everything she did. That was her. But she wasn't stupid. She gave me a slight nod. My words had struck home. I could feel the tension melt. "Do not worry, Pendragon. I have not lost sight." Her voice was softer. I still felt the intensity, but she was now in control. She was with me.

"Good," I said. "Now, where the heck are we going?"

Loor pointed ahead. I turned around and saw a single light glowing in the distance.

"That's as good a choice as any," I said.

Loor kept us headed for the light. I'd say we traveled for about half an hour. That's how big this underwater ocean was. As we got closer, we could see that it wasn't a single light at all—it was several. They were torches. Six of them. The flickering light illuminated enough of the surroundings that I could see we were approaching a shore. As we drew even closer, I saw that one torch wasn't lit.

"Six flaming torches surrounding one dark torch," I said. "I wonder if that's some kind of symbol?"

"The dark one is not a torch," Loor observed.

I squinted to try and see better, and sure enough, standing at the center of the ring of torches was a person. It was kind of creepy. The guy stood there, alone, stock-still, with the torches burning around him. Was it some kind of Rokador ceremony? He didn't seem to be dressed in the classic white robes of a Rokador. He was wearing all black.

"Should I land the boat near him?" Loor asked.

"I guess," I said. "I don't think it would be a trap because nobody knows we're—uh-oh."

My mouth went dry.

"What?" Loor asked.

I wanted to be sure I was right, so I didn't answer right away. As we drew closer and I saw the truth, I still couldn't answer because my brain wouldn't kick my tongue into gear.

"Pendragon?" Loor asked. "Could it be?"

I didn't have to answer. Loor knew. Standing in the sand, surrounded by torches, was a tall man wearing a dark suit. He was completely bald. We were still too far away to see the angry red veins that slashed across his head from front to back, like bloody lightning bolts. But even from this distance, I could see his eyes. His blue-white eyes. They caught the light from the flames, dancing like he was possessed by some evil, inner glow. Because he was. As we drew closer to shore, he actually smiled and lifted his hand to give us a slight wave.

We were being welcomed . . . by Saint Dane.

ZADAA

Loor had one hand on the tiller. With the other hand she went for her weapon.

"Don't," I warned.

"I can end this here, Pendragon," Loor said through clenched teeth.

"No, you can't," I said, trying to keep my voice calm. It wasn't easy since my adrenaline had just spiked too. "We gotta know what's going on."

Loor's eyes were laser-locked on to Saint Dane. This was the guy who was responsible for killing her mother, and possibly her best friend, not to mention all the other mayhem he caused on his mad quest to control Halla. Loor wasn't the type to negotiate with her enemies. She was more inclined to whack first, then not bother asking questions later.

"If he's showing himself like this, he wants to talk," I said. "We've got to listen. It's the only way we can find out what's been happening."

I knew we had to play this Saint Dane's way. There were bigger issues involved, not the least of which was the future of Halla. Picking a fight with Saint Dane wasn't going to help.

Imagine that? Me trying to protect Saint Dane from Loor.

Loor tore her eyes from Saint Dane and looked at me. "I will listen to him, Pendragon," she said, but it sounded like it physically hurt her to say it. I hoped she meant it. She guided the boat onto the sandy shore. I jumped out and pulled it up and out of the water. Saint Dane didn't lend a hand, in case you were wondering. He stood in the center of the circle of torches, watching. Not moving. He wasn't going to come to us. We had to go to him. Fine. Whatever.

"Be cool," I whispered to Loor.

The two of us walked up the beach and stood on the outside of the circle of torches, only a few yards away from the demon Traveler. Nobody said anything for the longest time. Maybe it was because nobody wanted to make the first move. I've been told that's not a good idea.

"I'm happy to see you are feeling better, Pendragon," Saint Dane finally said.

"Really?" I asked, heaping as much sarcasm into that one word as I could. "Then why did you beat me up in the first place?"

Saint Dane chuckled. I amused him. Swell.

"And now you're masquerading as a Ghee warrior," he said with a smirk. "What is it you say on your territory? Trick or treat? I'm afraid I have no candy for you, little boy."

He was trying to rile me. I didn't take the bait.

"Speaking of masquerades, you surprised me," I said. "Bokka knew your name. Your real name. That's not like you. Usually you're such a coward you have to hide behind other identities."

Saint Dane flashed his fiery white eyes at me and smiled. It wasn't a happy smile. The game was on.

"Ahh, yes. Bokka. The brave Tiggen guard," Saint Dane said. "I believe he was a friend of yours, Loor? Such a shame he turned out to be a traitor to his people. I do hope his death was painful."

Loor moved before I could react. She leaped at Saint Dane while pulling her weapon from its harness. Saint Dane didn't budge. He didn't have to. The instant Loor entered the ring of light, three Tiggen guards leaped from the shadows and tackled her. Two more Tiggen guards jumped me, holding my arms. Another stepped into the ring holding his crossbow full of steel arrows, ready to shoot. I recognized him. It was Bokka's killer.

Saint Dane said, "My friend here is such a fine marksman. I believe it only took one arrow to serve justice to Bokka. Though he fired several more, just to be sure."

Loor squirmed in anger, trying to get up, but the guards held her facedown in the sand. Saint Dane strolled over and leaned down to her.

"You want to kill me, don't you?" he said calmly. "And here I thought you and your friends were so righteous. You are just as capable of evil as anyone. Perhaps more so. Yet you believe your brand of evil is justified, so long as it serves your own misguided purposes."

Loor struggled to pull free. "Why did he have to die?" she growled through clenched teeth. "He is not part of this."

"That's not true, my dear," Saint Dane said. "Bokka made himself a very big part of this. Once the Tiggen guards discovered he was going to present a Ghee with a map that showed the route to Kidik, his fate was sealed." He walked to the Tiggen assassin with the crossbow and put a hand on his shoulder. "I can't say I was surprised, though. I knew Bokka would run to you. That's why I gave him the map."

Loor screamed and struggled, but the guards held her firm. I moved to go to her, but the Tiggen guards held me tight as well. I shot one guard a look straight in the eye and said firmly, "Let . . . me . . . go." The guard stared back, and a strange thing happened. He let go. I looked to the other guard, and yanked my arm away from him. The two guards stood there, looking at me like dummies.

"Nicely done, Pendragon!" Saint Dane said. "You are learning!"

I knelt down next to Loor and touched her back gently to try and calm her. I put my face down in the sand right next to hers and whispered, "Please do this my way."

Loor's eyes burned with anger and hatred. We locked gazes. Slowly I saw her regain control. She gave me a slight nod. I touched her hair, then stood up and looked at Saint Dane. "Let her go," I demanded calmly.

"Is your guard dog under control?" he asked.

"Let her go," I said again, just as calmly.

The Tiggen guards looked at Saint Dane. He gave them a nod, and they quickly backed away from Loor as if they were releasing a wild animal. They were ready to pounce back on her at the slightest sign of trouble. The assassin with the crossbow kept his weapon aimed at her. Loor didn't jump up right away. I think she was still trying to get her wits back. I leaned over and helped her to her feet. When we were face-to-face, I gave her a reassuring smile and a wink. She nodded. She was back with me.

I turned to Saint Dane and said, "Okay, so you gave Bokka the map to lure us to . . . wherever the heck this is. Nice job. Real clever. Why?"

Saint Dane chuckled and said, "To save your lives, of course."

I hadn't expected that. I didn't know what to say. Saint Dane reached into his pocket and pulled out a soft, black cap with no brim. He put it on his bald head to hide the angry red scars and said, "My time with the Rokador has been so refreshing. There has been no pretense, no trickery. I've presented myself to them as I am, and helped them forge their own future. It's been such a perfect demonstration."

"Demonstration of what?" I asked.

"Of my ability to control Halla, of course," he said as if I were an idiot for not knowing that.

"What's going to happen, Saint Dane?" I asked, trying not to sound as desperate as I felt.

"Pendragon, my boy," Saint Dane said. "Once the excitement starts, those fortunate enough to be on this underground island will be the only survivors. I've spared you because I wouldn't want you to miss seeing Zadaa's future. And why not? You helped create it." He turned to the Tiggen guards and said, "Please escort our guests to chambers." With that he smiled at me, turned, and walked away.

"What's going to happen?" I yelled at his back.

"Patience," he called. "Your answer will come soon enough." He stopped and turned back to say, "Oh yes, I nearly forgot. If you feel any guilt about spending so much time with Loor, don't. The lovely Courtney Chetwynde has found a new beau."

He gave a smug little smile and continued walking. His comment came from so far out of left field, I didn't know how to react. He had just jerked my head away from Zadaa, and thrown me back to Second Earth.

"How do you know that?" I shouted at him.

"Why, Pendragon!" Saint Dane teased. "Don't tell me you're jealous."

"Leave Courtney alone!" I screamed. I took a step to follow him, but Loor put her hand on my shoulder, stopping me. It was her turn to be the calm one.

Saint Dane motioned to the assassin with the crossbow and walked toward a group of huge boulders that lined the beach. The Tiggen killer followed. Saint Dane didn't turn into an animal or a bird or anything else. He simply walked away like a regular person. This may be weird to say, but it creeped me out. Seeing Saint Dane acting human was unsettling. I think maybe it was because it was easier to think of him as some impossible, supernatural being. It was harder to accept that someone who was capable of such evil, could be a normal person. It made me shudder.

"Be calm, Pendragon," Loor said softly.

"He's been to Second Earth," I said, my panic rising.

"Maybe," Loor said. "Or maybe he is trying to upset you."

"He's doing a good job," I shot back.

Before we could make another move, the Tiggen guards grabbed us, took our weapons, and pulled us along the beach in the direction that Saint Dane had gone. Loor gave me a look as if to say, "Should we take these guys out?" She wanted to start kicking some Tiggen butt in the worst way. I was beginning to think the same way. It took all I had to keep my emotions checked. Saint Dane was trying to get us to lose control. We couldn't let him.

I shook my head and said, "Not yet. We need to know more."

Reluctantly Loor backed off and let the guards control us. We passed the boulders that marked the beach and continued along a gravel path. It felt like we were in a huge field, littered with boulders. I couldn't tell for sure because it was so dark. I had the stupid thought that I wanted to see the place in daylight. Right. Daylight. There was no daylight here. Ever. How depressing was that? I had no idea what time of day or night it was.

The path continued up a hill. When we reached the top, we got a better view of our surroundings. Saint Dane said this was an island. We had to take his word for that. Because of the darkness, there was no way to see where the land ended and the sea began. What we did see, though, was a group of buildings. I'd say they were about a half mile farther along the trail. It was a sprawling, complex maze of steel and stone. There was one central square structure that was pretty big. It looked about the size of an airplane hangar. Scattered around it were lower structures of all different lengths and heights. It was easy to see these buildings because there were lights burning in hundreds of windows. This was the first sign of life we had come across since we left the surface. We had finally caught up to the Rokador.

"It is a fortress," Loor said in awe.

She had read my mind. The inner buildings were surrounded by others that ringed the entire complex, like a fort. For the Batu to attack, they would have to come across the ocean, unprotected, and invade this island stronghold. We were wrong before. The Rokador weren't going to make their stand in Kidik, they were going to fight the Ghee warriors right here on this island. This is where the battle for Zadaa would unfold.

The Tiggen guards hurried us down the path and quickly brought us into one of the outlying buildings. It was a long corridor of stone, with lights lining the walls. There were several doors on either side, spaced several yards apart. Doors with bars. It was a prison. They rushed us into one of the cells and quickly locked us in. Loor and I both turned back to see something strange.

The Tiggen guards had removed their hoods. Since they were underground, they didn't wear goggles. Like the other Rokador, these guys had incredibly pale skin and dazzling green eyes. They were all blond, too. That wasn't the strange part. What was odd was the way they looked at us. We were the enemy. We represented a tribe that was about to come down here to annihilate them. You would think they'd have hatred in their eyes. They didn't. It's hard to describe this, but it seemed as if they were looking at us with sadness. I swear they wanted to say something, but couldn't bring themselves to do it. All five of them. They stood in the doorway with these pained looks on their faces.

I took a chance and asked, "What's going on?"

The guards looked at one another nervously and left quickly, as if they had already stayed too long. One stayed outside to watch over us.

"That was . . . odd," I said to Loor.

She didn't look happy. "I listened to you, Pendragon," she said impatiently. "Now we are trapped. I cannot stay in here when the Batu attack."

"The trick is to stop this before they attack," I reminded her.

"How?" Loor asked quickly. "There is no time. When we left Xhaxhu, the Ghee were gathering. They were bringing in thousands of other Batu to join in the attack. They had no problem finding volunteers. They are angry and they are thirsty. When they discover this underwater sea, there will be no mercy."

"But Saint Dane has something planned," I reminded her. "He said the people on this island would be the only ones to survive. That didn't sound like he was betting on the Rokador to beat the Batu in a fair fight. He's more clever than that."

"All the more reason we must leave this prison," Loor said.

She scouted the cell. It was a good-size room, with two stone cots. There wasn't even a toilet or a sink. There was one window with bars that looked out onto . . . nothing. Loor grabbed the steel bars and shook them fiercely. They didn't budge. She left the window and hurried to the cell door. She grasped those bars and shook them as well. All she got for her effort was a minor clattering of the lock and a dirty look from the Tiggen guard outside.

"Saint Dane is putting on a show for us," I said. "He's not going to keep us in here. He wants us to have front-row seats for whatever it is he's got planned."

"And if he gets what he wishes, we will have failed," Loor said. She sat down on a stone cot, looking peeved.

I was beginning to think I had made a mistake. We were not doing any good in here. We needed to find out what Saint Dane was up to. What was he planning? He wasn't going to fight a war by himself. As usual, he was playing both sides. He made sure the one person who would have stopped the Batu from attacking was murdered. Then we found him down here being buddies with the Rokador. He wanted a war, all right, but there had to be more than that. There always was. The trick was finding it.

"Teek," Loor said.

"Excuse me?"

"Bokka's friend Teek," Loor answered. "You met him on the farm. I have known him as long as Bokka."

"Right, the guy who was afraid of bugs," I said. "What about him?"

"If he is here, he will help us."

I didn't know Teek from a hole in the wall, but if Loor said he would help, then I wasn't exactly in a position to argue. It wasn't like I had any other ideas. I walked to the door and looked at the Tiggen guard outside. He stood staring into space. Nothing was going on, yet he was breathing hard. He was upset about something, that much was pretty clear.

"Hello," I said.

The guy glanced at me, then quickly looked away. Yup, he was scared.

"You know something is about to happen, don't you?" I asked calmly. "It's bad, isn't it?"

The guy wouldn't look at me.

I was a Traveler. Uncle Press told me that we had the ability to persuade people. I had no idea why we had this power or where it came from, but I'd seen it work. Gunny was pretty good at it. So was Uncle Press. I never had much luck with it unfortunately. The only time it seemed to work for me was when I tried it on somebody who was under stress. Or upset. If their mind was someplace else, they were open to persuasion. The Tiggen guard outside our cell was definitely upset. If there was ever a chance for me to work the magic, it was on this guy. I did my best to clear my mind, take away any trace of emotion or doubt, and focus on the guard.

"We have a friend," I said to him. "He's a Tiggen. His name is Teek."

This got a reaction. He shot me a quick, surprised look. He knew Teek.

"Teek is a friend," I said. "He would want to know we're here. Do you know where he is?"

The guy fidgeted. I had no idea if I was getting through to him or not.

"Can you find Teek and tell him we are here?" I asked as sincerely as possible.

The guy was torn. He glanced at me a few times, as if he wanted to say something. I didn't push. I felt like I had a fish on the line, and if I pulled too hard, he'd get away.

"What you are asking," he finally said, his voice cracking, "could get me executed."

"I'm not asking you to do anything but let Teek know we're here," I said calmly.

The guy closed his eyes. He was really torn up. I didn't know if it was because I was being so persuasive or because he was holding something back. Finally he turned to face me. I saw his anguish. He was nearly in tears.

"Whatever happens," he said, "please know that most of us had no say. We are victims. I'm still having trouble believing it."

"Believing what?" I asked, letting urgency creep into my voice. "What happened?"

The guy turned and jogged away.

"Wait!" I shouted.

Too late. My fish was gone. I was afraid I'd pushed too hard. I turned to see that Loor was standing behind me.

"What did that mean?" she asked.

"That guy was scared," I said. "I don't think it's because the Batu are coming, either. He was truly shaken. Something else is going on."

"Do you believe he will find Teek?" she asked.

"I don't know, but right now he's our best shot at getting out of here."

There was nothing for us to do now. I needed to get my thoughts together, so I sat on one of the cots and took out the paper and pencil I always carry in my leather pouch and began to write this journal. I hoped that by putting it on paper, I might discover something we had missed. As I wrote, I went over ever detail, trying to unravel the mystery of Saint Dane's plan. What I kept coming back to was Bokka. He knew something was up. He said it was a nightmare. I figured that when he and the other Tiggen guards returned to Kidik, they discovered something so horrible, he had to come and tell us even though it meant putting himself in danger. Whatever it was, it had all the Tiggen guards on edge. What could it be?

I was writing for about half an hour, and was about to roll

up this journal and send it to you guys when I heard a small voice calling from the corridor.

"Loor?"

We both looked up quickly to see the Tiggen named Teek standing beyond the barred door.

"Teek!" Loor shouted, and ran to him. I was right behind her.

Teek looked bad, like he hadn't slept in a week. It was pretty obvious that whatever the big, scary secret was, he knew it. "Bokka?" he asked.

Loor frowned. "He was killed," she said. "By the archer with the silver arrows. I am sorry."

Teek dropped his head. I saw tears roll down his cheeks. "Bokka was coming to find you," Teek said, his voice clutching. "To warn you."

"About what?" I asked.

Teek looked between the two of us with red, teary eyes. "Who is Saint Dane?" he asked. "He says he is from a tribe on the far side of the desert. Could he be one of your enemies, Pendragon? The Red Sox?"

Under other circumstances I would have thought that was funny.

"He is not a friend," I said. "Not of the Batu or the Rokador."

Teek nodded. It seemed as if he already knew that, but my words confirmed it.

"Then why is he here?" he asked.

"That would take a really long time to explain," I said.

"Please believe me," Teek continued. "We did not know. Most of the Tiggen guards were spread far across the underground. We were lied to. We believed everything the elite told us."

"About the Rokador holding back the water?" I asked.

"That's only the beginning!" Teek cried. "There is so much more. It is horrible."

"Tell us, Teek," Loor said softly. "Maybe we can help."

"No one can help!" Teek cried. "It's too late."

"We can try to stop things from getting worse," I said.

Teek rubbed tears from his eyes and took a deep breath. He nodded as if he had made a decision. He unlocked the cell door.

"You must hear it for yourselves," he said. "After that, I will take you to see. Until you see, you will not truly understand."

"Where are we going?" Loor asked.

"First to the Rokador elite," Teek answered. "They are sharing a final meal with the one who calls himself Saint Dane."

ZADAA

When we stepped out of the cell, I saw that Teek had brought our weapons. Nice idea, but there wasn't a whole lot that a couple of sticks could do against an entire tribe of Rokador. Still, it felt good to have them back. I guarantee Loor felt the same way. Teek led us on a quick, twisted journey through the corridors of the stone building. I'm guessing we were in the basement since the hallways looked like the tunnels of the underground. There wasn't much to see except for stone walls and closed doors. Teek knew exactly where he was going, which was amazing because it all looked like a whole lot of the same to me. We made a few turns, dashed down a few more empty corridors, and stopped at a closed door.

"You must be quiet," Teek said softly. "Above us is the private dining quarters of the elite. This door leads to a small tunnel that provides air to the building."

"Who are these elite?" I asked.

"Our leaders," Teek answered. "They govern the Rokador, pass the laws, and sit in judgment."

"That's a lot of power," I said. "Are they elected?"

"They are descendents of the original Rokador—those

who first discovered the underground many generations ago." Teek stopped talking and closed his eyes. It was like he was suddenly overcome with emotion.

"Are you ill?" Loor asked.

"I'm fine," Teek said after taking a breath. "We can hear what they are saying, but if we are discovered . . ." He didn't finish the sentence. I figured that whatever would happen, it wouldn't be good. Note to self: Don't get caught.

He quietly opened the door and entered. Loor and I followed. We found ourselves in a space with a ceiling so low we had to duck down to walk. There looked to be two shafts that disappeared into darkness. Teek had explained that these tunnels provided air. I felt a slight breeze, as if the air were moving. But learning how they ventilated this building wasn't why we were here. Light shone down from above through several small slits that were about a foot long and an inch wide. Teek approached this light source quietly and pointed for us to look. We quickly saw that these slits were the openings through which the room above was ventilated. More important, we were able to look through them and see into that room. Judging from the angle, I guessed that the slits were at the base of a wall. It was the perfect vantage point to peek into the room and eavesdrop on the proceedings.

The room itself was like nothing we had seen in the underground. It was big enough to hold a long dining table. There was artwork on the walls and comfortable-looking furniture. Candles burned everywhere. The dining table itself was loaded with an incredible feast. There were silver bowls heaped with all sorts of strange-looking fruit. On one end of the table was a roast something. On the other end was another roast that looked like a turkey. There were tall goblets full of drinks. It was a pretty fancy feast—not exactly something you'd expect to see in a place where people were desperate for food and water.

Loor and I exchanged looks. I knew she was thinking the same thing I was: Where was the horror Teek was talking about? It sure wasn't in this room. This place looked pretty sweet. I counted ten Rokador. The ruling elite. I guess I expected to see a bunch of white-hairs who had centuries of experience between them to draw upon as they made the wise choices that helped guide the future of their people.

Well . . . no.

A couple people looked kind of old. One guy was so ancient he didn't look like he could get out of his chair. I think he was napping . . . and drooling. I swear, there was a line of drool dropping from his mouth that formed a puddle on his chest. Nice. But overall it was a totally diverse group. There were three people who looked like adults. Two women and a man. There was a guy and a girl who didn't look any older than I am. And then there were two little kids. I'm serious. Kids. They all had the pasty white skin and green eyes of the Rokador and wore the familiar white robes. This must have been a special occasion, because they all wore the fancy robes with the gold trim like I wore to the Batu Festival of Azhra.

Everyone was eating quickly, pounding down the food as if it were their last meal. Truth be told, it might have been. They stuffed their mouths with fatty chunks of meat before they had even finished chewing what they already had bitten off. They washed it all down with water from their fancy goblets. I was surprised at first, but that's before I remembered that in truth, there was no water shortage. At least, not down here.

Oh yeah. There was one other guest at the table. Saint Dane. He sat on one end, watching the elite stuff themselves.

He wasn't eating. Every so often he'd take a sip of water. The whole event seemed to amuse him. He watched them with a slight smile, like a spider who knew he didn't have to sweat because all the little flies were firmly trapped in his web. After watching this gluttony for a while, I was starting to feel sick to my stomach. I don't know if it was because I was scared, or disgusted, or just plain hungry. I think it was all the above.

Finally one of the adult women stood up and addressed the group. "A toast," she said, holding up her goblet. "To our friend from the far side of the desert. He came to us a stranger, but has grown to be a trusted friend, a wise council, and the angel who will be forever known as the man who resurrected the Rokador. To Saint Dane!"

"Saint Dane!" everyone echoed. They raised their glasses and cheered.

Saint Dane smiled and raised his hand modestly, as if to say, "Aw shucks, folks, it was nothing."

I wanted to puke. Whatever Saint Dane said to these people, he had them totally convinced he was there to help. It was an eerie feeling. The people in this room loved him. I saw it in their eyes. They offered him a toast, they fed him like a king, they thanked him for all he'd done. They were probably forming plans to build a statue to him. They had no idea that whatever it was he talked them into, it would lead them to ruin. It was chilling. Was this the horrible truth that Bokka tried to tell us about?

Saint Dane wiped his mouth daintily and stood up. "My friends," he said. "And I am honored to call you my friends. Today marks a new beginning. The wise decision you have made will allow you to put aside the recent dark past and look to a brighter tomorrow. Now, finally, the Rokador will be able to grow and flourish in ways that just a short time ago seemed impossible. After today nothing will be impossible for you. I applaud your courage, and your vision."

He raised his own glass to them as they applauded. It was a total lovefest, until one of the older guys stood up and raised his hand for silence.

"I share in everyone's gratitude to Saint Dane for offering us his insight and advice. We are on the brink of a new future. A safe future. But I must admit, I am troubled by the lengths we must go to in achieving it. As we sit here now, enjoying our feast, I think we should ask ourselves one last time if the drastic course we have chosen is the right one."

There was general murmuring of concern. Some of the people nodded in agreement with the old guy, others were shaking their heads no. The two little kids kept eating. I don't think they cared one way or the other. I half expected them to start a food fight.

Saint Dane stood again and took control. "You are a wise leader," he said to the old guy. "Your caution is further proof of that. All I can offer you as assurance is my own experience. My tribe was faced with a similarly difficult choice. Once the possibilities were discussed, we came to a conclusion that could not be denied. Details aside, we had two choices. To survive, or to perish. We chose to survive, and I am here today as proof that we chose the right course. You, the ruling elite of the Rokador, are faced with the same choice. The path you are on is not a pleasant one, I will not deny that. But what other choice do you have? I am the last one who needs to remind you how close you have come to the depths of oblivion. The wheels are now in motion. I suggest that if you do not want to be enveloped by the dark shadow of death, that you choose to break free . . . and live!"

"To Saint Dane!" shouted the really old guy, who had

been asleep and drooling. He jumped out of his chair, holding up his goblet. I couldn't believe he could move that fast. Or move at all.

"Saint Dane!" the others cheered, and jumped to their feet. Even the old guy who had just questioned their plan took his glass and raised it with the others. Whatever was about to happen, there was no stopping it now.

Teek touched me on the shoulder and led us back out of the ventilation room. Once we closed the door, I asked, "What the hell were they talking about? What's going to happen?"

"Follow me," Teek said, and led us farther into the building.

"That group of bozos was the elite?" I asked. "How did they get to be in charge? Eeenie, meenie, miney, mo?"

"As I said," Teek answered, "they are descendants of the original Rokador who discovered the underground."

"So, they get to be in charge because of their ancestors, not because they're any good at it?" I asked.

"That's one way of putting it," Teek said.

"That's the only way of putting it," I shot back. "There were a couple of kids in there! I'll bet Saint Dane had a real tough time convincing them to do . . . whatever."

I had to calm down. This was their show. The way the Rokador chose to rule themselves was none of my business— no matter how idiotic it was. I was more concerned about this big decision they had made. No, more like the big decision that Saint Dane maneuvered them into making.

Teek led us to the end of a long corridor, where a door stood out from all the others because it was made of steel. He stopped and turned to us. "We must be careful. There will be Tiggen guards inside."

"What's in there?" I asked.

Teek didn't answer, but he opened the door and entered.

I shot Loor a quick, nervous look. Were we about to see the nightmare that Bokka told us of? We followed Teek through the door and found ourselves on a narrow, steel catwalk that looked down onto a cavernous room. It was freaky at first, because I thought we had been running around the basement of this building. The room we had just entered dropped down another bunch of stories. I guess I shouldn't have been surprised. Digging holes is what these guys did best. Once I got my wits back, I tried to understand what I was looking at.

It was some kind of machine room. There were dozens of giant vertical silver cylinders lining the walls of this huge cavern that were connected by massive horizontal pipes. The center of the room was taken up by a single, huge horizontal pipe that ran the length of the room. This pipe had to be twenty feet across, with thick seams that were bolted together by thousands of fat rivets. The bottom half of the pipe was below the floor, so only the top half showed. Built onto the top of this pipe was a long platform. On the platform was the complex instrument panel that controlled the machinery. There were countless flashing lights, along with small dials and gauges. Three Rokador were on the platform, monitoring the gauges and making occasional adjustments to the small silver handles that controlled . . . whatever. As we watched, two more Rokador climbed the ladders to the platform and manned their own stations. The place had an energy to it. A physical energy. You could feel it. There was a low, steady hum. It felt like . . . power.

"This is the center of our world," Teek said. "It is the master control station for the rivers of Zadaa. From here we channel all the water, and create our power."

Hydropower. Of course! That's how the Rokador kept the lights on. They used the flowing water to create power.

"So, all the water can be controlled from here?" I asked.

Teek nodded and motioned for us to follow him to the far side. We snuck across the catwalk and left through the steel door on the other side, finding ourselves in another tunnel. Teek made sure the door was closed, then turned to us and said, "When the Tiggen guards returned to Kidik, we learned why the engineers had been closing down the satellite stations throughout the underground. We were told it was because of the drought. The truth was that they wanted all control to be here. It is how they plan to defeat the Batu."

We didn't have to ask him what he meant by that. He wasn't finished. He wanted to talk. I think he needed to talk. That was fine by us. We needed to hear. Teek looked tired, and sad. He took a deep breath and continued, "This is the plan Saint Dane brought to us. When the Batu attack, we will wait until they are on our doorstep to be sure that most of the Batu are in the underground. When the first wave of warriors reaches the shores of the Kidik Ocean, we will release the water."

Loor and I shot each other confused looks. "Explain what that means, please," Loor said quickly.

"It means we will flood the underground," Teek said with a shaky voice. "Every living thing beyond this island will be trapped, and drowned."

Loor fell back against the stone wall, stunned. I felt like I couldn't breathe. Saint Dane's evil plan for Zadaa had finally been revealed. He had found a way for one tribe to destroy the other. There wasn't going to be a war, there was going to be a slaughter.

"Every single Ghee in the underground will be killed," Loor said, numb. "Thousands will perish."

"Xhaxhu will belong to the Rokador," I said. "That's the nightmare that Bokka talked about."

"But it isn't," Teek said softly.

"Of course it is!" Loor shouted. "Why else would the Rokador wipe out so many Batu? You want the city. How can they make such a cruel decision? The Rokador used to be our friends!"

Teek was in tears. "There's more," he said.

"More than this?" I shouted. "More than genocide?"

"Yes," Teek said. "I promise you, we did not know. Bokka, me, and most of the Tiggen guards. We weren't here. We didn't see it. We knew the elite were preparing for war, but we didn't know why. It wasn't until we returned that we saw the truth."

"The truth," Loor said. "Bokka said we needed to know the truth. What is the whole truth?"

Teek wiped his tears and said, "I will show you."

We followed him through several more corridors until we had reached the far side of the large building. Teek stopped at a door and said to us, "Outside this door lies the truth, and the horror." He took a deep breath to prepare himself, then walked out. I wasn't so sure I wanted to see what was beyond the door, but I had to.

We followed him onto a balcony that looked out over a vast, flat field. It must have stretched out a mile in front of us, and almost as far to either side. The only reason we could see it so well was that the entire field was covered with small, round white stones. Thousands of them. I'm guessing they were about a foot in diameter. They were equally spaced in perfect rows for as far as I could see. On each stone was a small light. I didn't know what I was expecting, but it wasn't this. There didn't seem to be anything horrible about this place at all.

I was wrong.

"It started slowly," Teek said. "There was no warning. By the time there was serious concern, it was too late. We are not like you. We do not live our lives exposed to the elements. We do not have the same resistance to disease as you."

"What happened?" I asked.

Teek looked out at the sea of stones and said, "We were hit with a virus that caused a sickness. A deadly sickness."

I looked at Loor. Her eyes were wide, unbelieving. The two of us looked back onto the sea of stones. The thousands of lights had suddenly taken on a whole new meaning.

"It is a graveyard," Loor said softly.

It was too much to accept. There had to be some kind of mistake. There were so many! I asked, "Are you saying each one of those stones represents a Rokador who died from this sickness?"

"No," Teek answered.

It was a brief moment of relief. Very brief.

"Each one of those stones represents a *hundred* Rokador who have died," Teek continued. "Their ashes lie below those markers."

I was rocked. My knees went weak. The extent of the tragedy was mind-numbing. We were looking out over the remains of hundreds and hundreds of thousands of people.

"My family is gone," Teek continued. "Bokka's too. We didn't know any of this was happening until we returned. We had been gone for so long and it happened so fast. This is why there was so much secrecy. This is not just about the rivalry between two tribes. The survival of our entire race is at stake. We aren't running out of space. We're running out of people."

"How many?" I asked, stunned. "How many are still alive?"

"Perhaps a few hundred," Teek said, barely able to speak. "A thousand at most. The elite were protected. So were their families. The Tiggen guards were spared because we were not here. Many of the engineers survived who ran the remote control stations. Our ambassadors to Xhaxhu, as well."

"Is the disease still spreading?" Loor asked.

"No," Teek said. "The doctors were finally able to bring it under control. It had happened once before in our history. Thousands died before a cure was found. I don't know why it took so long to recognize it this time. It should have been stopped early, but it wasn't."

I felt as if Saint Dane probably had a hand in there somehow.

"We were told that if the Batu discovered our weakened state, they would invade us. The elite decided to strike first. We don't want to live in Xhaxhu. Our home is here. Underground. All we want is to survive."

"And who suggested this plan, as if I didn't know?" I asked.

"Saint Dane," Teek answered. "He has been advising the elite."

"It's perfect," I said, reeling. "He's taken advantage of a natural disaster and gotten the Rokador all paranoid. Then he's played the other side and pushed the Batu into attacking, which is exactly what the Rokador feared. Unbelievable."

"Why would he do this?" Teek asked.

How could I answer that? "Because he's a bad guy," I said. It was the understatement of all time, but I wasn't about to explain how Saint Dane was a demon from another territory, who was doing his best to destroy the past, present, and future of everything that ever existed. Teek was having a bad enough day as it was.

"Many of the Tiggen guards do not believe this is right," Teek said. "But when faced with extinction . . ." He didn't finish his thought. It now made sense why all the guards were looking at us with these long, sad faces. They were reeling from the horror they discovered on their return to Kidik.

They had lost family, they had lost friends. Their entire existence was threatened. Bokka was right. It was a nightmare.

"There's something I don't get," I said to Loor. "The Rokador are nearly wiped out by a horrible disease. They're afraid the Batu will finish the job, so they want to defend themselves by striking first. If it works, thousands of Batu will drown. It would be a double disaster of epic proportions. No question. But is it enough to throw an entire territory into chaos? I mean, where would it all lead?"

Loor leaned on the steel rail of the balcony overlooking the vast Rokador graveyard. Her mind went somewhere else, lost in thought, calculating the possibility. Finally she came back and said, "Zadaa is a violent territory. Many tribes fight to the death to defend their little piece of land."

"The primitive tribes," I said. "The cannibals."

"Yes," Loor said. "The cannibals. It is one of the reasons the Rokador went underground. It was safer. The Ghee warriors were created to protect Xhaxhu. In the past the Rokador have been our allies, so they fell under our protection as well."

"I know all that," I said.

"There is a fragile balance on Zadaa. Xhaxhu is one of the only civilized areas on the territory. The Batu and the Rokador are the future of Zadaa. If the Ghee are wiped out, along with most of the Batu, that balance would be thrown off. It would only be a matter of time before one of the marauding desert tribes attacked Xhaxhu. Perhaps more than one would lay claim. These tribes are barbaric. There would be no one left to defend the city. Generations of knowledge and progress would be wiped out. Zadaa would be sent spinning into turmoil."

I swallowed hard and said, "And these marauding tribes are, are—"

"Yes," Loor answered. "They are cannibals." She looked at me with fear in her eyes and added, "Saint Dane is very close to winning his next territory."

I'm finishing this journal deep within the core of the Rokador world—or what's left of it. Can it still be called a world if barely anyone lives in it? Teek has found a safe place for us. From here we must decide how to stop the Rokador. Which means stopping the Batu. Which means stopping Saint Dane. Which means we are in deep trouble.

I'm afraid things are too far along for us to do anything here that would help. It's all too huge. This isn't about changing somebody's mind, or stopping a small rocket, or even destroying a mine with explosives. It's about stopping an army. That's out of our league.

I can't believe I'm saying this, but I'm beginning to think the best choice for us is to give up Zadaa. As I've said so many times before, this isn't about any one territory. This is about Halla. If Loor and I stay here, we may not survive. Saint Dane may not want us dead, but I can't speak for the rest of the Rokador. If they're willing to drown thousands of Batu, killing us wouldn't make them blink.

We've already lost Kasha. Spader and Gunny are trapped on Eelong. If Loor and I become trapped here, or worse, the Travelers would become so weak I'm afraid we'd have no chance of stopping Saint Dane. As I'm sitting here writing this, I truly don't know what we will do.

Before I finish this journal, there's one last thing I have to write. I told you what Saint Dane said about Courtney. I don't know if he was telling the truth, or just trying to upset me. The more I think about it, the more it's got me worried. There's always some small shred of truth in everything Saint Dane says. The details of what he meant about Courtney finding a beau, whatever that is, don't matter. What matters is that he would know anything about you guys at all. I'm not saying this to scare you. I don't think you're in danger. My biggest fear is that he may have come to Second Earth to begin laying the groundwork for his attack on our home.

All I can say is . . . keep your eyes open and watch your backs.

I miss you guys.

And so we go.

END OF JOURNAL #22

● SECOND EARTH ●

Mark jumped up from where he had been reading on his bed and paced. Back and forth, back and forth, bed to desk, desk to bed. It was a totally useless activity, but he couldn't think of anything else to do. His palms were sweating so fiercely, he had to put Bobby's journal down for fear he would smudge the writing. A thousand random thoughts fought for control of his brain; none of them were good. Only one mattered.

Saint Dane was on Second Earth.

The demon wasn't taunting Bobby just for the sake of it. He was here. Mark was sure of that. Saint Dane knew about Courtney and that guy she met. What was his name? Wimpley? Whipple? Wittle? Whatever. How else would Saint Dane know about that if he wasn't here? Was this the beginning of his plot to control Second Earth? Up until that moment, Mark held out hope that by saving First Earth, the Travelers had saved all three Earth territories. That hope had just gone adios. Mark knew that if Saint Dane was here, it wasn't to sightsee and snoop on Courtney. He had plans. Bad plans. And Mark was the only one who knew it had to be true. Courtney was oblivious, and Bobby and Loor were trapped miles underground on an island of the dead where an assault was about to be unleashed that would wipe out the Batu—the tribe that was keeping the civilized people of Zadaa safe from barbaric cannibal marauders. Saint Dane was on the verge of winning another territory and turn his sights to Second Earth.

Mark's plan of watching *Comedy Central* and going to sleep was long gone. He wasn't sure if he could ever relax and sleep again. Or watch *Comedy Central,* for that matter. He felt as if he had to do something, but had no idea what. He checked his watch. It was almost midnight. Should he call Courtney? What would he say? "Hey, how's it going? How was your date? By the way, you didn't happen to see Saint Dane wandering around campus, did you? Bobby and Loor are about to die, and he told them he saw you messing around with that new guy. Sleep tight!"

Mark knew he had to get a grip. When he was excited, he couldn't think straight. To clear his head he went outside and walked around the block. A dozen times. Two dozen times. He had grabbed some carrots on the way out and gnawed on them nervously. Nobody was out that late at night, even the people walking their dogs. That was good. He didn't need small talk, he needed air. The walking helped him calm down and make a decision. He had to call Courtney. He felt sure that she sounded well enough over the phone to handle the news. The real question was, how much should he tell her about what was happening with Bobby? He couldn't lie about getting the journals anymore. That much was certain. How else would he say he knew about Saint Dane? It was going to be a tricky conversation.

It took Mark a solid few hours to figure out the exact right things to tell her. He decided not to go into detail about the hairy situation on Zadaa. There was nothing they could do to help, so he figured Courtney didn't need to worry about it. Besides, he was worried enough for both of them. He concocted a story that would let her know there was trouble on Zadaa, but didn't include all the gory details about the danger that Bobby and Loor were facing. He even decided to tell her a little about Bobby's feelings for Loor. He felt she had the right to know. After all, Bobby thought she was reading the journals anyway! Beyond that, he figured if Courtney started asking more questions about the Batu and the Rokador, he'd bring up Loor again and that would probably get her off the subject. It was kind of devious, but he figured it was the right thing to do to keep her anxiety level down and her antennae up.

Mark returned home with his story ready. He went to his bedroom, grabbed his cell phone and—his eye caught something. Could it be? No, it was impossible. Yet it was staring him right in the face.

His clock radio read 2:05.

There was no way he was going to call Courtney that late. He decided the best thing to do was wait until morning. Early morning. He dropped his cell phone back on his desk without looking at it and set his alarm for six o'clock. Courtney would be ticked about getting a call that early, but once she heard what was going on, she'd forgive him. Six was good. Anything earlier than six was still the night before.

Mark grabbed his cell phone again. He wanted it on his bedside table so he could make the call the instant the alarm went off. He placed it next to his clock radio. He was ready. He got into bed, fully clothed, and tried to sleep. It was impossible. His mind wouldn't shut down. He kept imagining what was happening to Bobby and Loor. Time seemed to slow down. He couldn't help but keep glancing at his clock radio.

2:44 . . . 2:45 . . . 2:46 . . .

Time. The concept of the territories existing in different times was a hard one to understand. Did Zadaa exist in the future of Second Earth? Or in the ancient past? Was the war between the tribes on the verge of happening? Or had it been over for centuries? Or did it all exist simultaneously? That was the strangest concept, but the one that was most probable. Halla was explained to him as everything—all time all places all people. Everything that ever was, or will be, all existing in some way, together. It was one of the reasons the Travelers were able to arrive on a territory when they needed to be there. Whatever grand power was controlling it all, it knew how to manipulate time. Or more precisely, it knew how to control their movements through time. That was how Mark and Courtney were able to be on Eelong for a month, and return to Second Earth only a few minutes after they'd left. He figured it was also what allowed Saint Dane to bounce back and forth between territories, messing with one while lurking around another. It seemed to Mark that time was actually some giant sea that you could swim around in and travel any which way. It also seemed to Mark that the more he thought about the whole bizarre concept, the less chance there was of him getting any sleep.

3:58 . . . 3:59 . . . 4:00 . . .

He wished he could take a couple of strokes forward in the sea of time and jump to 6:00. When the digital clock hit 5:00, Mark couldn't take it anymore. He got out of bed and decided to kill the last hour on his computer. He opened his Web browser and did a search for Stansfield in the Berkshire Mountains of Massachusetts. He found the Web site instantly and took a virtual tour. He decided it was a pretty nice place and a cool way to spend the summer. He wondered if Saint Dane felt the same way.

Finally, when his clock hit 5:30, Mark had had enough. He had practiced his speech to Courtney a thousand times. He had to make the call. He got up from his computer and sat back on his bed. Now that he actually had to do this for real, he had second thoughts.

He picked up the cell phone . . . and put it back down again.

He had to convince himself again that he was doing the right thing. He picked up the phone. He put it down. He picked it up. It was time. Courtney was on speed-dial: #1. He finally looked at the phone to make sure it was on and—

"Message waiting?" Mark said out loud.

Mark had never gotten a message on his cell phone before. He had no idea who could have called him. And when? He almost always had his phone in his pocket, how could he have missed a call? He stared at the blinking words. He didn't even know how to retrieve a message. He had to rummage through his cluttered desk to find the instruction manual. By the time he found the manual, waded through the table of contents, flipped through the French, Spanish, and Japanese sections to the English instructions, and finally found the right buttons to push to get his message, it was nearly six o'clock. Mark actually laughed to himself. He had made it to six after all.

The prerecorded voice over the phone said, "Message sent yesterday at seven forty-five P.M."

Mark realized he'd been downstairs eating dinner then. That's why he hadn't heard the ring. He continued to listen. There was a beep, followed by the message. What he heard made Mark want to fall through the floor.

It was Courtney. Her voice was weak, but it was definitely hers. In a frail voice she gasped, "Mark, he's here."

That was it. Abruptly there was another beep, and the prerecorded voice came back on, saying, "End of message." Mark stared at the phone, his heart racing. He played the message over and over and over again. There was no doubt in his mind. Courtney was in trouble, and he feared the reason why. He speed-dialed her number, but got the prerecorded voice saying, "The number you are trying to reach is not available." Mark wanted to throw the phone across the room. Courtney always had her cell phone on, except in class. But it was six o'clock in the morning! No class started that early. Something was very, very wrong.

The police! He'd call the local police! Yes!

No! And tell them what? That he thinks his friend is in trouble? Trouble from what? An interstellar dimension-leaping demon who wanted to trash the universe? Yeah, that would go over real big. He thought about filing a missing person report, but how could he say he knew she was missing? And was she really missing anyway? He didn't know. They'd laugh him off the phone. At the very least, they'd ignore him. He thought maybe his parents could help. He was about to leave the room to get them, but stopped when he realized he had no idea what he would ask them to do, either.

The more Mark thought through his options, the more he realized there was only one thing for him to do. He had to get to Stansfield as soon as possible. He needed to find Courtney so they could work this through together. Nobody else knew what they knew. Nobody else could help. They needed to be together.

Now that he had a plan, Mark felt better. He went online to check bus and train schedules between Stony Brook, Connecticut and Derby Falls, Massachusetts. He planned on telling his parents that Courtney invited him up to visit for a few days. If they wouldn't let him go, he'd go anyway. He didn't like to disobey his parents, but there were bigger issues at stake. He'd deal with the consequences later. Whatever they were, they would be easier to handle than Saint Dane.

He struck out with mass transit. The fastest combination of bus and trains wouldn't get him to Derby Falls until late that night. Twelve hours! According to Mapquest, it was only a three-hour drive! Mark began weighing the possibility of getting his mother to drive him, when another idea hit. The concept made him physically shudder, but he was desperate. He grabbed his cell phone and scrolled through the list of phone numbers from incoming calls. He didn't get many. He easily found what he was looking for. Before he had the chance to overthink himself out of it, he closed his eyes and made the call.

Two hours later Mark was riding shotgun on his way to Stansfield Academy.

Behind the wheel was Andy Mitchell.

⊘ SECOND EARTH ⊘
(CONTINUED)

"Let's do a little math here," Andy Mitchell said. "And I'm good at this, so you can't argue. I called you for help and it took about, what, an hour out of your busy schedule? You, on the other hand, call me at six in the morning and ask me to drive three hours up to the sticks, so you can see a chick I can't stand, and doesn't like me so much either. Is that about right?"

"Uh, yeah, that pretty much sums it up," Mark said sheepishly. "But you said if I ever needed a favor—"

"I did," Mitchell said, snorted, and hawked a lougie out the driver's window.

Mark nearly retched. He was grateful the window was open.

"All I'm saying is, this don't make us square," Mitchell said. "The way I see it, I'm in for six, seven hours plus here. After this, *you* owe *me*."

This was killing Mark. The idea of relying on Andy Mitchell for anything was worse than swallowing metal shavings. To know he was now indebted to the creep made him want to jump out of the car while they were doing sixty-five on the Connecticut Turnpike. To top it all off, since he helped Mitchell deliver the flowers that morning, there was nothing covering the rancid smell in the car anymore. What else did Andy use this car for? Stashing bodies for the mob? The only thing that kept Mark from losing it was knowing how important it was that he find Courtney.

"I'm really grateful," Mark said.

"Yeah, we'll see," Mitchell said.

Mark closed his eyes and pretended to be asleep.

"Why do you got to see her so bad?" Mitchell asked. "I thought she had the hots for Pendragon?"

"The truth?" Mark asked.

"No, I want you to lie," Mitchell said sarcastically. "Sheesh."

Mark had no intention of telling the whole truth, but it was going to be awkward once they got there. He figured he had to tell some version of the truth. "I'm worried about her," Mark said.

"Chetwynde?" Mitchell scoffed. "She's the last chick I'd worry about."

"Yeah, well, I think somebody might be giving her a hard time, and I want to make sure she's okay," Mark said.

"And you got this brainstorm at six o'clock in the morning?" Mitchell asked.

Mark shrugged and said, "I couldn't sleep."

Mitchell shook his head in dismay and said, "Some guy is giving Chetwynde grief and you want to swoop in like Batman to protect her?"

"I'm more of a Superman guy," Mark said.

Mitchell laughed. "You're nuts is what you are. Maybe it's a good thing you called me."

Strangely enough, Mark was thinking the same thing. He didn't want to be doing this alone. He wondered what Courtney would say when he showed up with Andy Mitchell. He hoped she'd get a good laugh out of it. He hoped to hear her laugh about anything.

Mark didn't hate the drive. Once the "you owe me/I owe you" conversation was over, they began talking about Sci-Clops. It was the one topic they had in common. Mitchell told Mark all about the process he went through to develop the elastic metal with the incredible tensile strength that he had demonstrated at his first meeting of Sci-Clops. Mark was fascinated to hear Mitchell describe how he was trying to find a way to create something with the durability of metal and the flexibility of plastic. The trick was to find the elements that would form an ionic bond on the atomic level to create an entirely new compound. Much of it was trial and error, and he said how he was still a long way off, but the professors at the university thought that what he'd done so far was pretty impressive.

Impressive was the word. It never failed to amaze Mark to listen to Andy when he spoke about his passion for math and science. It simply didn't jive with the slug personality of this guy who drove with one hand and kept pushing his greasy, dirty blond hair out of his eyes with the other. The guy was gross . . . and genius.

Not to be outdone, Mark told Andy more about the killer robot he had made that won so many competitions. He explained how the secret wasn't in the hardware, but the software. Mark had never told anyone about this before, but hearing about Mitchell's successes with his new compound, he felt as if he needed to show off a little too. He confided in Mitchell that he had been working on a new processing code that actually streamlined the binary flow through the processor of the computer that ran his robot. The result was that the clock speed of the standard microprocessor was dramatically increased, which translated to faster commands to the hardware, and therefore a robot that could react and attack way faster—with more programmed moves—than its competition. Mark admitted that it was all pretty crude at this point, but he hoped to develop it further so that at some point he might catch the interest of one of the big tech companies.

After hearing his story, Mitchell looked at Mark. He didn't say anything, he just looked at him.

"What?" Mark asked nervously.

"That's incredible," was all Mitchell said. "Absolutely incredible."

It sounded to Mark as if he meant it too. For the first time, Mark felt as if Andy Mitchell had respect for him. Not that it mattered. Impressing Andy Mitchell wasn't Mark's lifelong ambition. Yet it was an interesting moment. Mark actually felt a connection with this guy. Was it possible? Could they be friends?

He didn't have long to think about it, because a second later his ring began to twitch.

Mark didn't have time to fret about the bad timing. He quickly stuck his hand in his pocket and said, "I'm whipped. I'm gonna lie down in back."

Before Mitchell could react, Mark clicked open his seat belt and vaulted into the back of the ancient station wagon.

"Take it easy!" Mitchell shouted. "I ain't got no insurance."

Mark's ring was already growing. He pulled it off and crouched into a fetal position, trying to hide it and block the spewing light. He spotted an old, stained tarp in the back. Without a second thought he grabbed it and covered the ring, which had already grown. The tarp kept the light show hidden too. The only thing he couldn't hide was the music. The jumble of notes grew louder in spite of the fact it was muffled by the tarp.

"What are you doing?" Mitchell asked. "You got a Game Boy back there?"

"I-It's my watch alarm," Mark said, thinking fast. "It's a weird tone, I know. I think it's busted."

Andy Mitchell looked at his watch. "Why's your alarm set for eight forty-five?"

"Uh, th-that's when I get up. Usually."

The notes grew louder.

"Geez, turn it off, will ya!" Mitchell complained. "It's making me crazy!"

"Yeah, I'm trying. I can't find the button."

Mark prayed for the event to end. A second later he felt the ring shrink back to normal as the musical notes abruptly stopped.

"Thank you!" Mitchell said. "Jeez."

Mark felt around under the tarp until he touched the roll of paper that had come through the ring. Bobby's next journal had arrived. Mark was certain that contained in its pages would be the result of the war on Zadaa. But he couldn't read it. Not yet. It killed him, but he had to put it away until they found Courtney.

"You all right back there?" Mitchell asked.

"Y-Yeah, fine. I'm gonna sleep, okay? Let me know when we get close."

"Yes, ma'am."

Without looking at the journal, Mark slipped it into his backpack. In spite of the fact that he hadn't slept all night, he wasn't the least bit tired. But he had to play out the lie. So he lay there, wide awake, staring at the stained ceiling of Mitchell's station wagon. He tried not to think about the journal that was only inches from his head. First things first. He had to find Courtney.

The drive took a little over three hours. Andy Mitchell kept to the speed limit, which wasn't all that hard considering his beater of a car rattled like it was going to fall apart whenever they got up any real speed. Mitchell followed the directions that Mark had printed out from Mapquest. It got them to the front gates of Stansfield Academy shortly after ten in the morning.

"Nice place," Mitchell said. "I always figured Chetwynde had bucks."

"It is pretty nice," Mark agreed.

"So? How do we find her?" Mitchell asked.

Mark had already thought this through. He got the map of the school he had printed out from their Web site. They parked in the visitors parking lot and went to the registration office. Mark put on his most polite voice and introduced himself to the secretary as Courtney Chetwynde's brother. He said they were visiting and needed to know where her dorm was. Mark was so polite that the woman had no problem giving him the information. It helped that Mark had Andy wait out in the corridor. He was sure that if the woman got a look at Andy Mitchell, they'd be lucky not to be thrown out on their butts. With the information in hand, Mark and Andy walked quickly across the campus to Courtney's dorm. Within minutes they were standing in front of the old, ivy-covered brick building.

"One problem," Mark said. "It's an all-girl dorm. They don't allow guys in to—"

"Gee, yeah, that's a big problem," Mitchell said, and walked right in. Andy Mitchell wasn't big on following the rules.

It was an old building, with dark mahogany wood paneling everywhere and a wide staircase that led to the second floor. Courtney's room was #219. The guys took the stairs up, two at a time. Her room was at the end of a long corridor with old, thick carpeting that smelled kind of musty. Mark knocked softly.

"Courtney? It's Mark."

No answer. Mark knocked again.

"You there, Courtney?"

Still no answer.

Andy pushed Mark aside and pounded on the door a few times, yelling, "Hey! Wake up!"

Nobody answered.

"Now what?" Mark asked.

"Not a problem," Mitchell said. "I have a technique I developed for just such an occasion. It took me a while to master this. It's very precise. Observe."

Mitchell took a step back . . . and kicked open the old door.

"Andy!" Mark yelled.

"Hey, you said she was in trouble. What's an old door lock?"

Mark figured Andy was right. He truly didn't care about the door, so long as they didn't get arrested. They entered the room, quickly closing the door behind them.

Courtney wasn't there. Her single bed was made, her English lit books were stacked neatly on her desk. Mark took a quick look around and saw no other books.

"Her algebra-trig book isn't here," he announced. "She must be in class."

"Nice going, Sherlock," Mitchell said. "Let's go find it."

As they left the room, they ran into a girl who was wheeling her bike along the corridor, headed to the room across from Courtney's. She stared at them suspiciously.

"Hi," Mark said. "My name's Mark Dimond. I'm a friend of Courtney's."

"Oh yeah," the girl said, relaxing. "She's talked about you."

"I'm Andy Mitchell," Andy said, trying to be charming. "I'm her friend too."

"Yeah?" the girl said. "She never mentioned you."

The charming smile fell from Andy's face.

The girl asked, "Is she sick?"

"I don't know, why?" Mark asked back.

"Cuz she didn't show up for lit class this morning."

Mark's mind raced. Her lit books were still on her desk. He had to force himself to keep cool.

"I don't know. We just got here. Maybe she's with that guy she's been hanging out with. What's his name? Wimpy?"

The girl chuckled. "Whitney. Whitney Wilcox. Could be. They're always together."

"Where does he live?" Mark asked.

"I don't know," the girl answered. "Check with the registrar.

And when you find Courtney, tell her I picked up her assignment."

"Thanks," Mark said. "I will."

He grabbed Andy by the arm, and the two hurried off.

"Who is this wimpster dude?" Mitchell asked. "The guy we've got to rough up?"

"No," Mark said. "There's somebody else."

"Two guys?" Mitchell said with surprise. "Chetwynde's keeping busy. What's the deal?"

"Look, Andy, I don't mean to be mysterious, but this is Courtney's business."

"It was," Mitchell said quickly. "But you made it *our* business."

Mark was afraid it would come to this. He knew Mitchell would start asking questions he didn't want to answer, even if he could. But he knew he had to tell Mitchell something.

"All I know is that she's been seeing some guy, but then there's another guy who's been bothering her. I wanted to come up here to give her support. That's pretty much it." Mark thought that, in some simplistic way, that was the truth. He could only hope that Andy Mitchell would buy it.

"Whatever," Mitchell said. "Let's do what we gotta do and go home."

The two went back to the registrar's office to see if they could find Whitney Wilcox. After a long search by the secretary through the school's computer records, she announced to Mark that there was no Whitney Wilcox registered at Stansfield. Mark's radar instantly went up. A vague feeling of dread began to rise. There was no record of a Whitney Wilcox. But Courtney knew him. So did Courtney's neighbor. He was a real guy, but he wasn't. Was it possible? Mark's heart started to race again. His head went light. He had to run out of the registrar's office. Every bit of news he uncovered was bad, and getting worse. Andy followed him and stopped him on the stairs outside.

"What is going on?" Andy asked.

Mark had a double dilemma. He had to pull his thoughts together, and tell Andy what was going on in such a way that kept the truth hidden.

"I-I'm not sure," Mark said breathlessly. "I'm b-beginning to think that the guy who Courtney was seeing is the same guy who was giving her trouble."

"How much trouble could a guy named Wimpley cause?" Andy scoffed.

"Enough," was all Mark said.

Andy thought about that answer, then asked, "Is this big-time, going-to-the-cops-style trouble?"

Good question. If Courtney was missing, then they absolutely had to tell the police.

"I-I don't know," Mark said. "M-Maybe. I gotta think this through. Courtney called me yesterday. She said she had a date last night with this Whitney guy. They—they were going for pizza in town. She said she was riding to meet him."

"Riding. Not driving. She said riding?" Mitchell asked.

"Yeah, I'm sure of it."

"There wasn't a bike in her room," Mitchell offered.

"Right," Mark said. "Then she had an English class this morning, but her books were still on her desk."

"So you're thinking she rode her bike to meet this guy last night and never made it back to her room?" Mitchell asked.

"I don't know," Mark answered. "There's more. Later last night I got a phone message from Courtney. She sent it around seven thirty, right around the time she was supposed to meet Whitney. She sounded bad, like she might have been hurt. I didn't hear it until this morning. That's when I called you."

"What did she say?"

Mark had to lie. Her real message wouldn't have made sense to Andy. "I couldn't tell. It was garbled. But it was definitely her and she sounded bad . . . like she may be hurt."

"Are you serious?" Mitchell screamed, genuinely upset. "Why didn't you tell me that before? Never mind, it don't matter. I'm the last one to be saying this, but we gotta tell the cops."

"You think?" Mark asked.

"If she was riding her bike to meet some mystery guy and right about that same time she called you sounding like she was hurt, I'd say there's more going on here than a date for pizza."

Mark had to admit that Andy was making perfect sense. Right now this had nothing to do with Saint Dane's plan to rule Halla. Courtney was in trouble, for real, here on Second Earth.

"You're right," Mark said. "Let's drive into town and find the police station."

They both hopped into Andy's car and drove off campus, headed for town. Mark was grateful that Andy had actually taken charge. His mind was in so many different places, worrying about so many things, that he couldn't see the obvious. After what they had found at Stansfield, Mark felt certain it was time to report Courtney missing. He didn't think anybody would laugh at him now.

They drove along the quiet country lane that led through the beautiful farm country and up into the Berkshires. Mark stared out the window, in a trance, thinking that this would have been the same route Courtney took the night before. He didn't even register how lovely the countryside was. He was too busy thinking about Courtney. And Saint Dane. And doomsday. The road grew steep as it left the pasture and snaked along the side of a craggy mountain. Off to the right was a dense pine forest. Mark turned his gaze to the road in front of them. They were headed toward some blind curves. Mark's palms started to sweat. He thought that if another car were coming around the curve ahead, and took the turn a little too wide, there would be a head-on. Without thinking, he gripped the elbow rest of the car.

That's when he saw it.

"Stop!" Mark shouted.

Andy jammed on the brakes, skidding to an abrupt stop.

"What?" he yelled. "What happened?"

"Look!" Mark said, pointing ahead.

Andy looked forward and said, "Look at what?"

"The road," Mark said. "Look at those skid marks. There was trouble here."

Sure enough, there was a set of dark skid marks that started in the opposite lane, crossed over the center line into their lane, and stopped just before the steep edge that dropped off into the pine forest below.

"Whoa," Andy said when he registered the skid marks. "Those are fresh."

Andy pulled the car as far over to the side as possible. The two got out to examine the skid. Mark saw that the marks led to the shoulder just off the road, where there were two imprints from the front tires of a car.

"Looks like the car came down from above, hit the brakes, and skidded to a stop right here," Mark said.

"Lucky guy," Mitchell added. "Two more feet and . . . banzai!"

Mark walked to the edge of the road and looked out over the forest below. There was a short, steep clear section before the pine forest began. Mark saw what he thought might be a gouge taken out of a tree several yards below them. It looked fresh.

"What're you thinking?" Andy asked.

"Nothing," Mark said. "We should keep going before we get hit."

Andy started back for his wagon. Mark hesitated a moment. Something was keeping him here. He had no idea what it was. He was starting back toward the car when his eye caught something. It was off the side of the road, a few yards farther up the hill, stuck in a bush. The only reason he saw it was that it was bright red against the green foliage. He was ready to ignore it and get going, but something about it bugged him. Looking around, Mark realized that it wasn't so much that there was a piece of bright red trash on the side of the road, as that it was the *only* piece of trash. Living in a heavily populated area, Mark was used to seeing garbage strewn along the sides of the roads. It was a sad fact of life. Glancing around here, everything was as clean as Disneyland. Not a single piece of trash littered the road, except for this bright red something.

"What're you doing?" Andy asked. "Let's go!"

"Hang on," Mark said.

He carefully stepped down off the shoulder onto the steep pitch of the hill. He walked to the bush, tripping over rocks and getting thorns caught in his jeans. He reached into the bush and pulled out the piece of trash. As soon as he lifted it, he saw that it wasn't trash at all. It was a book. A textbook.

An algebra-trig textbook.

Mark's eyes went wide. His adrenaline spiked. He looked out onto the forest and screamed, "Courtney? *Courtney?*"

"Are you crazy?" Mitchell asked.

Mark threw the book to Andy. "She's here," he said breathlessly. "There was an accident. She's here!"

Mark tripped down the hill, headed for the forest and the tree with the gouge taken out of it. Andy Mitchell shrugged and followed. It was so steep, Mark nearly took a header. But he kept going. He got to the tree and saw that the gouge was definitely fresh.

"Courtney!" he yelled.

He looked around the silent forest, scanning for any clues. He got a big one. A few yards farther down the hill was a bike. Mark ran to it and quickly realized what had made the gouge in the tree. The bike's handlebars were bent into a right angle.

"Is it hers?" Andy asked as he ran to meet Mark.

"Yeah," Mark said, his panic rising. "If she was on this when it went over the edge, then she—"

The words froze in Mark's throat. A few yards to his left he saw a hint of something that was dark green. Courtney had a dark green backpack. Mark leaped for it, picked it up . . . and came upon the body of his friend Courtney Chetwynde.

"It's her!" he shouted. "Call nine-one-one!"

"Holy jeez," Andy said, stunned. He fumbled to pull his cell phone out of his pocket. He nearly dropped it. Twice. "What's the number again?" he stammered nervously.

Mark shot him a look. Andy nodded, feeling dumb. He dialed.

Mark bent down to Courtney. Her long brown hair was a tangle over her face. Her left arm was bent back at a strange angle. He could see that her right hand was on her cell phone. He now knew how she'd made the call to him. He bent down and brushed the hair out of Courtney's eyes.

"Is she . . . ," Andy asked. He couldn't bring himself to finish the sentence.

Mark summoned his courage and put two fingers to her neck, looking for a pulse.

"C'mon, Courtney," Mark whispered. "You're there. I know you're there."

He felt around. There was no pulse. Her skin felt cold to his touch. Mark's heart sank. If only he had gotten her message earlier! He began to cry.

"I'm so sorry, Courtney," he said softly.

"Yeah, this is an emergency," Andy spoke into the phone. "We're on a road between the fancy Stansfield school and the town. Derby Falls. There's been an accident. A girl is hurt off to the side. Bad. You can't miss my car—it's parked on the side of the road. We're down in the woods. Hurry, all right?"

He disconnected the call and looked at Mark. "What do you think?"

Mark was in tears. "I don't know. I can't feel a pulse."

Andy Mitchell bent down next to Courtney. He gently picked up her hand.

"Be careful!" Mark said. "If she hurt her back—"

"I know, I know," Andy replied.

He grasped Courtney's hand in both of his. Mark was surprised at how gentle he was. Andy Mitchell was definitely full of surprises. Andy held her hand in his for several seconds while looking at Courtney. He then moved his fingers toward the underside of her wrist. He placed two there, and waited.

Mark's heart was ready to burst.

"I got it," Andy said softly. "It ain't strong, but it's there."

Mark was stunned. There was hope!

"Keep her warm!" Mark said while taking off his sweatshirt. He gently placed it down over Courtney. "We gotcha, Courtney," he said. "Help is coming. You're gonna be okay."

Within minutes a fire truck and ambulance arrived from Derby Falls. The EMTs dove into the woods and went right to work. They quickly checked Courtney's vitals to find she was indeed alive. They expertly immobilized her by putting her onto a fracture board. With Mark and Andy's help, they carefully pulled her out of the woods and got her into the ambulance. Fifteen minutes after Andy put in the 911 call, Courtney was on her way to the hospital.

The next few hours were like a blur to Mark. He and Andy answered a ton of questions from the police, and made sure that Courtney's parents knew what had happened. Mr. and Mrs. Chetwynde were on their way to Derby Falls minutes later. Mark told the police about the mysterious guy Courtney was supposed to meet, Whitney Wilcox. He knew the police would question people at the school. He knew they'd find people who knew Courtney was hanging out with Whitney. He knew it would all be a waste of time. They would never find him, because he didn't exist. At least, not in the normal sense. He may not have been a student at Stansfield, but he was very real.

And he was out there.

Throughout this ordeal, there was one question that was more important than all the others. Nobody could say for sure if Courtney was going to survive. The only information Mark and Andy got was that she had some broken bones, but her real problem came from internal injuries. There was a lot of bleeding. She was in surgery, and it would be a while before anybody knew if she would live. All they could do was wait and hope.

Andy Mitchell wanted to get something to eat. Mark didn't want to leave the hospital, so Andy volunteered to bring something back. Throughout, Mark thought, Andy had been terrific. He was turning out to be a good friend. How strange was that? Once Andy left on his hunt for food, Mark was faced with a long wait before Courtney would be out of surgery. He sat in the quiet waiting lounge with nothing to do . . .

Except read the next journal from Bobby Pendragon. He took a quick look around to make sure nobody was watching, and pulled the journal out of his pack. He expected to see the familiar, crusty brown roll of parchment paper that all the journals from Zadaa had used. He didn't. This roll of paper was bright, lemon yellow and tied with a purple bow. It looked like something you'd get at a kid's birthday party. When Mark unrolled it, he saw that Bobby's writing was done in bright purple ink. He had no idea what the significance of any of it was, but didn't spend too much time wondering about it.

It was time to read.

ZADAA

I've now written twenty-two journals to you guys. I've described the amazing things I've seen and the impossible truths I've learned. This journal will be no different. I'm going to tell you about the invasion of the underground. It happened. We couldn't stop it. Zadaa has been changed forever.

Obviously, I survived. As I'm writing this journal, my hand is shaking. Nervous energy, I guess. I think it's because I'm having trouble understanding the truths I've learned since I last wrote. I don't know what to think. It's all so confusing. The battle may be over, but I'm more scared than before. It's because I'm afraid to face the person I've become. The frightening truth is that I'm not the same as when I left home with Uncle Press. I guess that goes without saying. Nobody stays the same forever, especially after having gone through what I have. But understanding that in my head, and accepting it in my heart are two different things.

What's actually bothering me more is that in reality, I may not have changed as much as I think. I know, I'm contradicting myself. Let me explain. The way I've always thought about what's happened to me is that I was a normal kid who, for reasons I have yet to figure out, was chosen to be the

Traveler from Second Earth. Nobody ever told me what those reasons were, but the decision was made and off I went.

Now I'm beginning to think it didn't exactly happen that way. Since I wrote you last, I've learned some things about myself that I can't explain. There are things I'm able to do that aren't exactly normal. At least they aren't normal for a kid who grew up in Stony Brook, Connecticut. I'm not just talking about the ability to be persuasive. Compared to what I've just done, that's about as impressive as a card trick. There's more. A whole lot more. That's why my hand is shaking.

I'm confused. But I'm also upset. Take my word for it, it's a strange feeling to realize you aren't the person you thought you were. One of the things that's kept me going this whole time has been my base. My home. You guys. Stony Brook. And of course, the hope that I will one day find my family again and get back to normal. Now I'm beginning to wonder if I truly belong on Second Earth. Or ever belonged there. What makes it worse is that if that's true, I have no idea where I *do* belong.

I don't mean to sound so sorry for myself. I think you guys know that writing this all down helps me sort it out in my own head. I wish it would help me find some real answers. So far those have been few and far between. All I can do is look ahead, and keep searching.

I've got to tell you what brought me to this point. I suppose I should stop whining about my own pathetic state of mind and be grateful that I'm still around to write at all. I've got to reset my head, back to where it was only a short while ago, so I can get this all down. I finished my last journal when Loor and I were hiding with Teek, the Tiggen guard. The fuse was lit. There was about to be an invasion that would determine the future of Kidik, the Batu, the Rokador . . . and the entire territory of Zadaa.

We were safely hidden in a remote room deep below the main building on Kidik Island. No Tiggen guard would look for us there, and if the Batu attacked and the water was released, we would survive. Hopefully. Teek was off trying to get more information about the elite's plan. That left Loor and me to regroup and plot our next move.

"We've got a couple of choices," I said. "We can warn the Batu that they're headed into a trap and hope they back off—"

"It is too late for that," Loor interjected. "They were preparing to attack when we left Xhaxhu."

"Okay. Then we can try to convince the Rokador elite that by wiping out the Batu, they would doom the rest of their tribe, because killing the Ghee warriors would leave them exposed to attack by the cannibal tribes of Zadaa."

"That is not likely either," Loor said. "Their hatred and fear of the Batu runs too deep."

"I agree," I said. "Which leaves us with the third option."

"And what is that?" Loor asked.

I hated to say what I was about to say. It went against all we had been doing to defeat Saint Dane, and against my nature. It definitely went against Loor's nature, but it seemed to be the only choice.

"We can leave," I said.

Loor shot me a surprised look. "Leave? I do not understand."

"I think Saint Dane has won," I said. "I don't know how we can stop this."

"You are suggesting we abandon Zadaa and allow the territory to crumble?" Loor asked.

I didn't answer right away because that's *exactly* what I was suggesting, and it sounded rotten. This was tough. We were talking about Loor's home.

"I'm sorry, Loor," I said. "But we have to look at the big

picture. We've already lost Kasha. Spader and Gunny are trapped on Eelong. The battle here on Zadaa is going to happen—"

"It will not be a battle; it will be a mass execution," Loor said coldly.

"You're right," I said. "But whatever happens here on Zadaa, you and I must survive to continue the fight against Saint Dane. We have to think of all of Halla, not just one territory."

Loor showed no emotion. She looked me square in the eyes. I wanted to be able to read her mind to know what she was thinking. Or maybe I didn't. She might not have had such a hot opinion of me just then.

"I understand, Pendragon," she said calmly. "Protecting all of Halla is of more importance than saving one territory. Your decision is a wise one. I will get you back to the flume."

"Good," I said, though I wasn't happy about it. "I know how you must feel—"

"I am sure you do," Loor interrupted. "That is why I know you will understand when I say that I cannot leave Zadaa."

"Why?" I asked in surprise. "You can't stop this."

"Perhaps not," she said. "But I could not live with myself if I did not try. I agree that losing you would be a crushing blow in the fight against Saint Dane. I, on the other hand, would not be missed."

"You are so wrong—"

"Please, Pendragon. My mind is made up. Perhaps I can stop some of the Batu from descending into the underground. Saving even a few lives would be worth the effort. Whoever is left alive will be needed to defend Xhaxhu from the marauders."

I knew it was useless to argue.

"Come," Loor said. "We must not waste more time."

I felt like a coward. Though my brain told me it was the right move, my heart wasn't so sure. I had never given up before. I guarantee Loor had never given up. Ever. She wasn't giving up now, either. I didn't feel as if I had a choice. I had to force myself to think of all of Halla. Losing a battle wasn't the same as losing the war. I tried to convince myself that I wasn't running away, I was running toward the next battle. I hoped that by the time we made it back to the flume, *if* we made it to the flume, I could convince Loor to leave with me.

We left the small room and moved quickly through the labyrinth of underground tunnels, looking for the way to the surface of Kidik Island. We no longer feared running into a Tiggen guard. We knew there weren't many left. Our plan was to get back to the beach, take the boat to the city of Kidik, and drive the dygo back to the flume. My biggest fear was that we would run into the first wave of Ghee warriors, and the show would be over. All we could do was keep moving, and hoping.

We finally popped out of the underground in a familiar area. We were on the ground level of the vast cemetery where most of the Rokador population was buried. Seeing all those white markers with the small flame burning on each was a gut-wrenching sight. It was hard to grasp the concept that so many had died—and so many more were soon to follow. The two of us stood looking out over the sea of death, humbled and sad.

"Why?" Loor asked. "Why is any of this happening?"

She didn't expect an answer. She knew I didn't have one. There was only one person who could answer that question. As it turned out, he was standing right behind us.

"Not guilty," Saint Dane said.

Loor and I both whipped around quickly, pulling out our weapons.

Saint Dane was alone. He stood there with his arms out, showing that he wasn't armed and not interested in fighting. "Please, there is no need for violence," he said. He circled around us, walking to the edge of the cemetery. He looked out over the thousands of markers with a small smile. I hated this guy.

"Such a tragedy," he said.

"Yeah, right, like you care," I said.

"Correct. I don't care," Saint Dane said. "The tragedy is that I had nothing to do with it."

Loor took an angry step toward him. I held her back.

"You're saying you didn't prevent these people from using the cure until it was too late?" I asked. "I don't believe you."

"It's true," he said. "The virus was a natural occurrence. I simply used the event to my advantage. It was the turning point on Zadaa . . . that, and the death of Pelle a Zinj. Thank you, by the way, for delivering him to the assassin. Without your help, the Batu may never have decided to attack. It was a nice little piece of insurance."

I could feel Loor's anger radiate from her like heat. I kept a hand on her shoulder to calm her.

"We know the plan," I said. "We heard your performance at the—"

"At the banquet with the elite, yes, I know," Saint Dane said. "I felt your beady little eyes staring at me through the hole in the floor, like rats. I thought I was quite remarkable, didn't you?"

His arrogance was pissing me off, but I couldn't let him get to me.

"I don't get it," I said. "What's different this time? Why haven't you taken on a disguise?"

"Because I didn't need to," he said casually. He turned to

face us. His expression grew dark. "And because I wanted you to see how simple it is for me to control these creatures. To me, that's what Zadaa is about, Pendragon. A demonstration. I wanted you to see, firsthand, how weak the people of the territories are. How stupid. How their emotions control their actions. You believe they have noble aspirations? That they would make sacrifices for the greater good? That they care for anyone or anything outside their selfish little orbits? I say the people of the territories are no better than common animals. Dangle raw meat in front of a starving rodent and he will kill his own to get it. That's who you're working so hard to defend, my misguided friend. You are surrounded by fear, greed, and envy. The Batu, the Rokador—all of them. The Milago and Bedoowan of Denduron. The arrogant agronomers of Cloral, those criminals on First Earth, the klee and gars of Eelong, and the escapists on Veelox. None of them seek the truth. None are willing to suffer or sacrifice for others. They all fear someone else will get more than they have, or they might experience pain, or their lives will be less than what they feel they deserve. You think you're fighting me, Pendragon? You're not. You're fighting the nature of the very people you think you're helping. All I've done is give them what they want."

"No," I said. "That's not what it's about. Of course people will defend themselves if they're afraid, but there's a lot of good in—"

"Good? What is good?" Saint Dane said dismissively. "It's easy for people to be good when they're comfortable and well fed. But that isn't what this existence is about, Pendragon. It's about challenges that you conquer, or fall to. Now the people of Zadaa are about to fall, and I will have made my point once again."

"No!" Loor couldn't take it anymore. She blew past me

and attacked Saint Dane. I have to admit, I wanted her to do it. Saint Dane wasn't fighting me this time. He was taking on the pro. Too bad for him. I wanted Loor to take the demon out. Loor lunged at him with her wooden stave, committing the cardinal sin. She made the first move. Saint Dane easily blocked her attack, reached into his jacket, and pulled out a metal, Tiggen weapon. Before I had a chance to react, he nailed Loor in the chest, sending her crashing to the ground, shaking with pain. I stood there, frozen. I don't know if it was because of the surprise of the sudden violence, or because I saw Loor beaten.

"You wanted her to kill me, didn't you?" he said. "Don't lie. You wanted her to beat me unmercifully like I beat you. You're no better than the worthless creatures you've dedicated yourself to protecting."

I couldn't move. His words hit me hard. He was right. I wanted Saint Dane to hurt as badly as he hurt me. Had I just proven his point? Was I no better than an animal who only knew to attack when threatened?

"What are you feeling, Pendragon?" Saint Dane seethed. "How will it make you feel when I touch this weapon to her head, and melt her brain?"

Saint Dane lowered the metal baton toward Loor. I was too far away to stop him. His white-blue eyes had frozen me in place. Loor was about to die, and I was too far away to stop it.

From the corner of my eye I saw a sudden flash of silver. An instant later Saint Dane screamed out in pain and dropped his weapon. Sticking from his arm was a silver arrow. I spun quickly to see someone standing on the balcony above us, holding a crossbow.

"Hello, Mallos," the guy said. "That is what you called yourself on Denduron, no?"

It was Alder! Standing next to him were Saangi and Teek.

Saint Dane clutched his arm, screaming in pain. It didn't last long. The demon turned into a liquid shadow. The silver arrow dropped from the inky cloud and clattered to the ground. The shadow re-formed itself into the same black bird I had seen flying away from the Manhattan Tower Hotel on First Earth. Saint Dane was about to get away. Again. The bird rose into the air, flapped its wings, and sailed off. We all watched it disappear into the darkness that enveloped Kidik Island.

"Ahhhh!" A scream of terror came from the balcony above. It was Teek. I guess he wasn't used to seeing a person turn into a giant crow. Go figure. I glanced up to see him back away from the edge of the balcony in confusion and fear. Alder and Saangi tried to calm him. Good luck. I had no idea what they were going to tell him. But that wasn't my concern. I ran to Loor. She was no longer shaking, but still looked pretty dazed. I knelt down next to her and put my hand on her shoulder, saying, "Relax. You're not hurt. It was just a small jolt."

"That . . . is . . . easy . . . for . . . you . . . to . . . say," Loor said through chattering teeth.

She was going to be okay. I kept my hand on her shoulder, more out of reassurance than anything. Shortly we were joined by Alder, Saangi, and a very nervous-looking Teek who was shaking almost as much as Loor. I stood and hugged Alder. "I can't believe you're here," I said. "Are you all right? When we left, you were barely conscious."

"I believe it was the medicine that made me sleep. I feel better now," he said. He flexed his stiff shoulder and added, "There is some pain, but it did not stop me from taking this from a Tiggen guard." He held up the multiple-shot crossbow. "Interesting weapon."

Loor moved to get up. She was quickly getting her act back together. Saangi helped her sit up.

"You were to take Alder to the flume," Loor scolded.

"Do not blame her, Loor," Alder said. "I would not leave, not while there was still work to be done."

Talk about making me feel guilty. Leaving is exactly what I was about to do.

"How did you find us?" I asked.

"It is my duty to help Loor," Saangi said. "To do that, I did something that will make you angry. Before you left, I copied the map to Kidik. Please forgive me."

Loor stared at Saangi in disbelief.

Saangi kept her eyes to the ground and said, "Once in the underground, we took a dygo and followed the route."

I had to hand it to Saangi. She never gave up. I said, "I guess it was a good thing we sprang all of those traps."

"I did not expect to see an ocean under the ground," Alder said.

"Yeah, no kidding," I shot back. "How did you know enough to cross it?"

"The city was dead," Alder explained. "You were nowhere to be found, and we saw lights across the water. We found a boat, followed the lights, and made it as far as this building."

"That is when we found Teek," Saangi said. "He brought us here. I know this is not what you wanted, Loor, but if we had not come . . ." Saangi didn't have to finish the sentence. We all knew. If they hadn't shown up, Saint Dane would have fried Loor.

"I am not angry, Saangi, I am grateful," Loor said. "Perhaps you should disobey me more often."

Saangi beamed. She had once again proven to be Loor's guardian angel.

"I did not really mean that," Loor added. "But thank you."

"Evil spirits!" a voice shouted. We all looked at Teek. He was standing away from the group, looking spooked.

"Are you okay, Teek?" I asked.

"Evil s-spirits!" he repeated nervously. "He is an evil spirit! Evil!"

Teek wasn't okay. I had to think of something to say that would keep him from going totally insane.

"He's no spirit," I said. "It was a trick. He's full of tricks to fool people."

"He . . . he transformed! And flew!" Teek chattered.

"All a trick," I lied. "But you're right about one thing: He is evil."

Loor got to her feet. She was wobbly, so Saangi had to help her up. "We must get Pendragon to the flume," she said. "He must be kept safe."

"No," I said. I looked at Loor, then Alder, and Saangi. "Saint Dane thinks he's proving a point on Zadaa? I can prove one too. We're seeing this to the end. All of us."

"Are you sure?" Loor asked.

I nodded. I could see her relief.

"The end may come sooner than you think," Saangi said.

"Why's that?" I asked.

"That is another reason we had to come," she answered. "The Batu have entered the underground. The attack has begun."

ZADAA

Loor knew the plans for war, as did Saangi. The Ghee had been preparing for this day for a long time. The invasion would be overwhelming.

"It will begin with dygos," Loor explained. "Ghee spies have stolen dozens of them, of all sizes. They have been kept hidden in the desert. The plan is to drive them into the underground and use them as shields against the defenses of the Tiggen guards. Each dygo will be followed by hundreds of warriors. The dygos will break through any resistance, whether it be rock or Tiggen, clearing the way for the Ghee warriors."

"How do they know where to go?" I asked. "I mean, isn't the underground like a huge spiderweb?"

"It is," Loor answered. "But there have been scouts. They know the general direction of Kidik. They know this is the seat of power. This is the target. They will travel through the tunnels that take them in the proper direction. If there is no tunnel, they will drill one. The attack will be relentless."

"Yeah, until they reach the ocean," I said.

"What will happen then?" Alder asked.

"It's a trap," I answered. "The Rokador are going to flood

the tunnels and drown every Batu who's in the underground."

Saangi shot me a look of surprise. Alder looked just as stunned. I hated to have to put it so bluntly, but we were way past worrying about tact.

"That will be thousands of Batu," Saangi said, her voice suddenly sounding like that of a frightened, little girl.

"Can they truly do that?" Alder asked.

I looked to Teek. He still looked shaken, but his senses were returning.

"What did you find out?" I asked him. "How is this gonna work?"

Teek answered with no emotion. It was as if he were in a trance. His world was crumbling around him, in more ways than one. "The Kidik Ocean is nothing more than a giant holding tank," he began. "It is fed from the north by many distant rivers. The engineers control how much water is let in with giant gates. To the south, near the city, there are many small gates that control the flow to the rivers beneath Xhaxhu. Those are the gates that have been closed to choke off the water and create the drought. The plan is to throw all the gates to the north open, allowing the ocean to rise. The engineers have already begun. I can see that the ocean level is far above normal."

"Isn't that dangerous?" I asked. "I mean, if they let too much in?"

"No," Teek continued. "The next step will be to open the gates to the south. The rivers of Zadaa will flow again, higher and faster than ever before."

I thought back to the deep, dry riverbed near the flume. When I first saw it, the water moved through quickly and powerfully, fed by the tall waterfall. Now the water was long gone, but I could envision water suddenly spewing from the top of the waterfall and crashing down into the dry trough, filling it with a violent, relentless surge. The same would happen to all the dry riverbeds. The water would quickly find its way up to the streets of Xhaxhu, filling the troughs and recharging the fountains. Some on the surface might think this was good news, signaling the end of the drought. They'd be right, at least about the drought being over. Those below would quickly learn that the return of water wasn't such a good thing.

I looked to Loor and said, "When the Ghee see the water suddenly return to the rivers, what will they do?"

Before Loor could answer, Teek said, "They will die. Even if they decide to call off the invasion, there will not be enough time to escape. That is when the final step will be taken. There are giant overflow gates throughout the underground that lead to runoff tunnels. They were designed to carry off excess water should there be a flood, or the control gates malfunction."

"I've seen those," I said. "Giant silver disks built into the tunnel walls?"

"Yes," Teek said. "Today they will be used for another purpose. When the control gates to the south are opened, the gates leading to the runoff tunnels will also be opened. These tunnels will quickly fill with water."

"There is enough water to do all of this?" Loor asked.

"So they say," Teek answered. "The gates to the north will all be opened. Thousands of water sources will be channeled into the ocean. It will take only minutes to fill the overflow tunnels. That's when the overflow gates will be opened, flooding the entire underground."

"Drowning every Batu below," I said.

"And leaving Xhaxhu open to attack by every marauding tribe on Zadaa," added Loor.

"It's a hideous plan," Teek said. "But the elite are convinced it's our only chance of survival."

"They are wrong!" Loor shouted. "Killing the Batu will be their own suicide!"

"Saint Dane has convinced them otherwise," Teek said. "I believe it is a horrible mistake. So did Bokka. He died trying to warn you. I would do anything to stop it, but it is too late."

"Maybe not," I said.

Everyone looked at me with surprise. As Teek was explaining the Rokador plan, I got an idea. It may have been a long shot, but at least it was a shot.

"We cannot stop the Batu," Saangi warned. "It is too late."

"She is right, Pendragon," Alder said. "Saangi showed me the dygo machines gathering in the sands outside of Xhaxhu. There were hundreds of them. We watched as they rose up on legs and began drilling into the ground. They are coming. The only reason we arrived here before them is we had a map. I would not be surprised if they are nearing Kidik as we speak."

Teek added, "With so little time, there is no way to convince the elite of their mistake. The water gates to the north are open. The ocean is rising."

"I know," I said. "We can't stop the attack and we can't stop the Rokador. Our only hope is to control the controller."

"I do not understand," Loor said.

"This all comes down to the water-control device in the center of this building," I said. "If we can't get the elite to stop the flood, maybe we can do it ourselves."

Loor's face brightened. She said, "You mean, seize control of the machinery?"

"Exactly," I said. "Shut it down. Reverse the flow. Whatever." I looked to Teek and asked, "Do any of the other Tiggen guards agree with you? Do they know what a mistake this is?"

"Many do," Teek answered.

"Find them!" I ordered Teek. "Bring them to the master control station. Now!"

"But—"

"Go!" I shouted.

Teek took off running. My mind was in overdrive. This seemed to be our only hope. There was no time for debate. We had to act.

"Wait, stop!" I called to Teek. He put on the brakes.

"Are there any dygos here on Kidik Island?" I asked.

"Yes, there are two housed on the far side of this building."

"Good. Go!"

"Why do you want a dygo?" Loor asked. "To attack the control station?"

"No," I said. "I want a chance of getting our butts out of here after it all hits the fan. We've got to do what we can to save Zadaa, but win or lose, if we're trapped here, Saint Dane wins. The whole thing. Halla. Before we make another move, you all have to promise me something. Whatever happens, there's going to be a point when we've done all we can. Promise me when that time comes, we'll all get out together."

"I agree," Alder said. "That is the wise thing to do."

I looked at Loor. She didn't answer right away. This had to be tough for her. Finally she said, "I understand, Pendragon. You are right. When you say it is time to go, we will go."

I looked at Saangi, and she nodded in agreement.

"Good," I said. "Saangi, can you drive a dygo?"

"I drove here, did I not?" she answered.

"Perfect. You heard Teek. Find one. Bring it here."

Saangi looked to Loor. Loor gave her a reassuring nod.

"Of course," Saangi answered brightly, thrilled to be part

of the plan. She turned and ran off. It was down to the three of us. Me, Loor, and Alder. We exchanged nervous looks. It was a brief moment of calm and a chance for us to catch our breaths.

"Seems like old times," I finally said.

The two nodded knowingly. We had been here before. The three of us. We had become different people than the three kids who fought to save Denduron. Though it had been only a short few years since that battle, we had each gained a lifetime of experience. I could only hope we would be as successful—and lucky.

As the three of us stood there, on the edge of that vast cemetery, there was only one thing I was certain of. These would be the last few quiet moments we would have for a very long time.

ZADAA

In spite of all my bold talk, I had absolutely no idea how we were going to take over the master water controller, or what we would do next if we were lucky enough to pull it off. There was no time to form a plan. No chance to weigh all the options and make the smart choice. We had to go for it, taking it one step at a time and making decisions as we went. One consolation was that I couldn't think of two better people to have with me than Loor and Alder. We had saved one territory together. It was time to save another.

We worked our way back through the maze of tunnels in search of the master control station. Loor's instincts and memory were incredible. With no wrong turns, we soon found ourselves outside the steel door that led to the catwalk over the massive room full of machinery.

Loor gave us both a cautionary look, with a finger to her lips as a signal for us to be quiet. We nodded in understanding. She opened the door, and we stole quickly onto the catwalk that ran high over the master control station. There was more activity going on below than when we were last there. Four engineers were at the controls. Even from as high up as we were, I saw the tension on their faces and in their body language. No big surprise. Carrying out genocide would tend to put people on edge. I wondered what they were thinking. Did they fully understand that their actions would result in the death of thousands? Were they convinced that killing so many was the only way they could save themselves? Or was the reality weighing heavily on them? It didn't matter. They had to be stopped.

Preventing us from doing that would be a handful of Tiggen guards. They stood on the floor of the control room, each at the bottom of a set of steel stairs that led up to the control platform. They seemed pretty relaxed. They weren't expecting an assault on the station. Good news for us.

Looking down on the control-room floor, I knew there would be guards. I knew there would be engineers. I didn't know we'd be joined by a third group. Seated together, in special chairs that had been put there for the occasion, were the ten members of the Rokador elite. They had been gathered, I suppose, to bear witness. Most of them sat attentively, looking edgy. I didn't blame them. The engineers up on the control platform may have been the ones flipping the switches, but the decision to destroy the Batu came from the odd group on the floor. The really old guy was slumped over in his chair again. Asleep and drooling. The two kids fidgeted and poked at each other. Unbelievable. I wondered if their votes counted as much as the others'. I also wondered if they were worried about Saint Dane not being there at the final hour. They must have thought it was strange. I, on the other hand, knew it was perfectly normal. I knew that their buddy, the architect of this horror, had probably hit the flume already, bound for his next territory after a job well done.

The last difference I noticed was the sound. I already told you how this room had a hum to it, like it was full of energy. Now the powerful sound was even more intense. It filled the vast space, making the catwalk vibrate. I could even feel it in the pit of my stomach. I was pretty sure that this machinery had never been put to this kind of test. It was staggering to think that it had the power to move the massive underwater gates that controlled the flow of an entire ocean. I had a brief hope that the machinery would malfunction and save us all a lot of trouble. But we couldn't rely on that. We had to act.

We heard a soft, screeching sound to our left. The door to the catwalk was opening. Loor, Alder, and I sprang to attention. We had been discovered. A second later two Tiggen guards entered. Loor and I pulled out our weapons. Alder shouldered his crossbow, ready to shoot. A third Tiggen guard entered—Alder fired—and I knocked his aim off with my elbow. The steel arrow flew, but embedded itself in the wall over the door, harmlessly. I had thrown off Alder's aim just enough so that he missed killing his target. It was Teek.

I instantly recognized the other two Tiggen guards. They were with Bokka when he brought us to the crossroads. They were friends. The three Tiggens looked up at the steel arrow in the door above them, then back to us with wide eyes that said, "What the heck did you do that for?"

Alder shrugged an apology. I nudged him and Loor to follow me and ran quickly and quietly toward Teek. We all left the catwalk and the machine room, closing the door behind us.

"The water level is rising," Teek said nervously. "And I hear sounds. Across the water. I believe the Ghee invasion is growing close."

"Are you willing to help stop this thing?" I asked, looking at Teek and the others.

Teek answered for the group, saying, "We have trusted Bokka since we were young. We have no reason to stop now. He knew this was wrong. It should be stopped. The question is, how?"

"Do any of you know how that control panel works?" I asked.

The Tiggen guards looked at one another. None seemed ready to jump in with expert advice. Finally Teek took the lead.

"Come," he said, and opened the steel door.

"Wait here," I said to the others. I followed Teek back onto the catwalk where we could look down on the control platform. As I wrote before, this platform was built on top of the huge, horizontal pipe that was half-buried beneath the floor. I'm guessing its deck was about twenty feet off the floor, with metal ladders that led up to it. The control panel itself was centered along the length of the platform, so that the engineers could walk around it. The panel had two sides, was angled like the roof of a house, and each side held a long row of steel handles that looked as if they could be turned one way or the other. Over each handle was some writing that I'm sure described what the control did. Above the writing looked to be gauges of some sort that measured . . . whatever. There were also three white lights over each handle. I saw that in some cases all three lights were lit. Others had only one, still others two or none. The only difference between the sides was that one had larger handles. There seemed to be twice as many of the small handles as there were large ones. Two engineers were on each side, monitoring the gauges, looking tense.

Teek whispered, "The way I understand it is that the larger switches control the giant gates to the north. They are all open now, allowing the ocean to rise. The small switches on the opposite side control the many smaller gates to the south. They are closed, waiting for the moment when the Batu arrive on the far shore."

"So they haven't started sending the water into the dry rivers?" I asked.

"No," Teek said. "They are waiting for the signal. There is a string of Tiggen guards, starting with boats on the ocean and leading back to here. They will pass the word when the Batu are in sight."

I nodded and snuck back to the door. Moments later Teek and I were again with the others.

"We've got a window," I said. "They haven't started the flood. Whatever we're going to do, it's got to be now." I said this while looking at Loor. She was the pro. She would have to come up with our plan of attack.

"Surprise is our best weapon," she said. "But that advantage will not last long. As soon as we make a move, I am sure there will be some sort of alarm. Tiggen guards will descend on us. Even if we successfully take control of the device, we will not hold it for long."

My big plan to take control was suddenly looking not so big.

"What if we seal the entry?" Alder asked.

"You mean, lock ourselves in?" I asked.

Loor said, "It might give the Ghee warriors enough time to arrive on the island and capture the Tiggen guards."

We all looked to Teek and the friendly Tiggen guards. They looked sick. Since returning to Kidik, they had been hit with a pretty harsh dose of reality. It wasn't getting any better. They said they wanted to help, but it now looked as if they would have to battle their own. I was afraid they were having second thoughts.

"You are asking us to fight our brothers and help overthrow our own tribe," Teek said solemnly.

"It's true," I said. "If we do this, the Batu will seize control of the underground. But if we don't, the Ghee warriors will be drowned. That leaves Xhaxhu wide open to be attacked by the marauding tribes of Zadaa."

"Soon after, they will come for you," Loor said.

"Not if the tunnels remain flooded," Teek said hopefully. "We can be safe here on Kidik Island."

"For how long?" Loor asked. "You will starve. All food comes from above. Soon you would have to drain the tunnels and move to the surface, where you would be slaughtered the same as the Batu."

"I know this is hard to understand," I said. "But that is exactly what Saint Dane wants. That's why he led the elite into this plan. It will mean the end of civilization on Zadaa."

"Why would he do such a thing?" Teek asked.

I looked to Loor, and to Alder. There was no easy answer to that question.

"Because he feels that once Zadaa falls apart, he can seize power himself and build his own world from the ruins." That was about as short a thumbnail explanation as I could come up with. I hoped it was enough. "The Batu and the Rokador once existed in peace," I said. "That can happen again. The Rokador can rebuild and grow, but not without the help and protection of the Batu."

Teek said, "I need a moment." He led his two friends away from us for a private chat. Loor, Alder, and I were left to do the same.

"Will they help us?" Alder asked.

"If they don't, it means they're against us," I said while pulling my wooden stave from its sheath. "The battle for the master control room might start right here."

It was a tense moment. We heard the three of them whispering with passion. Finally Teek approached us.

"We will help you seize the master controller," Teek said. "But we will not trap ourselves inside. Whatever fate holds for the rest of our tribe, we will join them and face it together."

Loor nodded and said, "That is both wise and noble. It is the way it should be."

"Okay," I said. "How are we gonna do this?"

Loor's plan was a simple one. We weren't worried about the engineers, or the elite. We had to go right for the Tiggen guards and get them out of the master control room. If anybody else wanted to leave, that was fine by us. The idea was to move fast, take charge, and lock ourselves in before they knew what hit them. And definitely before they started to flood the underground. Teek explained that there was a single entrance on the ground level. That is how we would enter. We decided that one of Teek's friends would remain on the catwalk to seal off the entrance from above. That's as far as our plan took us. After that we'd have to wing it.

With a quick "good luck" to the Tiggen guard who would remain, Teek led us out of the building. We had to quickly move across an open field, away from the sprawling complex, to get to the entrance that would lead down deeper underground to the floor of the master control room. Teek explained that the catwalk entrance and the ground entrance were kept separate in case of emergency. I didn't know what kind of emergency they were planning for, but I was pretty sure this wasn't it.

The entrance was nothing more than a small building, no bigger than a garage. We had gotten halfway across to it when we all heard an odd sound. I was going to keep going, because everything I saw and heard was odd, but Teek stopped short. Whatever was making that sound, it wasn't something he was expecting. Same with the other Tiggen. They stopped abruptly and looked at the sky. Actually, there wasn't any sky to look up at. Above us was the rock ceiling of the immense cavern that held the Kidik Ocean.

"What is that noise?" Alder asked.

I realized that it sounded familiar, though I couldn't place it. Nor could I tell where it was coming from. Since Teek and the others were looking up, I figured it was coming from above. But how could that be? There was nothing up there but a rock ceiling. The sound was a steady, rumbling noise that came from everywhere and nowhere. It actually sounded muffled, as if something were masking the true sound.

"Could it be?" Loor asked, looking up.

"Could it be what?" I asked.

A second later I had my answer. The sound suddenly grew louder, as if whatever was muffling it had been pulled away. The sound instantly became high-pitched and sharp. I realized where I had heard it before.

"It's a dygo!" I shouted.

The reason it was no longer muffled was because it had been drilling through rock and had now broken through. For a second I thought Saangi had found the dygo and was coming to join us. I couldn't have been more wrong. High above, off in the distance, a dygo had broken through the ceiling of the cavern.

"No!" Alder shouted. "They do not know they are drilling down into a cavern!"

"How can a Rokador not know there's a cavern here?" I asked.

"Because that is not a Rokador," Loor said solemnly. "The Batu have arrived."

The sick truth hit me. Whoever was piloting that dygo was drilling down, expecting to hit a tunnel. Instead they hit air. The drill came through first, followed by the familiar silver sphere of a dygo. A moment later gravity took over, and the dygo fell for what had to be a couple of hundred yards. The only minor luck was that it wasn't directly over Kidik Island. It was over water. The dygo plummeted down, its drill spinning uselessly. It was hard to watch. It only took a few seconds, and the dygo splashed down like a space capsule returning to earth without a parachute.

I winced. I couldn't imagine what the passengers were going through.

"Can they survive that?" I asked.

Teek answered, "It's possible. If they were securely strapped in."

Alder said, "But they will drown!"

"No," Teek answered. "The dygo will sink to the bottom. If they are alive and aware, they can drive it across the bottom. There is enough air inside for a short while."

We were still trying to get our minds around what had just happened, when things got worse.

"Look!" one of the other Tiggen guards said.

We all looked up to see the points of six more drills poking through the roof of the cavern. The Batu were arriving in force—and were going to meet with the same fate as their friend in the lead.

"This is horrible!" I shouted. "Is the whole invasion going to crash?"

"No," Loor said. "The plan is to come from many directions. Those Ghee have picked a most unfortunate route."

One by one the dygos drilled through the ceiling and tumbled through the air to splash down into the sea. I couldn't help but watch in horror and hope that the Ghee inside would survive. It was then that another horrible thought hit me.

"If the invasion is here," I said, "we're out of time."

ZADAA

Teek led us into the small building that was the topside entrance to the master control room. Inside was an elevator that took us straight down.

"The doors will open directly onto the control-room floor," Teek explained.

Loor added, "The moment they open, the surprise will be over. We have to move quickly and decisively."

I grasped my wooden stave. This was it. My bystanding days were over. I hoped I was ready. Loor had given us each a target. From the catwalk above, we counted five guards, two on one side, three on the other. If the guards were still at their same posts, we would come out on the side with the three guards. I was to take the first Tiggen guard to the right of the control platform. It was the easiest assignment. If we were fast, the guard wouldn't know what hit him. It would be different with the others. Loor and Teek were to move past me to knock out the guards farther along the platform. Those guards would have more time to react and protect themselves. Alder and our other Tiggen friend would have the toughest job. They had to cross to the far side to take out those two guards. By the time they got there, those guards would know something was going on and be ready. A second, one way or the other, could mean the difference between success and failure.

My palms were sweating. I suddenly had the sick feeling that if my hands got too wet, I'd lose the stave. I wished I had a couple of batting gloves. There wasn't time to stress about it, though. With a thump we hit the floor. The doors slid open. Without a second's hesitation the five of us bolted from the elevator. We didn't shout or scream out a war cry. Every extra second of surprise was precious.

My target's back was to us. He didn't have a clue as to what was about to happen. I ran up behind the guy . . . and hesitated. It was the exact wrong thing to do, but I couldn't help myself. It wasn't because of the whole "never make the first move" thing either. The first move was okay if your opponent was totally oblivious. In that case the first move would also be the last move. But I didn't do it. I couldn't bring myself to whack a totally defenseless guy across the head.

Big mistake. He wasn't oblivious for long. As soon as he saw Loor and Teek sprint by, headed for the other guards, he got unoblivious real quick. The guy was good. He must have quickly realized that if the attackers were ignoring him, there had to be somebody else coming up who wouldn't ignore him. Me. Without looking, the guy whipped out his steel baton and lashed back. It was so fast, he grazed the front of my leather armor. Another inch and I would have been hit with a jolt of electricity, and the show would be over before it even started. The adrenaline rush of the near miss shocked me into action. With my stave I knocked the back of his baton arm, forcing him to follow through and not backhand me. I spun, came around the backside, and cracked him across the back of his head with the end of the stave, sending him sprawling. He hit the floor and didn't get up.

I stood there for a moment, bombarded with emotions. I had hit the guy, hard. When I fought the Tiggen assassin at Mooraj, I had been tentative. I whacked that guy a few times with the stave, but never did any damage. I blamed that on the fact that I was more used to fighting with a bamboo stick and not a heavy wooden stave. The truth was, the idea of cracking somebody in the head with force went against the nature of my being. I wasn't a violent guy. As I stood there over the unconscious Tiggen guard, the realization came to me that maybe I was wrong. Maybe I was a violent guy after all. It wasn't a good feeling.

"Pendragon!" Loor shouted.

Her voice pulled me back into the moment. I looked quickly to see that both of the other Tiggen guards on our side of the control platform had been knocked unconscious. Loor and Teek were already dragging them toward me, and the elevator. I saw that the Rokador elite had jumped out of their chairs and were cowering together, terrified. For all they knew, we were the first wave of the oncoming Ghee army and their murderous trap was sprung too late. I wasn't about to tell them otherwise. The engineers stayed on the control platform, looking down on us in fear.

We were quickly joined by Alder and the other Tiggen ally. They too had triumphed. All five Tiggen guards were unconscious. I looked up to the catwalk high above, where Teek's other friend was waiting and watching. I waved. He waved back to acknowledge and ran off to lock down the doors. So far, so good.

"We will bring them up in the elevator," Teek said. "Once we have reached the surface, you can shut down the elevator from here."

"You have done the right thing, Teek," Loor said. "No matter what happens from here, you must know that."

Teek nodded. I think he believed her, but he wasn't happy about it.

"Good luck, my friends," Teek said. "I hope we will meet again and—"

Teek suddenly stopped talking. An instant before, I heard a short, sharp hissing sound, but didn't register what it was. Teek looked at us with wide eyes, then crumpled to the floor. Sticking out from his back was a silver arrow. We all quickly looked up toward the catwalk to see . . .

Another Tiggen guard. It wasn't Teek's friend. Teek's friend was dead. He lay on the catwalk, a silver arrow in his chest. Standing over him with both feet planted was his killer. He held a crossbow to his shoulder. He was aiming at us. He fired.

We scattered, taking cover behind the vertical steel tanks. Loor and I jumped to one side, Alder and our Tiggen friend jumped the other way.

"It's him!" I shouted to the others. "The assassin from Mooraj."

It was Bokka's killer. He was back. We were trapped. The instant one of us stuck our head out from behind the tank, the guy would fire another laserlike arrow.

"Open the southern gates!" the assassin called from the catwalk. He was yelling at the engineers on the control platform. The engineers weren't sure what to do. They were frightened and confused. The same went for the Rokador elite. They stayed huddled together in fear.

"Alder?" I shouted across the floor. I made a shooting motion, as if to say, "Where is your crossbow?" Alder shrugged and pointed to the unconscious Tiggen guards we had attacked. Lying next to the pile of bodies was the crossbow.

"I will get it," Loor said, and made a move to run into the open.

"No!" I shouted, and held her back. A nanosecond later another arrow shot by, barely missing her. If I hadn't stopped her, she would have been skewered.

"We must do something, Pendragon," she said. "The flood!"

It was a frightening moment. There was no way we could stop those engineers from flooding the underground from where we were hiding. But if we stepped out, we were dead.

"We'll all go at once," I said. "He can't get us all."

"Not you, Pendragon," Loor said. She looked across to Alder and motioned that both of them would go. Hopefully one would get the crossbow.

"We all go or nobody goes!" I shouted.

I pushed by her, ready to jump out into the line of fire. I'm not a hero. I didn't want to die. What I did wasn't so much brave as the result of being hypercharged on adrenaline, knowing disaster was seconds away. I didn't stop to think. I went.

But I didn't need to. No sooner did I leap out from behind the tank than I saw something nobody expected. Least of all the assassin on the catwalk. He was too busy keeping us pinned down to realize he hadn't finished his first job.

Teek had picked up the crossbow.

He rolled onto his side, took aim, and fired. The arrow shot upward, darting toward its target. His aim was dead solid perfect. The killer still had his own crossbow shouldered when Teek's arrow nailed him square in the chest. The force knocked him backward. He stumbled, hit his back on the rail, dropped his weapon over the side, and fell down after it. The assassin tumbled through the air and hit the ground with a sickening thud. We didn't need to check to know he wasn't going to be shooting at us anymore. Bokka's killer was dead. It was a fitting end.

We all ran to Teek. Loor got there first and knelt by him.

He was on his side, the arrow still in his back. His white Rokador tunic was saturated with blood. There was nothing we could do to help him.

"Hurry," he whispered. "You must stop the flood."

"Bokka would be proud of you, my good friend," Loor said.

Teek gave her a small smile. "Do not let our deaths be for nothing." Teek looked up at his friend, the Tiggen guard, and whispered, "Help them."

With those last words Teek closed his eyes and died. We couldn't mourn his death. There would be time for that later, hopefully.

Loor looked up to the last Tiggen and said, "Get the guards out of here."

The Tiggen nodded and began dragging the unconscious guards toward the elevator.

"I will help," Alder said, and grabbed two of the guards himself. He looked at us and said, "Go!"

Loor and I each grabbed one of the guards' baton weapons and ran for the first ladder that led up to the control platform. I was up first and saw that the engineers were all on the same side of the control board—the side with the small switches that opened up the southern gates.

"Stop!" I shouted.

The guys looked terrified, but didn't move. I may not have been enough of a force to intimidate them into backing off, but Loor sure was. One look at her charging toward them with her stave in one hand and the silver electric baton in the other was enough to get them to back away from the controls. The four of them huddled together like frightened children.

"Close the gates," Loor commanded, with her weapon held high.

The frightened engineers looked as if they were ready to faint, but they didn't budge.

"Do not listen to them!" came a voice from below. It was one of the older guys from the Rokador elite—the only one who was brave enough to leave the others. "If you obey them it will be an act of treason!" the guy called up.

The engineers did the one and only thing they were capable of at that point. They ran. Together they scurried to the ladders, climbed down, and ran to join the elite. The older guy stood there with his hands on his hips, looking up at us, smug. I ignored him. It didn't matter what he thought.

"We gotta stop it ourselves," I said to Loor.

We looked at the array of valves that controlled the gates to the south. It looked as if only a few of them had been opened. We weren't too late. We had to focus. Quickly I grabbed one of the handles and turned it counterclockwise. The needle in the gauge above it instantly dropped down. I grabbed the other two handles and did the same. The southern gates were now all closed again. It was just that simple. Or so I thought. This wasn't over by far.

"Okay," I said. "I don't know how long we can hold out here. If the other Tiggen guards break in before the Ghee arrive, they'll kill us and let those geeks back at the controls."

"What choice do we have?" Loor asked. "We must keep them away as long as possible."

Our victory was probably going to be a short one. We were in control, but for how long? That's when I looked back to the array of switches and got an idea.

"Or we can shut it down for good," I said.

"We cannot shut down an ocean," Loor countered.

"But we can make it so nobody else can take over."

"You mean destroy the controls?" Loor asked.

"If a slew of Tiggen guards comes crashing in here, we're

done," I said. "But if the controls are smashed, it might slow them down long enough for the Ghee warriors to arrive."

"That is risky," Loor said. "We do not know anything about this—"

At that very moment we saw something that made the decision for us. High above on the catwalk, Tiggen guards began flooding in from both sides. Our Tiggen friend who we'd left up there never got the chance to seal off the doors. The guards had a long climb down tall ladders before they would reach us, but they were on their way. We could put up a fight, but there were too many of them. They would quickly win back the control panel and turn it back over to the engineers to do their wet work.

Loor looked at the long line of small silver handles, took her Rokador baton, slipped it through a handle . . . and yanked. The silver handle popped off like the cap of a soda bottle. She looked at me and smiled. I took my Rokador baton and did the same thing. It felt good. The two of us quickly worked to break all the smaller handles off the panel, hopefully making it useless, at least for a while.

The Tiggen guards were halfway down the ladders to the floor. By the time they got to us, our work would be done.

One of the engineers down on the floor must have seen what we were doing. He left the elite and ran back to the bottom of the platform, shouting, "No! Stop! You don't know what you're doing!"

Yes we did. In no time, all the small handles that controlled the southern gates were gone.

"Is that enough?" Loor asked.

"Let's make sure," I said.

I picked up my wooden stave and began smashing the gauges. It sure felt good. Loor joined me. Together we totally trashed the controls.

"Stop! I beg you!" the engineer screamed as he climbed back up the ladder. Soon all four engineers were back on the ladders, headed up onto the platform. Their fear was gone. At least their fear of us, anyway. By the time they reached us, the controls were useless.

"There you go, Poindexter," I said. "Try to flood the underground now."

"Don't you see?" he cried. "That is exactly what you have insured!"

Huh? Two of the engineers ran to the controls on the other side, the side that controlled the northern gates. They tried to move the larger handles, but they wouldn't budge. They checked the gauges and gave a grim look back to the first engineer.

"We have never opened every gate to the north," the first engineer explained frantically. "But it was the only way to carry out the plan. Now they cannot be closed again."

"Why not?" I asked, not liking where this was going.

"It is the immense pressure!" the engineer said. "It would only be relieved once the gates to the south were opened. The timing had to be precise. After what you have done, the gates to the south cannot be opened in time."

"Exactly!" I said. "So the Batu are safe."

"But they aren't!" he exclaimed. "Now the pressure in the ocean will build until it collapses the southern gates anyway. But not before Kidik Island sinks under the rising waters. You haven't saved the Batu—you've doomed both tribes!"

ZADAA

Proof of what the engineer predicted came quickly. The powerful hum that filled the room grew even louder. The lights on the control panel starting going haywire. I heard hissing sounds coming from somewhere. It sounded like incredible pressure was building up inside the vertical steel tanks, which is exactly what was happening. An alarm sounded. It was a blaring horn that warned of disaster.

We backed away from the controls to let the engineers try to reverse the damage.

"It is futile!" the one engineer exclaimed. "We have no control."

A quick look to the Tiggen guards who were climbing down the ladders showed that they had changed their minds. Rather than streaming down the ladders to stop us, they realized what was happening and had changed direction. They were now desperate to climb back up and get the heck out of there.

"What is happening?" came a voice from below. It was the older guy from the Rokador elite. The one who had questioned Saint Dane's plan. He was joined by the others, who no longer wanted to be hiding in the corner anymore, or be anywhere near there for that matter.

"Get out now!" the engineer called down to them. "We can no longer control the waters."

The Rokador elite all stood there, not believing. The statement the engineer had made was a bold one. Controlling the water is what the Rokador did best. It didn't make sense to them that it was no longer within their power. Controlling the water was going to be their salvation, not their destruction. At least that's what they thought. Any doubt they had was blown away a second later. Literally. The joints of the giant pipe beneath the control platform were held together by massive bolts. There was a huge hissing sound, then a loud pop. One of the bolts had blown out. It shot across the room like the cork out of a champagne bottle. It nailed one of the steel tanks with a loud *clang,* putting a huge dent in it. If it had hit somebody, they'd be history. The seam it came from was now tearing open, spewing out a stream of high-pressure water.

The place was coming apart.

The elevator doors opened, and Alder ran out.

"The elevator!" screamed the elderly drooling guy, who had finally woken up. The ten Rokador elite charged for the elevator in a panic. The older people didn't even help the little kids. They pushed the little ones aside to get in the elevator first. They were followed by the engineers, who were just as eager to get out of there. There was a definite "abandon ship" vibe. The engineers slid down the ladders and ran to the elevator, but they were too late. With plenty of room left, the elite closed the door on them, leaving them to wait for the next ride. Nice guys to the end.

Alder quickly joined us at the control panel. "What happened?" he asked, wide-eyed. "The ocean is rising."

"Because it's got nowhere to go," I said. "Let's hope we do."

"The ladders," Loor yelled. "I do not trust the elevators."

The three of us ran for the giant ladders that led up to the catwalk. There were two. Loor jumped on one and climbed quickly. I was right beneath her. Alder took the other one. It was a hairy climb. Through the metal rungs I could look back into the master control room. More seams popped open. The pressure must have been monstrous. Water sprayed everywhere, making the rungs slippery. I felt like we were in the bowels of a huge ship that was going down fast. There was no question, their machinery was not built to withstand this kind of pressure. The underground worked on hydropower. There must have been pipes snaking all over the place. This room was what controlled the flow. If this room collapsed, there would be nothing to hold back the water, anywhere. The Rokador world could explode from the inside out.

I focused on climbing. It didn't do any good to think about the fact that when we got out of there, we would still be miles below the surface, in the middle of the maelstrom. We had to take one step at a time. We all made it to the catwalk, where a quick check showed us that our Tiggen friend was indeed dead. I bowed my head quickly out of respect.

"We must keep moving, Pendragon," Loor said.

Of course we did. But to where?

"The cemetery," Alder said. "That is where Saangi is to meet us with a dygo."

Of course! I had forgotten that Saangi's part of this mission was to get us out of here. My spirits rose. If there was one thing Saangi was good at, it was bailing us out of trouble. I hoped she wouldn't stop now. We ran off the catwalk, through the tunnels, and popped outside, back at the cemetery.

Saangi wasn't there.

"She will come," Loor said with absolute confidence.

"I know she'll try," I said. "But if all hell is breaking loose, who knows what happened to her?"

"My faith is in her," Loor said. "We must not abandon her."

"Okay," I agreed. "But not for long."

We finally had a chance to catch our breaths and plan our next move.

"How did this happen?" Alder asked.

"It's my fault," I said. "We busted up the controller so they couldn't open the gates to the south and flood the underground . . . which was the exact wrong thing to do. They were counting on those gates opening to relieve the pressure of the water building up, and now there's no place for the water to go."

"Will Kidik be destroyed?" Alder asked.

"I don't know," I said. "For sure it'll be flooded."

"The question is," Loor said, "how many will survive?"

I don't think it was until she said those words that the full impact of what we had done hit me. Instead of stopping the Rokador from killing off the Batu, all we did was push the Rokador off the cliff with them. I was beginning to think we had helped make Saint Dane's plan to destroy Zadaa even more successful than the demon had hoped. And just to make the whole event absolutely perfect, there was every probability that three Travelers and an acolyte would die right along with the tribes. I had to sit down. It was like the truth was too heavy to bear. This wasn't simply the battle for a territory. I felt as if here on Zadaa, Saint Dane may have won the battle for all of Halla.

Loor sensed my desperation. She stood over me and touched my head. "If we are alive, we are not done," she said.

I looked up at her. It didn't matter that we were standing on an underground island that was about to be swallowed by rising water, she looked as calm and confident as ever. As always, she gave me hope. Man, I loved her.

"Loor!" called Saangi.

We all looked as Saangi came running toward us. On foot. She was out of breath and excited. There was a definite lack-of-dygo going on.

"The water is rising!" she exclaimed. "The Rokador are leaving the island. They're on boats and dygos and anything else that will move. I've been hiding, trying not to be caught, but they are not interested in me now. They are fleeing for their lives!"

"What of the Batu?" Loor asked.

"I heard them say the Batu were in retreat," she said. "Is this the flood the Rokador promised?"

"Worse," I answered. "They're flooding everything, including themselves. What about the dygo?"

"Gone," she said, embarrassed. "The Rokador have taken them all."

"Then we're stuck," I said.

"No," Saangi said. "We still have the boat that Alder and I came over on. It was hidden. I have brought it closer."

I had to smile. "Where did you find this girl, Loor?" I asked. "She's incredible."

Loor said, "I did not find her. She is my sister."

I sputtered out, "Your sister? Why didn't you tell me?"

"Shall we discuss this now?" Loor asked.

Enough said.

The three of us followed Saangi back through the building and out the far side. As soon as we emerged, we were confronted with a horrifying sight. The island was shrinking. The water's edge was now a good half mile closer than it had been when we arrived. Gone was the beach and the trail. It wouldn't be long before the water reached the central building.

The water was strangely calm. There were no waves or whitecaps. It just kept rising and rising. On the surface were dozens of boats, all full of Rokador. I saw one boat that had all ten of the Rokador elite. Another had the engineers. Many were full of Tiggen guards. It looked as if they were doing all they could to help the other Rokador escape. They were doing their duty till the end. The whole scene looked eerily like lifeboats leaving a sinking ship. Except in this case there would be no rescue ship coming by. I could only hope that they had enough knowledge of the underground that they would find an escape route to the surface.

"Down here!" Saangi said.

We ran down a rocky slope where we saw, hidden behind a large boulder, another silver boat like the one Loor and I came across the water on. The four of us lifted the craft and quickly carried it to the waterline that was growing closer by the second. We launched the boat, jumped inside, and kicked over the engine as . . .

Boom!

The roof blew out of the central building. Jagged pieces of metal rocketed high into the air, along with multiple geysers of water that spewed from the massive pipes, now totally ruptured under the incredible pressure. Some chunks flew so high they ricocheted off the rock dome above.

"Look out!" I shouted.

I grabbed the tiller and made a sharp turn as a chunk of metal splashed down into the water a few feet from us. Before it sank beneath the surface, I saw that it was a piece of the master control panel. For the next few minutes metal and water rained down around us. It was a miracle we weren't hit. Once the deadly storm ended, our thoughts went ahead to the next step.

"There aren't a whole lot of options," I said. "I think our best chance of getting out of here is back through the city. At least we know that way."

Everyone agreed, so I steered the boat back in the direction of the abandoned city. Nobody said anything, but I knew we were all wondering how high the water had gotten. The southern gates were under the city. If the Rokador engineers were correct, eventually the water pressure would be so great that those gates would collapse, sending the millions of tons of water careening through the tunnels of the underground. After seeing the master water controller explode so violently, I had no doubt that the engineers were right, and those gates would soon be history. The only real question was, how much time did we have?

If it had already happened, we were dead. The underground would be flooded and there would be no way out. If it hadn't happened yet, we had to hope that the water level hadn't risen too high for us to find the opening into Kidik and make it up the wide stairs that led back to the main street. If we were lucky enough to make it that far, it would be a race to get out.

We soon drew closer to the massive stone cliffs that held Kidik City. When Loor and I were here before, we were able to see the lights of the landing at the base of the stone cliff. I held my breath. Had the water risen so high that it covered the opening to the landing? A few tense minutes later, Saangi pointed and said, "There!"

It was a thin sliver of light at the base of the cliff. The opening wasn't underwater, and the lights were still on. But it was much thinner than when we had left. The water had definitely risen higher. I gunned the throttle. Right now speed was everything. When we got to the stone wall, we saw that the opening was barely high enough for us to steer our boat inside without ducking down. This had once been a thirty-foot-high opening. Still our luck was holding. If we could maneuver our way inside and find the stairs, we'd have a chance of climbing up onto the dry ground of Kidik, and begin the race back to the surface.

Our luck didn't hold.

No sooner had we cleared the entrance of what was now a watery cave than the lights flickered. A moment later the lights of Kidik went dark. The power was gone. We were in pitch darkness, miles underground, with the water rising.

ZADAA

"Don't panic," I said. "We can find our way through."

I had no idea if that was true or not, but it felt like the right thing to say. It wasn't like we had a whole lot of options. I tried to hold a mental image of where we were when the lights went out. I had to compare that to my memory of this launch area when Loor and I were here before. It was next to impossible. In seconds my sense of direction was totally gone. I couldn't tell up from down, left from right.

"Careful!" Saangi shouted.

Bump! The bow of the boat crashed into a rock wall, making us all lurch forward.

"That's good!" I shouted. "Put your hands on the wall. We'll make our way along. Eventually we'll hit the opening that leads to the stairway."

Alder and Saangi sat on the left—port—side of the small boat with their hands out on the wall. I motored ahead slowly, so they could keep their hands in contact with the rock surface. My memory of the launch area was that if we could continue on like this, we would come upon the opening to the cavern at the base of the stairs. Nobody spoke. As we moved along in the total darkness, I began to worry about something else. I tried to visualize what the archway to the stairs looked like. The stairs were really wide, which meant the opening to the stairs was also wide. But width wasn't what we needed. It was height. If the water had risen to the top of the opening, we could be right in front of it and not know it. Even if the water level had risen to only a few inches higher than the opening to the stairs, we'd miss it. After puttering along for several minutes, my worry turned to fear. I felt sure we should have found the opening by then.

My fear didn't last long. That's because it gave way to panic.

"Ouch!" Alder shouted.

"What happened?" I asked.

"I . . . I hit my head," he said soberly. "We are out of room."

The water had risen so high that it nearly filled the launch area. There was no way we would find the opening to the stairs now. Soon the water would reach the ceiling—and we would drown.

"I'm going to try and get back out to the ocean," I declared. I had no idea what we'd do once we got out there, but staying in here meant death. "Keep your hands on the wall," I ordered. "It should bring us back around to the entrance." My fear was that this launch area was so huge that taking this roundabout route would take too long. But it gave us a better chance than if I simply took a guess as to where the opening to the ocean was and gunned it. We could easily go in the wrong direction and be lost. I knew that we might have to do that at some point, but I wanted to hold off for as long as possible.

"We do not have much room left, Pendragon," Alder warned.

He was the tallest on the boat and had to duck down to

keep from scraping his head against the rocky ceiling. Soon the tops of all our heads were grazing the ceiling. We were out of time. I had to take a chance.

"This is taking too long," I declared. "I'm going to make a guess and go for it."

Nobody said anything. I was sure they all had the same concerns I did.

Finally Loor uttered a soft, insistent, "Hurry."

"Hands in the boat," I commanded. "Stay low."

I made a best guess as to where the opening to the sea might be. I was fooling myself. I had no clue. I turned the tiller away from the wall and gunned it. I figured we were either going to get out, or crash trying.

We crashed.

A few seconds after we got up to speed, we hit something. Hard. The bow hit on the right side, and flipped the boat over. We were all dumped into the water. My first thought before getting wet was: *Loor can't swim*.

I went under with no idea of which way was up. The only clue was the hum of the boat's engine. I kicked my legs and broke the surface, shouting, "Loor!" My scream came back to me as an odd echo. I quickly realized that I had come up underneath the capsized boat.

"Is anybody here?" I called.

"Saangi," sputtered the acolyte. She sounded scared. "Loor cannot swim."

"I know. Is she under here?"

There was no answer, which meant no.

"I'm going out," I said, and didn't wait for her to acknowledge. I kept one hand on the boat, ducked underwater, and pulled myself out. When I resurfaced, I heard thrashing in the water.

"Loor!" I yelled.

"Here!" came a welcome voice. There was a slight, fearful quiver in it, though, which for Loor was the same as gut-clenching panic in anybody else. She was floundering. I pushed off into the darkness in the direction of the splashing. It only took a second to reach her. I wrapped an arm around her chest and flipped her over on her back. She trusted me. She relaxed.

"Alder!" I called out.

"Here!" the knight yelled. "I am holding the boat with Saangi."

I kicked toward his voice and reached forward with my free hand. Soon I felt the hard metal skin of the overturned boat. I pulled Loor up to it and made sure she was holding on.

"I am all right," she said.

There wasn't time to rest or discuss what had happened.

"We've got to swim for it," I said.

"Which way?" Alder asked.

I tried to figure out where the wall was that we had hit. We didn't want to go that way. I looked around, though I wasn't sure why. It was pitch black. There was nothing to see. As it turned out, I was wrong. There *was* something to see. Hovering just beneath the water, a few yards away from us, was a light. Saangi saw it too.

"What is that?" she asked.

"I don't know," I said. "Maybe that's what we hit."

The little bit of light helped me get my bearings. I let go of the boat and swam toward it. I kept my eyes focused on the strip of light. It seemed to be floating only a few inches beneath the surface. As I got closer I began to sense that this light was part of something much larger. It was so incredibly dark that I couldn't make out any real form, except for right around the light. I got to it and touched it. The light was embedded in something solid, and it was big—much bigger than the light itself. I brought my nose closer to the light to see that it was actually behind what seemed to be a glass window. The window rose above the water, though the light was still beneath the surface. I put my nose closer to this mysterious window, and came face-to-face with a Ghee warrior!

A *dead* Ghee warrior.

"Ahhh!" I screamed in surprise, and pushed away.

"What is it?" Alder asked.

I had swum quickly back to the boat in a panic. I clung to the side, trying to catch my breath and calm down. It didn't take long for me to realize what I had seen.

"It's a dygo," I said. "There's a Ghee inside. I—I think he's dead."

"It must be one of the dygos that drilled through the ceiling of the cavern," Alder said. "The rising water must have pushed it in here."

Nobody said anything for a moment. I think we were all trying to process the information. It was Loor who first put our thoughts into words.

"It is our last hope," she said.

"Can you open it from the outside?" I asked. "Without flooding it?"

"We will have to try," Loor said. "I will need help to get there."

I instantly swept my arm around Loor and pushed off of the boat, headed for the crippled dygo. Saangi and Alder swam right behind. In seconds the four of us were hanging onto the silver sphere.

"The hatch is on the other side," Loor said.

We all carefully moved hand over hand around the floating orb until Loor said, "Stop. The hatch is underwater."

"We have to spin it," I said.

It wasn't easy. Though the dygo was floating, it was big

and clumsy. It wasn't until Alder went to the far side and pulled down while we pushed up, that the section of the sphere that held the door broke out of the water. Loor ran her hands across the surface, which was no easy thing since the only light we had was the dim glow that came from the window. A few agonizing seconds later I heard the welcome sound of a latch being released and the hatch being raised. She had done it!

"Careful!" I said. "We don't want to flood it."

We maneuvered the dygo so the open hatch was directly on top. Alder came up from the back side and pulled the hatch fully open. It instantly hit the rocky ceiling. We only had a few feet to maneuver.

"Saangi first," Loor said.

Saangi didn't hesitate. She pulled herself up and slipped inside the dygo, head first. Loor slid in next. I was about to enter when Loor said, "Wait!"

"What's the matter?" I asked.

I was holding on to the edge of the open doorway. My answer came in the form of a cold hand that was laid across mine. It was the hand of the dead Ghee warrior. Loor and Saangi were pushing him up and out of the dygo.

"There isn't enough room," Loor said.

"Are you sure?" I asked. I wanted to be respectful.

"He was a Ghee," Loor said. "He died in battle. This is how it must be."

I pulled the body of the fallen warrior up and out of the craft, while Loor and Saangi pushed. It wasn't easy, for all sorts of reasons. He was heavy, and he was dead. I tried not to be too grossed out by the whole thing. I think I was too far gone for that. We finally got the body clear of the hatch. I pushed him away and the fallen warrior floated off into the darkness, never knowing that his sacrifice may have saved our lives.

"Hurry, Pendragon," Alder said. "We are nearly out of room."

Alder was holding the hatch, but he couldn't open it all the way, because we were getting closer to the ceiling as the water rose relentlessly. There was only about a foot-wide opening now. In a few seconds the hatch would be forced practically closed and the opening wouldn't be wide enough for us to get through. I dove for it and went in headfirst, falling into Saangi's lap.

"C'mon!" I shouted back to Alder.

Alder snaked around the hatch, dropped his feet and legs inside, then fell the rest of the way in. No sooner did he fall inside than the hatch was forced closed by the ceiling overhead. Saangi reached up and sealed it tight.

"Done!" she shouted.

Loor reached for the console and flipped a switch that lit up the interior. We could see! We were a jumble of arms and legs and bodies on top of one another, trying to figure out where to go. I was happy to see that this dygo was larger than the one Loor and I had driven before. It wasn't exactly spacious, but there were four seats, two in front and two behind. At that moment, however, it was on its side.

Loor took charge. "Saangi, next to me," she ordered. "Pendragon, Alder, to the rear." She was already moving herself around to get into the driver's seat, which is not easy to do sideways. After an awkward minute of maneuvering, we were all in our seats but still lying on our sides. Loor worked busily to power up the dygo.

"Does this work like a submarine?" I asked.

"No," Loor said. "We must sink to the bottom."

I didn't like the sound of that, but Loor seemed to know what she was doing. She toggled a few switches, and I heard what sounded like a burst of air bubbles being released. I could feel that we were sinking. Loor must have been taking on water so that we would drop down. Gulp. As we sank, the sphere gradually righted itself. We were heads up!

"I'm turning off the inside lights," Loor said.

A moment later we were back in black. It didn't last long. Loor hit the switch that turned on the outside lights. I felt like I was back in the hauler submarine on Cloral, with Spader. There wasn't much to see through the windshield, though. The water was too murky. No sooner had I gotten used to the sensation of floating in this big sphere than we gently landed on the bottom.

"We're treads down, right?" I asked.

Loor gave me a quick look, as if to say, "Give me a break."

She hit the throttle and the dygo crawled forward. It didn't feel much different from when we were on dry land. We had an unobstructed view through the windshield in front, which meant that the drill was behind us.

"I do not know which way to go," Loor said.

"We've got to find the stairs," I replied. "Keep going until we hit a wall, then we'll follow it like we were trying to do on the surface."

Loor pushed the sphere forward. We crawled along slowly. It wouldn't be smart to crash into a wall. A minute later the headlights reflected off a rocky surface directly in front. We had found the wall.

"Excellent," I said. "Let's go right. Keep the wall in sight. Eventually we have to hit the stairs."

Loor carefully moved the dygo along. She turned the whole sphere so that the window faced the wall, but the treads were ninety degrees the other way. We were actually moving sideways. For the first time I began to think we actually had a chance of getting out of this. We had been moving along slowly for a few minutes when suddenly the wall disappeared, and we were faced with nothing but water.

"This is it!" Saangi exclaimed.

Loor spun the dygo so the window faced the direction of the treads. She was about to turn the whole vehicle so we could move forward into the opening, when I realized something.

"Stop!" I shouted.

"What is the matter?" Loor asked.

"Can we look down from here?" I asked.

Loor spun the sphere back so the window faced the open water. She then tilted the whole sphere so the window gave us a view down. What we saw made each of our hearts beat a little faster.

"That was almost a very big mistake," Alder said.

What we saw was . . . nothing. The stone floor did not continue. It ended. We were not in front of the stairs. We were on the exact opposite side. It was the edge of the platform where we had launched the boat for Kidik Island. If we had gone forward, we would have toppled off the edge and sunk to the bottom of the ocean. We all let out nervous, relieved breaths.

"At least we know where we are," I said. "We need to go in the opposite direction."

Loor spun the dygo sphere a hundred and eighty degrees, lined up the treads, and followed the compass thing on the instrument panel to send us in the opposite direction. We still had to move slowly because visibility wasn't great

"What kind of air supply does this thing have?" I asked.

"There is no air supply," Loor said. "The vents are closed to keep out the water. When we use up the air, we suffocate."

"Oh. Just checking." I suddenly felt more urgency to find the stairs.

While Loor drove, Saangi worked the headlights. She

could direct them to scan in several directions. After driving for a few more moments, Saangi announced, "There!"

Up ahead and above us, we saw what looked like the top edge of an opening. We were passing out of the launch area, hopefully into the cavern at the base of the grand stairway. Loor pressed on. Alder and I leaned forward, desperate to see something that would tell us where we were.

"Look to the left," I said to Saangi. "That's the direction the stairs would be if—there!"

Through the floating particles, we could make out the bottom of the giant staircase. We had made it! We didn't celebrate. We were still far from safe. Loor turned the dygo. Saangi scanned the stairs with the light until she found one of the ramps that cut through the steps. Loor directed the vehicle toward the ramp and in no time we were climbing up. The treads were on a steep angle, but Loor kept the sphere upright so it felt kind of like rising in an escalator.

I want to say that I was relieved, and I was. But all we had done was get to the next hurdle. There was plenty more to worry about, not the least of which was the time bomb that was ticking beneath us. Had the floodgates collapsed? Were we going to find that Kidik was flooded? I didn't know how much air we had left in the dygo, but I didn't think it would be enough to get us to the surface. I was already feeling the effects of the air running out. It was harder to get a breath. All we could do was keep moving, and hope.

We climbed the stairs, higher and higher. I was trying to calculate how deep we had been underwater, which would be a good indication of when we should break the surface. That is, if there was a surface to break.

A minute into our climb, the windshield of the dygo cleared. We were out of the water. Kidik was still dry. It meant the floodgates hadn't been destroyed yet. Loor instantly opened the vents, and Saangi cracked open the hatch to let air rush in. Man, it tasted sweet. I didn't mind that it was tunnel air. I took in a huge lungful. I exchanged a smile with Alder. We had come so close to disaster, but were still going. As Loor said, if we were alive, we were not done.

When we reached the top of the stairs, we were met with more good news. The lights of Kidik were still burning. Only the lights at the bottom of the stairs had gone dark, probably because they were underwater. Up here, we could still see. At least for now. Loor drove the dygo away from the top of the stairs and stopped the vehicle on the edge of the main street. Nobody said it, but we all needed to get out, if only for a few seconds. We needed to get our bearings back. Saangi pushed open the hatch, and we all crawled out of the vehicle that had saved our lives. It felt good to be on solid ground again, even if it was in a deserted city miles underground. I stretched my legs, enjoying the feeling of standing on two feet.

"They were here," Loor said.

"Who was?" I asked.

She was looking at the ground. Sure enough, the fine sandy ground was covered with footprints that hadn't been there when we came in. There looked to be thousands of them.

"The Batu invasion made it to Kidik," Loor declared.

"Where do you think they are now?" Alder asked.

"Fleeing for the surface, I hope," Loor said. "If they saw the rising water, they may have realized the danger."

"So they might survive this after all?" Saangi asked.

My first thought was that Saangi was right. The thousands of Batu who came down into the underground might have dodged a very big, wet bullet. It all depended on where they were, and how much longer the floodgates would hold. If they survived, Saint Dane would lose.

That was my first thought.

My second thought was that we were still in the depths and a time bomb was ticking. I was about to point that out when the ground rumbled. It felt like a short, sharp earthquake. We looked at one another. Our sense of victory was short lived.

"Could that be?" Alder asked.

Another short earthquake rumbled the ground. This one was so strong, it nearly knocked me off my feet.

"Back in the dygo!" Loor shouted.

We all ran for the vehicle. As we were about to climb in, a building that was thirty yards in front of us exploded. It was as if an atomic water bomb had blown up beneath it. A huge blast of water shot up into the air, much like what had happened when the main building on Kidik Island had exploded.

"They're starting to go!" I exclaimed.

On cue two more buildings exploded, sending rock and sand and water everywhere. We were pelted with debris. This was the beginning of the end for the underground. The southern gates were giving way. There must have been so much force surging through those first collapsing gates that the tunnels couldn't contain it. There was more water than space for it to go, so it found its own way.

Kidik was about to be obliterated.

ZADAA

The world was exploding around us.

We piled into the dygo. Loor powered up while Saangi sealed the hatch. "Go!" she exclaimed.

Loor hit the throttle, and the dygo sped forward. She told me these buggies were fast. She was right. We bounced along the main street of Kidik as the buildings to either side began to crumble. It truly was like an earthquake. The ground was being torn apart by the force of the water as it sought space. There was no stopping it, because an entire ocean was behind it, pushing it forward. More buildings blew out, while those on levels above toppled. It reminded me of a giant, elaborate sand castle that was being torn apart by the incoming tide.

The street directly in front of us erupted, sending a blast of water high into the air. Loor was able to steer around it. All I could think of was if one of those geysers shot up directly beneath us, we'd be blown over like a toy. I wondered what would happen if we were knocked off our treads. That would be ugly.

To our left a building looked as if it were lifted up into the air a few feet. The whole building shifted in one piece and slid into the street in front of us. It was too late for Loor to avoid it.

"Brace yourself," she shouted. We hit the building. It was a hard jolt and we knocked around, but the dygo remained intact.

"We can't outrun this," I said. "Eventually we're gonna get nailed."

"There is only one thing we can do," Loor said.

I was happy to hear that there actually was an option, because I was fresh out of ideas.

"Whatever it is, do it," I shouted.

"Do we dig?" Saangi asked.

"We dig," Loor said.

Loor stopped the dygo. She toggled a switch on the instrument panel. I heard a whine and saw the drill drop from overhead and settle down into its front position.

"Dig what?" I asked.

"Dig out," Loor answered.

She toggled another switch, and the drill began to spin. She turned the dygo so we were facing one side of the street. In front of us was a stone house that was still intact. It wouldn't be for long.

"You sure about this?" I asked nervously.

"Brace yourself," Loor commanded.

She hit the throttle and drove the dygo right into the building. The drill dug through the wall as if it were made of paper. A second later we were in somebody's living room. Good thing nobody was home. We blasted through, moving past stone furniture, dishes, and even clothing hanging on racks. It was a twisted experience. We ate through wall after wall, room after room. The ceilings collapsed on us as we tore through, but the dygo kept moving. I realized that the many levels of stone buildings that could be seen from the street were nothing more than the front layer of this city. Like all of the underground, Kidik was like a massive beehive. We charged through open areas that looked like market squares. We passed a huge amphitheater with rings of stone seats that would never see another performance. Loor didn't stop to sightsee. We crashed through more deserted homes. I was feeling kind of guilty, but knew it would only be a matter of time before the surging water did a lot more damage than we were doing.

"Is there a plan here?" I asked.

"We need to get to the surface as quickly as possible," Loor said. "Following the route we took from Xhaxhu would be suicide. We could never outrace the flood."

"So what are we looking for here?" I asked.

"We are looking for nothing," Loor said.

"Excuse me?"

"Nothing," Loor repeated. "We need to get to the rock that Kidik was built on. From there we can drill our own tunnel."

Loor's plan was incredible, and incredibly simple. It didn't matter where we got to the surface, so long as we got there. She had decided to create her own route. From what I'd seen of the dygo, it was possible. The only thing stopping us would be time. We had to outrun the water.

I looked ahead to see we were no longer moving through open space. We had reached the bedrock of Kidik and were drilling our way through. There wasn't much to see. Looking through the hollow drill bit, all that was visible was the rock we were drilling through. If we were lucky, the next thing we would see through that hole was sky.

I felt myself being pushed back into the seat. A quick glance at the compass thing on the instrument panel showed me that we were headed up. It was like flying through a cloud. There was no way to know when we would come out of it, until we were out. A few times we hit an open air-pocket. I couldn't tell if they were tunnels, or natural gaps in the rock. It didn't matter. The treads of the dygo took over, moving us forward until we reached the far side, at which point the drill would go back to work. I didn't know how fast we were going; there was no point of reference. But I figured it couldn't be all that fast. The spinning drill cut through the rock like it was Jell-O, but even going through Jell-O took time.

I tried to get a sense of how long we had been sealed inside the dygo. Ten minutes? Fifteen minutes? Saangi, Alder, and I made a point of not talking. We didn't want to disturb Loor's concentration. She drove the dygo as easily as if she were driving along a quiet country lane. If she was nervous, she didn't show it. Then again, she never looked nervous.

We kept digging. My teeth were chattering from the constant vibration. I hoped the fillings in my teeth were strong. I had no idea where to find a dentist on Zadaa. A few minutes later I learned there was something more important to worry about. I felt something tickling the back of my foot. I looked down to see . . .

"Water!"

The floor of the dygo was wet. The flood had caught us.

"Close the vents!" Saangi shouted.

Loor quickly flipped the air vents shut, stopping the leak. I noticed a trickle of water creeping its way onto the windshield. I looked to the far side, where another trickle of water pushed across the outside of the glass.

"Do you see that?" I asked Loor.

"The water is filling up the tunnel behind us," she said.

"Is that bad?" I asked.

"I do not know, Pendragon," she said. "I have never done anything like this before."

Good point. This was a new experience for all of us. All we could hope was that the water wouldn't hit us with such force that the dygo couldn't take it and we'd be squished. I forced that gruesome possibility out of my head, only to realize there was yet another gruesome possibility to worry about. If we had to keep the vents closed, we had no air. We had to make it to the surface before our air gave out. It had become a race.

Loor angled the dygo steeper and drove it faster. The drill whined in protest. I saw smoke coming from the rock in front of us. Loor wasn't taking any chances. This was the final push. We had to get to the surface, fast. We were pressed back into our seats. I felt like an astronaut being launched into space. I was sweating. Breathing was getting difficult. There was no way to know how much air we had left, but it couldn't be much. The situation was dire. If we didn't break through the surface soon, we would suffocate. We all sat still, trying not to waste any energy that would burn precious air.

I was getting dizzy. I knew I was about to pass out. I closed my eyes and tried to think of something other than death. My head went back to Second Earth. Home. I didn't do that often; it was just too sad. But I did then. Why not? If these were going to be my last thoughts, I wanted them to be good. I thought of my family, and Marley. Man, I missed them. I thought of you guys. We were hanging at the beach. All of us. It was a beautiful sunny day. The sun was so bright, I had to cover my eyes. I felt its warmth on my face. This was a good last thought. The strange thing was, it was like I could really feel it. I wondered if this is what people talked about when they were at the moment of death? Was this the bright light at the end of the tunnel that I was supposed to walk into?

It wasn't, I'm happy to say. I opened my eyes to see bright

sunlight blasting through the windshield. For real. That's what I was feeling. We were out! But we weren't safe, not by a long shot. The dygo had stopped drilling, but we continued on upward, lifted by a powerful jet of water that was pushing us from behind. Rather than settle down to the ground on our treads, the force of water lifted us into the air. We couldn't have gone very high, but it was high enough to flip us over. We crashed back to the ground, upside down. It was a good thing we were strapped in or we'd be dead. The dygo hit, bounced, and flipped over more than once. With one final shudder, we landed . . . on our treads. It was a rude arrival, but we were upright and alive.

"Open the vents!" I shouted to Loor.

Loor flipped the switches, letting in fresh air. Truly fresh air. Surface air. We all took a deep breath to fill our lungs.

"Where are we?" Alder asked.

Through the windshield we could see that we were in the middle of the desert. Only a few yards away was the geyser of water that had rocketed us out of the tunnel. The ground rumbled. Right next to us another geyser burst out of the ground, shooting into the sky like a huge water cannon.

"It is not safe here," Loor said.

That turned out to be a huge understatement. We weren't even close to being safe. Geysers of water burst out of the ground everywhere. It was like the underground couldn't contain the massive pressure that the water had created. It had to go somewhere, so it blasted up. All around us. There was nowhere for us to go. Nowhere to hide. We didn't know if we were safe, or sitting on the next geyser. All Loor could do was react to what was happening.

We weren't alone. Dygos kept popping up out of the sand. It reminded me of when Bokka and Teek and the others had magically appeared out of the sand at the farm. I didn't know if the drivers of the other dygos were Batu or Rokador. It didn't matter. With each new dygo that appeared, it meant that more had survived. Now we could only hope that we would all live through the onslaught that was roaring up from below.

The ground continued to shudder. Loor came to a quick stop, barely avoiding a cave-in directly in front of us. Another dygo wasn't so lucky. It teetered on the edge and tried to reverse. The sand gave way beneath it and it tumbled over the edge, falling into the deep crevice that had appeared out of nowhere.

Loor positioned the giant drill bit directly overhead. It gave us a better field of vision. What we saw was Armageddon. The sand rolled in every direction like there were giant serpents moving beneath. Dygos were flipped around like pinballs. We nearly went over a few times, but Loor was able to keep us upright. I don't know how. All around us giant geysers kept spewing up from nowhere, without warning. One blasted up so close to us that it pushed us up on one tread. Loor drove us away from harm on the one tread before we bounced back down.

The most frightening thing of all was that we had no idea how long this would last. Every second seemed like a lifetime. If this continued, I was afraid that every dygo that had escaped from the underground would be destroyed here on the surface. How wrong would it be to make it this far, only to be scrambled inside the very vehicle that got us out. As it turned out, this frenzy didn't continue much longer.

It got worse.

We had rallied together with what looked like a dozen other dygos. The ground had stopped moving. There were no more geysers.

"Is it over?" Saangi asked.

Nobody answered. We didn't dare believe that we were safe. There was a rumbling. It was like nothing we had experienced so far. It was deep, and low, and coming from somewhere underground.

"Does anybody feel that?" I asked.

"I *hear* it too," Loor answered.

Sure enough, it sounded like there was a rumbling freight train coming closer. We looked around at the desert, but there was nothing unusual. Aside from the dozens of geysers that were spewing water into the sky, that is.

It was Saangi who saw it first. She didn't say anything; she simply pointed. We looked straight ahead to see something far in the distance. It appeared as a jagged line in the sand . . . that was headed directly for us. The line moved fast. Behind it, the desert opened up wider and wider like some giant, demonic zipper.

"It is tearing the desert in two," Loor said in awe.

"Move!" I shouted.

All the dygos reacted at the same time. Some moved left, some moved right. The idea was to get away from the growing chasm as quickly as possible. There was no telling how wide it was going to get. Loor spun the dygo and hit the throttle. We bounced over the sand, desperate for distance. I could lean forward and look out the far end of the windshield to see that some dygos weren't fast enough. The widening chasm caught up with them and they fell back into . . . what? We had no idea what was beneath this rip in the desert.

I said one word to Loor. I said it calmly, but I felt as if she needed to hear it. "Faster," I said.

Loor poured it on. There was a fine line between speed and loss of control. If we hit a rise in the sand that was a little too steep, we'd crash, and the crack in the earth would catch us. It was a chance we had to take. If the growing chasm caught us, we'd be doomed for sure. The point of the tear moved behind us and continued on. I looked out the other side of the window to see it continue to rip its way across the desert. We didn't dare stop. If the gap continued to grow, it would get us. We churned our way across the sand, along with more and more dygos that we picked up along the way. It became clear that there were many survivors of the disaster below. It remained to be seen how many would survive the disaster on the surface.

I don't know how long we rumbled across the desert. Five minutes? Ten? I had lost all track of time and reality. At one point I looked back at the chasm to see that we were actually pulling away from it.

"Look," I shouted. "I think it stopped."

Everyone else looked, but nobody wanted to quit moving.

"We will continue for a while, to be sure," Loor said. Nobody argued.

Another few minutes went by. Loor had gradually been slowing down. The other dygos around us were also slowing. We were pretty sure that the chasm had stopped growing. Finally Loor brought our dygo to a halt. The race was over. We had won. The four of us sat there, our senses tuned for any new sound, or movement, or rumbling or earth-wrenching disaster.

Nothing happened.

Minutes passed. We didn't move. If something new started, we wanted to be ready to roll. Saangi cracked the hatch open to get more air. Still, nobody moved. More time passed without so much as a tremor. After what felt like around half an hour, I couldn't take it anymore.

"I want to see," I said.

Before anyone could talk me out of it, I unclipped my seat belt and climbed over Alder to get to the hatch. I didn't even wait for Saangi. I pushed it open myself. The first thing I saw outside were hundreds of dygos all parked around us. Many hatches were opening and cautious noses were beginning to peek out. I saw many Ghee warriors. I also saw many Rokador. Neither cared that they were among their enemy. They had a much bigger enemy to deal with at the moment. It was an eerie sight, seeing so many dygos in the middle of nowhere like that.

I climbed out of the sphere, hopped onto the tread, and turned to look in the direction of the chasm. What I saw was impossible. It was made all the more bizarre by the fact that all around me, hundreds of Rokador and Batu were staring at the same thing, and probably thinking it was just as impossible as I did.

We were looking at an ocean.

It spread across the horizon in either direction. I couldn't tell how far on either side of us it went, but the shore began barely a hundred yards behind where we had stopped. What made it seem even more surreal were the dozens of powerful water geysers that continued to shoot into the air. It was like some incredible, natural display.

"It is the Kidik Ocean," Loor said. She was standing next to me. So were Alder and Saangi.

Alder said, "The ceiling of the cavern must have collapsed."

"Or got blown apart," I suggested.

As we stood watching in awe, the water geysers grew weaker. They no longer shot hundreds of yards into the air. One by one they lost power and shrank down. Within minutes they disappeared.

"It's over," I said.

"Is it?" Loor asked. "Or has it just begun?"

ZADAA

You've heard the term "earth shattering," right? I don't think I'll ever use that phrase to describe anything else again. How could I? Nothing could be more "earth-shattering" than what I witnessed that day on Zadaa. Literally. Or maybe it was more like Zadaa-shattering. Whatever. It was amazing. The underground realm of the Rokador was destroyed, and out of that destruction was born an entirely new world. I'll do my best to describe it to you, but I know that my words won't even come close.

We drove the dygo along the shore of the new ocean, headed back toward Xhaxhu. At least we thought we were headed there. The best we could do was make an educated guess based on both the route we had traveled to Kidik and the sun. We had survived, that much was certain. Many hadn't. As we sped along the shore, we had no idea what we would find in Xhaxhu. Had the flood and the cave-in also destroyed the Batu city? More important than the city itself was the question of how many Batu died in the underground? For that matter, how many Rokador made it out alive? This story was far from over.

The new ocean stretched for miles. It soon narrowed down

to a river. Yes, there was a new river on Zadaa. Above the ground. I looked through the water-spattered windshield to see that the new waterway continued on through the desert for as far as I could see, but not before skirting around what looked to be giant sandstone pyramids far in the distance.

"Xhaxhu!" Saangi exclaimed.

Yes, Xhaxhu. The city hadn't crumbled. We all exchanged relieved looks. The future seemed a bit brighter.

"If this waterway is being fed from the rivers to the north," Loor said, "Xhaxhu is no longer a city in the desert."

"I want to see this in a couple of years," I said. "I'm thinking farmland, trees, pastures for grazing—"

"Is that possible?" Saangi asked, wide-eyed with wonder.

"Possible?" I answered. "I think it's probable."

What we saw next was further proof of the possible. We abandoned the dygo outside the walls of Xhaxhu and walked into the city on foot. No sooner did we enter than Loor stopped cold. We all did. What we saw was truly incredible.

Xhaxhu was back. The troughs that lined the streets flowed with clean, clear water. The fountains around the statues had come back to life, spraying ornate patterns of water high into the air. The people of Xhaxhu weren't exactly celebrating. I think they were in shock. They lined the troughs, scooping up handfuls of water and drinking their fill. Children splashed and played. I saw more than one person crying with joy. Their nightmare was over. It seemed like it was almost too much for them to get their heads around. I wondered what they would think when they discovered that a river of fresh water was now flowing not far from their doorsteps.

Seeing the Batu reveling in their new fortune had another meaning. The tribe had survived. There were ordinary citizens in the streets, as well as Ghee warriors. That was important.

Whatever happened during the invasion, at least some of the Ghee had turned back before it was too late. The Batu tribe would survive. The Ghee were intact to protect the city against the marauding, cannibal tribes. Civilization on Zadaa would continue.

Saint Dane had lost.

"There is an irony here," Loor said.

"What's that?" I asked.

"Xhaxhu has been reborn, perhaps better than before, thanks to Saint Dane," she said.

It was true. Saint Dane had tried to destroy two tribes and ended up creating new life, and new hope, for the territory.

Saangi added, "It is only fitting that it happened during the Festival of Azhra!" The young acolyte gave us a huge, satisfied grin. I had to laugh. Alder did too. Even Loor chuckled and shook her head.

Of course, Saint Dane didn't act alone. The Rokador played a big part in this, and paid a steep price. Over the next few weeks we learned the extent of their misfortune.

Their underground civilization was no more. And more devastating than the destruction of their world of tunnels was the loss of life—multiple thousands had died because of the virus that swept through them like the plague. The Rokador had come within a whisper of being obliterated. But there was some good news. Most of those who survived the virus escaped the destruction of the underground. They used the thousands of escape routes that had been carefully dug for generations.

Ironically, it was determined that those same tunnels were the ultimate cause of the grand collapse. Miles of hard rock were honeycombed with so many tunnels, it had become unstable. The Rokador world was a disaster waiting to happen. When it was tested by the pressure from the rising ocean, it failed. The area that was most developed, Kidik, collapsed. The ruins now lay at the bottom of a brand-new ocean in the desert.

The Rokador elite survived. They were put on trial and sentenced to prison terms for attempted genocide. I wondered how those kids were going to do in jail. I figured they wouldn't be there long. They really had no say in what had happened. The engineers were put on trial as well. They tried to argue that they were only following orders. It didn't fly. They were sentenced to prison.

I thought the decision was sort of unfair. After all, it was Saint Dane who planted the idea in their heads. He should have been put on trial too. Yeah, right. Like that would happen. But I guess in the end it was the decision of the elite and the engineers to go forward with the horrible plot. There had to be some form of punishment. There was special consideration given to the fact that they were in such a desperate state due to the virus. Their sentence could have been worse. Way worse. The Batu weren't above execution. These guys were lucky. They would eventually be released and returned to their tribe.

The royal family of Zinj presided over the trials. Throughout, the family echoed the words and wisdom of their hero son, Pelle, who preached peace and tolerance. To that end, the surviving Rokador were promised help and protection, so they could rebuild their civilization—on the opposite side of the new river. There would be no more tunneling. The royal family of Zinj recognized the advances of the Rokador society, and how valuable the two tribes could be to each other. They hoped that this tragedy would begin a new era of cooperation.

Not all the Rokador were punished. Many of the Tiggen guards were proclaimed heroes. Most had no idea of the plot to destroy the Batu until it was too late. Once the destruction began, they were credited with saving every single Rokador who made it out of the underground alive.

More than that, we were surprised to learn that it was the Tiggen guards who saved the Batu invaders. Testimony from both Ghee warriors and Tiggen guards confirmed that the Ghee warriors had made it all the way to Kidik. They were preparing to cross the ocean and attack Kidik Island when they were met by a band of Tiggen guards. These guards had learned what was about to happen. They had been prepped by Teek. Teek had convinced them of how wrong the mad plan was. When Teek returned to help us take over the master control station, several Tiggen guards risked their lives to cross the ocean, meet the Ghee, and warn them of the impending danger. The Ghee leaders at first thought it was a trick, until the water started to rise. The order to retreat was given, and the Batu quickly fled to the surface. The Tiggen guards didn't flee with them. They risked their own lives by staying to help their fellow Rokador escape.

Bokka and Teek would have been proud. When I heard this story, I thought of Saint Dane's condemnation of all the people of the territories. He said they were selfish and weak. I wished he could have heard about the heroism of the Tiggen guards. Maybe he had.

I learned all of this during the trials. Alder and I stayed with Loor and attended as observers. We needed to know the final outcome of the conflict. After all, this wasn't just about a war between tribes, this was about our struggle with Saint Dane. Our part in the destruction didn't get much play, I'm happy to say. Some of the engineers testified that a few renegades had made it to the master control station, but since we didn't step forward to take credit, the story was discounted.

It was still semi-risky to look like a Rokador and walk around the city. We got a few odd looks, but there was no trouble. The Batu had had their fill of trouble. It helped that Loor was always by our side. It also didn't hurt that water was flowing freely. That diffused a lot of tension. At worst we were looked on as a beaten enemy. At best we were potentially new friends. Either way, we didn't have any problems.

It was amazing to see how quickly Xhaxhu healed from the drought. The rows of dead palm trees that lined the streets like dry matchsticks began to sprout new green growth. The giant stone buildings and statues that had been encrusted with desert sand were washed down. The same with the streets. The sand that was slowly encroaching on the city was turned back and cleaned away.

Xhaxhu was alive once again.

The massive farms outside the city walls were cleared of sand and replanted. Water flowed freely, irrigating the many rows that would soon sprout an abundance of food to feed the two tribes. We strolled along the bank of the new river, where small green plants were already starting to grow. We even took a trip out to the Mooraj training camp. I was expecting to have all sorts of bad memories, but it wasn't like that at all. The camp had been cleaned up and it was full of children, both Batu and Rokador, who played together happily.

I truly felt as if we were witnessing the birth of a new civilization that had every chance of becoming greater than the last.

It also meant that we had beaten Saint Dane. We had done that before, but this felt different. He made some pretty bold statements. He had nothing but contempt for the people of the territories. For him, Zadaa was meant to be a demonstration of how weak we all were and how we were so easily controlled by fear, greed, and envy. He was so confident in his victory that he didn't even resort to trickery with the Rokador. Of course, he didn't tell them the *whole* truth. He didn't admit to being a demon Traveler bent on destroying their world. The more I thought about what he had done and said, the more I realized that for him, winning Zadaa meant more than winning another territory. He wanted to prove a point. To the Travelers. To me. He wanted to demoralize us and show us that we were fighting a losing battle to save people who didn't deserve saving.

He was wrong. To understand that, you didn't have to look farther than Bokka and Teek and their Tiggen friends. They knew what was happening was wrong. Bokka and Teek sacrificed their lives for the greater good. Many other Tiggen guards risked theirs as well. In my mind, their actions were proof that Saint Dane was wrong. Instead of proving his invincibility, the events on Zadaa gave me hope, for the first time, that we could beat this guy. No, that we *would* beat this guy. I hoped he knew, wherever he was, that he was wrong about the people of the territories. They would triumph over his evil, and we would be there to help them.

I was left with only one troubling thought. Saint Dane said he had made a promise that he would destroy the territories and make the people of Halla suffer.

Who did he make that promise to?

As much as I wanted to think of Zadaa as the battle that turned the war against Saint Dane in our favor, his words bothered me. There was much more to learn about this war. We still had a long way to go.

Once we were confident that the trouble on Zadaa was over, it was time to think about moving on. Alder was the first to leave. We were all totally relieved to discover that the tunnels directly beneath Xhaxhu remained intact. Water once again flowed over the waterfall and through the underground river. That was important because it meant the waterways to and through Xhaxhu did not have to be rebuilt. For us it meant we could still get to the flume. If these tunnels had been flooded, we would have been stuck on Zadaa. Finding the flume clear was our final victory.

"Thank you," I said to Alder.

We stood in front of the mouth of the flume along with Loor and Saangi.

"There is no need to thank me, Pendragon," Alder said. "I am a Traveler." He put his big arm around me and added, "And if I weren't, I would still be there for you."

I hugged the big guy. I was going to miss him.

"Perhaps I should stay with you," Alder said. "This is not over."

"Thanks," I said. "But I don't know what I'm going to find next. Believe me, if I need you—"

"You know where I am," he said. "When this is all over, I want you to return to Denduron. You will be amazed by how the Milago and the Bedoowan have grown together. I can only hope that the Batu and Rokador will do the same."

Loor stepped up to him and gave him a hug. "They will," she said. "With thanks to you."

Wow. That was a surprise. Maybe Loor was getting to be a huggy-type after all. I guess total victory will do that.

Even Saangi got a hug from Alder. "Take care of her," Alder said, referring to Loor.

Saangi said, "I always do."

Alder stepped into the tunnel. He took a breath and bellowed, "Denduron!"

The tunnel came to life. Alder turned back to us and raised his hand to wave. "Until next time, my friends. I will be waiting."

A moment later he was gone.

I didn't follow. I had made a decision. I wasn't going to

leave Zadaa before talking with Loor. There was a lot on my mind that I had been holding back because the time wasn't right. I didn't have that excuse anymore. As terrifying as it may have been, I wanted to tell Loor how I felt about her. There was never going to be a better time. The three of us left the flume, headed for Loor's home. When we arrived, I asked Saangi if I could have a little time alone with Loor. She didn't seem too happy about it, but she agreed.

"Then we must now say good-bye," Saangi said.

I held out my hand to shake hers and said, "You know, you're my hero."

Saangi grabbed me in a big hug. "Loor told me to put my faith in you," she said. "At first I did not understand why, but I do now. You will defeat Saint Dane. I have no doubt."

I pulled away from her and said, "Are you serious? You didn't have faith in me at first?" I tried to sound all insulted.

Saangi frowned nervously. I smiled. She looked down, embarrassed. "Will I see you again?" she asked.

"I hope," I said.

Saangi jumped back at me, gave me a quick kiss on the cheek, then turned and ran away. I don't think she wanted me to see that she was crying. Loor and I watched her run off.

"You said she is your sister?" I asked.

"Not by blood," Loor answered. "She was orphaned, like me. Osa took her in when I was young. She has always been my conscience, and my angel."

Funny, that's the way I thought of Loor.

The two of us stepped inside Loor's home. My heart was racing. I was about to put myself out there in a way that I hadn't ever done before. I was terrified. With all that I had been through, with all that I had learned, nothing had prepared me for the most terrifying challenge of all—opening up my heart.

ZADAA

Loor fixed us a delicious dinner of bread, fruit, and some tasty potatolike vegetable. Even though the farms hadn't started to produce, the strict control on food had been lifted. The Batu no longer feared starvation. While we ate we talked about the future of Zadaa, about how the Rokador would rebuild and be governed, and about how the Ghee warriors would protect them from marauding tribes. We talked about everything but what I wanted to talk about. Finally, when the meal was finished, I had to step up to the plate.

"I'm going to leave tomorrow," I said.

"Do you want me to go with you?" she asked.

Oh man, did I? Of course I did. But the truth was, it was better that I learned about our next challenge before deciding which Traveler would be the best to help me.

"Of course I do," I said. "But not right away. I think it's best if you stay here to see how things progress."

Loor nodded. She knew I would send for her if I needed her. I had done it in the past; I wouldn't be shy about doing it again.

"Where will you go?" she asked.

"Home," I said. "Saint Dane's comment about Courtney has me a little spooked."

"Do you think his next target will be Second Earth?" she asked.

"I don't know," I said. "That's what I want to find out . . . and to make sure Courtney's okay."

"Ah yes, Courtney," Loor said. "Do you love her?"

Whoa! That was direct. I no longer had to stress about finding a way to slide into the topic. Loor had taken the lead. I shouldn't have been surprised.

"Yes, I do," I said. "Courtney is the best. I trust her the way you trust Saangi."

"Saangi is my sister," Loor said. "Is that the way you feel about Courtney?"

Oh man, she was really putting me on the spot—not only about revealing my feelings for her, but confronting my feelings about you, Courtney. Forgive me for writing about it here. This is the kind of thing that should be discussed in person. But as always, my goal is to document all that was happening with me. And something was definitely happening here.

"That's hard to answer," I said. "I don't think of Courtney as my sister. But since we're so far apart, it's hard to see where a real relationship might go. I think that if I never had to leave home, Courtney and I would be together. But with all that's happened, I've changed in ways that never would have happened at home. I'm a different person than the Bobby Pendragon who would have spent the last two years on Second Earth. And I have no idea what's going to happen from here. With all that, I don't see how Courtney and I can be together, and that makes me sad."

"It is sad," Loor agreed. "But you speak the truth."

"There's more," I said. This was it. Time to step off the

cliff. I had practiced a dozen different ways of saying it. I rehearsed in my head for every possibility. I needed to tell Loor exactly how I felt. But as I sat there on the floor with her, the words didn't come. She looked beautiful, like the night we had gone to the festival. There were candles burning on the table, which made her look spectacular. I loved her. I loved her strength and her compassion. I loved the way she was fiercely loyal and honest. I loved the way she looked. She was beautiful in every possible way. How could I say all that without sounding like a geek? As we sat there on the floor, in the candlelight, the answer came to me. I could say all that I wanted to say with one small gesture.

I leaned over to kiss her. It was the kiss that we almost had that night at the festival. That night wasn't the right time. Sitting there, in her home, the time felt about as right as possible. I leaned forward . . .

And Loor turned away. It wasn't a dramatic move, but it spoke volumes. I knew instantly. Loor didn't have the same feelings for me. It took only a few seconds for everything to change. I was crushed. I had gone from thinking I would profess my love for her and we would be together, to feeling totally rejected. We sat there quietly for a few seconds. Then I said, "Wow, this is uncomfortable."

Loor looked about as awkward as I felt. She stared at the candle flames. I wanted to jump up and say, "Oh well, see ya!" but that wouldn't have been fair. To either of us. As badly as this was going, it had to play out. Now the ball was in her court.

"Forgive me, Pendragon," she finally said. "My feelings for you run very deep."

"Not deep enough, I guess."

"That is not true," she said. "You told me that you could not be with Courtney because you had become two different people. I am saying that we cannot be together because we are too much alike."

"Uhh . . . huh?" I muttered.

"I love you, Pendragon," she said. "I love all that you are. But love is a powerful emotion. It can cloud thinking. I know you have been wondering if I loved Bokka. I did. I do. But we were never together because of who we were. I always knew that one day, either one of us might be killed."

I saw a tear grow in her eye. Her fear had come true.

"But it was his love for you that helped us save Zadaa," I said. "He helped us. He helped *you*. If not for him, Saint Dane might have won."

"And now he is dead!" she said, letting her emotions slip. She took a second, got her act back together, and looked me square in the eye. "We are on a mission, Pendragon. No group of people have ever been given such a monumental responsibility. We must prevail. We must stop Saint Dane. That is our quest. We are warriors. We will fight together again. We cannot allow emotions to cloud our judgment in any way. That is why I cannot be with you."

We let that thought hang there for a good long time. It felt so . . . final.

Loor added, "I know that when you think about what I have said, you will agree."

"Maybe," I said, and gave her a small smile. "But I won't necessarily like it."

Loor leaned over and hugged me. It was a bittersweet feeling. At least the tension was broken.

"We must enjoy our victory," she said. "We have earned it. Tomorrow you will leave, and we will take the next path on our journey. That is the way it was meant to be."

I wanted to ask her if things would be different once the war with Saint Dane was over, but I realized how pathetic that would sound. For one, it would make me sound needy. It would also put her on the spot, and that wouldn't be fair. But most of all, I couldn't think ahead to what life was going to be like when our mission was completed. I had no idea about how things might change.

As crushing as the whole experience was, I don't regret that it happened. I was honest with Loor, and that was good. Instead of blowing me off, she gave me a small peek into her own feelings. She wasn't the totally cold warrior she pretended to be. She cared. She cared about me. She was just better at suppressing her feelings than I was. In some odd way, I felt closer to her than before. I went to sleep that night knowing that we would be bound together forever. What that meant would be revealed in time. I closed my eyes feeling sad, yet somehow more complete.

I also had the satisfaction of knowing that our adventure on Zadaa was finished.

I was totally, absolutely wrong.

ZADAA

Loor brought me to the flume by herself. That was cool. I wanted the chance to say good-bye without Saangi there. I chose to wear the white tunic of the Rokador, rather than my Ghee armor. It was a heck of a lot more comfortable. Besides, once I got to Second Earth, I'd be changing into local clothes anyway. Loor and I made our way past the raging water at the bottom of the restored waterfall, through the abandoned Rokador tunnels, down into the trapdoor that was marked with a star, and finally down through the cleft in the rock that led to the large cavern, and the flume.

The two of us stood near the mouth of the tunnel, not sure what to say. We had triumphed. Again. In a big way. In spite of the awkward conversation the night before, we had grown even closer. Or maybe it was because of the conversation. Zadaa was safe, and I felt as if we had tipped the balance in the battle with Saint Dane. Still, there was more to come. We knew Saint Dane wouldn't crawl into a ball and give up. There were battles ahead, but our confidence was pretty high.

"I want to see Second Earth again," Loor said.

"You will," I assured her. "Let's hope it'll be to sightsee."

"Give my regards to Mark and Courtney," she said. "And rest, if you can."

"Yeah, like that'll happen," I said, chuckling.

I knew we would see each other again, so this wasn't a tearful good-bye or anything. I gave her a quick hug, and was about to step into the flume when the tunnel came to life on its own. I stood next to Loor, watching curiously as the light appeared in the distance, along with the musical notes.

"That's weird," I said.

"Could Alder be returning?" Loor asked.

I didn't know. Besides you two guys, Alder was the only Traveler who knew I was on Zadaa. Another Traveler might have decided to pay a visit, but I couldn't guess which one. The rock walls began their transformation into crystal as the light grew brighter. Loor and I took a step back from the tunnel to give the arriving Traveler some room. The sound of the musical notes filled the cavern. We shielded our eyes. A shadow appeared out of the light. The Traveler had arrived. Before the light had the chance to shrink back into the tunnel, the shadow leaped out at us. It happened so fast, there wasn't time to react. A moment later the light disappeared, and I saw who it was.

Saint Dane.

He jumped from the tunnel, directly at us, letting out a hideous, guttural scream. He had a sword. A very big sword. He held it high over his head, ready to strike. Loor pushed me out of the way. I stumbled and fell to the cavern floor. As usual Loor's first thought was to protect me. Like her mother before her, the price for saving my life . . .

Would be her own.

Saint Dane thrust the sword forward. Loor tried to dodge it, but wasn't fast enough. I watched in horror as Saint Dane ran his sword through her chest. I froze. My brain wouldn't accept what I was seeing. Saint Dane drove the sword through Loor. My Loor. The Traveler from Zadaa. I saw the blade come out her back, slick with blood. He drove the weapon so deep that his hands were pressed against her chest. He looked her square in the eye and said with a brutal anger that I felt to the depths of my soul, "Now *die!*"

He pulled the sword out just as quickly. Loor fell to the ground. For all I knew, she was already dead. Saint Dane turned to me, holding up the bloody sword. I saw the fury in his white eyes. I was next.

"You think you have won?" he seethed. "You think you have outwitted me? We haven't even begun."

I think I was in shock. Thirty seconds before, Loor and I were talking about her visiting Second Earth. Now she lay dead at my feet. I couldn't think. I couldn't breathe. It all felt so impossible. But it wasn't. Loor was dead, and if I didn't snap out it, I knew I would be next.

Saint Dane was out of his mind with anger. When I think back on that moment, I realize that our victories on the other territories had pushed him to the limit. Losing Zadaa had sent him over the edge. To win this territory, he had taken off the gloves. He used less trickery. He appeared as himself. He wanted to beat us straight up. He proclaimed this to be a demonstration of his strength. I think the person he was really trying to prove something to was himself. He had failed. He was ready to declare victory in the battle for Halla, but he underestimated the Travelers. He underestimated me. Most importantly, he underestimated the character of the people of Zadaa. He called them weak, and some were, but in the end we never would have saved Zadaa without the courage and wisdom of the people themselves. Saint Dane was losing. After his failure on Zadaa, he knew it. He was like a wild cat that was backed into a corner. In other words, he was dangerous.

He stalked me with the bloody sword. I got to my feet and turned sideways, taking a defensive stance that reduced my target area. Loor's lessons were well learned. As Saint Dane stalked closer, his body transformed. He changed from his normal image into that of the Ghee warrior who had beaten me so badly. My knees went weak. History was repeating itself. The moment I dreaded was here. I was going to have to fight this guy again. Saint Dane knew how to get into my head. I had nightmares about that fight. This time there was no chance of a last-minute rescue. One of us wasn't getting out of that cavern.

I wished I had decided to wear my Ghee armor. I didn't even have a weapon. Saint Dane didn't care. This wasn't about sportsmanship. It was about revenge . . . and death.

This is what I trained for.

"I will give you this much credit," Saint Dane seethed. "You are stronger than Press said. But that means nothing to me now. If killing you is meant to be, I am more than happy to be the executioner."

He lunged at me. I ducked and rolled toward Loor's body. I had to stay focused. I couldn't think about her. I needed her weapon. While jumping back to my feet, I grabbed her wooden stave. I was now armed. I spun to face Saint Dane, who held the sword high once more.

"You have been practicing," he said. "No matter. You are still a weak boy. I should have killed you on Denduron."

He came at me with the sword. This time his movements were shorter, quicker. He slashed the weapon back and forth. I deflected the blows with Loor's stave. He wanted me dead. I wanted me alive. If I was going to beat him, I was going to have to use his anger against him. But I had to be smart. The last time I tried that, it backfired and I landed in the hospital. This time I would end up dead.

I ducked away from his attack and spun toward the other side of the cavern.

"It's over," I said. "You can't outwit me. This proves it."

"Ahhh!" he ran at me and chopped down with the sword like a lumberjack. I ducked away, but couldn't counterstrike. He was too good. He may have been making bad attacks, but he kept recovering in time to block my counters.

"Go back to whatever cave you call home," I taunted. "You have no chance of controlling Halla. We're too strong. The people of the territories are too strong. You're in way over your head."

"Rahhhh!" he bellowed, and unleashed another attack. I blocked two of his shots, spun, and cracked him on the back of his head, knocking him off balance. My confidence grew. I had to force myself not to think of this as revenge. I had to stay in control. I couldn't think about how he nearly beat me to death. I couldn't think about Loor. I had to be the warrior she taught me to be.

"Your bravery is impressive, but foolish," Saint Dane said as he circled back for more. "You are not invincible. You will meet the same fate as Press, and Kasha . . . and Loor."

I attacked. I faked a shot to his gut, then spun and drilled the other side of my stave for his head. He was ready for me. He didn't go for the fake and knocked my second shot aside. He followed by lashing at me with the sword. I moved quickly enough so that I wasn't sliced, but the blade smacked me in the back, stinging. I had committed the number one mistake. He had goaded me into making the first move. It nearly cost me my life. I wouldn't do it again.

"You're running out of territories, Saint Dane," I said. "Your campaign is running out of steam. We are all over you. We know your tricks. We know how you think. And . . . we're the good guys."

Saint Dane thrust his sword at me. I knocked it away, spun the stave, and hit him square on the side of his head. I heard him bellow in pain. I didn't stop. I hit him again, straight in the gut. He doubled over and dropped the sword. I wanted more. All the anger, all the frustration, all the hatred for this guy poured out of me through Loor's stave. It was payback time. I had no sympathy. I pummeled him. I hit him in the head, the knees, the gut. I gave him every bit the beating he had given me, and more. I had won, but that wasn't enough. I wanted to kill him. Yes, I'll say it. At that moment I wanted to kill him.

I had lost control. I was in a frenzy, beating him mercilessly. It was exactly what he wanted. When I was in control of my emotions, I was in command of the fight. As soon as I let my emotions take over, Saint Dane turned it around. He took the beating, backing into the far wall of the cavern. He looked as if he were ready to pass out, but he wasn't. He surprised me by ducking down, reaching into his Ghee armor and pulling out a short, three-bladed knife. It was a weapon from Eelong, the three claws of a tang beast. He lashed out with the knife, catching my forearm. I screamed, and lost control of the stave. He lashed at me again and I dropped it. It clattered to the cavern floor, out of my reach. I was about to be skewered.

Without thinking, I threw myself backward. Saint Dane slashed with the knife again, catching and slicing the front of my tunic. I did a full backward somersault. Saint Dane got his feet back under him and charged. This was it. He was coming in for the kill. He let out a roar of bloodlust. I finished the somersault and landed on my back. I saw Saint Dane charging with the tang knife held high, ready to plunge down at me. I didn't move. There was no way I could get out of the way fast enough. He was coming in full throttle and I was on my back. I had only one chance left.

Without taking my eyes off him or moving my body, I reached out and grabbed the sword that had fallen to the ground. The sword that had killed Loor. Saint Dane's eyes were locked on mine. They were on fire. He had a single-minded purpose—kill Bobby Pendragon. I felt the handle of the sword . . . Saint Dane lunged at me . . . I brought the point of the sword up and . . . Saint Dane impaled himself square on the blade. His eyes stayed locked on mine. I saw his look change from rage to shock. The unthinkable had happened.

I had killed Saint Dane.

His body transformed from that of the Ghee warrior back to his normal self. But the agony and shock were still there. The blood-red veins on his bald head seemed to glow. His white eyes grew dim. It was over. It was all over.

Or so I thought.

Saint Dane hung there for a moment, then his body turned to black smoke before my eyes. The dark cloud floated away from me and moved quickly to the mouth of the flume. There it grew and transformed back into solid form. Saint Dane stood there, looking totally fine. He wasn't hurt. Not even a little. Making things worse, he was strangely calm. Gone was the anger. He even had a small smile on his face. I lay on the ground, still holding the bloody sword. My brain had frozen. I couldn't move.

"I see you are capable of rage," he said cockily. "I will remember that."

"How could you . . . ?" was all I could gasp.

"Didn't Press tell you how futile it would be to try and kill me?" he said with a smirk. He kept his eyes on me and shouted into the flume, *"Quillan!"*

The flume came to life. He was getting away. I didn't have

the strength, or the will to try and stop him. Truth was, I didn't know how.

"This has been such an amusing diversion," Saint Dane said. He was back to his old, confident self. "In spite of what you may think, Pendragon, this isn't over. I can lick my wounds and move on." He glanced down at Loor's body and added, "The question is, can you?"

The light from the flume enveloped the demon Traveler. He took a step back and was gone. As the light disappeared, I could hear his laugh fading away.

I dropped the sword. My mind was reeling. What had just happened? One minute Saint Dane was dead, the next he wasn't. One moment he was desperately trying to kill me, the next he was back to his old self, as if his attack had all been a planned stunt. Maybe it was. Maybe this was one more way of throwing me off balance. If that was the case, he'd done a pretty good job. I had discovered that under the right conditions, I was capable of taking a life. Or maybe I was only capable of taking Saint Dane's life. But his life couldn't be taken. My head hurt.

That's when I remembered Loor. I rolled over onto my knees and crawled to her.

"Loor!" I shouted. "Loor!"

The Ghee warrior lay still. The front of her black armor was slick with blood. Lots of blood. I lifted her head. There was no sign of life. I wouldn't accept that. I couldn't. I felt her neck for a pulse. There was none. I lifted her eyelid. She stared ahead, looking at nothing. It was impossible, but true.

Loor was dead.

I was brought back to the moments when life abandoned Osa. And Kasha. And my uncle Press. I had been there for all of them, and I was there for Loor. I cried. No, I sobbed. Not Loor. Never Loor. It wasn't right. I put my hand on the wound that Saint Dane's sword had made. The wound that had spilled her blood. It was warm.

"No," I whispered. "This can't be happening. I will not accept this."

So many memories of Loor came rushing at me. I remembered when I first met her on Denduron, and she wouldn't accept me as a Traveler. I had memories of nearly drowning her in the river when I thought I was rescuing her from an enemy that turned out to be Alder, of her holding her mother as she died, of standing by me on Cloral at Uncle Press's funeral, of meeting you guys on Second Earth, of jumping into Lifelight with me and battling the fantasy monsters in the Barbican, of standing with me in the rain here on Zadaa, hoping for a kiss.

I pressed my hand into her chest as if I could close the wound. Trying to bring her life back. Praying that she could be saved. This was her moment of victory. She had saved her home territory. I didn't accept that she could die at the moment of her greatest triumph. It wasn't right. I didn't believe for a second that this was the way it was meant to be. I wouldn't let myself believe. The tears ran down my cheeks, my eyes stung, but I wouldn't take my hand off Loor to wipe them away. I was determined to make this nightmare go away, but it wasn't going anywhere. This was real. Loor was gone and I was alone.

It was at that very moment, the instant when I believed that all hope was gone . . .

That I felt a heartbeat. It was weak, but it was there. Her heart was beating. I quickly took my hand away from her chest and felt her neck again. There was a pulse. I must have missed it before. She was alive! But for how much longer? I didn't know what to do. I had to get her to a doctor, but there was no way I could carry her up through the crack in the rock using the footholds dug into the stone. No way. I had to get help. My mind went into hyperdrive. Saangi. I had to get Saangi. But first I had to cover the wound so it wouldn't bleed anymore.

I quickly took off my Rokador tunic and with the sword, I cut the sleeve off to make it into a bandage. I cut the other sleeve off and wadded it up into a pad. My idea was to put the pad on the wound, then tie it down with the other sleeve to stop the bleeding. That's how you stopped bleeding. Direct pressure. The makeshift bandages were ready. I went back to Loor and untied the front of her armor chest piece to get at the wound. I pulled the two leather pieces apart and saw . . .

There was no wound. Huh? I checked around the area, but there was no wound to be found. How could that be? I saw Saint Dane impale her. I saw the sword come out of her back. I reached over and grabbed the sword—it still had her blood on it. There was still blood all over her armor. It was real. That had to have come from somewhere. What had happened?

"Pendragon?" Loor said weakly.

She was awake!

"Don't sit up," I warned. "You're hurt. Saint Dane—"

"I know," she said. "Saint Dane came at me with the sword. I did not move in time. He . . . he killed me." Loor's hand went to her chest. She felt the area where there should have been a wound. She looked at me with wide, confused eyes. I was just as confused as she was. Loor moved to sit up.

"Let me help," I said, and went to give her a hand.

"No, I am all right," she said. "Pendragon, what happened?"

"What do you remember?" I asked.

Loor sat up on the edge of the flume. She was shaken, but otherwise totally okay. "I remember him coming at me out of the flume. I remember the sword. I remember his white eyes looking right at me. He said 'Now—'"

"Die," I finished the sentence. "He said, 'Now die.'"

Loor continued, "I remember. I felt like I was falling. But it was not a frightening thing. I felt safe. There were people around me. I knew they were friends, but I did not recognize anyone. They were unfocused shadows. I said I was ready to go with them. A woman said that it might be my time, or not. We would know soon. They were all very happy to see me, and I was happy to see them as well. I liked being with them. I was happy. But I do not know who they were. Then somebody said, 'This is not the way it was meant to be, Loor.' It was a man. I knew who he was, but I didn't. The voice sounded familiar, but I couldn't see him. The next thing I knew I was here, looking up at you."

"I guess it wasn't time" was all I could add.

Loor nodded thoughtfully. "Pendragon," she said, "something has been bothering me."

"Yeah, no kidding," I said.

Loor ignored my sarcasm and continued. "There have been other times where things did not make sense to me. Did you not think it was odd how you recovered so quickly from your wounds after the fight with Saint Dane?"

"Well, yeah," I said. "But I figured I was a quick healer. I've always been a quick healer."

"But you were nearly killed," she said. "Your recovery was nothing short of impossible. And what of Alder? That arrow should have killed him, yet he was up and fighting with us so soon afterward. Did you not think that was unusual?"

"I had a few other things to worry about at the time," I said.

"And here," she said. "I should be dead. I *was* dead. Yet I am not. How can that be?"

Good question. I wished I had an equally good answer.

"Could it be because we're Travelers?" I asked.

"I do not know," she answered. "None of us knows our own true history. We were not born of our parents' blood. There is much we have yet to learn."

"Then why did Osa die? And Kasha? And Uncle Press? They were Travelers."

Loor gave this some deep, troubled thought. She said softly, "Maybe it was because you did not know you could heal them."

Those words stunned me. I let them sink in for a minute, then rejected the idea. I jumped to my feet and paced.

"No way," I said. "That's impossible. This isn't about me. I can't bring back the dead."

"Perhaps not," Loor said. "Or perhaps with Travelers, it is different."

"So you're saying I could have saved Uncle Press? And the others?"

"No, but only because you did not know. You told me that Uncle Press said to you that killing Saint Dane was futile, because he would only come back in another form. Saint Dane is a Traveler. We are Travelers. We may be more alike than you think."

The idea was incredible. I would have thought it was ridiculous, if not for what had happened to Loor. She was dead. I know she was. There was no heartbeat. She had a mortal wound. Yet there she sat, as good as new, and the wound was magically gone. I wasn't ready to accept the fact that I had incredible healing powers, but it would have been stupid to ignore the fact that there may be more to being a Traveler than we first thought.

I was about to suggest we get her back home, when the flume sprang back to life.

"You gotta be kidding me!" I said.

I helped Loor to her feet, and we backed far away from the tunnel. Neither of us wanted to be sitting ducks again. It was too late to climb out of the cavern. Whoever was coming, we had to face them. Though just to be safe, I quickly picked up the sword that Saint Dane had left behind.

The flume did its normal pyrotechnics with light and music. I squinted through the bright display to get a glimpse of who would be coming back at us. This time there were no shadows emerging from the tunnel, primed to kill. The light disappeared and the music stopped. Nobody was there.

"Look!" Loor said.

Resting on the bottom of the flume, near the mouth was a brightly colored square box. It looked like an elaborate gift. It had bright red and yellow stripes and looked about the right size to hold a big pumpkin. The whole thing was tied up with a bright red bow.

"I've lost my mind," I said.

Loor walked boldly over to examine the package. I was behind her, but without the same enthusiasm. There was a huge, yellow tag dangling from the bow. Loor looked at it, then held it out for me to see. There was one word written on the rectangular tag. In fancy letters was the word PEN-DRAGON.

"Oh, great," I said with absolutely no enthusiasm. "Is it my birthday?"

Loor pulled off the tag and found that it was folded in half. She opened it to see what was written inside. Her face fell.

"What?" I asked quickly.

She turned the tag around so I could read it. It said: "With my compliments. S.D."

"S.D.," I said. "Cute. Do I want to know what's inside?"

"Don't you?" Loor asked.

I didn't, but I had to. I thought back to the time Saint Dane had made a present of Gunny's hand in a bag. There was every reason to believe there would be something just as nasty in this box. I knelt down and pulled off the ribbon.

"This might be dangerous," I said.

"There is only one way to find out," Loor said.

I grasped the sides of the lid, winced, and pulled it off. Instantly a jack-in-the-box clown popped out. It was a scary-looking thing, with a garish smile and a jester's hat. It was on a spring, and bounced around while laughing over and over. I thought I recognized the laugh.

"There is something else inside," Loor pointed out.

Sure enough, there was an envelope in the bottom of the box. It was bright blue and looked sort of like a birthday card. Again on the outside was the word PENDRAGON. I rolled my eyes and opened the envelope. Inside was a single sheet of heavy paper. It was bright yellow, with fancy, red writing. It read:

> *Riggedy riggedy white*
> *Come and spend the night*
> *We'll play some games*
> *Some wild, some tame*
> *Cause if you will, you might*

> Your hosts on Quillan,
> Veego and LaBerge

"What does it mean?" Loor asked.

"It means I'm going to Quillan."

I'm writing this journal to you from the territory of Quillan, in very strange surroundings. More of that in a second.

I reluctantly left Loor in the flume cavern on Zadaa, convinced that she was healthy, but clueless as to why. Did I bring her back from the dead? Do I have that kind of power? Do all Travelers have that kind of power? Loor raised a lot of good questions. I've never been sick a day in my life. If ever I was injured, it never lasted. My coaches used to call me the Terminator, because no matter what happened to me, I kept coming back. I never thought twice about it . . . until Loor died. Or un-died.

Having the ability to heal quickly isn't what's got me freaked out. It's more about why. Healing that fast isn't normal. Neither is rising from the dead. Saint Dane is a Traveler with powers that defy the imagination. We're Travelers too, but we don't have those same powers. Or do we? I have to admit, I sat here trying to change myself into looking like somebody else. It didn't work. All I accomplished was feeling stupid.

Still, I can't ignore the facts. Loor was dead. Then she wasn't. Whether I did it, or she did it herself, or it was the combination of both of us, I don't know. But it happened. That leads me to the biggest, most troubling question of all: Am I human?

Don't laugh. Humans don't rise from the dead. Humans get sick. Humans don't have the power of persuasion. And most of all, humans don't shoot around Halla trying to stop Saint Dane. (I know, you guys did, but you weren't supposed to.) It raises other questions too. What happened to my family? Uncle Press said my mother and father weren't my real parents. Then who were? Where did I come from and why was I living in Stony Brook? How could all records of their existence have disappeared? That's impossible, isn't it? None of the Travelers know where they came from. They were all told that their parents weren't their biological parents, but were never told who their real parents were. I have to admit, it's got me all sorts of worked up again. I had put all those questions aside to focus on Saint Dane. Now they're coming back to haunt me.

And speaking of Saint Dane, he has led me to the territory of Quillan. Actually, he invited me. Or had me invited. I'm writing this journal from my room. It's in this monstrous castle where a couple of characters named Veego and LaBerge live. The castle is right out of the Brothers Grimm, but this room looks more like I'm living at the circus. The walls are purple and yellow striped; the ceiling is covered with balloons; I'm writing on a desk that looks like a giant hand; and the bed looks to be floating in the air. I have no idea what's holding it up. Oh yeah, there are hundreds of dolls in the room. Clown dolls. I hate clowns.

I'm supposed to have dinner with my hosts soon, so I should finish this journal. I have no idea what's in store for me here, other than some scary clown nightmares. But I feel certain this is where I should be. Saint Dane brought me here for a reason; I need to find out what it is.

As I wrote before, please be careful. Whatever he's doing on Second Earth, assuming he's really there, I've got to believe it's in the early stages. I don't think you're in trouble. That's not his style. It's not you he wants to beat, it's me.

The adventure on Zadaa has changed me in so many ways. I've learned some things about myself, and discovered some new and disturbing questions. Above it all, I still think we are closer to beating Saint Dane. He's starting to sweat. No, he's starting to panic. It's my job to keep the pressure on, so that's what I'm going to do.

I miss you guys. I love you guys.

And so we go.

END JOURNAL #23

● SECOND EARTH ●

"What are you reading there?" Andy Mitchell said. *"Highlights?"*

Mark quickly rolled up the yellow pages of Bobby's last journal. He had already read it three times.

"N-No. Uh, what's 'highlights'?"

Andy plopped down next to Mark with a bag full of burgers and fries. "You know, *Highlights.* That kid magazine they have in doctors' offices where you gotta find the picture of the pencil hidden in the tree and whatnot."

"Oh. No. This is just, uh, something I'm working on," Mark said.

"Yeah? Another one of them stories about Pendragon?"

Mark shot Andy a surprised look and asked, "What did you say?"

"You know, like that one you wrote about, what was that place? Da-doo run run?"

Mark relaxed. He had forgotten that Andy had seen Bobby's first journals. In fact, he had stolen them from Mark. Mark and Courtney had to pretend that they had written the story themselves so Andy wouldn't spread strange rumors about what really happened to Bobby . . . that weren't rumors at all.

"Denduron," Mark corrected. "No, it's just an article. Leave it alone."

"All right, jeez, lighten up." Andy handed the bag of food to Mark. "Here, eat something. You look like hell. Sorry it took so long. Nothing's close to anything up here in the boonies."

Mark took the burgers, but didn't feel like eating. His mind was in too many different places. Courtney was lying in an operating room, near death, from an accident that might have been caused by Saint Dane. They still didn't know if she would live or die. As horrible as it was, worrying about Courtney kept his mind from spinning to all the other things that had him so worried.

Saint Dane was on Second Earth. Was he there to lay the groundwork for his attack on their home? As much as he wanted to think there was another reason, Mark couldn't come up with one. His worst fear was about to come true. There was going to be a battle for Second Earth. That is, unless Bobby could stop Saint Dane for good.

That thought brought Mark back to the strange news from Bobby's latest journal. Of course, Mark was thrilled that Zadaa was saved. But that also brought bad news. With so many losses, Saint Dane was getting desperate . . . and violent. He nearly killed Bobby out of sheer anger. He *did* kill Loor, which brought up some truly unsettling possibilities.

Loor had returned from the dead.

How strange was that? It was good news, yes, but disturbing news just the same. How could it have happened? Other Travelers died, and stayed dead. Mark saw one die himself, Seegen, the Traveler from Eelong before Kasha. What was different about Loor's death? Was it Bobby? But Bobby was there when his uncle Press had died. The same with Kasha. Those two didn't come back from the dead. Whatever the reason was, it brought something to light that could not be denied. There was something unusual about the Travelers. The simple fact that they healed so quickly was enough proof that they weren't normal. Or at least normal by the standards of the territories they came from. That brought Mark around to the bottom-line question that disturbed him the most.

Who was Bobby Pendragon? Really? They had been best friends since either could remember. Now Mark was faced with the possibility that Bobby wasn't just randomly chosen to be a Traveler. He was different. More different than even he could imagine.

"Mark?" a woman's voice called. It was Mrs. Chetwynde. She entered the waiting room along with Mr. Chetwynde. Both looked tired and scared. Their eyes were red. They had been crying.

Mark jumped to his feet to greet them. "You made it!" he exclaimed.

"We've been here for a while," Mr. Chetwynde said. "We've been with Courtney."

Andy stood up and joined Mark. Mark asked, "How is she?" He wasn't entirely sure he wanted to hear the answer.

The Chetwyndes exchanged looks, as if they weren't sure which one of them should answer. That wasn't a good sign.

"Is she okay?" Mark asked more insistently.

"She's out of surgery," Mrs. Chetwynde said. "She's got problems. She lost a lot of blood. The doctors have done all they can; now it's just a matter of time."

Mr. Chetwynde continued, "She's really banged up. Broken ribs. Her left arm was broken in two places. She has a terrible concussion . . ."

"Wow," Andy said without even thinking.

"The real damage was internal," Mr. Chetwynde said. "There was lots of bleeding. That's why the surgery took so long. They think they repaired it all but, they just don't know for sure. The next twenty-four hours are going to be critical."

Mrs. Chetywnde said, "If you boys hadn't found her . . ." She didn't finish the sentence. The words caught in her throat.

"What happened, Mark?" Mr. Chetwynde said, holding back tears. "The police said it was a hit-and-run. How did you find her?"

Mark was prepared for that question. He knew it was coming. "It was luck, mostly," he began. "Courtney called me yesterday to say she was riding into town to meet some guy named, uh,—"

"Whitney," Mr. Chetwynde said. "The police told us. Nobody can find the guy. He's not registered at the school."

"Yeah, we found that out too," Mark said. "This is Andy Mitchell, by the way. He's a friend of mine; he gave me a ride up this morning."

The Chetwyndes smiled at Andy. Andy nodded. He wasn't used to being polite.

"Why did you decide to come up?" Mr. Chetwynde asked.

This was the tough part of the story. Mark couldn't say that he was warned by Bobby Pendragon in a journal from across time and space that an evil demon might have been stalking Courtney. That probably would have made their heads explode, along with Andy's. Mark decided to be as vague as possible.

"It was just a feeling," he answered. "Courtney talked about hanging around with a new guy, but for some reason it didn't feel right to me. I can't explain why. I'd been planning on visiting her anyway. It was lucky we decided to come up when we did."

The Chetwyndes nodded. They accepted his reasoning. So did Andy. It was close enough to the truth. Mark continued quickly to get past that rough spot. "When we got here, we found out that Courtney didn't make it to class this morning. She wasn't in her room and her bike was gone. That got me thinking the worst, like she never made it back from her date last night. So Andy and I drove into town. We saw the fresh skid marks on the road, and when we stopped to look, I saw Courtney's book in the bushes. That's how we found her."

Mrs. Chetwynde started to cry. "Thank you, Mark. Both of you. You are both angels."

Andy shuffled uncomfortably. Mark felt a little awkward too.

"It's getting late," Mr. Chetwynde said. "You shouldn't drive home. We can put you guys up in a hotel for the night."

Mark wanted to stay in the worst way. If they wouldn't know about Courtney for another day, he wanted to be here. He looked at Andy and said, "What do you think?"

Andy shrugged and said, "Sure, what the hell."

Mark winced at his language in front of Courtney's parents. He looked at the Chetwyndes and said, "That's great, thanks. But, uh, I gotta call my parents and tell them what's going on. They sort of don't know we came up today. If you could talk to them for a second and tell them you're here and all, I'd appreciate it."

"No problem," Mr. Chetwynde said. "What about you, Andy?"

"I'll call my parents," he said. "No problem."

Mrs. Chetwynde said, "But first you should see Courtney. She wants to talk with you."

"Really?" Mark asked. "She's awake?"

"For now," Mr. Chetwynde answered. "I don't know for how long, though. She's pretty drugged up. She's In intensive care, just down the hall."

"Awesome!" Mark said, and started to walk off. He suddenly stopped and turned back to Andy to say, "C'mon."

"Nah, it's cool. It's you she wants to see," Andy said.

Mark walked back to Andy and said, "If it weren't for you, she wouldn't be here right now. She should know what you did."

Andy looked at the Chetwyndes. They nodded encouragement. Andy shrugged and followed Mark. As they walked along the corridor toward the intensive care unit, Andy scratched nervously.

"Look, uh, Chetwynde's not exactly a fan of mine," he said. "I don't want to bother her or nothing."

"She should know how much you helped," Mark said. "Just say hi."

"Yeah, well, I've never seen a banged-up person before," Andy said nervously. "What if I do something stupid, like puke."

"Don't" was all Mark said.

The two guys found the nurses' station and asked where Courtney was. The nurses broke out into big smiles. They said that normally only family members were allowed to visit in intensive care, but seeing as Mark and Andy were the two heroes who saved Courtney, they'd be happy to make an exception. Besides, they said, Courtney had been asking to see Mark. The nurse led them through the corridor. There were only four rooms, and none of the others was occupied. Mark figured that in such a small town, it was a big deal to have somebody in intensive care. The nurse walked them to the last door at the end of the corridor and stopped.

"How is she doing?" Mark asked her.

The nurse frowned. That was a bad sign. "You'll have to ask the parents," she answered. "Don't be long, okay?"

Mark knew that was bad news. People were quick to give good news. It was time to see for himself.

◉ SECOND EARTH ◉
(CONTINUED)

Mark tentatively entered Courtney's hospital room. He motioned for Andy to wait a second. He wanted to see her first. When Mark rounded the curtain and saw her, he gasped. Courtney was a mess. Her face was black and blue. Her head was bandaged. Her left arm was in a full cast that was held in position by a steel rod that kept it away from her body. She was hooked up to all sorts of tubes and wires, with bags of various colored liquids dangling over her and monitors spewing out graphs and data. Numbers flashed that had no meaning to him. There was an incessant *beep . . . beep . . . beep* coming from one of the machines that Mark figured was her heart rate. He was grateful that he couldn't see the bandages from all the surgery. That would have put him over the edge.

He walked tentatively up to the bed. He couldn't tell if her eyes were closed because she was sleeping or they were swollen shut. That's how bad she was.

Mark leaned down and softly whispered, "Courtney?"

Courtney's eyes fluttered and she said with a weak voice, "You don't have to whisper, dork. This isn't a library."

Mark smiled, in spite of the fact that he wanted to cry. Courtney may have been hurting, but she was still Courtney.

"We gotta talk," she said with a raspy voice.

"I know," he said. "But first you gotta see somebody. I know this is weird, but if it weren't for his help, you'd still be out there."

Mark gestured to Andy, who reluctantly walked to the foot of the bed. He stood there, looking uncomfortable.

"Hey," he said to Courtney. "You look good. Seriously. Considering."

Courtney moved her head a few inches and looked at Andy.

Mark said, "Andy gave me a ride up here. That's how we found you."

"What happened, Mitchell?" Courtney said. "You get visited by three Christmas ghosts who changed you into a human being or something?"

Andy smiled. "That's funny, Chetwynde. Glad to see you still got such a hysterical sense of humor."

Courtney gave him a thumbs-up with her good hand. Andy backed toward the door. "I'll let you guys talk," he said to Mark.

"Hey," Courtney called to him in a weak voice. "Thanks. Seriously."

Andy nodded. "No problem. Get better, all right?"

Andy left, and Mark and Courtney were alone. Mark pulled up a chair and sat right by Courtney's head. He didn't want anyone to hear what they were going to say.

"You're going to be okay," Mark said. "I guess there was all sorts of internal stuff going on but they got it in time and—"

"He's here," Courtney said.

Mark nodded. "I know," he said soberly. "Bobby wrote that Saint Dane knew you were seeing a new guy."

"The new guy *was* Saint Dane," Courtney said.

"Yeah, I figured," Mark said. "He's gone. Nobody can find him."

"You got journals?" Courtney asked.

Mark smiled. He was prepared for this question too. "Bobby was on Zadaa. It's over. They saved the territory. You can read

400 ~ PENDRAGON ~

about it when you're feeling better. Things are looking real good."

"Yeah, real good," Courtney said. "Except that Saint Dane is here."

"Right," Mark said, deflated. "That."

The two sat there for a moment, the only sound coming from the steady beep of the heart monitor.

"Mark," Courtney said. "If I don't get better—"

"Don't say that! You're gonna be okay."

"Call Tom Dorney," Courtney said. "He can be an acolyte with you. I don't want you to be alone."

"I won't be alone, I'll be with you," Mark said. He was desperately trying to hold back tears.

"Yeah, maybe," Courtney said. She took a difficult breath and then said, "But if I make it out of here—"

"You will."

"Okay, when I get out of here, I want you to know, I'm done hiding and feeling sorry for myself." She drew another tired breath and said in a clear voice, "Mark, I want that bastard."

Mark looked right into Courtney's eyes. She may have been hurting and weak, but her eyes told the real story. The fire was there. She wasn't going down without a fight. Mark took her right hand and squeezed it.

"Me too" was all he said.

An hour later Mark and Andy were watching TV in their room at the Derby Falls Motor Lodge. It was a cheesy room with two beds that smelled like disinfectant, but they were comfortable. Andy was busy with the remote control, trying to figure out how to get the in-room movies for free. Mark's mind was elsewhere. He hadn't said much since they left the hospital. There was so much on his mind, most of which he couldn't share with Andy. He decided to focus on Courtney, and her health. At least everyone was on the same page there.

Andy gave up and flicked off the TV with the remote. He sat up and started putting on his sneakers. "I'm going out for a smoke."

Mark watched him for a second, then said, "This is weird."

"Gee, you think?" Andy said sarcastically.

"I don't mean Courtney," Mark said. "I'm talking about you and me. Let's be honest. We hate each other."

Andy struggled with his shoe, then said, "I don't hate you, Dimond. We're just on different frequencies."

"Yeah, well, I hated you," Mark said with a smile.

Andy smiled too and said, "I don't blame you. But hey, things happen for a reason, right?"

"I don't know what else to say but . . . thank you," Mark said sincerely. "If it weren't for you, Courtney might be . . ." He couldn't finish the sentence. "You're an okay guy."

Andy nodded. "Yeah, whatever." He stood and walked for the door. "You know," he said. "Maybe something good will come out of this."

"How do you figure that?" Mark asked.

"Bad things sometimes bring people together," Andy said. "You and I, we're pretty different. But when it comes to some things, like Sci-Clops, we click."

"True," Mark said.

"And we didn't kill each other on this trip. Not yet, anyway." Mark chuckled.

Andy continued, "Maybe we should think about working together on something."

"Like what?" Mark asked, surprised.

"I don't know. We both got our own projects going—you got the code thing and I'm working on the plastic steel. Maybe there's a way to, like, combine them. You know, two heads are better than one and all that."

Mark nodded thoughtfully.

"Think about it," Andy said, opening the door. "I'll be right back."

Andy closed the door behind him. Mark chuckled again to himself. As if he didn't already have enough to deal with. Never in a million years did he ever think that he and Andy Mitchell would become friends. The idea of actually working together on something was an even bigger stretch. Yet for Mark, neither seemed out of the question. Andy wasn't the guy he'd thought he was. There was more going on there. Mark wasn't a psychologist. He had no idea why some people became bullies and others victims. So much of what Andy had done to him over the years, all the torture, seemed so trivial now. There were bigger things to worry about. Way bigger things.

With all that Mark and Courtney and Bobby had been going through over the last few years, the one thing that helped keep Mark sane was Sci-Clops. It got his mind off the troubles of Halla, and let him relax and have fun. He didn't want to give that up. He needed it. The idea of working together with Andy Mitchell on a project—the brilliant Andy Mitchell, not the bully Andy Mitchell—suddenly sounded like it would be a whole lot of fun. Mark lay back on the bed, put his hands behind his head, and smiled.

Life, he thought, was full of so many strange surprises.

Courtney Chetwynde lay alone in her hospital bed. She was a fighter, and now she was fighting for her life. After Mark and Andy left the hospital, after her parents had said good night, after the nurses had changed shifts, she had taken a turn for the worse. Her blood pressure had dropped dangerously low. Her heartbeat slowed. The nurses feared that the internal bleeding had begun again. After a quick deliberation, the nurses decided to call in the doctors. If Courtney was going to survive, she would have to go back into surgery. Fast. The little hospital of Derby Falls wasn't used to handling this much excitement. The nurses scrambled to find the doctors, contact the Chetwyndes at their motel, and prepare the operating room. It was the night shift. Fewer people were on duty, which meant everyone had more to do. It wasn't chaos, but it was close. A patient was dying.

In all the frenzy nobody noticed that a young man with blond hair had entered the intensive care wing. He strolled casually down the corridor as the nurses hurried about, trying not to bump into one another. They were too busy to ask who he was. They didn't care. They had a patient to save. The young man walked calmly past the nurses' station toward the end of the corridor and stepped into Courtney's room.

Courtney was alone, and asleep. She had been given the first stage of anesthesia to prepare her for surgery. The guy walked up to the bed and looked down on the broken girl. He glanced at the vital signs monitor. She was barely alive. The guy reached out and gently put his hand on Courtney's chest. He pressed his flat palm over her heart firmly. All his attention was focused on Courtney. He closed his eyes. The only sound in the room was the steady, slow *beep . . . beep . . . beep* of the heart monitor. Outside in the corridor nurses raced around furiously, trying to cover all the bases while fearing it was already too late.

The young man took a deep breath and exhaled. His entire focus was on Courtney. Slowly, ever so slowly, the weak *beep . . . beep . . . beep* of the heart monitor, grew stronger. Courtney's blood pressure increased. The young man didn't take his hand away. He stayed focused. Courtney's breathing grew deeper. Vital oxygen was getting to her blood.

In a few minutes the doctors would arrive. They would find that Courtney's vital signs had not only stabilized, but improved. She would not need surgery. The nurses would be at a loss as to what had happened. They would have to scramble to explain why they turned the hospital upside down and got so many doctors out of bed for nothing. The Chetwyndes would arrive and be shaken by the ordeal, but grateful that Courtney was doing so much better.

None of that would happen for a while, though. The young man needed to finish his work first. He glanced once more at the monitors to see Courtney had turned the corner. She was going to live. With a satisfied smile he took his hand off her chest and folded his arms.

"Like I told you," the young man said, "I give, and I take away."

He heard a nurse out in the corridor yell, "Last room on the right! Hurry!"

The young man glanced at the door. Soon the entire emergency staff of Derby Falls Hospital would descend on the room to discover their patient had made a miraculous recovery. The young man glanced back to Courtney and chuckled. "I've been working such a long time to get this far, you didn't think I'd let you slip away so easily. This is just getting interesting."

The team of nurses and a doctor hurried into the room, stopping short when they saw the young man with the blond hair standing next to Courtney's bed.

"What are you doing in here?" a doctor demanded. "How did you get in?"

"I was just checking on my friend," the young guy answered innocently. "Is she okay?"

"Let's hope so," the doctor said, pushing past the guy, headed for Courtney. "Get him out of here! Do your parents know you're here?"

"It's cool," he answered. "I'm a friend."

"What's your name?" the doctor demanded.

The young man casually brushed back the dirty blond hair from his eyes. "It's Andy," he said. "Andy Mitchell."

To Be Continued

PENDRAG⊕N

QUILLAN GAMES

QUILLAN

I like to play games.

Always have. It doesn't matter if it's a simple game of checkers or something more brainy, like chess. I like board games like Stratego or Risk, and pretty much every team sport that exists. I like playing computer games and card games and charades and Scrabble, and when I was a kid, I was known to play a killer game of red rover. I like to win, too. Doesn't everybody? But I'm not one of those guys who has to win constantly or I get all cranky. Why bother? When I lose, I'll be upset for about half a second, then move on. For me, playing a game is all about the fun of the contest and seeing the best player win, whoever that may be.

At least that's the way I *used* to think.

What I found here on the territory of Quillan is that games are a very big part of the culture. All kinds of games. So given the fact that I like games so much, you'd think hanging out here would be pretty cool, right?

Wrong. Really, really wrong. Games are about being challenged and plotting and developing skills and finding strategy and having fun. That's all true on Quillan . . . except for the fun part. There's nothing fun about what goes on here. On this territory games are deadly serious. When you play on Quillan, you had better win, because the price of defeat is too high. I've seen what happens when people lose. It's not pretty. Or fun. I'm only beginning to learn about this new and strange territory, but there's one thing that's already been seared into my brain: Whatever happens, don't lose. It's as simple as that. *Do not lose.* Better advice would be to not play at all, but that doesn't seem to be an option here on Quillan. When you live here, you play.

You win, or you pay.

As ominous as that sounds, I've got to accept it because I know these games will somehow factor into the battle against Saint Dane. He's here. This is the next territory he's after. It doesn't take a genius to figure that out. He sent me a big-old invitation. I already told you about that in my last journal. But there's more—something I didn't write last time. You see, another Traveler was here before me. I'm not talking about the Traveler from Quillan. I mean someone from another territory. I don't want to tell you much more about it until I reach that point in this journal. My story should play out on these pages as it happened. The way I saw it. But I will say this much: I'm angry. Angrier than I've ever been since becoming a Traveler. If Saint Dane thinks challenging me to playing games is the best way to bring down Quillan, he's in for a big surprise. He picked the wrong battleground, because I like to play games. I'm good. And I'm mad. Bring it on.

Mark, Courtney, the last time I wrote to you guys was from a fairytale-like castle here on Quillan. There was way more I wanted to write in that journal, but I didn't think I had the time to get it all down. Besides, the information I gave you in my last journal was pretty intense all by itself. I needed to write all of that down while it was still fresh in my memory. I'm not sure why I was so worried. There's no chance I could ever forget what happened during my last few minutes on Zadaa. No matter how many different ways I look at it, or try to understand it, or search for a reasonable explanation for what happened, I keep coming back to the same undeniable fact:

Loor was killed, and she came back from the dead.

No, let me rephrase that: I think I helped Loor come back from the dead. If I live to be a hundred, I can't imagine a single day going by without reliving what happened in that cave deep below the sands of Xhaxhu. I know I already wrote about this, but I can't get it out of my head. Those few minutes keep coming back to me like a movie that only gets so far before it automatically rewinds and plays again. Of course, the outcome never changes. Saint Dane murdered Loor. I saw it. He blasted out of the flume and drove a sword straight through her heart. She didn't have time to react, let alone defend herself. He killed her in cold blood. Though she was gone, I didn't get the chance to grieve, because I wanted revenge. What followed was a fight to the death between me and the demon Traveler. Or so I thought. The thing is, I beat him. I fought him like a crazed madman because, well, I was a crazed madman. I guess seeing someone you love murdered in cold blood would send anybody off the deep end.

Saint Dane and I fought as if we both knew only one of us was getting out of that tunnel alive. It was a vicious, violent battle that could have gone either way. But in the end he made a fatal mistake. He thought he had won, and charged in for the kill. I grabbed the very sword that he had used to kill Loor and swept it into place. My aim was perfect. Instead of finishing me off, he drove himself into the weapon. To the hilt, just as he had driven the sword into Loor moments before. I won. Saint Dane was dead. The nightmare was over. But my victory didn't last long. His body transformed into a black mist that floated away from the sword and re-formed at the mouth of the flume. I looked up to see the demon standing there calmly, not looking any worse for wear. He stood there in his original form, standing well over six feet tall, wearing that dark Asian-looking suit. The lightning-bolt red scars on his bald head seemed to pulse with blood. It was the only sign that he had exerted himself at all. But what I couldn't stop looking at, as usual, were his blue-white eyes. They locked on me and held me tight, taking away what little breath I had left. We stayed that way for a long moment, staring, waiting for the other to make a move. But the fight was over. He gave me a cold, knowing smile as if to say everything had happened exactly as he had planned.

"I see you are capable of rage," he said cockily. "I will remember that."

"How could you . . . ?" I gasped in shock.

"Didn't Press tell you how futile it would be to try to kill me?" he said with a smirk. He kept his eyes on me and shouted into the flume, *"Quillan!"*

The flume came to life. I didn't have the strength, or the will, to stop him. Even if I had, I wouldn't have known how.

"Zadaa has been such an amusing diversion," the demon said. "In spite of what you may think, Pendragon, this isn't over. I can lick my wounds and move on." He glanced down at Loor's lifeless body and added, "The question is, can you?"

The light from the flume enveloped the monster. He took

a step back and was gone. As the light disappeared, I could hear his maniacal laugh fading away.

Have I told you how much I hate that guy?

When I turned to Loor, I saw that I was too late. She was dead. I'm no doctor, but it didn't take one to know that she was gone. Blood was everywhere. She wasn't breathing. She had no heartbeat. I stared down at her, not believing that it was true.

It was only the night before that I had told her I loved her by trying to give her a kiss. But she turned away. I was crushed. It had taken every bit of courage I had to admit I had such strong feelings for her, but with that one small gesture she let me know that it was not meant to be.

She told me, though, that she had deep feelings for me too. She said, "We are on a mission, Pendragon. No group of people have ever been given such a monumental responsibility. We must prevail. We must stop Saint Dane. That is our quest. We are warriors. We will fight together again. We cannot allow emotions to cloud our judgment in any way. That is why I cannot be with you."

It hurt to hear that, but she was right. We would fight together again. Letting our emotions get in the way of that, even in a small way, would be a mistake. Whatever feelings we had for each other would have to be put aside until the time was right. Or so I thought at the time. The next day I watched as Saint Dane killed her. As I sat there in that cavern, with my hand over her mortal wound, a million thoughts and feelings rushed through me. None were good. I had lost my friend. She was not only someone I loved, but my best ally in the battle against Saint Dane. The gut-wrenching realization began to settle in that the time for us would never be right, because she was gone. I found myself wishing with every ounce of my being that it wasn't true.

And she woke up. Simple as that, she opened her eyes.

Her wound was gone too. Like it had never been there. But it *had been* there. I swear. The drying blood on her black leather armor was proof of that. It was un-freaking-believable. Since that moment I've tried to make sense of what happened. But how can you make sense of the impossible?

Sorry for repeating all of that, but as hard as it is for me to understand what actually happened in that cave, it's almost as troubling to wonder what it might mean for the future. My future. Up until then a few things had happened with the Travelers that made me think we aren't exactly, oh, how should I put it? Normal. I had been injured pretty badly on Zadaa, and healed faster than seemed possible. The same happened with Alder from Denduron. He was hit in the chest with a steel arrow that should have killed him. But his wound healed quickly, and he recovered so fast it was like it had never happened. But healing quickly and coming back from the dead are two different things. Still, it's not like we Travelers can't die. We can. If we were invincible, then Uncle Press, Seegen, Spader's dad, Osa, and Kasha would still be around. It's not like we can't be hurt, either. I've taken the lumps and felt the pain to prove it.

But I've seen three Travelers take mortal wounds . . . and live to tell the tale. Loor, Alder, and Saint Dane. I hate to put my friends in the same category as that monster, but after all, he is a Traveler too. On the other hand, Saint Dane is capable of doing some things that the rest of us can't. I can't transform myself into other people. Believe me, I tried. Once. I felt pretty stupid afterward too. How do you "will" yourself to become somebody else? I closed my eyes, concentrated my thoughts, and said to myself: *Become Johnny Depp*. Nothing happened. Maybe I should have been more specific and thought: *Become Johnny Depp in* Charlie and the Chocolate Factory *as opposed to Johnny Depp in* Pirates of the Caribbean. It all seemed so silly.

Especially since nothing happened. I didn't even bother trying to think: *I want to become black smoke and drift across the room.* If I couldn't become Johnny Depp, no way was I turning to smoke. Bottom line is, Saint Dane may be a Traveler, but he's operating on a whole nother level than we are.

Still, both he and Loor came back from the dead. There was no getting around that. I wondered if it was possible that I had something to do with Loor's recovery. But I was with Uncle Press when he died. Same with Kasha. Neither of them came back. When I try to relive each of those final, horrible moments, the only thing I can think of that was different with Loor was that it happened so quickly, and I was so totally stunned that I didn't allow myself to believe it was real. It sounds crazy, but it was like I wouldn't accept her death. I didn't want to let it happen . . . and it didn't. She woke up. I know, impossible, right? But it's true.

I suppose I shouldn't be so upset about it. The ability for a Traveler to "will" another Traveler into staying alive is a pretty good thing. To be honest, it gives me a lot more confidence in our battle against Saint Dane. Not that I want to try it out again. No way. Testing death is not high on my "to do" list. As nifty as that might be, the idea leads me to some truly disturbing thoughts. I've always questioned the reasons that I was chosen to be a Traveler. I don't think you'll find a more normal guy than me. But after this whole healing/coming back from the dead thing, I'm beginning to wonder just how normal we Travelers really are. Uncle Press said that my mom and dad weren't my real parents, but he never told me who my real parents are. That starts me thinking. Where exactly did I come from? Knowing that my family disappeared along with every scrap of evidence that any of us ever existed defies every law of nature, yet it happened. It seems as if all the Travelers have had similar experiences. Each of us was raised on our own territory, yet none of us has a history to show for it.

I guess the overriding feeling I'm left with is sadness. Ever since I left home, my goal had been to get back to my normal life. It was the single biggest driving factor in everything I'd done since stepping into the flume for the first time.

I'm not thinking that way anymore.

This is tough to admit, but I'm beginning to wonder if I truly belong on Second Earth. I miss you guys more than I can say, but my family is gone. It's as if some grand cosmic entity highlighted everything to do with Bobby Pendragon, and hit the delete key. What would I say if people asked me where I came from? What would I say? "Well, I grew up in Stony Brook, Connecticut, but my entire history was wiped out, and my family disappeared right after I left through a flume to battle a demon who was trying to crush all of existence. Pass the salt." I don't think so.

I don't say this to make you guys feel sorry for me. Just the opposite. These journals are about writing down all that happens to me as a Traveler, so that when this cosmic battle with Saint Dane is over, there will be a record. And for the record, I'm fine. But there's nothing more important to me than finding the truth. About me, about my family, and about Saint Dane. I have to stop this guy. Not only for the sake of Halla, but for me, too. I have absolute faith that once he is stopped for good, the journey will lead me to the truth. That goal is what keeps me going. I'm going to try to not question so much, keep my head down, and get it done. Getting it done means stopping Saint Dane. That's why I'm on Quillan.

I wrote to you in my last journal how, shortly after Loor rejoined the living, she and I stood at the flume while it activated and deposited a brightly colored square box in front of us. It had red and yellow stripes and was tied up with a big red bow. Hanging from the ribbon was a yellow tag with the word PENDRAGON written in fancy red lettering. Loor unfolded the tag and we saw that written inside were the words: "With my compliments. S.D." Right. Saint Dane. (It was either that or South Dakota, but that didn't make any sense.) I didn't know what to make of the box. The demon had just murdered Loor, had fought me to the death, was killed and had come back to life, and now he was sending me a birthday gift. And it wasn't even my birthday. Compared to that, maybe getting a present from South Dakota wouldn't have been so odd. Welcome to my twisted world. Fearing that something nasty would be inside, I squinted when I pulled off the top. What jumped out was nasty indeed. At least to me. You remember, right? Springing out was a jack-in-the-box clown. It was a scary-looking thing with a hideous smile and a court jester's hat. In fact, pretty much all clowns are scary-looking to me. I hate clowns. I wondered if Saint Dane knew that. The clown laughed with some recorded cackle as it bobbled on the spring. It sounded familiar. Swell.

At the bottom of the box was a blue envelope with the word PENDRAGON on it. I quickly opened it to find a single sheet of bright yellow paper with fancy red lettering. It was an invitation that read:

> *Riggedy riggedy white*
> *Come and spend the night*
> *We'll play some games*
> *Some wild, some tame*
> *Cause if you will, you might*

Your hosts on Quillan,
Veego and LaBerge

Veego and LaBerge. I had no idea what that meant. I had no idea what any of it meant, but one thing was very clear: The next stop for me was Quillan. Alone. Loor wanted to come, but I needed to learn what Quillan was going to hold before deciding which Traveler could best help me there. Besides, Loor had just come back from the dead. She needed the rest. At least I thought she did. What did I know? I'd never seen anybody come back from the dead before. So I reluctantly left Loor at the mouth of the flume on Zadaa, stepped into the tunnel, and shouted, *"Quillan."*

And that's where my latest adventure began. . . .

QUILLAN

The flume.

As impossible an experience as flying through time and space may be, it has become the only time when I can totally relax. There are no surprises, nobody lurking around the corner waiting to pounce, no Saint Dane. I hope it stays that way. Once I announce the territory where I'm headed and get swept into the crystal tunnel of light and music, I can relax. I think back to that very first flume ride from Second Earth to Denduron and how flat-out terrified I was. Now I'm at peace. It's almost like a flume ride recharges my batteries. I do think there's a whole lot more to these magical tunnels than simply being highways across the cosmos, though. There has to be some kind of intelligence at work here. How else would the flumes know where to send us? More importantly, how else would they know *when* to send us? We always arrive where we need to be, when we need to be there. Even if there are two gates on a territory, we always end up at the gate where we need to be. I'm sure that when I learn the truth about the Travelers and Halla and Saint Dane, I'll also learn all about the flumes and how they can do what they do. Until then, I'll accept the flume rides as being my little vacation away from reality while speeding me to my next destination.

Still, there is one thing that haunts me about the flumes. Ever since Saint Dane won the battle for Veelox, I've been seeing strange, ghostly images floating through the starfield beyond the crystal walls as I travel through the cosmos. The black sky full of sparkling stars is now littered with near-transparent living pictures of people and things that exist on the various territories. I've seen the *Hindenburg* from First Earth, along with Jinx Olsen's flying seaplane. I've seen the white-skinned Novans of Denduron marching in line, and underwater speeders from Cloral being chased by bloated spinney fish. Batu warriors from Zadaa have floated alongside zenzen horses from Eelong. I've seen immense Lifelight pyramids from Veelox and even small animals that look like cats from Second Earth. Many things I don't recognize. I've seen swarms of people holding spears in the air, cheering for something or other. I've seen stiff-looking muscular men, running quickly, with stern faces and sharp jaws. I wouldn't want to get in their way. I've even seen some clown faces, laughing maniacally. I hate clowns. Have I mentioned that?

There are thousands upon thousands more images that I won't bother to describe, because I think you get the idea. Many I recognize, but just as many I don't. They are ghosts from all the territories, floating together in the sea of space. That's why it makes me uneasy. We all know that elements from the territories are not supposed to be mixed. We've learned that the hard way over and over. Yet here in space, or wherever it is, the images of all the territories are jumbled together. It's not like they are interacting or anything. It's more like I'm watching movies projected all over the place.

But seeing these images right next to one another makes me realize just how different each of the territories is. They all have their own histories and their own destinies. That can't change. Mixing them would be like throwing random numbers into a perfect equation. The result won't be the same. I think that's what would happen to the territories if the cultures were mingled. None of the territories would be the same and that could be disastrous.

Which is exactly what Saint Dane wants. He's played fast and loose with the rules about mixing elements between territories, and I'm beginning to realize why. The more he can throw a territory off balance, the easier it will be for him to send it all crashing into chaos. I believe he's not only working to push the turning point of each territory toward disaster, but he's helping his cause by mixing them together as well. What does that all mean to me besides making my stomach twist? Nothing, except that it's all the more reason he must be stopped. As I was speeding through the flume toward Quillan, I couldn't help but wonder if those images floating in space were there as a warning, or evidence that the worst had already begun and the walls between the territories were beginning to crumble.

It was the first flume trip that I didn't enjoy.

I didn't have time to sweat about it for long, though. I heard the jumble of sweet musical notes that always accompany me on a flume ride begin to grow louder and more complex. This familiar song signaled that I was nearing the end of my trip. I took my focus away from the images in space and looked ahead. A bright light shone at the end of the tunnel. I was about to arrive on Quillan. The time for theorizing was over. The show was about to begin.

As the cushion of light gently deposited me on my feet, every sense instantly went on alert. I stood there for a second to get my bearings. It was dark, but that could have been because I had just been sailing along in a shower of light. I needed a few seconds for my eyes to adjust. I waited with my knees bent, ready to jump at the first sign of trouble. After only a few seconds I heard an odd noise. It sounded like chattering. I'm not sure how else to describe it. There was a series of high-pitched clicking noises coming from somewhere off to my right. They didn't sound dangerous or aggressive. Just . . . odd. I strained to hear, but it stopped. Silence. All I heard was the faint echoing of the musical notes as they receded into the depths of the flume. I didn't move. I didn't want to step into something stupid. I waited a solid minute, but the noise didn't come back. Whatever it was, it was gone.

Looking around, I saw nothing but black. Swell. I would have given anything for a flashlight . . . assuming they had flashlights on Quillan. Another minute passed, and I figured I wasn't doing any good standing in the dark, so I took a tentative step forward and . . . *smack!* I walked right into a wall. Head first. Ouch. I took a quick step back, feeling more stupid than hurt. I reached out, more carefully this time, and eased forward until my hand touched the wall. At least I thought it was a wall. It sure felt like one. It was hard. It was flat. It stretched out to either side of me. You know . . . wall. The space between the opening to the flume and this wall seemed to be only a couple of feet. It was the smallest gate area yet. Of course, I knew there had to be a way out, the trick was finding it. I took a few steps back into the flume to get some perspective. I stood there for a few seconds until, slowly, I began to make out cracks in the wall. Actually, they looked more like seams. The lines were straight, crossing one another, forming a grid pattern with two-foot squares. I didn't see this at first because I was so close to the wall and my eyes hadn't adjusted to the dark. The light coming through was very faint. But it was there. I knew there had to be a way out, so I slowly scanned the wall, looking for anything that might be a doorway, or a window, or a hole. I didn't care. I was starting to get claustrophobic.

I heard the clicking sounds again. This time to my left. I shot a look that way to see . . . nothing. But there was no mistake. Something was there. I had no way of knowing how far off in each direction this wall stretched. The seams disappeared off to either side. It's not like they ended abruptly, they just kind of faded out into the dark. This wall could have gone on for miles for all I knew.

The chattering stopped. Whatever it was, was creeping me out. I wanted out of there. Out of desperation I walked up to the wall, put my hand on it, and started pushing. I reached up over my head and pushed on one of the squares that was marked off by the seam of light. It didn't budge. I moved my hand down, pushing on the square below it. Nothing happened. My thinking was that maybe one of these squares was also a doorway of some kind and . . .

It didn't take me long to find it. The fifth square pushed out. One side was on a hinge. Instantly light flooded in. I glanced back to the flume to see the big, round mouth of the rocky tunnel. I looked off to the sides to see if I could catch a glimpse of whatever it was that was doing all the clicking, but my pupils had already contracted because of the light. All I saw was pitch black. The mystery would have to wait. The door was about at my waist and just large enough for me to enter. I put one leg through, then ducked down and put my head through, and finally I dragged my other leg behind.

I was out! Great. But where was I? I turned around to see that the wall I had come through was made of cement, or stucco. Whatever it was, it was definitely man-made. That answered one of my questions. Wherever the flume was, it wasn't in some natural cave or tunnel. It was in a building. I suppose the hinge on the door should have been a tip-off too. Duh. The face of the wall was covered with what looked like a grid of metal. That accounted for the pattern of squares I'd seen inside. It looked to me like some kind of support to keep the wall secure. It was one of the sections of this grid that was actually the gate to the flume. I was about to close the hatch behind me, when I realized I needed a way to figure out which of these squares was the gate once it was closed. They all looked the same. Of course, I needn't have worried. They *didn't* all look the same. I saw a small star burned into the upper right corner of the open panel. It was no bigger than a quarter, but it was there. It was the mark that showed this was a gate to the flume. I knew how to get back. I closed the two-foot square secret door, then quickly opened it again, just to make sure I wasn't locking myself out. If I had to get to the flume fast, I didn't want to have to monkey with a temperamental door. After closing it again, I put my back to the wall to get my first look at Quillan.

The adventure continues in

PENDRAGON ⊕

BLACK WATER

Having left the futuristic territory of Veelox behind, Bobby
Pendragon now finds himself in a beautiful, primitive territory
called, Eelong. Covered in lush, green tropical jungle,
Eelong is inhabited by the Klee, a ferocious half human, half
cat species. The humans on Eelong are kept as pets and
are treated as one of the lower life forms much to Bobby's
alarm when he tries to communicate with the inhabitants.
But something is terribly wrong on Eelong, and when Bobby
discovers what is happening to the doomed territory he is
faced with some hard choices. Bobby realises that to save
Eelong he must break the rules of a Traveller. Can he do it
before it's too late?